Robin

Brides of a Feather 1

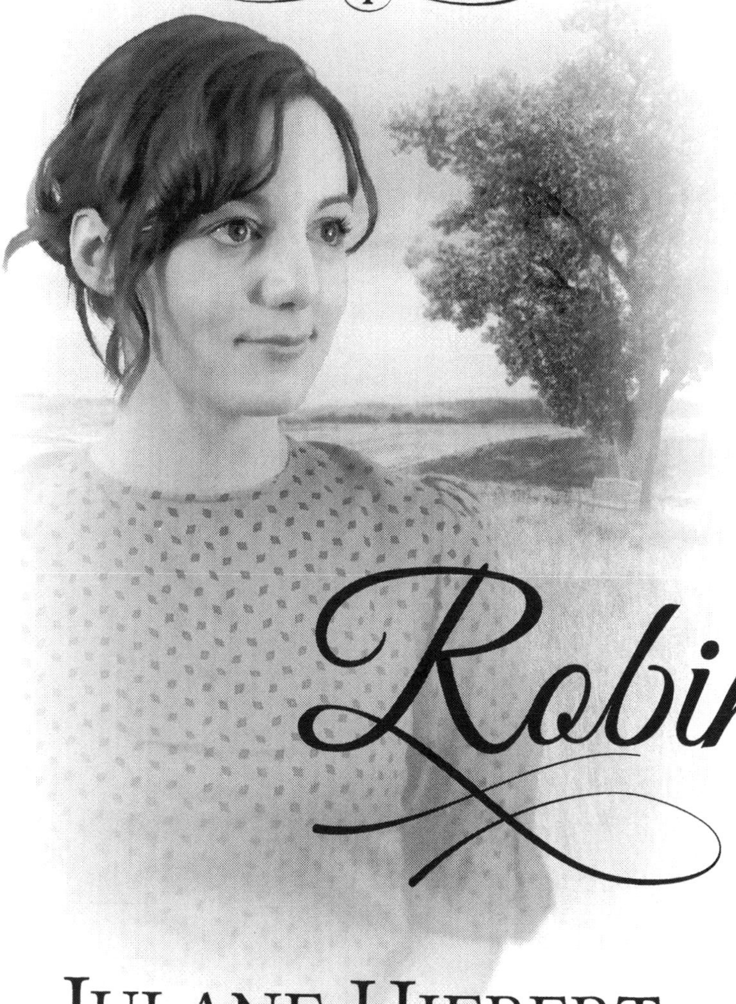

Robin

Published by Wings of Hope Publishing Group
Established 2013
www.wingsofhopepublishing.com
Find us on Facebook: Search "Wings of Hope"

Printed in the United States of America

Hiebert, Julane
Robin / Julane Hiebert
Wings of Hope Publishing Group
ISBN-13: 978-1-944309-00-8
ISBN-10: 1-944309-00-4

This is a work of fiction. Names, characters, incidents, and dialogues are products of the author's imagination and are not to be construed as real. Any resemblance to actual events or people, living or dead, is entirely coincidental.

Photography, cover design and interior layout by Vogel Design in Hillsboro, Kansas.

To my *Bob*, who has made our family rich, not with money or things, but because he is a man with a good name.

And to the memory of our daughters: *Tamara Jill* and *Lori Julane*, who are with Jesus, but who will remain in hearts and minds until that day when we will see them once again.

A good name is rather to be chosen than great riches.
Proverbs 22:1 KJV

ONE

Cedar Bluff, Kansas
Late April 1877

He didn't come. Now you're alone. We told you so. Now you're alone.

Her sisters' admonitions taunted in rhythm as the big iron wheels of the steam engine began to roll, and the train hissed and chugged past Robin Wenghold. She braced herself against the strong, hot wind and gripped the handle of her valise so tight her fingernails dug into the palm of her hand.

Squinting against the afternoon sun, she limped to the end of the platform that ran the length of the stone depot. Heat shimmered above the silver tracks that stretched as far as she could see in one direction, and a twist of dust skittered down the street when she peered toward town. Why wasn't he here? He promised. Had he discovered her infirmity and changed his mind?

A sleek, black cat occupied the one long bench on the platform, and Robin pushed it aside so she could sit. Her bad leg throbbed, and she longed to rub the pain away, but even after all these years her mama's voice echoed in her mind. *You needn't draw attention to yourself, Robin. Your infirmity is obvious. Learn to bear your cross without pity.*

The cat nudged its head under Robin's elbow. "And for whom are you waiting, mister bad-luck kitty? Have you been jilted, too?"

A steady purr vibrated beneath her hand while she stroked the cat's warm back. If her papa were here he'd no doubt make a joke about his little bird and a cat occupying the same space like long-lost friends. But then, if Papa were here she wouldn't be in this predicament—stuck in hot, windy Kansas waiting for an uncle she'd never seen to come to her aid.

Robin sighed. *Sittin' in a stew won't fill a man's belly.* Papa's words. And Papa was right. Worry wouldn't get her any closer to her intended destination. She stood, and the cat jumped to the floor then sat on his haunches, switching its long tail against the splintery boards. Robin bent and patted the downy soft head. "Suppose you could take me home with you if my uncle doesn't come? At least I'd have someone to talk to." She straightened, adjusted her bonnet, picked up her valise—determined not to panic—and sidled into the depot.

One window on the far wall provided the only light in the dark room. The aroma of old tobacco smoke and mildew added to the dread, which lay like a cold biscuit in her stomach. Except for the steady ticking of the large black-framed clock that hung beside the window, silence hovered like a cloud. Even the skinny man behind the counter made no move to acknowledge her presence.

"Ahem." She eyed the empty room. He had to be aware she was the only one there, didn't he? She drummed her fingers on the counter under his nose. Hot and tired, she had no patience for such nonsense.

"Ahhemm. Sir?"

He didn't raise his head, but pointed to a crudely lettered sign next to the window separating the tiny office from the waiting room. *Ring wonce to git my atenshun. Ring twice if I don't ansur the first time. If you kant see me, I ain't here so jist take a seet and wate.*

This was absurd. Robin tapped the bell with the palm of her hand. Nothing. He didn't even wince. "Sir?" She stared in disbelief as one bony finger underscored the instruction to ring twice. She dropped her valise to the floor, moved the bell in front of her and with determination hit it two times.

"Name?" The little man licked the end of his pencil and peered from under a green visor balanced on protruding ears.

"Name? Why do you need to know my name? I only want to ask you a question."

"Can't answer no questions 'til you tell me your name. It's my job."

"But I only need to . . ."

The man straightened his visor and thumped his chest. "This here says it all, ma'am."

She moved closer to read the badge, which hung from a frayed ribbon pinned to his vest. "It says, Ticket Agent."

His eyes crossed and forehead puckered as he peered at it upside-down. "Whooee, that do hurt them eyeballs." He blinked, then gave a crooked grin and turned the button to the other side. "Sorry. Now, read it again and tell me what it says."

Robin rubbed her temples. Her head hurt. Where *was* her uncle? "That side says Carl Rempel, Stationmaster."

"See, what'd I tell you?" The little man shook his finger. "It's my job, as the stationmaster, to mark off the names of all them what get off at this here station. Gotta make sure ever'body who had a ticket used it at the right gettin' off place."

"But no one else . . ."

"Don't matter. No, siree. Last week I put my mark beside five names. Next thing you know, I'm gonna need me a new pencil." He tapped the stubby writing instrument on the counter. "Now accordin' to my list here, you must be . . ."

"Robin Wenghold, sir. R-o-b-i-n. Perhaps you know my uncle, John Wenghold?" She retrieved a letter from her reticule and waved it in front of the man's face. "He wrote he'd meet me upon my arrival." She sucked her top lip between her teeth.

Mr. Rempel's bald head turned red and his shoulders shook with laughter. "Well, what do ya know? Kinda late ain't ya?" He winked.

"Pardon me?" How could she be late? Had she misread the ticket? That couldn't be. The silly man had marked her off his list.

He rested his elbows on the counter and stuck his head through the little window. "Most robins what come in here fly in 'long about the first of March. Here 'tis late April, and you come in by train. Something happen to ruffle your feathers, did it?"

Robin closed her eyes and counted to ten. "Indeed, sir. I don't think it's all that funny."

"Oh, it ain't just your name what's ticklin' my funny bones." He yanked a red bandana from his pocket and mopped his brow. "No, ma'am. You see, the real laugher is . . . Oh my. See, your uncle owns a ranch they call the Feather. And it got its name from the creek running through it—Pigeon Creek, they call it."

Robin gritted her teeth and waited for Carl Rempel to quiet his funny bones. She knew all about the silly ranch name. Papa thought it quite humorous to tell anyone who cared to listen that his family included a nest of little birds—Robin, and her sisters Wren and Lark. But his one and only sibling's claim to fame was a feather.

"What d'ya know. Robin. Feather. That do make me laugh." Mr. Rempel slapped the counter with his hand.

Robin clenched her teeth. A lady could only take so much. Uncle John didn't keep his word. She wouldn't keep hers, either. She would take the first train home and forget she ever heard of Cedar Bluff, Kansas.

She rummaged in her reticule. "Mr. Rempel. I would like to purchase a one-way ticket to Chicago, please." She counted the money and plunked it on the counter.

The man sobered. He took his watch out of his pocket, tapped it on his hand a couple of times, then peered at it from arm's length. "Oh, I'm sorry Miss Robin, ma'am. I can't sell it to you." He removed his visor.

"What do you mean you can't sell it to me? I have the money."

"Well now, you see, according to my granddaddy's pocket watch, the ticket agent is off duty 'til t'morrow mornin'."

"But . . . but . . . *you're* the ticket agent, aren't you?" She pinched the bridge of her nose.

"I *was* the ticket agent when the train came in, but weren't nobody what needed a ticket, and ain't no more trains comin' or goin' today so that makes me the stationmaster, and his job ain't to sell tickets. His job is to . . ."

"I know, I know. His job is to take names." A lump worked its way up her throat, but she would not let this little man get the best of her. "Mr. Rempel. Please try to understand. I don't know what to do. I have nowhere to go."

He sidestepped around the counter, closed the half door, and hung his visor on a peg on the wall. One crooked finger beckoned her to follow him out of the station; then he locked the door behind them.

"Sorry to leave you all alone like this, but it's the rules." He plopped a tattered black hat on his head and bow-legged his way down the steps. Tiny puffs of dust followed him as he shuffled a few steps away, then stopped and pointed to the sky. "Storm a brewin' I'd say. Hope John gets here before it hits."

"Wait! What if he doesn't come? Where can I go if it storms?" *Don't they have gentlemen in Kansas? Does he plan to leave me here all alone in this strange town?*

"Don't suppose you need to get fretful, ma'am. That there weather change has a whole lot of hills to cross before it gets to Cedar Bluff. If John Wenghold told you he'd come get ya, he'll be here. Never knowed the man to whistle a windy." He scratched his head through a hole in his floppy hat. "Reckon if you have to, you could go to Emma's Mercantile down the street a ways. That'd likely be the first place John would look if ya wasn't at the station."

He pursed his lips and kissed the air. "C'mon, cat. We best see what Mrs. Rempel fixed us good to eat." The black cat hopped from its seat on the platform, then arched its tail and marched behind the man as he shuffled away from the depot.

So much for taking me home with you, fickle kitty.

Robin waited until she could no longer see the stationmaster and his cat, then checked the gold watch pinned to her lapel. Four-thirty. One hour since the train chugged away, but it seemed a lifetime. Uncle John still had time to get here before dark. She rotated her shoulders and moved her head from side to side. No need to panic.

She sat on the long bench and massaged her left leg. She would give Uncle John another hour. Mr. Rempel said the storm remained a long way off, and her leg was too painful to attempt to walk any distance.

She leaned her head against the rough stone. Did her uncle know she was crippled? Surely Papa mentioned something to him over the years. But what if he hadn't? Would Uncle John send her back to Chicago? *Oh, Papa. If only you could tell me what to do.*

Hot wind stung her cheeks, and she closed her eyes against the glare of the sun in her face. It wouldn't do any good to pray, but she did so want Uncle John to get there before the storm.

Robin jerked from unbidden sleep. Heat radiated from the stone wall of the station behind her, and perspiration trickled down the side of her face. She limped to the end of the platform to search once more for any sign of her uncle. Another glance at her watch revealed a mere forty-five minutes had passed. Yet, in the short measure of time, the storm had crossed Mr. Rempel's whole lot of hills.

Ever-changing clouds scudded low across the prairie toward her. Behind them, a roiling, seething mass of green-black turbulence advanced above the horizon and flattened into a seemingly impenetrable wall as it continued its march across the prairie. An eerie silence hovered over the little Kansas town like a pall, yet belied the fury of activity up and down the dusty street.

Men ran to untie skittish teams from the hitching rails. Conveyances of all sizes careened past her. Many held wide-eyed women clutching open-mouthed babes in their arms—infants' cries swallowed by the pounding of hooves and clatter of iron wheels.

She gulped down the growing knot of fear. To venture forth amongst such bedlam would be foolhardy. She needed time to navigate any distance, and time evaded her.

Lightning snaked from cloud to cloud, occasionally spearing the ground. Thunder reverberated through the dusty streets. It reminded her of a Fourth of July parade she'd witnessed once—the boom of the bass drum and the vibration of marching feet sensed long before the band could be seen.

The sky darkened and long fingers of hot wind hurled handfuls of grit and dirt at anyone who dared to remain within range. Her eyes stung from the debris, and salty tears added to the pain. As quickly as the heat of her tormentors passed, large drops of rain began to fall. She hid her face in her hands and sought refuge against the side of the building.

Tiny pebbles of ice assaulted her, then larger and larger ones. She hunched her shoulders to ward off the attack, but they pummeled her painfully. No longer able to contain the storm of fear warring inside her, Robin screamed.

Without warning, strong arms wrapped around her middle and pulled her along the wooden platform.

"Don't fight me, ma'am. I don't mean you any harm. But you must get out of this storm before the hail beats you to pieces."

The arms tightened, lifted her over the side of the platform and planted her, without ceremony, on her feet.

"We've got to hurry. If we can get to my wagon we might still have a chance to outrun this thing."

"I can't run." Robin yelled above the fury of the storm.

Strong hands whipped her around. Her breath caught in her chest. Black hair hung to the stranger's collar, but curled at the ends, even in the rain. With his face so close she could see the ring of blue around his otherwise dark eyes. A shadow of a beard covered his square jaw.

"You've got to, ma'am. We're going to get hit hard if we stand out here like this. "A frown settled between his eyes. He leaned toward her and put his arms around her shoulder, urging her forward.

"Please." She twisted away from him. "I can't run."

A sudden stillness dropped like lead around them, and in an instant she lay against the rough stone foundation of the depot, the weight of the stranger heavy across her. A rivulet of muddy water slid past her cheek, and the scent of bay rum filled her otherwise numb senses.

"I'm not going to hurt you, but when the wind stops like that it's a sure sign of a fierce storm, most likely a twister. We need to stay as low to the ground as possible and pray the monster won't suck us up in it, or blow something—"

A roar like an approaching locomotive, accompanied by a cacophony of splintering wood and breaking glass sent fear coursing through her.

"It's a twister for sure," he yelled. "But it's headed for open country. It's only going to hurl its wreckage our way. I'll tell you when it's safe."

When the storm at last subsided, he rolled away from her and helped her to her feet. "Terrible way to meet, isn't it?" He smiled. "You *are* John Wenghold's niece, aren't you? Miss Robin Wenghold from Chicago?"

Robin nodded. "I thought he would meet me." Silver flecks danced before her eyes, and her back and shoulders hurt from the barrage of hailstones. She ran her tongue over her teeth to remove the dirt. What must she look like?

"I know. I'm Ty Morgan, your Uncle John's neighbor."

"Is he ill? He knew I would arrive today." She pressed her fingers against her forehead.

"He didn't forget you, ma'am. I guess he figured, since I planned to come in for supplies, it would save him a trip if I agreed to bring you back to his ranch."

Save him a trip? What kind of man issues an invitation to visit then sends a neighbor in his stead so he can save a trip? If only she could sit before her legs buckled.

Gentle hands rested on her shoulders, and dark eyes peered into hers. "Miss Wenghold, do you need . . ."

Though his lips moved, the swish of her pulse drowned out his words. She attempted to smile as a dark veil dropped over her eyes.

Ty managed to catch the girl before she crumpled to the ground. *Now what?* Rain continued to pelt them. Thankful the station remained intact, he balanced her in his arms and climbed the stairs, one rickety step at a time. Satisfied the wooden porch had not been damaged, he proceeded to the door and kicked it open. Splinters of glass covered the floor beneath the broken window, but otherwise it would provide shelter.

He laid her on the waiting bench and shook her gently. "Ma'am?" He couldn't leave until she responded. Shouts came from the streets. There was likely a lot of damage and perhaps even injuries. "Miss Wenghold?" He dropped to one knee beside her.

She blinked and turned her head toward him. "Is the storm over?"

"The worst of it. I reckon you had a pretty bad scare, but you're safe now."

The girl smiled and a dimple perched at the corner of her mouth. Long lashes curled against her cheeks and freckles sprinkled her nose. Cinnamon colored hair, tangled and muddy, lay across one shoulder.

Ty swallowed. Few would describe her beautiful, yet he found it difficult to take his gaze away from her. "You rest. I'm going to see if anyone needs help. I won't leave without you. Are you okay here? I need to take a look around."

Good lands. He was chattering like a schoolgirl. Would she notice? He clenched his fists to resist thumbing a smudge of mud from her cheek.

She nodded. "You go. I'm fine. I hope no one is injured."

"Me, too." Ty stood and walked to the door. "Don't go away." *Well, that was smart, Ty. And exactly where did you think she might go?*

She smiled again and sat up. "You will take me to Uncle John's? Do you think the twister hit his ranch?"

Ty shook his head. "I don't think so. I watched the storm build as I came into town and figured it would go south and east of our ranches."

"You in the depot, Morgan?" A voice called from the street. "Doc says he could use ya if you got time."

She swept a strand of wet hair away from her face. Eyes as dark as the storm clouds that threatened a short time ago met his. Black pools so deep he could drown. "Mr. Morgan, please see who needs help. I'm fine."

He bumped into the door on his way out.

TWO

Robin wrapped her arms around her middle and paced—five . . . six . . . seven, turn. How many times had she counted the distance from the tiny ticket office to the wall? A gust of wind blew through the broken window and a shard of remaining glass tinkled to the floor. The door rattled and a shiver slithered across her shoulders. She peered into the deepening dusk and held her breath, then when no one entered she resumed pacing—one . . . two . . . three . . .

Where is he? Mr. Morgan said he would return. Voices, which at first had called to one another after the storm, stilled. She longed for the sound of other human beings, even if she didn't know them. Instead, unfamiliar noises assailed her imagination.

Home. She thought of her sisters in Chicago, their evening routine so predictable it swelled the lump in her throat with the thought. Wren would flit in the front door and straighten the picture of Mama's great-uncle Alfred that hung above the table in the entryway. On her way through the parlor she'd rearrange the candelabra on the mantel, then make three turns around the large oval dining table to ensure the tablecloth hung evenly. And with each flit she'd flutter her hands and trill her day's events.

And Lark—dear Lark would scold. *Nothing changes, little Jenny Wren. The picture will wiggle crooked when you close the door in the morning. You never light the candles, and Mama would take to her bed if she knew you kept her best cutwork linen cloth on the table when we have no guests to entertain.*

Robin smiled. If only they could have made the trip with her. But Wren still made the daily excursion to the Wesleys'—as nanny to their children—and Lark had her piano students at Winford Lucas Ladies Academy of Voice and Piano. No. It was best this way. Between the three of them, Papa's debts would be paid in no time, and the sisters would join her to make their home in Kansas. Though it remained a mystery why, after all these years, John Wenghold made such an offer to nieces he didn't know.

A snuffle outside the window sent Robin cowering against the wall. She lowered herself to a sitting position and drew her knees to her chest. Darkness shrouded her from her foe. Crouched in the corner, she clasped her arms around her knees and locked her gaze on the door. Her heart drummed in her chest.

Sing, Robin. Mama said fear and song don't abide together.

A bump against the outside wall sent another shard of glass ringing to the floor.

"O for a faith that will not shrink, tho' pressed by every foe." She searched her memory for the words then raised her voice. ". . . Tho' pressed by every foe." A low moan rumbled outside the window. She took a deep breath. "That will not tremble on the brink . . ." With each new phrase the awful noise grew louder. "That will not tremble on the brink of any earthly wo-o-oe—" A furry head with long flapping ears poked through the open window and bellowed, took a long suck of air then brayed again. Robin screamed.

She released one more piercing cry before the door slammed open. A lantern in Mr. Morgan's hand gave enough light for Robin to make out the older lady with him. Oh, how good to be in the company of another female. The woman was tall and thin as a willow branch. One long braid wound around her head like a crown, and her face crinkled in smile lines when she strode past Robin to the window.

"You cantankerous old sister." The woman grabbed the intruder by the ear and the terrible noise stopped. The lady turned to Robin. "Crazy mule. The old dear thinks she's human."

Robin gazed from Ty to the woman. Mr. Morgan's eyes watered with restrained laughter. The older lady covered her mouth with the hem of her apron.

Her legs shook, but Robin managed to push herself to her feet. She was neither impressed nor amused. Hands on hips, she opened her mouth to inform them of such when soft arms enfolded her

"I'm Emma Ledbetter, dear. And this obnoxious critter is my mule, Dolly." Emma wiped tears from her eyes. "You must've been so frightened. Were you, by chance, trying to chase your fears away with a song? Dolly here thinks she can sing. You ought to hear her on Sunday mornings when it's warm enough to have the church windows open."

That was singing? The scraggly ears of Emma's mule, flashed back and forth like signal flags. Then Dolly curled her lip, gave a toothy grin, and backed away from the window.

"Sorry we took so long, Miss Wenghold." Ty stepped toward her. "It took a while to get through town and make sure everyone was okay. Then when Emma couldn't find Dolly I couldn't leave without helping her. As soon as we heard that silly animal singing we knew we'd better get here and rescue you. Again."

"Were people injured?" She managed to squeak.

"Only a few cuts and scratches." Emma led Robin back to the bench. "Doc Mercer was able to patch 'em up fine. And don't you fret none about your Uncle John, dearie."

"How did you know I'm worried?" Robin welcomed Emma's arm around her shoulders and scooted closer.

Emma laughed. "My late husband, George, always said I was the knowingest woman he ever did see—said I knew everybody's business, and a lot of business I shouldn't. I think it comes from listening to my customers. After a bit you learn to look at their faces when they're talking, and you begin to understand that sometimes what's coming from their mouth and what's showing on their face is two different conversations." She leaned toward Robin. "You have a great big frown between those pretty eyes. A furrow that deep says worry to me."

Ty knelt by the bench. "I know this day has been long and hard for you, Miss Wenghold. If you can hang on a few hours more, I think it will be best for us to wait until morning to head for John's ranch."

"Won't he be anxious if I don't come tonight?"

"John seldom gets anxious about anything. He'll figure I had sense enough not to head out onto the prairie with the storm still brewing." Ty smiled.

"But what will I do tonight? I only have my valise. The train left, and it took my trunk with it. They didn't unload it. I don't want to stay here alone." Heat bathed her face. She didn't want Ty Morgan to think she issued an invitation for him to linger.

"Oh, I have plenty of room at my place, Miss Wenghold." Emma patted Robin's hand. "And as far as your trunk—you have to do the unloading yourself, dear. But don't worry. My store is full of ready-made clothing, and you can have your choice. That is, if you don't mind."

"No, I don't mind at all. But I don't—"

"You needn't fret about paying me. We'll take care of all that later. In fact, after I have a talk with John Wenghold, I would imagine you won't owe me a penny."

"He must be a very generous man."

Ty and Emma chuckled in unison.

Emma shook her head. "Generous is not a word I would use to describe the man, but he is practical. You leave him to me."

"You know him well?"

"John Wenghold is as old as dirt, and I've known him since he was a speck of dust." Emma groaned as she got to her feet and offered Robin a hand. "Let's get home and settled in for the evening, then I'll try to answer your questions. Where will you stay, Ty?"

"I told Doc Mercer I'd bunk with him tonight in case someone wanders in. I think the twister missed most of the ranches, but never can tell who might have strayed into its path once it passed here."

He held the lantern as the women descended the rickety steps.

"It's muddy, so might be slippery. Watch your step."

Robin grasped Emma's hand and tried to match her stride. She feared her halting gait would soon be noticed as her hand jerked against the older woman's with each step.

"You okay, dearie?" Emma stopped. "Why, girl—you're limping. Ty, did you hurt this little gal trying to save her?"

Even the dim light didn't hide the frown on Ty's face. He handed the lantern to Emma. "Here, you take this, and I'll help Miss Wenghold over the rough part. You go ahead. We'll follow." He tucked Robin's hand in the crook of his elbow and leaned toward her ear. "We'll go slow. I promise."

Robin swiped at unwelcome tears. "I'm sorry, I—"

"You told me you couldn't run. Is this why, or *did* I hurt you?"

She sighed. "No. You didn't hurt me. I was born this way."

"You don't have to explain, you know. Not to me. Not to anyone. Emma will no doubt question you, but only out of concern. She doesn't have a mean bone in her body. You can trust her, Miss Wenghold, and she'll want to be your friend."

"Will Uncle John send me away when he finds out I'm crippled?"

"He doesn't know?"

She shook her head "We've never met."

Ty smiled. "That would explain why he couldn't describe you."

"After Papa died we received a letter from Uncle John saying he could use help around the house and would gladly pay for it. We think perhaps Papa wrote to him when the doctor told him he was near death."

"We? You have other siblings?"

"Come on, you two." Emma stood with one hand on her hip, the other one swinging the lantern. "We can talk over a cup of coffee. Ty Morgan, get that dear lady out of the muddy street."

Ty put his arm around her shoulders. "You don't have to say more than you're ready to tell, you know. Lean on me. I won't let you fall."

He won't let me fall? Robin's heart pounded. Maybe he wouldn't let her fall to the ground, but on the inside she'd already toppled. She'd tuck this conversation away for now. A man like Ty Morgan would never be attracted to her.

THREE

Robin settled onto the wagon seat and tucked her skirts around her legs. A ride across the Kansas prairie sitting on a hard slab of wood was not how she envisioned her journey. The uncertainty of meeting Uncle John, coupled with Ty Morgan's proximity for the trip, caused her palms to perspire.

"Here, dearie." Emma handed her a paper-wrapped bundle "I packed a few extra items. I doubt you'll find enough in John Wenghold's kitchen to last more than a few days. You'll be needing supplies soon, so don't let that old man keep you penned up out there, you hear?"

Robin's lips twitched with her attempt to smile. "Emma, whatever would I have done without you? Thank you. I'll make sure you get paid."

"You'll do no such thing. Now, lean down here so I can give you a peck on the cheek, then you two best be on your way."

"Thanks, Emma." Ty embraced the older woman, then climbed in beside Robin. "Ready?" He grinned.

Robin straightened her shoulders and nodded.

Ty flicked the reins, and when the wagon lurched, Robin clutched the seat with both hands.

"Sorry, I should've warned you." He smiled. "You might want to hang on tight. Can't always avoid the bumps."

Robin peered over her shoulder one last time as the town slipped from sight, then turned and set her face toward the hills. The road stretched before them in two long brown ribbons as far as she could see, while tall grass swayed and danced with the passing wagon. A brown and black bird sporting a bright yellow bib perched on a rock and warbled as they rolled past.

They traveled in long stretches of silence, broken only by birdsong and the occasional nicker of one of the horses. Grateful Mr. Morgan didn't seem to require a lot of conversation, Robin relaxed with the rhythmic roll of the wagon. The prairie revealed constant change. Great expanses of flat land gave way to unexpected rocky cliffs and valleys that plunged so deep shadows obscured the bottom. It was a far cry from the bricked streets of Chicago, but she was fascinated. Would she ever get used to the vastness, the sense of being as small as one of the insects that *whirred* from the grass as they passed? The wagon slowed, and the horses strained against their harness as they trudged their way up a steep incline. Robin's eyes widened when they reached the summit.

Ty reined the horses to a halt. "Quite a picture, isn't it?"

Trees, absent thus far, meandered through the valley below, then melted into purple shadows. The solitude was palpable.

"I didn't know grass and hills could be so beautiful." Robin whispered. "How can it change so quickly? Last night it blew wild and dangerous, and now"—she swept her arm in an arc—"this is so peaceful. Chicago has storms, too, but the only things to show for it the next morning are a few puddles and broken branches. Here, everything is so green and new. Even the sky looks washed clean."

"The old-timers say Kansas is like a woman. You never know when she's going to up and throw a fit, then the next minute she's smiling and happy as can be. You love her, or you leave." He wrapped the reins around the brake handle and jumped from the wagon.

"I take it you love her?" Was it appropriate to talk about love? Mama would make her recite the three L's of proper conversation with someone of a different gender: A lady doesn't *laugh aloud*, nor speak of *limbs* or *love*. If only she could fan herself. Past experience warned her that when she had a sudden gush of heat her face was also bright pink.

"She's in my blood. I don't suppose I'll ever leave. I've simply learned to live with her little temper tantrums. Would you like to walk a bit?" He removed his gloves and laid them on the seat.

"Now?" She peered at the sea of tall grass that surrounded the wagon. It was hard enough to navigate well-worn paths. How could she shuffle through such unmarked terrain?

"Here, let me help you." He circled her waist with his hands and lifted her from the wagon. "This is perhaps my favorite spot on the ranch."

Robin straightened her skirts. "Why? Though I must say, it is beautiful."

"This is Morgan Hill. When I reach this plateau I know I'm almost home. I never tire of the sight."

"I don't know anyone who has a hill named after them. I'm impressed." Robin glanced sideways at her escort.

"My grandfather gets that distinction. The story goes that he and Grandmother braved heat, storms, and occasional encounters with Indians to cross these plains. Then came the day they topped this hill and knew they would stay. They dreamed of a big family, but my father was their only child. I'm also a lone offspring.

Robin sucked on her lower lip to keep her mouth from gaping. "Then all of this is yours? Oh my. I don't believe I've ever seen so much open space. And to think it belongs to only one person."

Ty gave her a crooked smile. "I suppose it's hard for a woman to understand, but my sole claim to owning this ranch is my name on the deed. In reality, Miss Wenghold—the land owns me."

She'd heard the same awe in Papa's voice the few times he reminisced about his childhood on the Feather.

Ty peeked around the brim of her bonnet. "You still here, Miss Wenghold?"

She nodded. "I'm sorry. Your regard for this wild country brought back memories of my papa. I'm trying to imagine him as a boy in these hills."

"Maybe I can help. We're not far from your uncle's place, and we've time. I'd like to show you our fair prairie."

She grinned. "I have eyes, you know."

"Ah, but you're only able to see the surface. This is beautiful country but full of risks. I survive out here because I'm aware night and day of the dangers that exist."

"More dangerous than Chicago, Mr. Morgan? Have you ever been to a big city?"

He chuckled. "Believe it or not, Miss Wenghold, I've been to many a big city and am well aware of the hazards they hold. But out here it's not the people that pose the perils—it's the land itself. Come with me." He placed her hand in the crook of his arm and led her to a rocky overlook.

Large slabs of rock jutted from the hillside below and scrawny bushes obscured the depth. Robin tightened her grip on his arm. Would he think her forward? But peering over the edge caused her knees to tingle. Or was it Ty Morgan's bay rum? "How far down does it go?" She shuddered. "A person could tumble over the edge before they know it's here."

"And this is one of the more obvious ones. A man can get killed if his horse happens to step in a hole hidden among the grass while they're galloping across here. They say not so many years ago, the Indians killed buffalo by running them off a ledge like this. Look." He pointed to a large rock below them. "See that stick lying there?"

"You want to show me a stick?" She peeked over the edge once again. "We have sticks in Chicago, too, you know."

"It's not what you think. Watch." Ty picked up a stone and hurled it onto the rock.

She shrieked when the stick slithered into an S-like shape then coiled.

"Listen closely. Can you hear it?"

Robin pulled the bonnet away from her ear and leaned forward.

"You mean that buzzy sound?"

"That's it. Memorize that sound because it signals danger."

"Is that a rattlesnake? I've read of them." She shivered and rearranged her bonnet. Her pulse buzzed in her ears with this man standing so close. Was *he* dangerous?

"Yes, and believe me, your horse will hear it and most likely shy away from it. If you're not paying attention, you'll go off his back faster than you can think. Rattlers are poisonous. Don't ever mess with them."

"But what if I'm not on a horse?" Dare she tell him she couldn't ride?

"It's best you carry a stick with you when walking through tall grass. And if you should happen to meet a snake, stand still. More than likely it will slither away. But you can't be too careful."

Staring at the tall grass around her she quivered and willed her voice to remain steady, "Do they come close to houses?"

"Yes, they'll come close to a house. You can also find them along anything rocky. In woodpiles. Around the well. Just learn to watch for them. Until you've been here for a while, assume any snake is dangerous."

"Could we please change the subject?" Whatever made her think she could live in this wild place with hailstones the size of her fist, wind so fierce it could topple buildings, and now creatures that slithered and could kill you? And tall grass separated her from the wagon.

"I don't mean to frighten you, Miss Wenghold. In time, I think you'll love it here. This land has a rhythm and beauty all its own. It will talk to you, but you need to listen. See the trees in the distance? They're telling you something now."

Robin patted a handkerchief across forehead. "Like perhaps it's cooler down in the valley?"

"That—and more. Remember how Emma said she learned to *look* at a person's face to *hear* what they were ındeed saying? This land is the same way. Sometimes it's what you don't hear that's telling you something. Take a good look at her, then tell me what she's saying."

"You keep referring to Kansas as a female. My introduction to this land was anything but ladylike."

"She threw a tantrum last night." Ty gave her a crooked smile. "See how repentant she is today? Kansas is very much a lady. See how her long prairie tresses blow in the wind. She births new grass every spring and cradles the hills like a mother with a newborn babe."

Robin avoided his gaze. Mama's idea of proper conversation between a man and an unmarried woman didn't include mention of a woman's tresses or giving birth to anything. But she'd admit he did have a way with words. He might even make a good preacher, though no preacher she'd ever known made her heart do such funny things.

"Shield your eyes a bit so the sun isn't directly in them, then let the lady have her say."

Robin stepped away and positioned both hands above her eyes. She cocked her head then giggled when a gleam of light sparkled through the trees. "Water. She's telling me there's water down there." She glanced at him. "Did I *hear* correctly?"

A slow grin spread over his face. "You did, indeed, Miss Wenghold. That's Pigeon Creek. In fact, that branch of water is how your uncle's ranch got its name."

"Then why do they call his ranch the Feather? Is it a joke? Mr. Rempel found my name funny enough."

Ty tugged a clump of grass from the ground then smoothed the dirt with the toe of his boot. "From what we can tell, if we were flying like a bird—and I'm not teasing about your name, Miss Wenghold—but if we could fly, Pigeon Creek would look something like this from the air." He drew a long curving line in the dirt. "That's the main creek, but then there are these other branches that jut out from it." He drew several lines away from the original one. "This big one here, protrudes onto your uncle's land and becomes his water supply. Guess somebody thought it resembled a feather the way it was shaped."

"Do you get your water from the same source?" She studied the way his shirt strained across his shoulders. If he caught her staring and could read faces like Emma, she'd be in a heap of trouble.

"My land follows the entire course of the creek. As far as anyone knows, the Pigeon has never gone dry so there's always been plenty of water." He dusted his hands on the back of his britches.

Robin bent and traced the drawing. "It's kind of funny when you think of it—Pigeon Creek. The Feather. Robin. You want to hear something even funnier?" She might as well get it over with. He'd find out in time.

"And what would that be?" Ty lifted his hat and wiped his forehead on his sleeve.

"I have two sisters named Wren and Lark." She dared him to laugh.

He smiled and plucked a long stem of grass. "Want to hear something even funnier? My ranch is called the Hawk."

"You're making that up."

"Nope, every word is the truth." He laughed and stuck the stem in the corner of his mouth.

The grass cushioned their footsteps as they walked back to the wagon. In the stillness, Robin feared Mr. Morgan could hear her heart beat like a drum. She wanted to smile, but her tongue clung to the roof of her mouth. It would be her luck for her lips to stick to her gums and she'd grin like Emma's old mule. At least she should say something. Silence was golden, but it was also awkward. "Do we have to go down in that gully to get to Uncle John's ranch?" The image of the snake coiled in the sunshine played in her mind, and she kept her eyes focused on the ground on the way back to the wagon.

He helped her onto the seat. "No, we'll stay on the trail you can see. That's another lesson. Until you learn your way around, don't venture off this road. This will take you from town to your uncle's place. I'll show you where it veers off to my ranch. That's all you need to know for now." He gathered the reins in his hands. "Ready? You might want to hang on this—wait." He stood and cupped his hand around his ear. "Listen. Do you hear voices?"

"Is this another quiz?" Robin tucked a stray wisp of hair behind her ear. If only she could think of something witty.

"Shh. Listen." He looped the reins around the brake handle, jumped to the ground, and stepped further into the knee-high grasses. "Can you hear anything?"

Robin untied her bonnet and strained to hear above the wind. "Is there a ranch close by? It sounds like someone yelling. Or crying." She put one foot on the wheel.

"Stay put, Miss Wenghold. I'm going to take a look."

He disappeared over the crest of the hill, and she lowered herself to the ground. A trickle of perspiration escaped from her forehead. The distance from wagon bed to ground took much more energy when she maneuvered it herself. She propped her back against the wheel and wiped her face with the hem of her skirt. The vast terrain swallowed both time and distance, and she scanned the horizon for Ty's return. Only the steady rush of wind and an occasional thud as one of the horses stamped its foot to protest the flies that swarmed on its legs broke the silence. Had it been their imagination? The wind did sound like someone crying.

If only she could find something to poke through the grass so she could venture away from the wagon. To stand in one position soon tired her, but she didn't care to consider the option of sitting among things that buzzed or slithered, and to climb back into the wagon would take more energy than she cared to attempt.

What would her sisters think of this land? Life itself presented a new challenge each day for Wren, and she flitted and fussed to control every minute. But poor Lark hated change so much she preferred her dresses cut from the same pattern, and insisted they all be the same brown muslin. Robin laughed out loud, glad no one could hear her. Lark's red hair prompted Papa's teasing—*You're more a little house finch than a lark my dear, but what Papa in his right mind would call his daughter Finch?* Lark failed to see the humor of Papa's fun-making, but then Lark chose to ignore humor altogether.

"Miss Wenghold!" Ty's frantic yell interrupted Robin's musings.

He strode toward her. "Hurry! I need your help."

Had he forgotten she couldn't hurry? She limped her way to him, and he dropped to his knees, his arms wrapped around a dirt-covered little boy who wrestled against the confines.

"Let me go, mister. Let me go." The tyke kicked and hollered and pummeled Ty's chest. "Turn me loose. My mama will be mad when she wakes up. You wait and see." He stretched his arms toward Robin. "Please, lady, don't let him take me away."

Robin reached for the child then plopped to a sitting position under the boy's weight. "Here, little man." She cupped his face with her hands. Two big eyes peeked through a mud-splattered face and stared, unblinking, into hers. She smiled, and his shoulders shook with tearless sobs as skinny arms encircled her neck.

"I . . . I need to go back." Ty swiped beads of perspiration from his brow. "Will you be okay here for a bit?"

"His family?" She mouthed.

Ty shook his head, then strode to the wagon and returned with a blanket and shovel. His gaze met hers for an instant before he trudged away, shoulders slumped.

Her chest tightened. His lack of words answered her question.

She buried her face in the child's hair and wept the tears his dry eyes held.

Ty patted the fresh mound of dirt with the back of the shovel then stepped back and surveyed the area one last time. Had he overlooked anything—or anyone? He'd found the woman under the overturned wagon, and the child about fifty yards beyond. Though men's clothing lay scattered about, there was no sign of a man, alive or dead. Various tools—those a man used—mixed with cooking utensils and women's garments. An iron bed lay mangled among the wreckage, its mattress soaked beyond use. There was no sign of the team that pulled the wagon, but it was obvious they had broken loose. Hard telling where they might be, but at least they would have water and grass. He could only hope they weren't injured. The child seemed the only survivor.

He removed his hat and bowed his head. As the preacher of the only church in Cedar Bluff, this was not the first time he'd stood over the grave of a young mother. But it was different when he was acquainted with the deceased and those left behind. Today there was no grieving husband present. No heartsick ma or pa. No neighbors to mourn the loss of one so young. Only one small boy, who'd somehow managed to survive the fury of a Kansas twister and was now left to face the storms of life motherless.

"Lord, I don't know where this woman was headed or what happened to her husband. All I know for sure is she didn't make it, and there's a little boy who no longer has a ma. If I should be looking for her man, then, Lord, don't let me rest until I find him. And God, please take the sting from that little boy's heart."

He took one last look around, slung the shovel over his shoulder, and headed back up the hill. It didn't make sense to turn around. He'd go on to the Feather and deliver John's niece. Maybe by then he'd have an idea what to do with the boy.

He took a deep breath as he approached his wagon. Robin sat, nearly hidden in the tall grass, with the child cradled in her arms while she rocked from side to side. Why did women always move when they had a child in their arms? The ladies in his congregation often swayed in rhythm as they visited after Sunday service, sleepy babes clutched to their hearts. The scene before him seemed so peaceful—so natural. Who would suspect the artist to be the cruel hand of fate?

You know better, Ty Morgan. You're the man in the pulpit Sunday after Sunday declaring there are no words such as luck *or* fate *in God's vocabulary. He's sovereign. Remember? With Him there are no mistakes. He knows your days. He will supply. Perhaps you should start believing what you preach.*

He fastened the shovel to the side of the wagon then squatted beside Robin. "We'll go on to your uncle's ranch and take the boy with us for now."

"I ain't leavin' my mama," the boy mumbled against Robin's chest.

Ty cupped his hands around the boy's shoulder. "Sure would like to know your name, son. My name's Ty, and this lady is Miss Wenghold."

The boy shrugged away from his touch. "Jacob."

"A fine name, Jacob, and you're a very brave boy. It must've been real scary to be out here all alone in the storm." Ty patted the child's head.

"I wasn't alone. Mama stayed with me." He pushed Ty's hand away.

"Can you tell me if your pa was with you? If he's hurt somewhere, we need to find him."

"Don't have a pa." He drew his knees tighter to his chest.

Ty rubbed his forehead. Why did the boy allow her to hold him without protest, yet resisted any contact with him? He stood and attempted to take the child, but Jacob clung tight to Robin.

She motioned for him to back away. "I'm not going to leave you, Jacob. But I need to get off the ground. Mr. Morgan will take you long enough to help me to my feet and into the wagon, then I promise you can come right back to me. I'm not going anywhere without you."

Jacob loosened his grip around Robin's neck and allowed Ty to take him, but he kept his eyes scrunched tight.

Ty reached with his free hand and pulled Robin to her feet. She staggered against him, then righted herself and limped to the wagon. He groaned. He'd forgotten about her limp.

She climbed into the wagon then straightened her skirts and turned to reach for the boy. "Maybe you should give me lessons in wheel climbing, Mr. Morgan." She smiled and gathered Jacob close to her.

"You did fine, Miss Wenghold. Real fine." He hoisted himself in beside her.

The wagon lurched forward, and Jacob lunged from Robin's arms. "I can't leave Mama."

Robin dropped to the floor of the wagon, wrestling with the child.

Ty braced his feet against the front of the wagon and reined the horses to a stop. Why hadn't he considered the boy's grief? He'd been a grown man when his own mama died, and it still hurt. How could they expect this child to understand?

"Please, don't leave Mama all alone." Jacob kicked the side of the wagon. "Let me go."

Ty grabbed the boy's legs. "Jacob, listen to me. Your mama would want you to come with us."

"No! I promised I would stay put, and that means I can't go away."

"Your mama would want you to be safe. We can't leave you here all alone."

"No! No, let me go. I didn't tell her good-bye. She won't know where I am." He pounded at Robin with both fists. "Please, don't make me leave my mama."

Robin's face glistened with tears. "Mr. Morgan, I think we should take him back. We need to help him say good-bye. Uncle John can wait."

Ty nodded and turned the team in a wide circle.

Robin held the boy's fists. "Jacob, listen to me. We'll go back so you can say good-bye to your mama. But you will still need to go home with Mr. Morgan and me. Can you understand that?"

Jacob backed against Robin and pointed at Ty. "I don't want him to go with us." He hiccupped. "Can't you take me by yourself? Mama likes ladies."

Robin leaned her back against the sideboards and arranged her skirt like a nest. "Mr. Morgan needs to drive the wagon, Jacob. He's a nice man. He won't hurt you, and he won't let anything else hurt you." She settled the boy on her lap. "Agreed?"

Jacob frowned, but he nodded.

She wrapped her arms around the boy. "There, now." She held his head against her chest. Ty stole a glance at Robin. Her hair, no longer wet or muddy, tumbled from the confines of her blue and white bonnet. Slim fingers made minute circles on the boy's shoulders while she hummed a nameless tune. He swallowed a lump of memory. His own mama used to sing to him when he was afraid. If only she were here now, to tell him what to do next. The wagon bumped through a mud hole, a remnant of last night's storm, and Robin opened her eyes. Their gaze held for an instant, then the dimple accompanied her weary smile.

He tightened his hands on the reins. Only one other woman had ever made him desire a family. What irony that Robin Wenghold should storm into his life one year to the day after that one stormed out.

FOUR

John Wenghold crammed his hands into his pockets and waited for Ty's wagon to stop in front of his gate. *Well, old man. You've done did it now, ain't ya?* The only woman to ever lay her head at the Feather was his ma, and now he'd invited a female he'd never set eyes on to live here. If only he'd accepted his brother's yearly invitations to visit Chicago. At least then he'd have an idea what the little gal looked like.

He pulled a handkerchief from the pocket of his britches and cleaned his glasses. *Jumpin' bullfrogs. There ain't no spot on these spectacles, and that gal ain't so little. Besides that—she's got a kid on her lap.*

"Is that my niece, Ty Morgan?" Why, with her head cocked to one side she sure 'nuff resembled a robin. John stepped sideways to the large rock that served as his front step. "She never said nothin' about havin' a little one, you know."

Ty scowled and held a finger to his lips.

Now what'd I do? Ask a simple question and get frowned on and shushed all in one swoop. This ain't startin' out so good.

Ty met him before he could get to the wagon. "It's your niece, John, but it isn't her child."

"Then what's she doin' with it? Don't tell me she brung a kid along for company."

"Did it storm out this way last night?"

"Something fierce. I was a hopin' you weren't caught in it between here and Cedar Bluff." John pointed to the barn. "Lost me some shingles is all, but the worst of it passed to the south. And—doggone it—you done changed the subject on me."

"I thought maybe it would miss you by the way the clouds were building." Ty lowered his voice. "We found this little guy on the way here. It appears his folks got caught right out in the open. Can't find hide nor hair of any man, and the boy says he doesn't have a pa. His ma was dead, no sign of the team, and most everything they had was in shambles. I don't know what kept the little one alive, except he was tucked up under an overhang pretty good."

"Who you reckon put him there? If it was his ma, why didn't she stay with him?"

"There was only room for one very small person. I'd say she was willing to take the risk out in the open, but wanted to spare her child. I can't imagine how hard it was to make a decision like that."

"Doubt she even thought about it. Your ma would have done the same thing for you. Is he hurt?" John shuffled past Ty. "Well, don't just sit there, girl. Get the kid in here so's we can have a look-see.

"Wait, John."

"What now?" He waited for Ty to catch up with him. "You got another surprise in that wagon, do ya?"

"Don't go rushing up to the boy. For reasons we don't understand, he doesn't take much to me, seeing I'm a man."

John laughed. "So you're a thinkin' if the kid don't take to you, he surely wouldn't want my wrinkled old face a lookin' at him. Is that it?"

"I don't even like your old wrinkled face looking at me, John." Ty punched him on the shoulder. "Let me and your niece get him settled before you start growling."

Ty took the boy from the Robin's lap, and the tyke pummeled his shoulders. John chuckled. "You're a doin' a good job of gettin' him settled, Mr. Morgan."

Ty frowned and slung the boy over his shoulder like a sack of flour.

John hooked his thumbs under his suspenders while the girl

climbed from the wagon and limped toward him. *What's wrong with her? Never see'd anyone so awkward walkin'.* "You hurt, too, girl?" He turned to Ty. "What happened to make her hitch along like that?"

Robin glared. "You might as well know right from the start, Uncle John—I'm crippled." She dipped her head for an instant, but when her eyes met his again, there was determination in her gaze. "I've walked like this since taking my first steps. If you'd accepted Papa's numerous invitations to visit Chicago, you'd have known about my infirmity before you wrote that letter."

"Well, . . . I—" John stepped backward as she stomped toward him.

"Now, you can send me back if you want. I'll understand." She limped past him then returned with her hand extended. "Forgive my manners." She took his hand in both of hers.

Jumpin' bullfrogs, her hand is soft as a kitten, but she's spunky as a wildcat.

"I'm Robin, Lionel's oldest daughter." She motioned for Ty to follow her.

Ty shrugged and motioned to the boy. "His name is Jacob." He shifted the child to his other shoulder and followed Robin onto the porch.

Jacob opened one eye and wrinkled his nose as he passed by.

Well, if that wouldn't kick Granny's cat. I think the kid wants to play. John tweaked the child's nose, then held his thumb between two fingers and waggled it. "Lookee here, what I done got."

Jacob's blue eyes widened, and a lopsided grin wiggled loose from his clamped lips. He shook his head and covered his face with one hand.

John pointed at the kid's nose then wiggled the thumb again.

Jacob squirmed higher on Ty's shoulder. "Huh-unh. See?" He crossed his eyes. "It's mine."

John shook his head. "Nope, I got it."

"Could you give it to me, please?"

Robin turned to face him. "Do you have something of his, sir?"

John stuck his hand behind his back. "Well, not—"

Jacob pointed. "He gots it behind him. Look."

Robin held out her hand. "Hand it over, whatever it is. The child has already lost so much." Tears puddled in her eyes. "Please."

"Now, wait a doggone howdy-do. I don't have nothin' of his."

"Then what do you have behind your back?"

"He's only a boy." Ty scowled. "Whatever you have, please give it back to him."

John stuck his fist in Robin's face and wiggled his thumb "His nose. I got his nose." He winced. *There's some things a growed man shouldn't be caught doin'.*

Jacob giggled behind his hands.

Robin rubbed her forehead. "Oh, for—" She shook her head. "I don't know which one of you is the child. Would you mind giving Jacob his nose so we can get him settled?"

He examined his extended hand, thumb still protruding through the next two fingers. *This is plumb foolish.* He stepped closer, and in a flash, Jacob reached for John's nose and pulled. Hard.

"Rosy, posy, I got your nosey." Jacob clasped his hands. "I have to squish it real hard cuz it's so big. See?" He smashed his hand against his own face. "There, now I gots your nose on me."

Tears sprang to John's eyes and he rubbed his face. *Tarnation that hurt!*

Ty tapped his foot. "John? Do you mind telling me where you want everyone for the night?"

"Well, there ain't nobody but me livin' here, so I reckon most anywhere upstairs would suit. Will need some doin' up. Sheets on the beds and all. And if you plan on stayin', you best bed down in the barn, Ty. Wouldn't do for you to be a sleepin' upstairs with my niece."

Robin turned pink as a morning sky.

Jumpin' bullfrogs. This havin' a female in the house ain't gonna be easy.

"I've got supplies I need to unload, and I'd like to check for damage at my place. I'll take Jacob with me and give Robin time to get things ready here." Ty turned to leave.

"No! Put me down. I don't wanna go with you." The boy bucked in Ty's arms.

"I'll bring you back, Jacob." Ty set him on his feet.

The boy gave Ty a shove that sent him reeling backward.

The child hurled himself at John's legs, and his knees buckled.

"Watch out, kid—" His rear hit the porch floor, and his upper teeth clamped onto his bottom lip.

"Don't let him take me." Jacob's arms encircled John's neck so tight it hurt, but he wouldn't mention it. It was the first time a child had ever run into his arms. He'd ignore the fact that his lip throbbed like it had been stepped on and that it would no doubt swell bigger than the nose the kid pretended to pull off.

"Yep, Ty. You shore know how to settle a kid, don't ya?" He patted the boy's back, and the kid squeezed even tighter. Much more and he'd be gasping for air. "Don't worry, little man," he managed to squawk. "He ain't takin' you nowhere." John stretched his legs, and set the boy on his lap. "I surely do wish you'd give a thought to stayin' here for a spell. I could use me some help a gatherin' eggs and haulin' wood, and things like that. I reckon you're man enough for a job, don't you think?"

Jacob swiped a pudgy hand under his nose. "How come my nose is so drippy?"

John scratched his head. "Well, there's a real good reason for that. That's my nose on your face. Remember? And it's tryin' to run off so it can come to me again."

Jacob scrunched his hand around his nose then poked a fist in John's shirt pocket and wiggled his fingers. "There. Now can I have *my* nose back please?"

John laughed and hugged the boy. His arms had never been so warm or so full. "You surely can, my boy. You surely can." He wiggled his thumb on Jacob's face. "Now, I think you need to stay here with me 'til we can be sure that little thing I gave you is gonna stay on your face." He winked at Ty.

Jacob grinned. "Do you for real got eggs?"

"Sure do. You like eggs, do ya?"

The boy nodded. "Fried, with the insides all runny. Then Mama lets me sop it up with my bread." He sniffed and picked at his fingernails.

John held the boy close. *He can't fool an old man. It ain't a big nose that's makin' the little fella's face drippy. No siree. He's missin' his mama for sure. Strange he don't talk about a pa.*

"I'm a little short on bread right now, but I reckon Miss Robin could stir us up some biscuits." He stood the boy on the floor. "Now, you stay right there while Mr. Morgan helps me up."

John groaned when Ty pulled him to his feet. "You go on about your business, Ty. I think the kid likes me."

"Uncle John? Where might I find—"

He turned to Robin. "You'll find flour in the can behind the blue curtain in the kitchen, and soda's in the cupboard. Make yourself to home. Me and the boy got eggs to gather."

"Here, don't want to forget this." Ty handed Robin the package Emma had sent along. "I'll be back tomorrow, if that's okay with you. Looks like John has made a new friend, though I don't understand why the boy took to him so readily, yet pushes me away." Ty's voice held a twinge of awe. Or was it jealousy?

Robin tucked the package under one arm. "Uncle John wasn't the man who made him leave his mama. If he stays long enough, I'm sure he'll learn to trust us." She smiled. "If Emma were here she'd likely tell you that scowl on your face says you're worried."

Ty wiped his hand across his forehead. "Sure hope his pa isn't injured and lying out there waiting for help. I'll go on to my place. Maybe my men have seen someone. I'll see you in the morning."

Robin waited until he was no longer in sight then stepped into the kitchen. A large round oak table occupied the middle of the spacious room, and a line of cupboards occupied the wall to the left of the door. White curtains billowed in the breeze blowing through the open window above the sink, and open shelves flanked either side. The work surface of the lower cupboards was oak, worn smooth, doubtless from years of wear. The curtains covering the shelves below were—Robin shook her head—blue. *Well, Uncle John. I'm sure the flour is here somewhere, I just have to find behind which blue curtain you meant.*

She hung her bonnet on a hook beside the door then searched until she found the flour. By the time she'd found the ingredients and a bowl to mix them in, Jacob had returned with eggs cradled in his shirt pulled above his waist.

"We got lots of 'em, Miss Robin. See?" He counted six eggs and laid them on the counter. "Will you fry 'em?"

"I will. Thank you." She peered around the boy. "Where's Uncle John?"

Jacob shrugged and plunked down in a chair at the table. "Can I watch you fry 'em?"

"You may. But we'd better wait for Mr. Wenghold. Why didn't he come in with you?"

Jacob scratched his head. "He said he had some business to tend to. That's all I know."

"Well, I imagine he'll be in before long. You go wash your hands, please, then you can set the plates on the table for me." Robin measured the ingredients for the biscuits.

Jacob followed instructions, then sat at the table and rested his head on his arms.

"You're tired, aren't you? As soon as Uncle John comes in I'll pop these in the oven." The heat from the big cookstove was stifling. She'd need to remember to do her baking in the morning instead of so late in the day. That is, if Uncle John let her stay. Surely he wouldn't turn the boy out, would he? "Jacob, was my uncle with you when you came from the chicken coop?"

He propped his elbow on the table and rested his head on his hand. "No, ma'am. He already left to do something different."

"Did you remember to latch the door?" As a child she'd failed to shut the gate to the chicken coop and, consequently, chased chickens all through their neighborhood, much to the dismay of their uppity neighbors.

"I don't remember. Should I check?"

"That would be good. You should always remember to latch doors behind you so wild animals won't get into the buildings."

A few minutes later, Jacob returned, puffing. "I runned real fast and did what you said. I latched every single door I found." He settled back in his chair and swung his legs. "Can we eat yet?"

"*May* we eat?"

Jacob cocked his head, a frown deep between his big green eyes. "I just asked you that."

"I know. I was correcting you. *May* is the correct way to ask that question. Not *can*. Did you see Mr. Wenghold when you went outdoors?"

"Did I see him?" He shook his head. "No, ma'am. I didn't see him."

Robin busied herself looking through cupboards. It would take some time to learn what supplies Uncle John had on hand and what she would need to purchase on the next trip to Cedar Bluff. When the sun slipped below the trees that shaded the west side of the house, she lit a lamp and tried to still her imagination. If only she had checked on her uncle sooner. *What if he's hurt? How would I get help?*

Jacob was sound asleep at the table with his head on his arms. She moved the braided rug from in front of the sink, then gathered him in her arms and laid him atop of it so he wouldn't fall. He tucked one hand under his cheek and drew his knees closer to his chest, but didn't awaken. She patted his shoulder, then straightened and let herself out the back door. Uncle John had to be found.

If only she knew where to start searching. She gathered a handful of skirt and headed down a well-worn path through the grass. Intent on the lookout for snakes, she jumped when a loud voice broke her concentration.

"Hey! You let me out of here, you scamp."

She stopped, lifted her head, and her gaze rested on the weathered outhouse beneath the trees. She shook her head. Surely not. "Uncle John?" How in the world did he manage to lock himself inside the outhouse?

"That you, Robin? Get me out of here, and you best be tellin' that scalawag to head for the timber."

Robin hesitated. It didn't seem proper for her to hold a conversation with a man outside a place like this. "He said he didn't know where you were. Have you been here long?"

"Let me out. I ain't gonna keep shoutin' through this door."

Robin unlatched the door and stepped back as her uncle roared out of the small building. "How . . ."

"What do you mean—how?" Uncle John stabbed the air with his glasses. "That devil-child did it, that's how."

"When he came back with the eggs he said you told him you had some—"

"Did you think I was gonna spell it out for him? A man's got a right to some privacy, you know."

"Of course, I know. But how did you get locked in?"

Uncle John dug a red bandana from his pocket and cleaned his glasses with a vengeance. "He came a hollerin' for me, and I answered him. Then the kid latched the door, that's how. Said you told him to make sure all the doors was hooked so no wild animal could get in."

"Yes, I did tell him that, but I . . ."

"Did you think to tell him that if someone was in them buildings he was to leave the doors alone?"

"No, I thought . . ."

"Ya didn't think at all, girl." He hooked his glasses behind his ears and jutted his chin. "I yelled at him to get away, but he said he was followin' orders. You send that kid back out here, and you go on about puttin' some grub on the table."

"I asked him if he saw you, Uncle John, and he told me he had not." She tried to hide the smile that wanted to come. "I'm sure he didn't understand."

"Well, I'll give him that much. He didn't see me because the door was shut. Send him out."

"He's sleeping, and you're angry. I won't have you hurting the boy."

"Him and me have some talkin' to do out behind the barn. That's all."

Their conversation was interrupted when a lone horse and rider thundered from the shadows beyond the timber. Ty. He reined to a halt, and the horse slid in the still muddy ground. "Where's Jacob?"

"What you doing back already, Ty? Got a lot of damage, do ya?" John patted the horse's neck. "Got this creature plumb lathered, son."

Ty dismounted. "Sorry to sound abrupt, John." He turned to Robin. "Where's the boy?"

"He's asleep in the kitchen."

Ty handed the reins to John. "Mind if I put my horse in your barn, John? I'll take care of him after I've had a chance to visit with the two of you."

"I'll take care of the horse. You see that Robin gets back to the house without stumblin' in the dark. I'll tell you one thing for sure, the Feather has never been ruffled like this before. What I wouldn't give for a little peace and quiet again."

A knot gathered in Robin's stomach as Ty joined her. He hadn't planned to come until morning. Was there news of Jacob's pa?

Ty took her arm. "John seems a bit irritated. Is there trouble?"

"Jacob locked him in the necessary. He's quite angry. Before you rode in, he threatened to take the boy behind the barn to have a *talk*."

Ty chuckled. "Any other time I'd side with your uncle. But I think we might have a bigger problem." He helped her onto the porch and patted the space beside him as he sat in the swing.

"Was it bad at your place?" She reached for the rope to let herself down easy.

"About like here. Shingles from the barn scattered across the prairie, and one building lost part of its roof, but no one hurt. The fellas checked the line shacks this morning, and all were accounted for—men and animals alike. But there was one bit of disturbing news."

"And it concerns Jacob?" Robin's stomach fluttered, and she used her good foot to still the sway of the swing.

"I don't know. It might. Rusty, my foreman, said a stranger rode in a little ahead of the storm. He asked how far it was to town and if they knew of anyone needing a hand."

"Did he say anything about a wife or child?

Ty put his arm across the back of the swing and shook his head. "He said the man never let on like there was anyone but him, but he seemed real agitated. Rusty told him how to get to Cedar Bluff and warned him about the storm. He offered to give him shelter in the root cellar and told him he could wait until I got home to see about working, but he mumbled something about not being a snake or a beggar and rode off to the north."

"Do you think there's some connection? What if Jacob is lying about not having a pa? Did the man look mean? Maybe that's why Jacob seems to be afraid of you." Robin turned to face him. "What shall we do?"

"That's a lot of questions to answer, Miss Wenghold. I don't think we should do anything until we pray."

Robin shook her head. "You go ahead." She fiddled with a loose thread on her cuff. When she raised her head she met his gaze. "You're staring, Mr. Morgan. I get most uncomfortable when someone stares at me."

"I didn't mean to make you uncomfortable. By staring. Or by suggesting we pray."

He sat so close his breath tickled her ear.

"Just so you know . . . I believe there *is* a God, Mr. Morgan. But I think He's tired of me asking Him the same questions over and over again. I'm not sure He even hears me when I pray. He never answers."

"Oh, Robin . . ." Ty leaned closer. "God never tires of His children talking to Him, and He always listens. But sometimes, for our own good, He doesn't grant us the answer we want."

Robin bristled. "Oh really, Mr. Morgan? It wouldn't have been for my good to be born with two good legs? And what about that little boy? Don't you believe his poor mama prayed when that storm bore down on them?"

Ty moved to the wicker chair and reached for her hands, stilling the swing. "I can't give you an answer why God chose to allow you to be born with a bad leg. And for the life of me, I'll never have the answer why He would allow a little child to lose his mama right before his eyes. But I will say the storm keeping us in Cedar Bluff for the night probably saved Jacob's life. Who would have heard his cry if we hadn't stopped for that short time?" He ran a hand over his face. "You might not think God is listening, or that He cares, but He does."

Robin pulled her hands from his. "Then you pray, Mr. Morgan. And when God answers, you let me know." She stood and allowed the door to slam behind her. He sounded more and more like a preacher, and she'd learned at ten that preachers couldn't be trusted.

Come, little children. Come meet Jesus. He will forgive your sins and heal all your infirmities. The visiting evangelist seemed so confident—so promising. She ignored the frown on her mother's face and the tittering of other children as she limped down the aisle that night. They could laugh all they wanted. Jesus was going to heal her. They'd see.

Only He didn't. The preacher was wrong.

And it took fifteen bumpy steps to return to her parents.

FIVE

Ty stepped off the porch and took a deep breath of summer air. Could there be a sweeter scent than dew-drenched, sun-warmed prairie? With luck, he'd be able to leave before anyone could question him. But a clatter of feed buckets, followed by his foreman's long-legged stride toward him, signaled he'd waited too long.

"You headed for the Feather again today, boss?" Rusty raised one eyebrow.

Ty scowled. "What do you mean, again?" He loved this guy like a brother, but the hitch in his eyebrow was more than a question—it was an insinuation. And he didn't like it.

Rusty shrugged. "Every day last week, third day this week, and it bein' Wednesday. Can't say I blame ya none. Right cute little boy. Probably more than John can handle by hisself. But that fishin' pole ya got in your hand should help."

Ty grinned in spite of himself. "All little boys deserve to know the thrill of pulling a three-pound catfish out of a creek. Didn't your pa ever take you fishing?"

"Ever chance we got to sneak away from Ma and my sisters. But sure don't remember Pa ever smelling so sweet or wearing his white shirt on a weekday. You got special orders today?"

Ty removed his hat and ran his hand through his hair. "None we've not already talked over—keep an eye out for anything or anyone strange. Still can't believe a man would up and leave his wife and child alone with a storm approaching. Would've thought the woman was traveling alone if I hadn't found men's clothing among the debris."

"The boy still won't talk about it?" Rusty set his buckets on the ground and propped one foot on the bottom rung of the corral fence.

"I haven't questioned him. Robin . . . er, Miss Wenghold thinks we should let him take his time about what he wants us to know. He doesn't trust men, that's for sure, except for John."

"Not even you?"

"He's slowly coming around. That's why I've been going so often. Miss Wenghold says if he can see that she trusts me, it might help. And you can wipe that smile off your whiskery face."

Rusty smoothed his long mustache. "Oh, trust is important, boss. Almost as important as woman-cooked meals, walks down the lane, and poundin' posts in the ground to string wire across so's there'd be a place to hang a man's britches."

"You been spying on me, have you? How much longer do you want to work on this ranch?"

Rusty moved away from the fence. "Look, Ty. I ain't been spyin'. You know me better than that. I met John on the road yesterday. He seemed quite pleased with the whole affair."

"There's no *affair*. Can't a fella show a little bit of kindness without a big fuss?"

"Ain't nobody fussing. I can tell you for sure, every man on this place is happy you might be filling your mind with somebody new. You ain't gone around smiling like this since that . . ."

"Leave it be, Rusty. You go on about your business, and I'll take care of mine." He shouldered past his foreman.

"I already saddled Tag for ya. Thought it would save some time." Rusty matched his stride. "I'm serious, Ty. I know you're my boss, but you're also my friend. No need to fight what might be comin'. No need to deny it, neither." He nudged Ty's shoulder.

"I'm not going down that road again, pal. Some places don't need to be revisited." Tag gave a little hop when he mounted. *You're as eager to run as I am to get away from this conversation, aren't you, old boy?* He nodded at Rusty. "Take care of things. I'll be back early, unless the fish are biting."

He spurred his horse and settled into the saddle for the ride across familiar prairie to the Feather. *Don't fight it, he says.* He wasn't fighting, was he? What was there to fight? Jacob was the common denominator between him and Robin. One man, one woman, and a boy didn't add up to anything to make a fuss over. He was helping. That's all.

Jacob waved when Ty approached. Why did that make his pulse quicken? *Helping, that's all? Careful, Ty.*

"Hey, buddy. You ready to go fishing?" He wrapped Tag's reins around the hitching post in front of the house and retrieved the fishing pole from behind the saddle.

Robin laughed. "He's been ready since sunup. He must have asked a hundred times when you would get here. Would you remember to bring a fishing pole for him? Would you bring one for me? The questions didn't stop until he saw you riding in."

Ty handed the pole he carried to Jacob. "I brought one for him, but I'm afraid I don't have one for you."

"Oh, that's fine. I thought maybe only the two of you would enjoy a day together. I have things to do here."

Jacob's face clouded. "I . . . I have things to do, too." He handed the pole back to Ty and scooted behind Robin's skirts.

Ty scowled but was determined not to let this day end before it had a good start. "Well, then—how about I help you do what needs to be done then we can all go fishing together. Would you agree to that, Miss Wenghold?"

"My plan was to surprise you, but I like your idea better—that is, if you don't mind spending the morning in the kitchen." She crossed her arms. "Do you know anything about baking cookies, Mr. Morgan, or frying chicken?"

Ty leaned against the porch pillar across from her. This was a side of Robin he'd not witnessed. She was bantering with him. And she seemed right pleased with herself. "For a fact, Miss Wenghold, I'm quite a good cook. Don't know much about sweet stuff baking, but can fry a real mean chicken."

Jacob emerged, arms crossed in replica of Robin. "*Our* chickens aren't mean."

Robin giggled. "Mr. Morgan is bragging about what a good cook he is, Jacob. He didn't mean the chickens were mean. What do you think? Could he make better fried chicken than me?"

Jacob shook his head. "Mens don't cook gooder than ladies, do they, Robin?"

Ty knelt so he would be eye level with the boy. "What say we let her cook and bring us lunch, then we'll catch fish for supper. Think we can do that?"

Jacob turned to Robin. "Will you come for promise?"

"I promise, Jacob. Ty and I will always keep our promises to you."

Ty's chest tightened. She'd never called him anything other than Mr. Morgan. Did his face reveal his surprise? His pleasure? Why did it please him? It wasn't like he'd never had a woman use his first name.

Jacob slung the pole across his shoulder and reached for Ty's hand. "I'm ready now."

Ty squeezed the boy's fingers. "Can you whistle, Jacob? A fella needs to whistle when he's going fishing."

Jacob puckered his lips and blew. Lots of air escaped, but no noise.

"That's okay, buddy. You keep practicing. You'll be whistling by the time we reach the creek." Ty glanced over his shoulder as they stepped from the porch. Jacob's hand was warm against his, and the smile on Robin's face warmed his heart. He'd told Rusty he wasn't going down this road again.

But this was a different journey. Wasn't it?

Jacob squished an ant that crawled across the tattered quilt Robin had spread on the ground for their picnic. "Thank you for the lunch, Robin. It was good, and I'm sorry I got pickle juice on your dress. May

I be excused, please?" Jacob swiped his hand across his mouth. "Can you come fishing now?"

Robin brushed cookie crumbs off Jacob's cheek. "Thank you for using your manners, Jacob. Yes, you may be excused, but I'm going to sit for a bit before I go fishing."

"Aww. Why do big peoples always have to sit still after they eat?"

Ty ruffled the boy's hair. "When I was a boy my mama made me take a nap after lunch. Doesn't that sound like a good idea?"

"Not very." Jacob's lower lip jutted.

"Come here, buddy." Ty pulled his watch from the pocket of his britches. "Here, you take this and lie down here beside Miss Robin and when that big hand—see the big hand?—when it gets to this number with a one and a two, then we'll go fishing."

Jacob sat on the blanket and crossed his legs. "But that will take a long time."

"No, it won't. Lie here on your tummy and put my watch by your head so you can count the ticks. It won't take long at all."

Jacob flipped to his stomach and put the watch to his ear. He rubbed the blanket between his thumb and forefinger then closed his eyes.

Ty stretched out beside Jacob, propped on one elbow, and rubbed the child's back. "Works every time." He grinned at Robin. "Quiets kitties and puppies, too, when they've been taken from their mothers."

"Or their mothers taken from them," she whispered.

"That, too. But he seems to be adjusting, don't you think? At least he lets me touch him now." Ty brushed at a fly that swarmed around Jacob's face

"He likes you, Ty. He told me so last night, and again this morning—several times. He said, 'Ty can do everything. He can even spit, cuz I saw him.' Thank you for that demonstration, by the way. I'm sure he'll need to try it for himself." She moved the picnic basket to provide shade for Jacob's face.

He grinned. "Well, since we're telling tales on Jacob, you want to know what he said about you while we were fishing?"

"Only if it's worth repeating.

"He said you cook even gooder than his ma, and you can sing, and you sweep floors, and you make real funny faces right before you sneeze."

Robin laughed. "He brought me a bouquet of some kind of little yellow flower. I don't know what they call it, but it did make me sneeze."

"I must say, your list of accomplishments impresses me." He stood and stretched. "Would you care to walk along the creek? We'll stay where we can see Jacob. But if I don't move around I'll be the next one asleep, even without the watch ticking in my ear."

Robin swallowed. Why didn't she think before this picnic idea? The walk to the creek with the basket and blanket was almost more than she could manage, but Ty and Jacob had been busy fishing and hadn't observed her near fall. Oh, she wanted to walk with this man. Yet, the years of taunts and ridicule had taken their toll on her confidence. She and Ty had been together nearly every day since her arrival. But this was the first time he'd suggested time alone. He'd invited her to accompany him to church last Sunday, but she'd managed to change the subject when Jacob interrupted their conversation. She certainly didn't want to divert his attention now. But how could she explain that she'd need help to even rise from the ground.

Ty knelt in front of her. "Robin? Was I being too forward? I thought maybe . . ."

She shook her head and made herself look at him—a lesson learned at her papa's insistence—*face your fear Robin, and often it will become your friend.* "I . . . Mr. Morgan, we've been sitting for a long time, and it will be difficult for me to stand. Only two men in my life have ever helped me in such a manner."

"Have you forgotten that day on Morgan's hill, when we found this little tornado?" Before she could object Ty bent and placed his hands under her arms and lifted her easily to her feet. He steadied her against his chest with one arm against her back. "Promise me you will never hesitate to ask me for *anything*."

The rumble of his voice against her ear vibrated through her senses. William Benson had tugged her to her feet more than once, but she'd never had her heart tugged—until now.

As a young girl she'd imagined being swept into the arms of a handsome prince. As a young lady of coming-out age, while she sat on the sidelines and watched her girlfriends glide across the dance floor in the arms of a beau, she would tap her foot and hope Mama wouldn't see her. And she would tell herself that her prince would still come someday. And later, at the girls-only party that followed the soiree, her heart thrilled while her friends tittered and blushed their way through whispered accounts of stolen kisses and promises made in darkened hallways. Then—one by one, as her friends married—her prince became only an idle hope. And Mama no longer gazed with disapproval while she sat on the sidelines with widows and maiden ladies many years her senior. Nor could she remember the last time she'd tapped her foot in anticipation.

But now—now, in Ty Morgan's arms . . . *This is silliness, Robin. He helped you up . . . nothing more. He was only being a gentleman.* Yet, the thrum of his heart matched the cadence of hers. And though she had both feet on the ground, he did not release her from his embrace.

"Got your bearings? I don't want to let go of you until you do." His arm tightened around her shoulders. "Who were they?"

Robin pulled away to look at him. "Who were they?"

The space between his eyebrows crinkled. "The other two men who helped you. Who were they?"

Did it truly matter to him? "My papa and a friend of the family."

"Not a man friend? A friend friend. Right?"

This was new territory for her—this sensation that someone like Ty Morgan might be interested in her. Did she dare imagine even a bit of jealousy? Her limited intuition about such matters told her this was not the wisest time to expound on her relationship with William Benson. She smiled. Perhaps Ty wouldn't sense her hesitancy. How could she explain William to another man? "An old friend."

He leaned closer. "And how would you describe me to this old friend?"

She took a deep breath. Oh my, but he smelled good; however, she'd resist the urge to sniff again. Warmth tingled her toes, swirled through her tummy, and moved right on up. She wanted to fan herself, but that would be a bit awkward. Besides, the fan would doubtless send a whiff of pickle juice right to his nostrils. "I suppose I would say you're a *new* friend."

Ty chuckled. "I expected something a bit more eloquent, like—dashing or handsome." His arm moved to her waist. "Let's walk. I have something I want you to see. Maybe then you will even say I'm special."

"Is it far? I don't want Jacob to be frightened if he wakes up and doesn't see us right away."

"Not far, and we'll be able to hear if he calls. Promise." Ty led her around the other side of the tree that sheltered their picnic spot.

The large trunk, on the side not previously visible to Robin, was hollowed out, a depression large enough for only one person. Ty loosened his grip on her waist. "This is my 'leaning' tree. I hid in here for the first time after my pa scolded me for not keeping my word. I rolled a pair of socks together with a clean shirt, got my fishing pole, and ran away from home."

Robin laughed. "And you knew this place was here?"

Ty nodded. "John showed it to me one day. I came down here often when I was a boy. Your grandmother Wenghold made the best molasses cookies in Kansas, and she was just as sweet. I wouldn't be surprised if John hid in this same tree when he was a lad."

"Did your papa know where to find you?

"Now that I'm older I'm quite sure he knew all about this place. He left me out here the first night to teach me a lesson. I sat on the ground with my bundle of clothes until it grew too dark to see."

"Were you afraid of the dark?"

He shook his head. "Not the dark around me, but the dark eyes I'd encounter when I faced my pa. I knew he would be disappointed and that was worse than any spanking he could have administered."

"You said it was your 'leaning' tree." Robin scrunched herself into the cavity and leaned against the rough bark. "It is comfortable, isn't it?"

"I got too big to huddle down on the ground inside, but I could lean against it all day. It's my 'safe' place. This old tree knows more about me than anyone living. When my pa was dying, I would come here and let the familiar notch embrace me. It frightened me to think of taking over the responsibility of running the ranch myself. I spent the night after Ma died in here, listening to the night sounds and watching clouds sweep across the face of the moon. I needed the familiar noises and scenes that I'd experienced with her, sitting on our porch or walking down the lane in the dark. And that night after . . ."

Robin put her fingers on his lips. She didn't know what memory she interrupted, but with each remembrance his eyes darkened, and the furrow on his brow deepened. "Didn't you ever come here in happy times? Has this tree ever seen you smile?"

He placed his hands on either side of the entrance and leaned toward her. "*This* is a happy time, Robin." His gaze met hers. "And I'm smiling."

He was so near she could hear the steady *tick, tick, tick* . . . She closed her eyes. *Oh, Robin, you silly girl.* It wasn't his heart.

"The big hand is on a one and a two, Ty. Now can we go fishing?" Jacob wiggled his way between them, the watch held high in his hands like a trophy.

Ty waited for Jacob's rhythmic breathing to signal the tyke was asleep before he blew out the lamp and made his way downstairs. He didn't want to take a chance the little scamp would interrupt his conversation with Robin again. He'd come close to telling her about his one and only love, until now. Why? He'd never even shown her his tree. Why was it important for Robin to know his past?

John met him at the bottom of the steps. "You get the boy down for the night?"

"I think so. He was pretty tuckered from his day of fishing."

"Robin's on the porch if you would rather talk to her than me." John grinned.

"Thanks, but you're welcome to join us."

" 'Bout as welcome as a cricket chirpin' under your bed."

Ty chuckled. For a man who'd never had a wife, John Wenghold understood the ways of courting. Could a man become wise without experience? He smiled at the mere thought of John wooing a lady. But is that what *he* was doing? Courting? Wooing?

He stepped to the porch and leaned against a pillar. Robin sat sideways in the swing, her head resting against the high wooden back. Were her eyes closed? It was hard to tell in the light of the crescent moon. Maybe he should get on Tag and ride home.

"You're staring."

"I thought you might be sleeping. I didn't want to disturb you."

She opened her eyes and sat up. "Just thinking about today. Thank you for showing Jacob such a good time.

He joined her on the swing and put one arm across the back. "And how about you, Miss Wenghold. Did you have a good time, too?"

She turned to him. "I did have a good time. I especially liked your leaning tree. But I wish it held more happy memories for you."

"Oh, it's full of happy recollections. I just didn't get around to telling you about them before we were joined by a certain little boy."

"I was thinking perhaps your tree would be a good place for Jacob. He doesn't want to talk about a pa, but maybe he'd tell the tree."

"You mean spy on him? Listen to him?"

She shook her head. "No, nothing like that. You could tell him how special it was and how you could tell the tree anything. Maybe it would give him a safe place."

"But, Robin, it wasn't the tree I talked to when I went there—I talked to God. God was my safe place."

"That's not what you said. You said that tree knew more about you than anyone."

"Because when I was there I prayed. I learned early that I could tell God anything. It isn't a popular idea among many people, but my parents believed it with all their heart. I've never been afraid to voice even my deepest . . ." He took a deep breath, much like he used to do before jumping into water he knew was over his head. The only difference now—he didn't dare hold his nose.

He moved his arm so his hand rested on her shoulder. "Robin, a year ago I was . . ."

The door flew open and Jacob bounded onto the porch. "Ty, Ty, don't leave. Please don't leave. Please." The boy threw himself against Ty's legs.

Ty groaned. Was this child destined to always wiggle his way between him and Robin? Could he never have more than ten minutes alone with her? He lifted Jacob onto his lap. "I'm not leaving forever, Jacob. I'll be back tomorrow, remember?"

Jacob clutched Ty's arm and curled into his lap. "I wished you could stay here all night. Don't you Robin?"

Robin's foot pushed against the porch and the swing lurched.

Ty wrapped his arms around the boy. Was this tyke's mama glad when he learned to talk?

SIX

John grimaced when he entered Emma's Mercantile. Henrietta Harvey, of all people, stood chattering and waving her hands like a travelin' preacher. Why, she was the biggest gossip in Cedar Bluff.

"Good morning, John." Emma stepped from behind the counter. "What brings you to town so early? How's that niece of yours?"

Henrietta bustled his direction, chirping like a peahen. "Oh yes, I want to hear all about that girl, John Wenghold. Now Carl Rempel told me about her nearly two weeks ago. I says to him, I said, 'Carl, I've been praying ever so long for a nice girl for my Albert and look how the Lord answers.' Why, who'd think John Wenghold would have . . ."

John raised his hand. "Well, Henrietta, I don't know as how God has answered your prayers at all. Seems to me if the Good Lord was a wantin' my niece to be hitched up with your son He would've let me in on it, don't you think?"

"I don't know, John. I don't suppose He'd have anything to tell you unless you were in the habit of listening." Henrietta shook her finger under his nose. "It's a real shame you haven't brought that girl to church. There's many a young woman who would jump at the chance to be with my Albert."

John snorted. "Then what you doin' prayin' for someone? Ain't Albert old enough to say his own prayers?" He propped his hip against the counter and stuck one hand in his pocket. He'd keep the other one free to snitch a gumdrop if Emma would move away from the big glass jar that held them.

Emma laughed. "Listen, if you two are gonna tangle with one another you can do it somewhere else. Now, what can I help you with today, John?"

He shook his head. He had no intention of talking about the tyke they'd taken in where Henrietta could hear. "Oh, thought I'd just look around. Maybe see what you got new since the last time I come to town."

"You do that. I have some pretty new hand painted teacups. Not another woman in the area has anything so nice."

"Oh, but you're mistaken, Emma Ledbetter." Henrietta scrunched between them. "I saw some real bone china ones over at Florence Blair's when she served our ladies missionary meeting last week. Did you ever say why you weren't there? Well, I suppose you had a good excuse. The teacups had a gold rim, too. Do yours have a gold rim? John, now tell me your niece's name. Carl Rempel said it was a bird name but couldn't remember which one."

Jumpin' bullfrogs, the woman don't even take a breath before she starts waggin' her tongue again.

She tittered. "He got quite a chuckle out of it, though. Said she was a feisty little thing. I says to him, I said, 'Now, Carl, I would think *spirited* might be a better word for a young lady. And I don't imagine her mama thought it one bit funny to name her after a bird.' Though I do have to say I've never heard the like. It is a bit strange, don't you think?"

"Don't seem so strange to me, *Hen*-rietta." The look on Mrs. Harvey's face gave him a good belly laugh, but he'd have to wait until she harrumphed her way to the door before he could turn it loose. He nearly choked on his own spit when Henrietta turned, her hands cupped around her mouth, like they was a mile away.

"Emma, I almost forgot what I came here to tell you."

She paraded toward them, her skirts flapping around her ankles.

If she got tangled he'd be the one to catch her. He took a step back.

"Florence told us at the meeting Anna is returning to Cedar Bluff. She'll arrive two weeks come Saturday. But she wants to keep it a surprise for Ty." She shook her finger at John. "And don't you tell him, either." She lowered her head and marched to the door, elbows flapping against her plump sides.

John groaned as Henrietta did another sashay and headed back his direction. It seemed she was winding up again.

"Behave yourself," Emma hissed. "You make her mad and she'll never leave."

Henrietta puffed to a stop and tapped one pudgy finger against his chest. "Did you ever tell me the girl's name? Oh, don't you never mind. You bring her to church on Sunday and I'll ask her myself."

He shook his head. "Nope. Ain't gonna promise nothin' of the kind. It'll be up to Robin when she's ready."

"Ooh. So it's Robin? Well, how quaint. Hmm. I do wonder how they came up with that name. Never mind. The poor girl can't help what her parents called her. Besides, Albert will be so excited to meet her." She fluttered her eyelids and wiggled her fingers. "Oh my. How exciting. I can't wait to tell Albert." The bell above the door jangled as she departed.

John rested his elbows on the counter and shook his head. "Now what should I do, Emma?"

"You'll do what you said. When she's ready, you bring her to church." Emma grabbed her feather duster.

"It's not that easy. Let me tell you what's happened." He motioned for Emma to move closer.

Thankful no one came in while he filled Emma in on the details about the boy, John sighed and wiped his forehead with his bandana. "So, I need clothes that would fit a youngster about as tall as my belt line here, and some boots and—well, doggone it, Emma, I don't know what all a kid needs."

"Why didn't you send Robin sooner?" Emma ran the duster over the counter and rearranged the candy jars.

"She and Ty been too busy with the boy to leave."

Emma cocked her head. "She and Ty?"

"For some reason the youngster don't seem to trust men, though he took to me right off." John winked. "Course, I'm one of them fellas what people tend to favor and all."

"If the boy chose you over Ty I'm concerned he maybe got hit in the head during the storm." She poured a sack of gumdrops into one of the empty jars. "So, how does that fact keep the both of them so busy your niece doesn't have time to visit our fair little village?"

"Ty's been spending ever' wakin' minute at the Feather. Dug up some worms and took Robin and the tyke fishin'. Dug up a small plot for flowers for Robin. Reads and prays with the boy every night. It's payin' off, too. Saw Jacob give him a big ole grin and a hug after Ty hung a swing from the tall cottonwood tree out back of the house." John inched his fingers toward the jar of gumdrops.

"Sounds like he might also be trying to win Robin's approval."

"Yeah. I think he might be—" He slammed his hand on the counter. "My lands, Emma. Did Henrietta say Anna Blair was a comin' back?"

Emma nodded. "I'm afraid so. Bad timing, isn't it?"

"No time would be good as far as I'm concerned. Never did like the idea of Ty hitchin' up with that girl. She's too uppity."

"And you've already decided Robin and Ty would be a better hitch?" Emma smiled.

"Don't know as I've been decidin' anything of the sort. Gave you my thinkin' on the Blair girl, that's all." John flicked at an invisible crumb. "Missed one."

"Did no such thing, and you know it." Emma waved the duster in his direction. "Just because Anna is coming back to town doesn't mean Ty will take up with her again. Time changes things. Most likely Anna has a beau back East. She's a beauty."

"Yeah, she's a looker. No doubt about that. That's the funny thing, Emma. Robin—she's stuck about as far on the end of the pole as you can get from Anna, but Ty seems taken by her."

"What would you know about a man being taken by someone?"

Emma swished the feathers across his shoulder.

John plucked the duster from her hand. "What I knows might up and surprise ya, Emma girl." He grinned and grabbed a piece of licorice."

"You put that back, John Wenghold—or else pay for it."

He bit off a chunk. "Can't put it back. I done et some of it, but you can put it on my ticket." He tickled Emma's cheek with the feather duster and grinned when she turned pink.

"You get out of here." Emma shooed him away with a flick of her wrist. "I'll have some things ready for the boy when you get back."

John stepped onto the street and puffed out his chest. *That Emma's some woman.* He smiled to himself and tipped his hat to a passerby. *Yes, siree. Quite a woman.*

A floorboard squawked as he entered the building that doubled as post office and living quarters for Albert Harvey and his mother. Curled in a patch of sunshine, a fuzzy yellow cat opened one eye when John approached the counter. It stretched, bared its claws, then settled back into a purr.

"Albert? You in here?" The place seemed deserted. John adjusted his glasses to read the notices on the wall while he waited. One in particular caught his eye. *WANTED: Women willing to settle in Colorado to live and work on ranches. Can promise husbands. Only healthy young women need apply.*

"Oh, it's you, John Wenghold." Henrietta waddled from behind the curtain. "Why, fancy seeing you two times in one day. Oh my. Albert is feeling poorly, dear boy. I says to him, I said, 'Albert dear, it's a good thing I'm still living with you, otherwise you would have to lay abed all day without anyone to even care.' You know, what the boy needs is a wife. Unfortunately, until your niece arrived there simply has been no one in this town worthy of my son."

John sighed. Until Henrietta, he'd never known a female could tucker a man just by opening her mouth. How could she get so many words out of one suck of air? He pointed to the notice. "Surely women don't answer such a thing, do they?"

"Why, of course they do."

"Ever think of Albert advertising for a wife like that there?"

Henrietta sputtered and took such a deep breath her second chin popped above her lace collar.

Whew! If words come with that swallow of air, I'll never get out of town. "Sorry to hear about Albert. I suppose you can give me my mail?" He didn't want to wind her up again. Besides, he was teasing about Albert ordering a wife.

"Albert has no need to resort to such tactics. Why, any girl in her right mind would be proud to be the wife of the postmaster. You wait and see. I came right home from Emma's and told Albert all about your niece. I didn't say much about her name, though. He'll find out about that soon enough, won't he? Why, hearing about her made the poor boy feel so much better. I could tell by the way he smiled. A mother knows the ways of her son." She clutched her hands to her bosom. "Oh my goodness, I do believe the Lord gave me a wonderful thought this very minute."

He stepped back as her hands fluttered as if she were doing some kind of dance. Hopefully her whole body wouldn't join in.

"Did you ever think about ordering you a wife? Some even wonder why I don't marry again." She smoothed the sides of her hair with both hands and fluttered her eyelids.

Well, *he* never wondered. No siree. "The mail, Henrietta? Have you forgotten about my mail?" The tiny room closed in on him. He needed fresh air. Her sputtering about marriage with him all alone in the same space made him downright queasy.

"Oh, of course. Silly me." She fanned herself with the sheaf of mail she pulled from the W box. "I could help you write the advertisement. Some say I have a real way with words."

"Henrietta? The mail. Please. I do believe it's right there in your hand."

Henrietta tapped the mail against her chin. "John, do you ever hear from Eunice Parker? You were sweet on her once, as I recall. Now my sister, Maude Everly—I'm sure you remember Maude. She was older than me, but not near so comely—well, she's kept in touch with Eunice all these years. She could give you her address if you'd like. It would be so romantic, don't you think? I hear tell she never married."

John reached across the counter and pulled the mail from her hand. "Thank you, Henrietta. I'll be goin'."

Henrietta pushed the cat out of the way and propped her elbows on the counter. "You know, John. You would make Eunice such a good husband. She was always a bit . . . oh, I don't know. I suppose I would have to say a bit plain. I always thought the two of you would go so well together."

John let the door slam behind him. *Plain? So that's how she'd describe me? Plain?* Well, he'd do everything in his power to warn Robin about Mr. Albert Harvey and his wife-huntin' mama.

He stopped and peered at his reflection in the window of the barbershop. *Don't know who he is, but that guy standin' just a starin at me—now, he's a plain one.* He smoothed his eyebrows with his fingertips then twirled an imaginary mustache. *A real smart aleck, too, tryin' to imitate me. Bet the fella never had him a girl.*

John returned to the mercantile, and Emma smiled when he approached the counter.

"I have your purchases all packaged."

"How much this gonna cost me? Robin said somethin' about needin' to pay for some things ya gave her." John sidled to the counter. "Can already see havin' this woman around is gonna be a high-priced arrangement." He reached for the gumdrops, but Emma pushed them away.

"Not gonna cost you anything you can't afford, John Wenghold. But in case I'm wrong, I'll not charge you a penny for anything I gave Robin or bundled up for the little fella."

"Well, suppose I buy you a steak for lunch. Would that be about even?"

"Only if I eat the whole critter." Emma laughed.

"Do you know Henrietta tried to give me Eunice Parker's address?

Said she always did think we would be good together." *Well, jumpin' bullfrogs. Is that a scowl on Emma's face? Hmm. Now what's a fella supposed to think of that?*

Emma tapped John on the shoulder. "You bring Robin and that little guy to church. And don't pay Henrietta Harvey any mind. Think about the boy. Maybe someone will know something about the stranger who showed up at Ty's ranch."

"Yeah, I suppose that would be best. Now, where'd you put the stuff for the kid?"

Emma pointed behind the counter. "It's back here. Didn't want to have to answer a bunch of questions if someone came in before you got back."

John eyed the box of packages then squinted at Emma. "What did you put in them bundles, anyway? There's gotta be more stuff in there than I got hangin' on my own hooks at home."

"Oh, hush. There isn't anything there a boy his age doesn't need. I don't suppose it occurred to you that he might like something to call his own."

"He's got the whole ranch, Emma. What more could a kid want?" John grinned. No doubt Emma was building up a head of steam. But she was right. Beyond seeing that the boy had three square meals a day, he hadn't given a thought to more than some new clothing.

"Go on with you now. You make sure they get back for church when Robin's ready." Emma stacked the packages in John's arms. "Take care you don't stumble on your way out. I sent some special things for Robin and some of them are breakable." She opened the door for him and followed him as far as the porch.

John loaded the packages, then crawled into the wagon and tipped his hat. "Thank ya. Oh, say, Emma?"

"Forget something?" She shielded her eyes against the sun.

"Uh . . . well, I was a wonderin'. Would you say I was . . . plain?"

"Plain?" Emma laughed so hard tears flowed down her cheeks.

"I don't think it was all that much to laugh about." John mumbled.

She took her handkerchief from her sleeve and wiped her eyes.

"No, my friend—I say you're plumb."

"Plumb? Well, if that don't kick granny's cat. What does that mean . . . plumb?"

"It means you're plumb crazy." Emma laughed and waved.

John flicked the whip across the back of his team, and the wagon lurched. *Why did I bother asking a woman, anyway?*

SEVEN

"Jacob, quit jumping around. Here take my hand so you don't get your new clothes dirty before we even get inside." Robin gathered her skirt in one hand and attempted to match strides with her uncle. "Does the bell ringing mean we're late?" There didn't seem to be anyone else lingering in the churchyard, and the last thing she wanted was to walk into Sunday meeting after everyone was seated.

Emma had sent a new dress with Uncle John, along with assurance that the soft gray cotton was suitable for all occasions. She didn't want to stand out in the crowd, but this seemed less than stylish. Its square neckline lacked any hint of adornment. A row of small pearl buttons, the only embellishment, marched from the neckline to the waist, and also closed the plain, straight sleeves. The skirt didn't have enough yardage for fancy petticoats, nor sufficient length to cover her shoes. Would people notice she walked on tiptoe with her left foot to accommodate her bad leg?

"Never been late for church in my life, girly. Don't aim to start now."

She pulled on his arm. "Then could we please slow down? I limp more when I have to hurry, and I don't care to hobble down the aisle my first time here. I'm sure we'll create a stir as it is." She glanced around the churchyard again. "I thought perhaps Ty would wait for us. He said he'd be here."

Her uncle gave her a strange look. "Of course he's here. Ty ain't never late for meetin'. Not with him being the . . ."

"Uncle John? Robin?" Jacob tugged Robin's skirt and jumped from one foot to the other.

John scowled at him. "Stop that prancin' around, boy. You promised to sit still once we got here, so start practicin'. Now."

Jacob stopped and crossed his legs. "But I gotta . . . I got some business I need to take care of."

Robin groaned and turned to John. "Could . . . you?"

"Oh jumpin' bullfrogs, boy. Why didn't you tend to that before we left home?"

"I did, but that was a long time ago." He pulled his hand from John's and pointed. "Who's that bossy looking lady with her face all mad? Am I in trouble?" He reached for Robin.

"Oh, there you are, John Wenghold. Don't you dare make a move until I get there."

Robin stared at the stern-faced lady charging in their direction. "Uncle John?"

"Oh, girly. Plumb forgot to warn you about Henrietta Harvey. She's—well, there's no time to explain now. You'll find out soon enough."

The woman huffed her way to them, her mouth moving as fast as her legs. "I was afraid you were going to be late, like you always are. I laid my Bible on our usual pew so nobody would sit there. Room enough for all of us. Come along, dear. I'm Henrietta, by the way, but then I'm sure your uncle has told you all about me."

Robin glared at her uncle.

John rubbed the side of his nose. "I gotta help the boy. Catch up with you later."

The woman grabbed Robin's elbow and propelled her toward the church. Her leg ached as she limped—and Henrietta puffed—their way to the little white building among the trees. How the pudgy lady managed to trot and still have breath enough to talk was beyond her.

"You'll notice right off, Miss Robin, that my Albert is such an important part of this church. He's the one who rings the bell every Sunday. Why, I suppose people would hardly know it was the Sabbath if Albert didn't faithfully remind them each week." She leaned toward Robin. "It would please him if you would mention his silk necktie. He bought it yesterday, over at Emma's. I told him, I said, 'Albert, we're going to have a new young lady at church tomorrow, and it wouldn't do for you to show up in that same old raggedy brown thing you been wearing since your papa's funeral. Now you hike on over to Emma's and get you a new one.' He didn't much see the need, of course. You know how men don't like to spend money on themselves. Well, at least my Albert never wastes a penny if he can help it. Thrifty, he is." She ground to a halt and made a circle around Robin. "And I see you're frugal, too. One can always change out the pearl buttons for something a bit less showy. I saw some that would do nicely over at Emma's the other day. Oh, I knew it. I knew it. It's a match for sure."

They stepped into the vestibule, and Robin's gaze fastened on the bell-ringer. Despite his lanky height, Albert stood on his toes to reach the bell rope. His back was turned, and his hat rocked back and forth like a seesaw with each pull of the rope. Robin bit her cheek to keep from smiling.

"What did I tell you? See how smoothly he's able to do that?" Henrietta whispered. "It was my idea to shorten the rope, you know. Shows Albert's manly form as he pumps up and down, don't you think?" Henrietta folded her arms across her ample bosom. "*Psst.* Albert. She's here. This is Miss Wenghold. You know—the young *un*married woman living with John Wenghold. You can stop ringing the bell now."

Albert released the rope, pulled down his jacket then turned and took off his hat. Thinning hair lay in a giant sweep from one ear to the other across the top. One large strand slipped forward and seemed as if given a chance it would return quickly to the fringe around his ears. Wire-framed glasses revealed watery blue eyes. He ran his tongue over his teeth, then smiled and extended his hand.

"Pleased to meet me, I'm sure . . . no, pleased to meet *you*." He took three quick sucks of air that escaped his nose in a snort.

Robin's heart went out to him. Poor man was as nervous about this encounter as she was. "It's nice meeting you, Mr. Harvey."

Albert withdrew his hand and deliberately straightened his necktie.

Never in her life had Robin seen such a neck dressing. Had Emma helped him? If so—bless her dear heart. Purple with large orange stripes.

Albert leaned toward Robin. "Emma said she'd been saving this for some handsome young man. Only one she had, and she thought of me first off."

"How nice of Emma. I don't believe I've ever seen one quite like it." *Thank goodness Uncle John is busy with Jacob.*

Henrietta smiled so big her cheeks plumped like little pink pillows. "Ooh, I knew you would be impressed. Oh my. Yes, well, let's go in and get seated, shall we? I can't wait to show you off, Miss Wenghold. Why, you and Albert will cause quite a stir." Henrietta grabbed Robin's hand and pressed it to the inside of her son's crooked elbow. "There, you show her in, son. My Bible is in our pew. I'll sit by Robin. And Albert, you sit on the other side of Robin. Now, where did John go?"

"He's helping Jacob, I believe." Robin smiled at Mrs. Harvey. "I'm sure he'll find us."

Henrietta straightened Albert's collar. "Of course, he'll find us. The Harveys have had their own pew since Father Harvey donated the land for the church. Now, who is John helping? Who is this Jacob? Was he the little boy dancing around out there?"

"Yes, that was Jacob. You see . . ."

"Miss Wenghold. Is this . . . this Jacob your child?" Henrietta fanned herself with her handkerchief.

Robin glanced at the people gathered behind them. Standing in the aisle did not lend itself well to this conversation. "Perhaps we should sit down, Mrs. Harvey."

"Well, my goodness, I suppose so. I wish John would have said something about the boy. Oh my. I don't suppose there's anything I can do about it, though we'll need to talk about it later. On second thought, Miss Wenghold, you take my arm and Albert will lead us to our bench. Are we ready?"

Ready or not, Robin would either need to sprint or be dragged down the aisle. Albert's long legs took one step to her two, and Henrietta followed close on his heels. Robin no longer worried about her limp—it seemed more like a gallop on their way to the Harvey pew.

"Service doesn't start until the bell stops ringing. Albert's that important. Even the preacher waits on him, you see." Henrietta nudged Robin when they reached the bench with the Bible in the seat. "There, scoot right on in ahead of me. I had this all planned. I wanted you to sit by Albert, but now—oh my, what with the child and all."

Robin thought it best at this point not to explain Jacob. The little boy may have given her a way out of a rather prickly situation.

"Preacher will come from that little room back there." Henrietta smoothed her skirt and retrieved a fan from her reticule, which she unfolded with a flick of her wrist. "He's young, but surely knows how to give out God's Word. Sad, though. Such a big ranch to run, and then the duties of the church. He surely does need a helpmeet. Had a lovely local young lady destined to become his wife, but she left almost exactly a year ago. Oh, but is he ever going to be surprised today."

Henrietta's fan sent a spicy waft of cloves in Robin's direction, and she wrinkled her nose. Cloves always made her nose twitch. Papa would laugh and call her his funny bunny, but it wasn't at all humorous. Pinching her nose shut was the only way to stop the twitch. An inappropriate gesture, given she was seated beside Henrietta Harvey in church.

Other than Mrs. Harvey's rather dated green taffeta, it relieved Robin to observe that most women in the congregation were dressed in a similar fashion as she. And her pearl buttons were less showy than most. She must remember to thank Emma. Mama would be pleased to know she'd not made a spectacle of herself. *You must be careful, daughter. One can draw attention from both directions, you know. It's important you not appear aloof, nor one to be pitied. There's no need to cause others to feel uncomfortable for you.*

Oh for goodness sake, Margaret—Papa would reply—*let the girl be. All little birds preen now and again.* Happy memories of her papa squeezed Robin's heart. She'd not preen, to satisfy Mama. But would Ty notice?

"I do declare"—Henrietta elbowed Robin's rib—"the preacher's in for the surprise of his life today. Why, I can hardly wait. Oh, here comes John and that . . . that boy." Henrietta scooted her hip against Robin, forcing her closer to the end of the bench. "I do hope John remembered to wash the child's hands."

Albert leaned across his mother and gave Robin a wan smile as Jacob climbed across his feet and scrunched between her and Henrietta.

Robin returned the smile. *Poor Albert. He looks every bit as miserable as I feel.* She patted Jacob's knee. Henrietta's full skirt nearly hid the poor tyke.

Jacob wiggled into position to face her and his elbow poked into her hip. "Is it over, yet?"

Robin laid her finger on his lips and shook her head.

"This is the day the Lord has made." A familiar voice broke the hush.

Henrietta motioned for her to stand with the congregation as they chorused in unison "We shall be glad and rejoice in it."

Robin's breath caught, and tears clouded her eyes when they locked onto Ty Morgan's face.

"How come Ty talked?" Jacob's words seemed to bounce from the walls.

"*Psst.*" Henrietta tugged on her skirt.

Robin's knees shook and she sat with a plunk.

"For pity sakes, girl. If you don't know what to do, follow what everyone else is doing. And keep that child quiet. Hasn't he ever been in a church before?" Henrietta shook Jacob's shoulder.

Robin sat Jacob on her lap and gave the woman a withering stare. *How dare she touch this child in such a rude manner?*

She should have known. Ty as the preacher explained a lot of her questions the past two weeks. His efforts to win Jacob's trust. Their long talks after the boy was in bed—the words he spoke and the words he left unspoken. Had she imagined what those words were and what they meant? What she dreamed might be attraction for her was nothing more than a preacher fulfilling his obligation. Call it what you like . . . in reality it was pity. She bit her lower lip in an effort to control a sob. How could she have been so confused? Was she so eager to be loved and accepted that she mistook a preacher's kindness for affection?

"I don't like that lady," Jacob pointed at Henrietta, but at least he managed to whisper this time.

Bless his heart. She didn't much like her either.

She closed her eyes. The next time the congregation stood she would take Jacob out and leave. The ranch was too far to walk, but perhaps she could make it to Emma's.

A murmur through the congregation interrupted her thoughts. An older lady and a younger woman slid into the row in front of her. The woman wore a deep blue dress that matched her eyes and accentuated her white, stylishly coiffed hair. A single strand of pearls lay atop the pin-tucked bodice. A flawless complexion belied her probable age.

If the girl was her daughter, it was evident she'd inherited her mother's beauty. Hair the color of ripe wheat coiled like a crown, and a small pink hat perched on top matched the elegant silk gown she wore. One white feather arched down to frame the right side of her face. Large, blue eyes sparkled behind long lashes.

"That's Florence Blair and her daughter, Anna." Henrietta whispered. "You know . . . the wonderful surprise for our preacher."

Robin stared at Ty. This girl was a wonderful surprise for him? Was this the woman the preacher had been destined to marry? Her fingernails dug into her palms. She wanted to run but couldn't move. She couldn't even walk out without making a scene.

"Oh, how exciting." Henrietta stood and waved at Ty. "Pastor Morgan? Oh, Pastor Morgan?" She didn't wait for him to acknowledge her. "We all know this is the most wonderful surprise for you—and for us all—to have Anna back in our midst. Don't you think it would be a blessing if she played and sang for us again?"

A hum of agreement met Henrietta's suggestion. Robin's stomach churned. Anna Blair slipped off her long gloves and on her left hand a diamond and ruby ring sparkled in the sunshine streaming through the window. A soft murmur of excitement accompanied the beauty as she made her way to the front. She reached Ty's side and grasped both his hands in hers, then proceeded to the piano.

"What a friend we have in Jesus . . ." Soft and clear, her voice stilled the murmur.

Robin had sung this song, long ago, but never where anyone could hear. Only when others ignored her or jeered at the funny way she walked or chased her home from school for a chance to laugh at her attempt to run. Papa said Jesus would always be her friend even when others forsook her. *Oh, Papa, He doesn't feel like a friend right now.*

"Oh, what peace we often forfeit . . ."

She wanted to go home—back to Chicago. Her sisters loved her, and they'd love Jacob.

"Oh, what needless pain we bear . . ."

Why does it hurt so much? It wasn't Ty's fault she was crippled, or that she had silly thoughts about him.

". . . All because we do not carry, everything to God in prayer."

Robin squeezed her eyes shut as tears leaked down her cheeks. It seemed a bit late now to do her praying. Heat rushed to her face as she recalled her own words: *God doesn't hear my prayers.* What must He think?

Jacob twined his arms around her neck. "Robin, please don't leave me here," he whispered.

How did he know her thoughts? Had she said it aloud?

"Oh, little man. What makes you think I would leave you here?" she whispered.

"Cuz your eyes are crying and Ty looks all funny." He sniffed and snuggled closer to her.

Robin dared to look at Ty, but his eyes were on Anna Blair.

"If I leave, Jacob, I promise to take you with me." She hugged the little boy and rocked until Henrietta frowned and poked her in the side with her elbow.

"Excuse me, Mrs. Harvey. I'll take the boy out so he doesn't bother you." Henrietta's puckered eyebrows didn't stop her as she climbed over Albert's legs. She ground her heel on John's toe as she reached the end of the row, but refused to acknowledge the question he mouthed.

Once outside she stood Jacob on his feet. "You're too heavy for me to carry."

"Where're we going? Was I naughty?"

Emma stepped beside them. "You're not going anywhere, and no, young man, you were not naughty." She patted his shoulder then pinned her gaze on Robin. "Needing some air, were you?"

Robin shrugged. "Why didn't anyone tell me?"

"Tell you what?" Emma hooked her arm in Robin's.

"I didn't know Ty was a preacher, too."

"What difference would it have made, Robin? You know, most of us around here don't even think about Ty being anyone other than a fine young man. He grew up out there on the Hawk, stayed on after his folks died and took on the preaching when the congregation couldn't afford to hire a full-time man. I suppose that's why we don't think about it much."

She led Robin to a clearing where they sat on a fallen log. "I'd get to the ground, but you'd have to go back in and ask for help getting me up again." Emma smiled. "Now, how about answering my question?"

Jacob squatted beside them and dug in the soft earth under the trees.

"Don't get dirt on your white shirt, Jacob."

Emma patted Robin's knee. "*Pshaw.* Let the boy be. He's probably the only one in this whole mess with a good enough reason to run.

By the looks of you and Ty a while ago you were both ready to bolt."

"If Ty ran any direction it would be toward Miss Blair. Did you see her ring sparkle? Was it an engagement ring, Emma? And did Ty give it to her?"

"Is there something between the two of you I don't already know?"

Robin shrugged. "I hoped, Emma. I only hoped."

"And now, because Anna Blair shows up with a ring on her finger and a song on her lips, you quit hoping?" Emma clasped Robin's hands. "That's not hope, girl—that's wishing. And there's a whole lot of difference between the two."

"Did you see how he looked at her, Emma?"

"I did. I also saw him looking at you. And girl, what I saw in that man's eyes . . ."

"Pity, Emma. Pure, plain pity. He feels sorry for a poor crippled girl who wears clothes someone bought for her, living with a relative to earn enough money to pay off her papa's debts and playing mama when he knows she'll never have the opportunity to ever become one. That's what you saw." She swiped at her tears.

Emma cupped her hands around Robin's face. "Now you listen to me. You're as sweet as they come, but you might as well be living in the middle of a thorny bush. You've built a wall around you full of sharp things—pride and presumption—then you defy anyone entrance."

Robin stared, her mouth agape, at the older woman.

"Oh, Robin . . . shutting people out will only keep you alone, not safe. A turtle hides in his hard shell when he senses danger, but it doesn't keep a wagon wheel from crushing him. If he'd face the foe and move on, he might could save himself a whole lot of hurt."

"You think I was wrong to leave the service? That's moving on, isn't it?"

"No. That's running away. You move on when you acknowledge who or what is blocking the road, and you find a way around it."

"Who is this Anna Blair?"

Emma raised an eyebrow. "Do you consider her an enemy or a

roadblock?"

"I don't know. Maybe both. Did she and Ty have—an agreement?"

"I'm not going to answer that. You can talk to Ty about it if it's that important to you, but I'll not say anything."

Robin picked at her fingernails. "Is it a secret?"

"Not at all. But the two of you need to be talking, Robin. I won't fill your head with stuff only Ty has the right to tell you. Now, I suggest you dust Jacob off, wipe the tears off your face and get ready to finish the morning. If truth be known, I suspect Ty's as worried about you and Albert Harvey as you are about Anna Blair."

"Did you help Albert choose his necktie?" Robin grinned.

Emma's eyes twinkled. "I sure did. Like it, did you?"

"It's awful." Robin kissed Emma's cheek. "How will I ever face all those people again? Papa always told me I act before I think most of the time."

"You did nothing wrong, Robin. You were a bit hasty perhaps, but nothing to be ashamed of. You wipe your eyes, straighten your shoulders, and smile at everyone you meet. Now, help me off this log and I'll go with you."

Robin hooked her arm in Emma's as they sauntered to John's buggy. "I don't think Mrs. Harvey likes Jacob. And probably doesn't have much regard for me now."

Emma smiled. "Henrietta's awkward with kids. I don't think she even liked Albert much until he got old enough to know when to speak and when to keep his mouth shut. Mostly he keeps it shut now that Herman is gone. Strange family, but Henrietta means well."

"She's very proud of him. You should have heard her bragging."

"He's all she has. I think if Jacob ever wrapped his little skinny arms around her soft neck she'd melt like butter on a hotcake."

"What do you think Uncle John will say about my leaving the service?"

Emma put her arm around her shoulders and nodded toward the church. "I have an idea you'll find the answer soon enough. They're singing the benediction."

"Jacob?" Robin scanned the area for the boy. "Jacob? Where did you go?"

"I'm up here."

She followed his voice and spied him perched on a branch much higher than she could reach. "Jacob, however did you get up there?"

"I climbed up, but I don't know how to climb backward. Maybe Ty can catch me."

"We're not going to bother Ty, but here comes Mr. Harvey. Perhaps he can help."

Albert was headed across the churchyard, but before he could reach them Jacob had shinnied down the tree. He grabbed Robin's hand and held so tight it hurt.

"Thought you didn't know how to climb backward." She brushed at his shirt with her free hand. She'd have to remember white shirts and little boys weren't a good match.

"I didn't want Mr. Harvey to catch me."

Robin smiled and squeezed the boy's hand. She understood. She didn't want Albert to catch her either.

EIGHT

Ty hurried to the privacy of the church's small cloakroom, sat on the floor, and leaned against the wall. Under different circumstances he would be at the door, shaking hands, greeting each of his friends and neighbors as they made their way out of the church. But he couldn't have put two more words together in a sensible fashion. Only God knew what he managed to utter from the pulpit after Anna made her way to the front—and Robin exited.

"I've missed you so much," Anna had whispered when she clasped his hands before singing.

Why had she chosen now to come back? A year ago she'd vowed never to return. He'd only recently made peace with that choice. He slammed both hands on the floor and welcomed the accompanying sting. At least his body wasn't as numb as his mind.

"You in here, Ty?" John propped his shoulder against the doorframe. "Hidin' away, ain't ya?"

Ty shrugged. "Unfortunately there wasn't a crack big enough for me to fall through. Yeah, I'm hiding. What would you do?"

John sat beside Ty. "Can't tell ya what I might do in a situation like you're in. Never had me any woman worries. But I reckon hunkered down here in the cloakroom ain't gonna solve anything, now is it?"

"Is Robin still here . . . somewhere?" Ty wiped his forehead.

"Don't rightly know, but Emma followed her out, so I'm guessin' she'll take care of things. Did you ever tell her about Anna or that you were the preacher?"

Ty shook his head. "I wanted to tell her. But any talk of God and she recoiled like a wounded animal. And every time I tried to tell her about Anna, Jacob would find a way to interrupt. I tell you, the kid's timing is profound."

"Looks like ya could've found some time these past couple of weeks. Jacob weren't talkin' the whole time, was he?"

"What would you have me say, John?" He cleared his throat and made a grand sweep with his arm. "Oh, by the way, missy, my first and only love walked out on me last year—and oh, yeah, I'm the preacher man in this territory, so you better watch out."

John gave a wry smile. "No, don't reckon that was necessary. But you had to have done some thinkin' on the fact she were new to these parts. First off, Henrietta done pounced on her like a cat on a rat. Jacob had Henrietta in a frazzle—"

"You and I both know it doesn't take much to put Henrietta Harvey in a frazzle."

"Shore. We knows it, but that little gal don't. Then Florence Blair and her daughter come prancin' in, then—"

"You don't need to go into detail." Ty rubbed his temples. "I was there, you know."

"Well, nobody would a knowed it. You stood there with your mouth hangin' open like a barn door somebody forgot to shut. Ya should've stopped Henrietta when she got up yammerin' about lettin' Anna sing and all."

"What was I supposed to do? Trying to stop Henrietta from talking is like trying to stop the wind from blowing. You know that. I had no idea Anna would ever show up in this church again, John. Did you know she was back?"

John hung his head. "I heard tell she was a comin'."

"You knew?" Ty leaped to his feet. "You knew, and you didn't tell me? Why? You had to know, especially with Robin here, what this might mean."

John stood, too. "Henrietta told me she wanted to surprise you. Said I weren't to tell you."

"And you listened to her? You and Henrietta tangle every time you're within shouting distance of one another. Why in the world would you buckle under for something like this?"

"I didn't want Robin to suffer no more'n she already has. I seed she was gettin' right fond of havin' you around."

"I wouldn't hurt her for anything, John. You know that, don't you?"

John shook his head. "Don't make no difference what I know. It's Robin you need to be talkin' to about such things. Lest ya forget, there's a little boy involved, and I ain't about to let him get caught up in another storm. And mind you, young man, there surely is one brewin' or I don't know my name."

Ty reached for the older man's hand. "Put in a good word for me with your niece, will you?"

"Nope. Any good word is gonna be comin' from you, I reckon. You take some time to think about it, then you come walkin' outta here like a man." John clapped him on the shoulder and strode away.

Ty waited until John left, then walked into the sanctuary. He knelt and leaned his head against the apron of the small square table used as the altar. "Lord, what is it you want of me?"

"I know what I want of you, Ty."

Anna. Had she been there the whole time? For a moment the old excitement of hearing her voice surged through his veins. Then the memory of their last minutes together raised its ugly head, and his shoulders tightened. He turned to her. "Do you, Anna? We've had this conversation before, you know."

Anna knelt at the altar beside him. "I was wrong and I'm so sorry." She reached for his hand.

The ring on her finger caught his eye. "Why do you still wear the ring, Anna?"

"You said you didn't want it back, remember?" Anna twisted the piece of jewelry. "I tried to give it to you, but you wouldn't take it."

"If I remember correctly, the last time I saw that ring you'd sent it flying across the prairie. It wasn't like it meant anything to you. How'd you ever find it?"

"Mother paid the Johnson boy to look for it. She knew there would come a day we would both regret our foolish actions."

Ty stood. "*Our* foolish actions, Anna?" He clenched his jaw.

Anna bowed her head. "Sometimes a person has to make a terrible decision before they recognize how bad they are at making a good one."

"This is no time to try to make up for a year's absence, Anna. If you'll excuse me—"

"Is someone waiting for you? I noticed John Wenghold sitting in his buggy with that young lady and her child, but they left when I told them Mother was expecting us. She fixed your favorite—fried chicken. You will see me home, won't you?"

Ty rubbed the kinks in his neck.

She hooked her arm in his and laid her head on his shoulder. "I don't like your hesitation, Ty Morgan. It isn't at all like I imagined it would be when you saw me again. Is there someone else?"

Was there? He couldn't answer.

Her brow furrowed. "Your silence tells me something I don't care to hear. Is it that niece of John Wenghold's? And her child?"

Ty led her to the front pew and motioned for her to sit. "I'm not sure why I need to explain anything to you, Anna—especially my relationship with Robin Wenghold—but to quiet any suspicion you might have, you need to listen."

He told her briefly about meeting Robin and finding Jacob. Anna's eyes brimmed with tears.

When he finished his story, she swiped at her cheeks with the back of her hand. "I must say I'm most relieved. For a moment I worried you had forgotten our engagement. I know now that it's only your ill-conceived sense of duty as a pastor I observed." She kissed his cheek. "Mother will wonder what's keeping us."

His ill-conceived sense of duty? Is that what attracted him to

Robin? Not her gentleness with a child? Not her spunk with an old man? She wasn't beautiful like Anna. She couldn't glide in step with his. Would she even be able to stroll along the banks of Pigeon Creek without tiring? Or climb to the top of Morgan Hill to watch the sun set?

But this beauty standing in front of him was not the Anna he'd known—the Anna who claimed preaching to be God's highest calling. That Anna would have begged to take in the boy herself. And Ty's so-called ill-conceived sense of duty was the very thing she'd encouraged. *You're their shepherd, Ty. You must care for them.*

He frowned as she tugged on his hands, her full lips—lips so freely given in the past—only inches from his.

Lunch with Anna and her mother proved awkward. Even the gracious Florence Blair seemed tense with her daughter's constant rehearsal of plans for him. They would marry and return to Philadelphia. If he insisted on preaching there were a number of good churches. He could always find employment at a bank. What a shame to spend the rest of his life herding cattle and battling the elements.

Whatever happened to their dreams for the Hawk? They would fill the spacious house with children. It would be a place of rest and refuge for any weary soul passing their way.

Later, as Ty rode toward John's ranch, lightning flashed behind the hills. He wanted to get there before dark, but an occasional roll of thunder warned of a gathering storm. He reined Tag to a halt and dismounted at the edge of Pigeon Creek. A blacksnake slithered from the bank and skimmed silently across the water. Overhead crows cawed a warning, though he wasn't sure if it was him or the reptile they didn't want in their domain. Mere humans should be so accommodating. Having two women like Robin and Anna in the vicinity was certainly cause for alarm.

He squatted at the edge of the creek and splashed cool water on his face. Anna's reason for leaving remained a mystery. Her return baffled him even more.

Robin's arrival had filled a void he refused to acknowledge. Her leaving . . . He shook his head. What would her leaving do? If only he could talk with his ma again.

Thunder grew more persistent and a bank of darkening clouds slipped over the ridge of the hill. He reached for Tag's reins. No matter the cost, he would ride to the Feather and pay his dues.

The big gelding stepped sideways as Ty put his foot in the stirrup. "Hold still, fella. This is no time for games. We need to get to the Feather before this storm hits." He patted the horse's neck and swung into the saddle. Tag nickered and threw his head. "Yep, gonna let you run for a while at least." Ty squeezed his knees, and the animal lunged forward then settled into long, easy strides.

When they reached the summit of the hill the horse threw his head and humped his back, but Ty managed to keep his seat. A haze of smoke blanketed the valley floor. A lone rider sat atop his horse at the edge of the timber. Ty dismounted and laid his hand across Tag's nose. "Shh, old man." He nudged his shoulder against the horse to move him back behind the crest of the hill then hunkered down on his haunches to observe.

When the storm and the gathering darkness edged close enough to hinder his watch, Ty mounted Tag, determined to approach the stranger. Not only should he warn the man about the coming storm, but he also didn't like the idea of anyone camped so close to the Feather.

The man's horse stood a distance away, ground-tied. A small coffeepot sat on the embers of a dying fire.

"Hello, the camp," Ty shouted, staying mounted.

The stranger jumped to his feet, his hat tumbling to the ground. "Who's there? I ain't meanin' no trouble, whoever you are."

"I'm not going to give you trouble, mister. Just want to ask you a few questions." Ty rode in, one hand on the lariat looped across his saddle horn, the other reining Tag who pranced and threw his head.

"I ain't wanted for nothing, if that's what ya need to know." The man reached for his fallen hat, his gaze locked on Ty. "Any law says a man can't camp out along this creek?" He plunked the hat on his head and widened his stance.

"No law, but if it's shelter you're needing, there's a ranch not two miles away. Looks like a storm might be pushing our direction. Under this stand of trees is no place to bed down for the night. Ever ride out a Kansas thunderstorm?"

"Been in plenty of storms. Thought the trees would give more protection than the open prairie." The stranger stood with both arms loose at his sides.

The stance of a gunfighter. Yet he wore no guns. Ty made a mental note. Could just be a fella down on his luck. "Trees draw lightning. Best place would be in a cave, though in these parts you take a chance of having a rattler for a neighbor should you choose to go that route." Ty smiled. The man appeared to be about his own age, tall, slim hipped with a slight bow to his legs, as if he'd spent more than one day on the back of a horse.

The stranger's green eyes followed Ty's every movement.

"You passing through, or looking for work?" He admired a man that eyed you straight on.

"Work, if I can find it."

Ty loosened his grip on his lariat and extended his hand. As he did, the fella slapped his thigh, as though drawing a gun, then shook his head. "Well, mister, I guess you might wonder about that dumb move." He wiped his hands on his britches.

Ty dismounted. "My name's Ty Morgan, and I'd be obliged if you gave me something to call you.

"Sam Mason." He reached for Ty's hand.

"That your real name? I'll forgive the act of drawing on me, but I'm not so quick to overlook a man who lies."

The stranger nodded. "My real name."

"Then I'll shake with you. You ever work on a ranch, Sam?"

"Here and there. Was hopin' to get a place of my own someday." He wiped his hand across his face.

"Something happen to stop you?"

He shrugged. "Guess you could say I up and got homesick. My ma died when I was just a sprout. Got me a sister and pa in Missouri. That's where I come from."

"I surely could use some of that coffee if you could spare it." Ty squatted by the fire.

Sam handed him a cup of the dark brew. "Sorry, only got one cup. Got a couple of biscuits in my saddlebags."

Ty waved off the offer. Thunder grew more persistent and lightning streaked from cloud to cloud. He took a swig and handed the cup back to the young man. "Tell you what, Sam—you put together your belongings and come with me. We'll head for that ranch I mentioned.

Sam wiped his mouth. "You got any work, by chance? I've gone about as far as I can on what money I brung along."

"We'll talk to my foreman. He's always looking for good help, and I let him do the hiring."

Sam stood and reached for Ty's hand. "Mighty grateful, mister. Was about to give up on life out here."

"Well, you don't know what kind of work you'll be doing yet, so better not set your hopes too high. But I can give you a safe place to sleep and some grub." Ty helped him gather his meager belongings. "This all you got, man? Not even a change of clothes?"

A slight frown wrinkled across Sam's forehead. He emptied the remains of the coffeepot on the hot embers, scuffed them around with his foot, then mounted and waited for Ty to lead out.

"Mind if I ask a question, Morgan?" Sam moved his mount up next to Ty's.

Ty shook his head. "Fire away."

Sam laughed. "Well, you saw my weapons."

"Only an expression. What's on your mind?" He would ask him about his guns later. Even a tenderfoot should know you needed to carry a firearm in this country.

"I passed a new-dug grave back yonder. The only name on the marker was *Mama*. Any idea who it might have been?"

Ty frowned. "You looking for someone, Sam?"

"Nah, curious is all. Seemed kind of a lonesome place for a grave. That's all."

A raindrop splattered on his forehead, and Ty spurred Tag forward. "We better ride, fella. Not much farther." The horses loped in rhythm. Any further questions could wait.

NINE

"Will Ty come talk to me before I go to sleep?" Jacob climbed into bed and flipped onto his back.

"I don't think we can plan on Mr. Morgan coming tonight." Robin drew the thin sheet up to Jacob's waist and bent to give him a hug. "You're a big boy. You can put yourself to sleep without Ty reading to you." She ruffled his hair, then straightened and massaged her lower back with her fists.

"We have to pray. Do you know how?"

Robin sighed. Of course she knew how. But she hadn't done it for a long time. "Why don't you pray, and I'll listen." She pulled a small rocking chair closer to the bed.

"Ty listens, then prays. It's real easy, Robin. It's just like talking. I'll go first, okay?" He folded his hands under his chin and scrunched his eyes. "You don't have your eyes shut. You have to close them real tight."

She smiled as one little eye peeked up at her. "How do you know I don't have my eyes shut, Jacob?"

"Sometimes when I squeeze 'em shut real hard they kinda wiggle open." He rubbed his eyes with his fists. "Will Ty get all hurted when the storm comes? I don't want him hurted." A flash of lightning pierced the room, and he held his pillow over his face.

"Oh, little man. Ty knows what to do. Don't worry about him."

He turned his head away from the pillow. "Where's Uncle John?"

"Uncle John is downstairs. I'll stay here with you for a while. How's that?"

"Good. Okay, I'll pray now. He scooted up in the bed then folded his hands again. "Dear Jesus, thank you for Robin and Uncle John and Ty, but I don't much like the other lady that squeezed my shoulder so hard. Please have Ty come before the storm hurts him. Oh yeah, and could you please let Robin be my new mama because I know my other mama would like her a lot. Amen." He peeked up at Robin again. "It's your turn now."

She swallowed. It seemed so simple when this little boy prayed. He even dared to voice his dislike for Henrietta. Oh, she'd voiced similar complaints many times, but never in prayer. What if Ty didn't make it through the storm? As for her being Jacob's new mama—

The pounding of hooves echoed through the open window, interrupting her thoughts.

"Horses coming!" Jacob bolted to the window. "I bet it's Ty. He's here, isn't he?"

She shrugged. Why would he come this late? Surely he knew Jacob would be in bed by now. She bit her bottom lip. If he thought he could come riding back into their lives after everything that happened today, he could think again.

"Can I go see him?" Jacob scooted past her and grabbed the doorknob.

Robin pulled him away from the door. "No, young man, you stay right here. We don't even know it is Ty, and even if it is—if he wants to see you he'll come up. Now, you crawl right back into that bed."

Jacob complied with a huff. She smiled at the boy's obvious frustration, but was in no mood to see Ty Morgan tonight, or perhaps any other night soon. She would talk to Uncle John in the morning about returning to Chicago with Jacob. She had no right to take the child, but what other option did she have? He needed her. And the truth be known, she needed him.

John held onto his hat and ducked his head against the pelting rain as he made his way to the barn. No one sat a horse like Ty Morgan, but someone had ridden in with him.

He reached the barn and shook the rain from his hat as he entered through the still open door. "I knew it were you as soon as you rode in, Ty. Go ahead and put your horses in the stalls, and throw 'em some hay if you want." John pulled the door shut behind him and fumbled in his pocket for matches to light the lantern hanging on a hook nearby. "That lightnin' pert near makes enough light to see by, don't it?"

"It does at that, friend." Ty slid the saddle off Tag and hung it over the edge of the stall. "John, this is Sam Mason. I met him down on the Pigeon not far from here. Told him he could come along to get out of the storm."

Sam peered over the back of his horse and nodded to John.

"I reckon anyone Ty's comfortable with is welcome here, too, young man. Where you come from?"

"No one place, sir. Here and there mostly." Sam shook hands with John, then continued rubbing down his animal. "Thanks to you both. Didn't fancy ridin' out a storm in the open."

Ty stuck his hands in his pockets. "Is the boy still awake?"

"Don't rightly know but suppose you could go check. You know where he sleeps." John made a circle in the loose hay with the toe of his boot. "But if I was you, I'd be waitin' a spell."

"Is Robin okay?"

John leaned against the rough boards of the stall. "Little late to be worryin' about that, I'd say. I think she's a bit embarrassed. That Blair gal done put a hitch in her plans when she told us you'd be goin' home with her. Guess Robin figgered you'd be here for Sunday dinner like ya were last week. Fried a chicken and baked a pie yesterday. Just give her some time."

Ty hung his head. "I had no idea—"

"I know." John clapped him on the shoulder. Aware of the stranger, he wanted to change the subject. No need for the newcomer to know business that weren't his to know. "Can bed you boys down in some fresh hay. There's blankets hangin' in the empty stall."

He pushed the door open with his shoulder and nodded to Sam. "Glad to meet you, young man. Likely our paths will be a crossin' again come sunlight."

Sam Mason sat with his back against the side of the stall, arms wrapped around his knees. "Uh . . . you married, Mr. Morgan?"

Ty shook his head. "Nope."

"Got a girl?"

Ty hesitated. Did he? This morning he thought he did. Before noon it seemed he might have two. Right now he wasn't sure he had any. "Do you, Sam?"

The newcomer grinned. "Not no more. I did have, but guess she favored big men with tin stars. Only woman in my life now is my sister. But like I done told ya, I ain't seen her for a long time."

"Always kinda wished I had me a sister. A younger one though. I'm thinking an older one could get mighty bossy."

"Mine's younger. After our ma died, Sis thought she was the boss. I left home about then. Decided I didn't want to take orders from a woman. Seems pretty childish now." Sam stretched out on the hay and put his hat over his eyes. "Maybe if I can't see the lightning I can get some sleep."

"Good luck with that one. But it's worth a try." Ty lay on his back and put his arms behind his head. He didn't feel much like talking—at least not to a stranger—and John wasn't going to listen. Would Robin still be awake if he went to the house for a pot of coffee? No, that probably wasn't a good idea. And besides—how would he explain this morning?

Sam turned to his side and propped himself with his elbow. "Mr. Morgan? Is your ranch far? Sorry you didn't make it home because of me."

"Don't worry about it. An easy ride from here. I was coming to the Feather anyway."

"That John fella, is he related to you? Seems like a nice man."

"John Wenghold is as genuine a man as you'll ever meet. Likes to grumble, but has a heart as big as the prairie."

"Is he upset with you over a woman? I couldn't help but overhear some of your conversation."

"Like I said, it's a long story. Yes, I think he's upset with me, but it's nothing that can't be worked out." Surely a new day would bring an opportunity to make things right with Robin. But what about Anna? According to her, they were still very much engaged, and she had the ring to prove it. She'd reminded him numerous times during the afternoon that they'd planned their wedding for this coming Christmas. How could he forget?

Oh, Anna, if only you knew how hard I worked to forget.

Ty stood and walked to the door. A light still shone from the kitchen. Maybe he should try . . . No, he'd wait until morning. He blew out the lantern hanging at the end of the stall and settled down in the corner. Sleep might elude him, but the Lord never would. He'd pray. God would listen.

Robin tossed the sheet aside. A warm, humid breeze added to her discomfort. She sat up, twisted her hair into a coil and reached for pins to secure it on top of her head. She'd convinced Jacob that Ty was safe. Now she needed to convince herself. She fumbled her way down the dark stairway then leaned against the wall at the bottom. A light in the kitchen frustrated her plans. She hoped she'd be alone, but Uncle John sat at the table with pencil and paper in front of him.

"You couldn't sleep, either?" She took a cup from the cupboard and poured herself some coffee. "Need more while I'm here?"

"Nah. It's cold. Didn't want to heat the house any more than necessary."

Robin turned up her nose. Her papa drank cold coffee, but she'd never developed an appreciation for the stuff. But she'd drink it. At least it would give her something to do besides fret about Ty Morgan.

"On second thought, I'll join you." John held his cup. "Ty rode in after you and the boy went up to bed." He spooned sugar into the coffee.

"Jacob heard someone. I thought Ty would've come up to tell him good night." Robin rummaged in the cupboard for the few cookies left and put them on a plate.

"He brought a stranger in with him. Said he found him on the Pigeon."

"You didn't know this man?"

"Nope. Never seen him before in all my days. Good-looking young fella. Seemed nice enough. I think Ty aims to put him to work." John reached for a cookie and stirred another helping of sugar into his coffee. "Robin. I think we need to talk about somethin'."

Robin sank to her chair. Did he plan to send her back to Chicago? That's what she wanted, wasn't it?

"When I was in at the post office the other day there were a Wanted notice on the wall what got me thinkin'."

"You're interested in Wanted Persons?"

"You might call it that. Actually, it was an advertisement askin' for women to go to Colorado and marry up with ranchers out there."

Robin's heart plunged. "Please don't tell me you're sending me to Colorado."

"No, no, girl. Now that I got to know ya', I ain't about to let you leave the Feather. But it did set my mind a wonderin'. After today, I been givin' it even more thought." He pushed the paper toward her. "Here, take a gander at this and tell me what you think."

NOTICE: Looking for a strong young man, between the ages of 25-40, willing to come to Kansas and marry my niece to help run the Feather ranch. Niece young, hard worker, good cook. Will pay top wages. Send letter to John Wenghold, Feather Ranch, Cedar Bluff, Kansas. P.S. No drunks or crooks need to bother writin'.

Robin put her elbows on the table and cradled her head in her hands. "You're not serious. Surely you don't intend to advertise to see if you can get someone to marry me. Oh, Uncle John."

"It might not be all that—"

"No, let me tell you how it will be." Robin pushed away from the table and coffee splashed from their cups. "I will save you the hassle of deciding what to do with me. I intend to take Jacob and go back to Chicago—soon—very, very soon."

John's forehead wrinkled. "You can't take the boy away, Robin. We still don't know if he has a pa. What if someone comes lookin' for him? Besides, I need you here."

She grabbed a towel from above the sink and mopped at the spilled coffee. "If someone comes looking, then you can always tell them where to find him. And as for you needing me here, Uncle John—nonsense. I agree you could use help around here. So why not advertise for a hired man? Why does it have to include me in the bargain?"

John shook his head. "Never had much luck with hired men. Besides that—don't think it would be real proper for you to be the only gal livin' here with a single man, 'cept me of course. Truth be known, girl, I don't want you or the boy to leave. Never thought I'd get so used to havin' somebody else in the house. Knew I took a chance when I offered you a place to live. But . . ."

"But you felt guilty, right? Poor Lionel. Poor Lionel's daughters. Well, let me tell you, Uncle John, it may take longer than I expected, but I will find a way to pay off Papa's debts."

"With what, Robin?"

"This may surprise you, but I did have a proposal for marriage from a young man before Papa died. I turned him down. Perhaps I should reconsider."

John raised one eyebrow. "Did you love him?"

She threw the towel into the sink. "No, but at least I knew him."

"You'd settle for marriage without love?" John spooned more sugar into his nearly empty cup.

"And you think advertising for a husband will bring me love?" She tapped her temples with her forefingers. "What are you thinking? What kind of decent man would even consider a wife on those conditions? They'd get out here and see I wasn't the bargain you made me out to be. Oh yes, I can cook, and I can work hard, but you never mentioned my infirmity, or the fact there was a young child to consider." She blinked back tears.

"I thought ya understood, when I sent that there letter askin' ya to come, what I needed was help around the house."

Robin stared at her uncle. "That's what I've been doing, isn't it? Cooking. Cleaning."

John shook his head. "That's inside the house, Robin. I been doin' that myself all these years. Don't need no help with that. I admit it's been mighty nice to sit down to your good cookin', and I rightly 'preciate all the scrubbin' and dustin' you been doin'. But you see, girly—it's *around* the house I need help." He swung his arm in an arc. "Out there. Outdoors. In the yard. Out amongst them hills, lookin' for strays, huntin' where all them mama cows done decided to hide their babes. Gatherin' rock for the fence lines. Things like that."

Robin sank to her chair. "You thought I would be able to help you, Uncle John? You believed a girl from Chicago, even without a bad leg, would be able to do all that?"

"My ma did it ever day." John wiped his hand across his face. "Reckon it never occurred to me any other gal would find it strange."

"Is that what the women who answer the ad will be expected to do?"

John shrugged. "Reckon so, but don't rightly know what them men might've had in mind."

"Are you're saying the only way you will let me stay on here, and do what I've been doing, is if I let you try to get me a husband?"

"I can't make you stay, Robin. You're a woman growed. But you can't take the boy. That's final. Not until we know for sure there won't be someone come ridin' in a-lookin' for him."

Robin spread her palms on the table. "You have me trapped. You know I won't leave Jacob here alone, and you won't let me go unless I leave him. Uncle John, look at me."

John ducked his head and stirred his spoon around and around in his empty cup.

"Look at me, Uncle John. I'm a woman—a living, breathing, human being—not a dozen eggs you can trade or a horse you can sell to the highest bidder. I do not belong to you. Why do you think you can pawn me off on the man who makes you the best offer? Some who-knows-what-kind-of-man hoping to get his hands on a woman and a ranch all in the same deal?" She rubbed her temples. Her head throbbed and she thought she might be sick.

"Well, tell me this, girl. This fella what asked you to marry him. Was he your beau?"

Robin stood and tucked a strand of hair behind her ear. "Not a beau, exactly—a very good friend. His name is William Benson, and his father was Papa's banker."

"Well, then he probably didn't want you for your money." He chuckled.

She sighed "I don't think he wanted me for love, either, Uncle John. At least it was never mentioned."

John shook his head. "Never intended for ya to have to marry up with any old body what happened to come along. Mentioned it first off to Ty, seein' as how he seems to be taken by the boy."

"What?" Heat flooded her face and she laid her head on the table.

"Ty would've been a good man for ya, if that Blair women hadn't showed up when she did."

Robin wanted to crawl under the table. He'd talked to Ty about marrying her? And what did the good Reverend have to say about that? She could only guess. Well, she could play this game, too. She would have to pull on every Wenghold bone in her body, but she would not let her uncle get the best of her

She stood and leaned so close to her uncle she could count his whiskers. "Okay, Uncle John. I'll stay, but you will not send for a husband. I will learn to do anything and everything you want. But there's one thing I insist on."

John blinked and nodded. "Let's hear it, girly."

"First thing tomorrow morning I'd like to leave Jacob with you and take the buggy to town."

"What do you mean? I can't let you go wanderin' across this prairie alone."

Robin sat and reached for John's hand. "I drove a horse and buggy every day in Chicago, Uncle John. Papa couldn't afford a driver, and it frightened Mama so she wouldn't try. I can drive better than I can walk."

"But you don't even know your way to town."

"Ty told me the first day to stay on the road I could see. I'll get there without any problem."

He squeezed her hand. "I done messed up real good, didn't I? But I thought with the boy and all you'd be wantin' a man to help."

"I have you, Uncle John. But I do need a woman to talk to. I'd like to go see Emma. But please understand—I'm not looking for a husband. Especially not one you bribed to marry me."

She patted his hand, then spun around, and pushed open the door. It slammed behind her, and she sank into the porch swing. Only an occasional flash of lightning in the distance remained of the storm that swept across the hills earlier, but her stomach was twisting and her head was spinning.

One of Uncle John's barn cats padded across the porch, casting long shadows in the lamplight that filtered from the kitchen window. It stopped, crouched, then pounced onto the swing beside her and rubbed its head against her thigh. She scooped it up and settled it onto her lap, scratching under the soft chin and stroking the length of the cat's calico body. Its purr vibrated contentment against her hand.

Robin laid her head against the high back of the swing and closed her eyes. It had all seemed so simple—agreeing to come to Kansas. She'd keep house for Uncle John and save her money. And when they were able, her two sisters would join her.

A gust of wind rustled the branches of the lilac bush near the porch and sent a shower of rain droplets cascading around them. The cat shook its head in protest and Robin laughed. "You don't like that, do you, kitty? Did the cold water interrupt your sweet dreams? Well, guess what. I know how you feel. Uncle John just doused my hopes, too."

The cat lunged from her lap and scampered down the steps—no doubt off to search for a dry place or to hunt for its breakfast. Robin wrapped her arms around her middle. If it weren't for Jacob, she would leave, too.

TEN

The morning sun perched on the hills as John made his way to the barn. In a short time it would begin its climb and bathe the prairie with the scent of warm dirt and dry grasses. John took a deep breath before entering the barn. He loved Kansas summers. The heat soothed his bones. And he could sure use a good soothin' this mornin'. Considering his conversation with Robin last night, he figured he'd better warn Ty it'd be best if he and that Sam fella rode on to the Hawk before breakfast.

He probably shouldn't have told the girl he'd mentioned marriage to Ty. But then, Ty had never given him an answer, so maybe he was still thinking on it. If only that Blair gal hadn't come back.

He pulled the big barn door open and tripped over a cat as he entered. "Git, you mangy rattrap. I ain't gonna milk yet so you can go huntin' for your breakfast."

"You callin' me a rattrap or are you talkin' to yourself?" Ty pulled on his boots. "You're up early. Not hardly even light."

"If I'm needin' good company, I talk to myself. And I know what time it is, young man. I stayed up pert near all night." He stuck his hands in his pockets and waited while Ty stomped one foot then the other to get his pant legs in place.

"Don't suppose Jacob is awake?" Ty brushed the hay from his britches and nudged Sam's sleeping form with the toe of his boot.

The stranger groaned, then sat up and rubbed his eyes.

John nodded at the young man. "Mornin', Sam. And no, Ty, Jacob's still sleepin', leastways he hadn't come down the stairs yet. And I'm thinkin' it might be best if the two of you were out of here before Robin gets up."

"Is she angry?" Ty tucked his shirt into his pants

"You best take my word for it and skedaddle on home. Give her a couple of days."

"What about Jacob? He'll wonder why I don't show up."

"I reckon he'll get used to you not being here so much. I'll keep him busy. He's not too young to have a few chores to do." John grinned. "Bet you cleaned out horse stalls when you was his age, didn't ya?"

"You knew my pa." Ty peered over the stall. "What about you, Sam? You ever muck out a barn?"

Sam got to his feet and hung the blanket over the stall door. "Pitched more straw in my day than I want to brag about." He grinned. "Right now I reckon I'd as soon be doing that as going hungry another day."

John ran his tongue over his teeth. Common courtesy dictated he feed the two men, but for reasons he couldn't explain, he thought it best not to be in a hurry for this new fella to get acquainted with Robin or the boy.

The men finished saddling their horses and led them to the door. "Thanks for the use of the barn, John." Ty plopped his hat on his head and mounted.

"Any time, neighbor. You're welcome any time." John turned to the stranger. "Good to meet you, Sam. Hope it works out for ya to stay around a spell."

Sam shook John's hand. "I'm mighty obliged to the both of you."

"Wait!"

John whirled at Jacob's voice.

"Wait, Ty! Don't go yet." The boy ran barefoot, still in his nightshirt.

Ty hipped around in the saddle. "I thought you were sleeping, buddy."

"I got something for you." Jacob held up his arms and Ty pulled him onto the horse.

"For me? Now, what do you have for me?"

Jacob handed him a folded piece of paper. "I made you a picture. But don't look yet. It's a surprise."

John edged closer to the men. *Now where did the kid come up with paper?* He rubbed his forehead.

Ty slipped the missive into his shirt pocket. "I surely do thank you. I like surprises."

Jacob grinned. "I gotta go back in or Robin will be mad with me."

"Well, we certainly don't need Miss Robin mad, do we?" Ty lowered him to the ground and winked at John.

Jacob raced ahead and peeked around a porch post as John reached the house.

"You ain't hidin' from me, you know. I can see your eyes."

"I'm not hiding. I'm looking." Jacob pointed.

John followed the boy's gaze and caught his breath. The stranger hadn't moved. Hands crossed on the saddle horn, he peered toward the house.

"Jacob?" John kept his voice low. "Do you know that man?"

The boy shrugged. "I don't think so." But his gaze didn't waver.

"Jacob?" Robin stepped onto the porch. "What are you doing out here in your nightclothes?"

With Robin's arrival, the stranger turned and rode after Ty.

She pulled the boy away from the post and gave him a swat on his behind. "Get upstairs and get dressed. I'm going into town, and you're going to stay here and help Uncle John today." She straightened and shielded her eyes against the rising sun. "Who just rode away?"

"Uh . . . Ty wanted to get on to the Hawk."

"That wasn't Ty, Uncle John. I was at the window when Ty rode off and this guy stayed behind. Do you think he was watching Jacob?"

John shrugged. "Don't know what he was a lookin' at. Ty ain't no dummy, though. I reckon he knows he stayed behind."

"You didn't tell Ty about your silly idea, did you? You promised, you know."

"Nary a word."

"What did you do with the ridiculous advertisement? I came down early thinking I would get it before anyone found it."

"I thought you had it. Didn't you take it with you when you slammed out the door?" He was surprised his hat didn't blow off with the wind he done let fly out of his mouth. He'd deliberately left it on the table, in plain sight, hoping she would rethink the idea.

"No, I did not take it with me. You'd better find it. You should've torn it up last night. I can't believe you would leave it lying around for anyone to see. What if Ty had decided to come in?"

"Well, he didn't, and I don't reckon Jacob can read, so don't see no reason for you to get so worked up. Probably find it in some rat-hole. Pesky pack rats will take most anything, you know."

Robin wiped her hands on her apron. "Even paper?"

He was already in so deep he reckoned one more step wouldn't make a whole lot of difference. "Oh, 'specially paper. See, they like to hear it crinkle up." He ran his tongue around the inside of his mouth. Ma always told him if you told a lie a blister would pop up on your tongue and hurt until you confessed.

Robin pulled a dish towel off her shoulder and brushed a spiderweb from between the porch posts. "I have seen signs of a mouse in the cupboard. Perhaps you're right. I'll ask Emma what she does to keep them away. Breakfast is on the table if you're ready. And since you're so used to doing the inside work, I'll leave the cleanup for you. I'd like to get an early start."

"You're sure you want to go to town alone?" He'd welcome a reason to go back to the barn and get the buggy ready. He certainly could use the time to figure out what to do next. Ty needed to know about Sam peering at the boy. But he'd already sent the preacher away with a warning not to show up for a couple of days. And he couldn't risk taking the boy over to the Hawk with him until he knew for sure what was going on.

He crossed his arms and stared out over the prairie. If the Good Lord had any mercy, He'd be sending a horde of pack rats about now.

He didn't know if Emma would have advice on getting rid of mice—but it'd be worth begging a ride to town to see if she had some kind of concoction for mouth sores.

The sun had not yet reached its zenith when Robin climbed out of the buggy in front of Emma's Mercantile. She had stopped once to allow the horse to drink and another time to soak in the scenery. A meadow of purple and yellow flowers bloomed not far from where Jacob's mama was buried. She would stop on the way home and gather a bouquet to put on the grave.

Emma nodded when Robin approached the counter but continued to measure a length of fabric for another customer. Robin smiled in return and busied herself choosing items from her list. She'd wait to ask about the men's clothing until she and Emma were alone. She'd finish her errand, go to the post office then stop at the train station on the way out. With luck, the ticket agent was on duty, and not the stationmaster.

The bell above the door jangled when the lady left, and Robin moved to the counter and unloaded her basket.

"This is why you came to town, dear girl? Two jars of peaches?" Emma's skirts swished as she rounded the corner and wrapped her arms around Robin.

Robin's resolve to remain silent about what had transpired the previous night melted with the embrace, and she buried her head on Emma's shoulder and wept.

"I wondered how long it would take you to do this, Robin. Now, you have a good cry; then we can get to the real reason you're here. I take it John isn't with you?"

Robin shook her head. "I made Uncle John stay home." She hiccupped.

Emma dug a handkerchief from her sleeve and handed it to Robin. "Oh, dearie, nobody makes John Wenghold do anything he doesn't want to do. But if you got him to agree to your wishes then you came closer than most." She laughed and led Robin to a chair behind the counter. "Now, if anyone comes in, slip behind that curtain. There's no need for the whole town to see your tears. Most every woman that stops here, stops at the post office on the way home. Need I say more?"

Robin dried her eyes. "Oh Emma, I told myself all the way here that I was a big girl and didn't need to let another soul know what was happening. And I threatened Uncle John. But I don't have my sisters to talk to and . . ." Fresh tears coursed down her cheeks.

"That bad, huh?" Emma sat on a cracker box across from her.

Robin nodded then told her the story. ". . . And he even had the nerve to suggest to Ty that he marry me. Without me knowing it."

"So you drove to town by yourself to purchase two jars of peaches. That'll show him."

Robin wound Emma's handkerchief around her fingers. "I can't prove it, but I'm pretty sure the only reason Uncle John ever agreed to have the Wenghold sisters venture his direction is because he promised Papa. I hate being more of a hindrance than a help. And I abhor the thought of paying someone to marry me."

Emma patted her cheek. "You have your grandmother Wenghold's spunk. A lady through and through but worked alongside those men on the Feather like she was a hired man. And those same men adored her. I take it your plan involves a bit more than jars of fruit."

"I'm going to purchase two one-way tickets to Chicago for me and Jacob, in case I decide to leave for sure. But I also need some men's pants and a pair of boots and some shirts."

"Men's? Whatever for—" Understanding came to Emma's eyes and she slapped her knee. "Oh my lands, Robin. I'll be able to hear that old man hoot clear in here if you come downstairs some morning wearing men's clothes. Are you sure you want to do this?"

"I can't move fast, and I don't move with grace. I've suffered more than one tumble when my feet got tangled in my skirts when I tried to hurry. He wants a hired man, Emma, but he won't hire one. So I'll do the job, even if it means dressing like a man. Will you help me?"

Robin stood and put her hands on her hips.

"I'll not only outfit you, but I promise to pray every morning, noon, and night. But you have to promise me one thing." She placed her hands on Robin's shoulders. "Promise me if he expects more than you're able to do without hurting yourself, you'll come scooting right in to me. Will you do that?"

She smiled. "I'll come. If I can't do it, I'll come. But you have to promise me something in return—not a word of this to anyone. Not to Ty Morgan or Anna Blair, and especially not to Henrietta Harvey."

Emma crossed her heart and planted a kiss on Robin's cheek. "Nary a word, except to Jesus. Him and me is gonna be doing a whole lot of talking, Robin girl. Now, let's see what we can do about getting you all fixed up—like a man." She laughed. "Wish I was going home with you, just to see the old codger's face."

Robin sighed with relief when Albert stood at the counter in the post office and not Henrietta. The bell jangled, and he turned and swiped his hand from one ear to another, captured a stray strand of hair, and patted it into place.

"Good afternoon, Miss Wenghold." He nodded in her direction. "I suppose you want your mail?"

"If you don't mind, Albert. Thank you."

Albert leaned across the counter and handed her two envelopes. "Miss Robin, I want to . . . I want to say I'm sorry about yesterday. My mother can be quite determined at times, if you know what I mean?" He pulled a handkerchief from his back pocket and proceeded to clean his glasses. Clear, kind eyes met Robin's. "Your little boy is a handsome lad."

"Albert, I'm sorry if—"

"Oh, you needn't apologize."

"Thank you. Jacob is a handsome lad, but he's also quite a busy child. I'm sorry if his presence caused you any discomfort."

"Not me, Miss Robin. You may not believe this, but I was once a rather busy child myself. At least that's what my mother tells me." He took three short sucks of air, but this time Robin didn't feel like laughing. Away from Henrietta's influence, Albert Harvey was a very pleasant gentleman.

"Uh . . . Miss Wenghold, might we talk?" Albert stepped from behind the counter and motioned for Robin to sit in the only chair in the room "I . . . well, I think you should know I'm not looking for a wife. At least not one like . . ."

"One like me, Albert?" She bit her lower lip.

"Oh, no, no. That's not what I meant at all. You're a very lovely lady."

"Let me assure you that I am not in the market for a husband, either. I came to Kansas for the sole purpose of helping my uncle on his ranch. I'm afraid the role of mama to young Jacob is rather by chance, not choice, though he has captured my heart."

Albert mopped his handkerchief across his brow. The poor man seemed so relieved it angered her that Henrietta Harvey would put her son through such turmoil.

"Miss Robin, do you play the piano, or perhaps sing?"

She shook her head. "Oh, Albert. I do neither. I've always envied anyone who could carry any resemblance of a tune. My sister, Lark, is quite accomplished in both piano and voice. In fact, she stayed in Chicago to continue with her music pupils until the end of the term, and then she will join me here with Uncle John. I take it you have an interest in music."

Albert gave a furtive glance behind him then bent to whisper. "My desire is to one day play and sing for the church. But Mother would not approve of my confession in this regard. She's quite adamant that I not make a spectacle of myself."

Robin's heart went out to him. How well she knew that admonition. "Albert, I hope to one day hear you do that very thing. I've often wondered why more men don't participate in the worship service in this manner. I must admit, as a younger girl I would giggle behind my hand at what the pastor announced as the *special*. Some of it was not very special at all."

Albert leaned against the counter and laughed. "I haven't been this encouraged in years. Mother has managed to frighten away most single ladies—I'm sure with the threat of marriage to her son—and I've never cultivated many men acquaintances. Do you think we might perhaps be friends, Miss Wenghold? Just . . . friends?"

Robin stood and reached for his hand. "I would be pleased to call you my friend, Albert."

"I hope you'll come back to church, Miss Wenghold." Albert blushed and wiped his hand on the front of his vest before extending it to her.

"I live at the Feather, Albert. I'm sure we'll be back." The strength of his grip when she took his hand surprised her. "Thank you again for the kind words."

She stopped on the porch and turned her attention to the letters Albert had handed her. One addressed in her youngest sister's flowery script sent shivers of excitement down Robin's spine. The other bore William Benson's return address. Her heart lurched. Surely her sisters were seeing to Papa's business. Why would William be writing, unless the bank intended to demand full payment? Her heart sank. She'd wait to open the letters at home. The last thing she needed was for Henrietta Harvey to observe her reaction to bad news while standing in front of the post office. Oh, but she did so wish to read the latest happenings from her sisters. She would savor every word, every wiggly curlicue Wren penned. She climbed into the buggy and gave the reins a flick. She'd find a place to pull over so she could read the letter away from prying eyes.

When she reached the meadow of flowers again, she reined the horse to a stop. Though the letter was burning a hole in her pocket, she picked a bouquet to place on the grave of Jacob's mama. Fluffy white clouds played hide-and-seek with the sun as she laid the purple and yellow arrangement on the small mound of prairie that marked the grave. Who was this woman, this *Mama* who'd never again see her fine looking, busy little lad? Robin knelt beside the grave and straightened the cross that stood askew from some unknown force. A smattering of paw prints were visible after the overnight rain, and she smoothed them away, angry that animals would invade the privacy of this woman's final resting place.

"I wish I knew your name, dear one. But Jacob only wanted us to put *Mama*, and that was good enough for us. Where were you headed? Were you following a dream? Where is Jacob's pa? Was he with you? I have so many questions." She swallowed.

"Me and Ty Morgan found him the day after the storm. He's fine. At first he didn't like Ty, but they're friends now. We're going to do everything we can to find the answers. And we'll take good care of your boy. You'll be so proud of him."

She wiped her tears and lowered herself amidst the carpet of wildflowers and long grass. The rain-dampened ground seeped through her skirt, but she didn't mind. She couldn't wait another minute. She would succumb to the temptation of her sister's correspondence.

Dear Sister Robin:

Lark has another one of her bad headaches and put herself to bed, but she said I must write to you this afternoon. I miss you something fierce. Lark is her usual bossy self, and I can't seem to do anything right. I burned only a very small hole in the kitchen tablecloth and you would think I committed a crime. I sat the spoon holder over it, and it doesn't even show, but sister says I am to never light the candles again. I only lit them because my chicken got a little too brown and I thought it would look better in the dim light. But you know sister. She said I needn't try to impress anyone with my fancy ways, especially since she could taste what was burned without having to see it.

Robin sighed. Maybe she should have insisted Wren come with her to Kansas, but that would have left Lark alone. No, it was a decision they'd made together—Robin had no other obligations in Chicago so it only made sense for her to come first.

I went to the bank yesterday to make a payment on Papa's note and William Benson inquired about you. Lark said we shouldn't tell anyone why you are gone. She said it would bring shame on Papa's name if people knew he left so much debt. So I told him you'd accepted an invitation to go West. Oh my, Robin. He was dressed in his black banker suit and his white shirt was so stiff it crackled. And he had a big gold ring with a red stone on his finger. He looked absolutely delicious.

Robin laid the letter in her lap and laughed aloud. *Delicious?* Only Wren would use a word like that to describe a man. Papa used to say Wren eyed every eligible male as though he were the fattest worm in the apple. And as for not telling about Papa's debt, William's father was the banker. He surely was more than aware of their predicament.

I almost forgot what Lark said I should tell you. It was the strangest thing. One day a wagon pulled up in front of the house and this man carried a trunk to the porch. And it was yours, sister. He said it was left at the station and they were tired of working around it. It's a good thing you had your name on it. But Lark thinks we should keep it here until you tell us what to do. You know Lark. She doesn't trust anyone.

Robin sighed. She'd intended to stop at the station to purchase tickets, but forgot all about it in the joy of receiving the letter from home. She must write and tell them to send her belongings. It would be so nice to have her own things again.

What is Uncle John like? I told Lark we probably wouldn't hear from you until you had your nest feathered. She wasn't amused. Do write to us soon. I miss having fun talking and laughing with you. I send hugs to you.

Sister Wren

P. S. Please don't be angry, but we gave Mr. Benson Uncle John's address. He acted like it was very important.

Robin rested her head against the buggy wheel, thinking of home. Wren got home sooner than Lark most nights so would be bustling about attempting to fix the supper meal. Poor thing. She could only imagine the frustration Lark's critical spirit caused her little sister.

A movement among the grass caught Robin's attention and her heart skipped. Had she been foolish to venture out alone? She turned her head ever so slightly and searched her surroundings. A short distance beyond the grave lay a dog, its muzzle poised on outstretched legs. Big brown eyes followed her movement as she stood, yet the animal stayed motionless.

"Where did you come from?" Her gaze swept the area, but she observed nothing to indicate the dog's owner was near. She knelt and held out her hand. "Come. You're friendly, aren't you?"

The dog's tail rustled the grass and his ears perked.

Robin stood and took a step. "Have you been here long, fella?"

Its ears perked again, and the animal stood, then with a whimper turned and disappeared into the cover of the prairie.

Robin's skin prickled. Perhaps it was her imagination, but she sensed someone watching her. She crammed Wren's letter into her pocket and clambered into the buggy. *Take a deep breath, Robin. It was a dog, that's all.* She gripped the reins with both hands, gave a flick of her wrist, and willed herself not to look back. She'd not mention this incident to Uncle John. Not yet.

ELEVEN

Ty's mind whirled with unanswered questions on the ride back to his ranch with his new acquaintance. Ty knew the new fella had trailed behind when they left John's this morning, and he'd observed Sam watching as the older man and Jacob headed for the house. Until Rusty had a chance to meet this man, Ty would hold his peace. Was this the same person who'd sought shelter the night of the tornado?

If not—then who was he? Why the curiosity about the gravesite, and why the interest in Jacob? Caution tightened Ty's chest, and he determined not to let the sun set with unanswered questions. Sam was friendly, willing to work, and unarmed. But why did he hope the man's curiosity was simply that? Was it because if Jacob's pa showed up, he might lose the connection with both the boy and Robin? He patted his pocket to make sure the paper was still there. Little scamp. Probably used Robin's writing tablet without her knowing. He couldn't imagine she would have given the boy paper if he'd told her his plans.

"Mornin', Boss." Rusty strode toward the men as they dismounted and tied their horses. "I was about to send a couple of hands out to find you, then figgered you must've holed up somewhere out of the storm last—why, look what the wind blew in." Rusty closed the gap between him and the stranger in two wide steps. "Sam Mason. You're a mighty good sight for sore eyes. What in the world brung you all the way to Kansas?"

Ty propped one foot on the bottom rail of the fence as the two men greeted one another with slaps on the back and awkward embraces.

Ty eyed his foreman. "You know this man, Rusty? I found him making camp in the timber along the Pigeon. The two of us waited out the storm at John's."

Rusty laughed and threw a punch at Sam's shoulder. "Should have left him there, Boss. Hard-headed ole' cuss like this deserves to be lightnin' struck." Rusty slung one arm around Sam's neck. "We worked together on the Queen ranch, down Texas way. Neither one of us dry behind the ears, but we thought the world was real lucky to have us."

"He's looking for work. You have something he could do?"

"Got a barn what needs muckin'." The foreman laughed. "Course, we'd have a hard time decidin' which pile was what at the end of the day."

Sam grinned. "Rusty, you old cow dog. If I'd a knowed you was anywhere near I would've turned around and hightailed it outta here. But honestly—it's mighty good to see ya again."

"One thing ya gotta know about this sidewinder, Boss. He's worser than an ole' mama bear if he ain't got food in his belly. You et anything at John's this mornin'?"

Ty shook his head. "Not this morning, nor last night. Think we better feed him before he trees us?" Ty laughed and followed them to the house as they punched and shoved like a couple of puppies.

Ty squirmed to scratch his back against the porch railing. A full moon hung like a lantern in the eastern sky above the hills, and in the distance a coyote howled. He used to sit with his ma, on evenings like this, and listen to the night sounds. Ma had made a game of most everything, and darkness never frightened him. If only he could ask her about the ways of a woman. She'd known Anna since birth, but what would she have thought of Robin Wenghold? She'd love little

Jacob, but she'd for sure send the men scouring the countryside to find the child's pa.

"Got a minute, Boss?" Rusty stepped from the shadows and came up on the porch to sit beside Ty. "Figgered you'd have some questions about Sam."

Ty nodded. He did have questions but wasn't sure this was the time to ask all of them. "Is he gonna work out for you? Seems like a nice enough fella."

Rusty laid his hat on the porch. "Couldn't ask for a better hand. Still can't believe you found him like ya did. Lost track of him about five years ago, around the time I left the Queen and headed north."

"Then this isn't the fella who came looking for work the night of the storm?"

"Nope. Sam Mason would never leave a woman and child to fend for themselves, even in bright sunlight." Sam hitched one knee up and wrapped his arms around it.

"Do you know anything about his family? Where'd he come from when you knew him on the Queen?" Ty turned to face his foreman. "He asked about the grave of the boy's mama."

"Cowpokes don't usually ask a lot of questions. You know that, sir. Only find out things about family and such by listenin', but I don't recall Sam ever talked much about his. I remember him writin' a couple of letters once—I helped him spell some words—but don't know that he ever got mail of any kind. Don't think he finished school. Leastways we was both awful young down on the Queen."

Ty sighed. "Wish we could have found a Bible or papers or anything that would give us a clue about those travelers—the boy's folks, I mean. Lots of other stuff blown all around, but nothing with any names."

"You thinking Sam might know something since he asked about the grave? I suppose I'd do the same thing if I happened on it sudden-like. Maybe he was only makin' conversation."

"Maybe. But when we left John's this morning he rode back and watched John and Jacob go to the house. The youngster ran out of the house as we left and wanted to give me a picture he drew, so Sam got a good look at him. I got the impression he recognized the boy."

"You want me to ask him?" Rusty stood and put his shoulder against the porch post. "He's a mighty good ranch hand, Boss, and I'm glad to see him again. Probably the closest one I ever had to call a brother. If you think there's something we need to know, then I'll flat-out ask."

Ty shook his head. "No, don't do that. But keep your ears open, Rusty. If Jacob has a pa running around the country somewhere, then we need to know. And if Sam knows something, then sooner or later he'll spill it. You do trust him, don't you?"

"With my life. He put himself between me and a feisty range bull one day. Big ole' spotted critter gouged my horse and knocked me off. I was on the ground scootin' for all I was worth to get my feet under me so I could get mounted again. That long-horned devil had his head down, slobber flyin' every direction, and before he could charge again that spunky Sam—wasn't more'n about sixteen at the time, skinny as a broom straw—roped him around the horns and dragged him to a mesquite bush. He circled that fella around the bush a couple of times, got him so tangled up he was usin' all his fury to get loose. Gave me time to get on my horse. Me and Sam both lit out like we was runnin' from fire. Never did get his rope back, neither."

"Thanks for coming by, Rusty." He stood and shook his foreman's hand. "I'll sleep better tonight with this much information. Keep your eyes and ears open, though. I know Sam's a friend, but if he's hiding something, we need to know it."

Rusty stuck his hands in his back pockets. "If Sam's hidin' anything, I'll find it sooner or later. You can count on that."

He disappeared into the shadows, and Ty settled on the bottom step. Rusty's confidence in Sam relieved one concern. But there was still Anna. And Robin. And Jacob. He reached to pluck a piece of grass and the crinkle in his pocket reminded him of the picture he promised Jacob he'd look at when he got home.

Ty stepped back into the kitchen and poured a cup of coffee.

Moving the lamp closer to the edge of the table, he turned sideways and propped his feet on a chair. He unfolded the paper and adjusted it so he could see. *NOTICE: looking for . . .*

His heart lurched as he finished reading the advertisement. His boots hit the floor and he stood and paced, paper in hand. Was this some kind of joke? John had mentioned him marrying Robin. Was this his around-the-barn way of getting him to answer? Did Robin know what the old man planned? At least the paper was in *his* hands. John evidently hadn't had time to post it yet. But now what? Would he get Jacob in trouble if he said anything? He wadded the paper and threw it on the table.

Ty slammed the door behind him and marched toward the barn. He'd ride to the Feather and get to the bottom of this. Surely John wouldn't use the boy in such a scheme—would he? But he stopped before he reached his destination. So he would go riding in like a madman. Then what? Humiliate Robin more?

He shuffled back into the house and sat at the table again. He smoothed the crumpled paper and turned it over. He hadn't even bothered to look at the other side. The boy's picture consisted of two big round circles, and a smaller one between them—all with wiggly stick legs and arms that connected. And in one corner a twisty scribble hung from a long pencil-line sky.

Ty propped his elbows on the table and put his head in his hands. *Did this little man draw a picture of his family and the storm—or do the three figures represent him, Robin, and me? And what about the advertisement? Would Robin allow such a thing to happen? What was John thinking? What should I do? Lord—what shall I do?*

Much later, the clock on the mantel in the living room struck three times. Though sleep failed him, he did have an answer, and his heart quieted.

"Trust in the Lord with all thine heart; and lean not unto thine own understanding."

TWELVE

Robin pulled her sleeping gown over her head and sat on the edge of the bed to survey her choice of apparel for the next day. A pair of stiff-looking britches hung across the back of the chair, and a blue long-sleeved shirt rested on top of them. Under that, hidden from Jacob's sight, lay gray stockings and a pair of men's underwear, of all things. She vehemently opposed such a purchase, but Emma convinced her the new britches left no room for the fancy tucks and lace she was accustomed to wearing.

She fluffed her pillow and propped it against the head of the ornately carved bed. The letter from William and the bank could no longer be ignored. Wren said he acted like having her address was very important. It could only mean one thing, but how would they ever come up with more than the pitiful little they paid each month to satisfy Papa's debtors? Could she dare approach Uncle John?

She tucked her gown under her feet and slid her finger under the seal.

My Dear Robin:

Dear? Did all requests for money begin so . . . familiar?

It saddened me to learn of your departure to Kansas before I had the opportunity to make known my wishes, once again. After much cajoling and—I'm afraid—becoming rather a nuisance, I got your sisters to agree to give me your Uncle John's address.

I've had ample time to reflect on our last meeting and am embarrassed and ashamed at the way I conducted myself. I chose my words with little regard as to how they might sound to you. To assume that you would agree to become my wife at a time when you mourned your father's impending death was most inconsiderate of me, and I beg your forgiveness.

Robin sighed. Papa had been gone nine months. There'd been ample time for Mr. Benson to contact her before she left Chicago. It wasn't the timing, or the choice of words—it was the lack of them.

I can only hope you will be willing to see me again, and perhaps reconsider my proposal of marriage. It would not be fair for me to assume you would give an answer without a proper courting. Therefore, I have seen fit to purchase a ticket to come to you. I shall arrive in Cedar Bluff on July 1 and will plan to stay one month. I have also purchased two return tickets to Chicago and will flatter myself to think that, by the end of my stay, you will make a favorable decision to accompany me home.

Until then, I remain

Sincerely, William Arthur Benson, III

Robin closed her eyes and lay back against her pillow. William was coming to Kansas? One month. Could one month accomplish what twenty-two years failed to do? William, her forever friend and protector, now desired her to consider becoming his wife? Never once, even with his proposal, did he mention loving her. Oh, he brought her punch and sat sipping on the sidelines with her while they watched their friends dip and twirl the night away. And one year, at the school's annual ice-skating event at Manning's pond, he pretended to have a sprained ankle so she needn't huddle around the fire alone. Yet, he never mentioned love.

Daily, Papa had loudly proclaimed his affection for Mama. She would blush and fuss—*Lionel Wenghold, the neighbors will think you a madman.* And his reply remained the same until the day Mama died—*Ah, my dear Margaret, without question I am mad. Madly in love with the loveliest girl to ever grace the streets of Chicago.* Then he would pull Mama to her feet, tell her he loved her more that day than yesterday and kiss her soundly on the mouth, against her protests that it was indecent behavior in the presence of their impressionable daughters. Robin and Wren had eagerly awaited this evening ritual, but Lark would push her glasses higher on her nose, turn away, and scold the sisters for giggling.

Robin stuffed the letter back into the envelope and slipped it under the picture of the Wenghold sisters on the table by her bedside. She blew out her lamp, padded in her bare feet, and knelt by the open window. A soft, warm breeze billowed the lace curtains. She pushed them behind her shoulders to gaze across the prairie unhindered. If God answered prayer, this would be the time to ask Him for guidance. But she'd not bother Him.

She propped her elbows on the sill and cupped her chin in her hands. The moon gleamed full and bright across the grass. How far could one see on such a night? Forever, it seemed. As her eyes adjusted to the distance, a lone rider emerged from the shadows beyond the barn. Thankful for the darkness of her room, she watched until the silhouette melted into the night. Then she scrambled to her feet, her heart pounding as she grabbed her wrapper. She'd not told Uncle John about the dog. She must tell him about the stranger.

Robin trailed one hand along the wall while descending the stairs. In Chicago she knew the number of steps and could navigate them even in the dark, but she'd not yet mastered it here.

"Robin?" Uncle John's voice drifted through the open door. "Don't light a lamp. I'm on the porch leanin' against the wall if you care to join me, but I'm not hankerin' to be seen right now."

She stepped onto the porch and made sure the door didn't slam behind her. "Then you're aware—?"

"Yeah, was watchin' him. Didn't do much but sit."

"Did you recognize him?" Robin strained to read her uncle's face in the dim light. Most of the time, his eyes spoke volumes more than his words.

"It weren't Ty, that's for sure."

"Could it be the stranger he had with him last night?"

Her uncle shrugged "Don't know. Haven't seed that man enough to tell from afar. Funny thing how you get used to the way a fella sits a horse and can tell, even from a distance, if it's a body ya know." He led her to the swing. "Here, sit a spell. Been doin' me some more thinkin."

Robin moaned. "Uncle John, I don't much like it when you think."

He chuckled. "I been thinkin' on how I don't want you strayin' too far away from the house. I know I told ya I wanted help out and about, but—well, seein' as how this fella come a snoopin' around here tonight, and we still don't know nothin' for sure about Jacob's pa, I think it best you stick close."

"Couldn't we work together? You said your mama helped your papa every day. Did he stay with her all the time?" Robin put her foot down to keep the swing from swaying.

"My pa wouldn't allow her to work out on the prairie all by herself. No sirree, she stayed within his look-see most all the time. Me and your pa right there, too."

"Then why can't we make it work like that? In Chicago, we three sisters divided chores. I know I have a lot to learn, but you can teach me. I'm a quick learner. And I'm stronger than you think, Uncle John. I limp, but I can work hard. And Jacob isn't too young to have chores."

"You'd be willing to do that, girly? I think it only fair ya know I ain't completely given up on the hope of findin' ya a husband. Don't know how I'm gonna work it—being as how you won't let me mail out that notice—but I'm most certain gonna try."

"There's something you need to know." She studied her hands. "I received two letters when I picked up the mail today. One from my sisters, and the other one from William Benson."

"*The* William Benson what wanted you to marry him before you came here?" John frowned. "And what did the young man have to say? Did he want you to hightail it back to the big city?"

"No, William plans to come here. He wants to court me."

John jumped to his feet, and the swing flung in a crazy swaying motion. Robin's head thumped against the wooden slats.

"He's coming here? To the Feather? And when is this blessed event going to take place?"

Robin rubbed her head and put her foot down to stop the swing and settle her queasy stomach. "He says he'll arrive in Cedar Bluff on July 1. He plans to stay one month and hopes I will agree to return to Chicago with him at the end of that time." Thank goodness she couldn't see her uncle's eyes. No doubt they were shooting fire.

John punched at the porch post. "Well, now, isn't this a fine feather on granny's bonnet? And what are we supposed to do with a tenderfoot from Chicago for a whole month, I'd like to know."

Robin went to her uncle. "I'm a tenderfoot from Chicago, Uncle John. You have two weeks to break me in before the next one comes." She giggled and squeezed his arm. "And before you get any silly notions, I have no intention of making a snap decision. There's too much at stake—my sisters, Jacob, and—"

"And what, girly?" He put his arm around her shoulders. "Are you terrible disappointed that Blair woman came when she did?"

"I was thinking of you, Uncle John. As silly as it sounds, and as crazy as I think you are, I rather like it here. And I don't know what William will think of Jacob. There's so much more to consider than merely agreeing to become Mrs. William Arthur Benson the Third."

John turned her shoulders toward the door. "You'll have to admit—that's an impressive mouthful. What say we go in and finish this discussion over a glass of warm milk."

Robin wrinkled her nose. "Cold buttermilk sounds better to me. I think there's still some hanging in the well."

"You go on in, I'll fetch it. Never could pass me up a good cold glass of buttermilk."

"What if that man is still out in the shadows somewhere?"

He stepped off the porch, silhouetted by moonlight, and cocked his head. "Hear them night birds a chirpin'? And them coyotes a barkin'? Them's all signs there ain't nobody around. Ya gotta learn to listen, so when it's too dark to see ya still know what's goin' on. God made them creatures a whole lot smarter than He made most men. Take my word for it."

Robin clenched her hands. This morning she'd planned to leave, and tonight she longed to stay? Not that she wanted him to find her a husband. But Uncle John reminded her of Pa. And she loved her pa.

"Uncle John, there's something else I should tell you."

"Land's sake, girl. You're gettin' downright chatty. What is it now?"

"I stopped at the grave of Jacob's mama today on the way home. While I was there, a dog came. He wasn't wild or anything, but I . . . had a strange feeling someone was watching me."

"You didn't see nobody?"

"No. I didn't wait around though. I didn't want to say anything before, but now since that man was out there . . ."

"Don't know as the two is addin' up to more than one, but I don't want you a goin' off by yourself again. You need somethin' from town, I'll go with you. Ain't gonna leave you here alone, neither. Now, let's have us that there cold drink before we say our good nights."

John whistled as he made his way to the well. So the banker's son was thinkin' he could ride in here and court Robin away. Proud fella, wasn't he? One month wasn't a lot of time to come up with a plan, but he was sure gonna try. It helped to know Robin didn't want to leave. It would give him a whole lot more comfort if Miss Blair would leave. Maybe it wouldn't be such a bad thing if the boy *had* drawn his picture on the back of that notice. Might make the preacher quit straddlin' the fence.

A dribble fell from the bucket he'd pulled from the well and plinked in the water below. He frowned. Funny how one little drip of water would be loud enough for him to hear it plink. It was quiet as a church. Had he let his guard down too soon?

Something hit his leg hard, and he jumped.

"John, it's me . . . Ty."

He dipped his shoulder toward the direction of Ty's voice.

"No, don't let on I'm here." Ty kept his voice low. "Keep pulling on the rope and listen."

John rubbed the spot on his shin. "What'd ya pitch at me, a boulder?"

"I've been following a fella but lost him somewhere not far from here. Have you seen anything or anyone?"

"You lost him? You gettin' old, Ty? There was a time you could've tracked dirt in a dust storm."

"Crazy horse spooked."

"Throw ya, did he?" John chuckled and busied himself with the bucket emerging from the well.

"No, he didn't throw me, but I had to run him in circles to settle him down. You didn't answer my question. Did you see anyone?"

"As a matter of fact, I did. So did Robin. Fella sat out by the barn for a spell then sorta disappeared into the shadows. Didn't seem to be in any hurry, or mind that he might be seen. First thing came to my mind was this Sam guy. Don't it seem funny we'd have two strangers hangin' around all of a sudden?" He lowered the bucket.

"I know it looks suspicious, but as it turns out Sam and Rusty worked together down on the Queen ranch in Texas. They're good friends. Sam isn't the guy who rode in the night of the storm."

"That don't say he couldn't still be a snoopin' around. Men change, Ty. And not always for the good. You know that."

"Rusty would bank his life on the man, and I'd bank mine on Rusty. As a matter of fact, Sam put me onto the intruder. I was headin' out to check on a horse that got snake bit, and Sam had been watching the guy for a while. Said about the same thing as you—didn't seem real intent on hiding, yet didn't come riding in, either. I don't like it.

Don't like it at all."

"Seems if he's up to no good he'd stay in the shadows more. Maybe he don't know no better. Notice anything strange at all about him?" He brought the bucket up again.

"Just the horse. It seems bigger than any of our cow ponies. Looks more like something you might hitch to a wagon, not put a saddle on. Another good reason for me to know it wasn't Sam."

"Well, if he's still watchin', he's gonna wonder why I'm a yammerin' to myself while I'm a crankin' this bucket up and down this here well. I'm gonna go on back to the house like nothin's wrong. You see somethin' more, might as well come a knockin'. No need for us to be hidin'. We ain't the ones sneakin' around." He turned to leave.

"Wait, John." A slight rustling came from where Ty hid. "Uh, you know that paper Jacob gave me this morning?"

John groaned. "Now, before you go—"

"Would you tell Jacob I liked the picture?"

John breathed a sigh of relief he couldn't see Ty's face. *Sure as granny has a cat that young man done laid his eyes on the notice I writ and ain't gonna say nary a word about it. He'd rather watch this old man squirm.*

"Reckon you should be a tellin' the boy yourself, Ty. But suppose I could mention it. Now, if you're done flappin' your gums, I best get this buttermilk in the house before it gets warm. Robin done turned up her nose at warm milk."

He hunched his shoulders against Ty's laughter followin' all the way to the house. *By sugar, you wait 'til after July 1, young man. We'll see if you're still a snickerin' then.*

THIRTEEN

Robin turned sideways and lifted her leg onto the bed. Is this how men got dressed every morning? She should've put her stockings on first. The heavy fabric of the new britches didn't want to bend, and by the time she encased both feet in her shiny new boots she panted with the effort. Emma told her it would be awkward at first. How she knew, Robin didn't ask.

She stood in front of the mirror and clamped her hands over her mouth to keep from squealing. Mama would have rolled her eyes and ordered her to go change at once. Wren would want a matching wardrobe, and poor Lark would probably take to her boudoir in humiliation. From a distance she supposed people could mistake her for Uncle John. Maybe she should rethink wearing men's clothing, but her uncle said he needed outside help and her feet tangled too easily in a dress.

She bent at the waist and let her hair fall forward, then twisted it into a rope before coiling it on top of her head. It took more pins than usual to hold. But Emma said if she wound it tight, then pulled her hat down snugly over it, most likely it would stay in place even in a strong wind. One last turn in front of the looking glass made her blush. It didn't seem decent to look at herself packed into such snug quarters. She picked up her hat, slapped the side of her leg with it, and willed her stiff-legged britches to bend on her way down the stairs.

Robin stood on bottom step and sucked a breath, then exhaled with a whoosh. Dirty dishes sat on the table. Both ends of a loaf of bread appeared to be chewed off, and crumbs littered the floor. Broken eggshells adorned the top of the stove, along with a big iron skillet that held the remains of what appeared to be scrambled eggs.

She gritted her teeth so hard her jaws hurt. If Uncle John insisted he could very well take care of the inside chores, then so be it. He could start this morning, as far as she was concerned. She plunked the hat on her head, tightened the strings under her chin, slammed the door behind her, and stomped to the barn.

She squeezed through the partially open door, and a clump of straw hit her face then slid to adorn the front of her shirt.

"Jacob?"

Another pile landed at her feet.

"Jacob, stop—or at least watch where you're throwing that stuff."

"Uncle John said I should scrunch my eyes when I pitch it so the loose stuff don't paste 'em shut." A forkful of debris flew past her ear.

Robin grabbed the pitchfork. "Stop. Where's Uncle John?"

Jacob wiped his hands on his pant legs. "He's out behind the barn doing this—" He bent forward, hands behind his back and his face close to the floor. "He says he's trackin'. I'm supposed to tell you to get a fork and help me." He pointed over his shoulder. "There's one hanging on the—"

The boy's eyes widened, and he put his hands over his mouth. Giggles tumbled around his fingers. "Robin! You look like a boy." He turned and ran out the door. "Uncle John! Uncle John, come look at Robin. She looks like you."

Robin stood against the wall and waited for the inevitable. Might as well get it over with so they could get on with the day.

"What do you mean she looks like me?"

Jacob dragged the older man into the barn by his hand. "See?" He pointed.

A scowl buried itself deep in John's forehead. "Now if that don't send granny's cat up the wall. What do you think you're a doin', girly?

I never seed anything so . . . so wrong in all my born days."

She moved away from the wall and squared her shoulders. "Did you expect me to clean up this stuff in a dress, Uncle John?"

"My ma did. She'd a never let another soul look on her dressed like a man. No, siree. You ain't gonna look like that around here." He shook his finger in her face. "Now, you git right back in that there house and put you on some woman clothes."

Robin crossed her arms. "You don't seem to understand. I'm the new around-the-place help you need. And it doesn't matter what name you put on this . . . this *job* you want done. I'm not doing it in a dress. Nor will I pick up rocks or go huntin' for little baby cows in woman clothes. I thought you agreed I could help."

"Calves," John mumbled. "And I never agreed to you lookin' like a man."

"What?"

"They's called calves, not baby cows. And the job, if you want to know, is called cleaning out the barn. And you can do it just as well in lady's clothes."

"That's not what you told me, Uncle John." Jacob mimicked John's stance—hands on hips, legs apart. "You told me we was gonna muck out horse—"

John slipped his hand over the boy's mouth. "That's enough outta you, son."

Robin planted her hands on her hips. "What difference does it make?"

John's frown deepened and one eyebrow shot up to his hairline. "What difference does what make?

"What I call a baby cow."

"Cuz they're not baby cows, they's calves. Besides, it makes you sound like one of them city fellas. That's the difference."

"I *am* a city fella—or rather, a city girl. That's what makes this whole thing so ridiculous."

"What whole thing? And nobody could tell you was a girl—city or otherwise—by lookin'."

"Ohh." She stomped her foot. "I know I have a lot to learn. And I agree I look ridiculous in this getup. I feel that way, too. But you need a hired man and that's what you're getting. Now, if you don't mind"—she wielded the pitchfork—"I have some stuff to put in a pile somewhere."

John grabbed the fork from her. "No, ma'am. Not 'til you go back in that house, like I told ya, and put on somethin' what makes you not look so much like . . . like me. Ya hear? I ain't about to have somebody come drivin' onto this here yard and be a squintin' their eyeballs tryin' to decide if you're a man or a woman. Hard tellin' what could happen."

Robin clenched her fists. "You can stand out here and growl and grumble all you like, but by what I observed in that kitchen, you have a lot of work to do. Now, if you don't mind, me and Jacob here have a barn to clean. We'll be in at noon for lunch. If there's gonna be bread for the table you better get it measured out and starting to rise. And since I made a trip to town yesterday, the washing didn't get done. Take care you don't throw Jacob's white shirt in with your dirty pants. It'll need to be scrubbed separately." Her pulse raced, but she faced him eye to eye.

"You tryin' to shame me, girly? You think I ain't scrubbed clothes before? I done washed a whole lot more clothes than you've made straw piles, I'll have you know."

"You haven't scrubbed boy's clothes or woman things. Before I came, I would imagine you lived on biscuits and pickles. And Emma probably gave you the pickles." She grabbed for the pitchfork. "Give that to me, Uncle John."

John gripped tight. "Nope, not gonna do it 'til you put on somethin' decent." He pulled on the fork.

"Then we can stand here and do this all day because I'm not changing clothes." She yanked the fork from his hands, turned her back so he couldn't reach it again, and plunged it into a pile of straw and whatever else was under there.

"So now what'cha gonna do, girly? That there load is heavier than you."

Robin withdrew the fork and realigned her hands. "I can handle it . . . Just you watch." She would show him she could work as hard as his ma. Bless her soul. She tucked her bottom lip between her teeth.

"Yeah, well—you best be the one what's watchin. Some of that stuff is still fresh . . ."

She swung her arms back along her side, then with all her strength lunged with her left foot as she brought the fork forward. Oh dear, that was the wrong thing to do. She scolded herself as her foot slid on the loose straw. Her bottom hit the ground, and her teeth clamped onto her lip. She tasted salty blood. The strings around her neck choked her when the hat flew off, and her hair tumbled around her face like a mane. The fork, full of . . . *debris,* flew over her shoulder. Uncle John moaned.

Papa's oft-quoted admonition flew through her mind so fast she wanted to duck. "Pride goeth before destruction, and an haughty spirit before a fall." Today she fully understood the meaning. She guessed the Lord would rather remind her of her failing than answer her prayers.

"Uncle John?" Did the pitchfork hit him? Had she killed him with her stubbornness?

"Jacob? Where are you? Can you see Uncle John? Is he hurt?"

Two eyes peeked over the wall of the nearest stall, and his fingers gripped the splintered boards.

"Answer me, Jacob."

One finger wiggled.

She swiveled on her bottom and came face to face with her uncle, sitting on the barn floor behind her.

Muck covered her uncle's face. Clumps of dirty hay stuck in his hair and draped across his shoulders. His hat lay at his feet, flattened. He spit out a piece of straw. "You can handle it, eh? Just watch, you said. Well, missy, look what ya done did. I oughta turn ya over my knee and give you a good whuppin'. That's what I oughta do." He heaved himself to his feet.

"You. Wouldn't. Dare." *Ohh! Wrong thing to say.*

His eyes darkened. "I wouldn't dare? I won't back away from nobody's dare. But never let it be recorded that John Wenghold paddled a gal while she was down. Let me help you up and then, by jumpin' bullfrogs, we'll see how high and mighty ya sass me." He grabbed her hand.

"Stop it!" Jacob butted with his head to get between them and kicked at John's shins. "Stop it. You're mean. You can't hit my mama!" he screamed. "I won't let you hurt my mama no more." He pummeled John's stomach with his fists and continued to kick. Tears ran down his face.

"Oh, Jacob." Her heart lurched. "Your Uncle John—"

"What's going on in here? Miss . . . Miss Wenghold? Is that you? Do you need help?" Anna Blair stood in the doorway armed with a pitchfork. "I'll keep the old man busy, you crawl away as fast as you can."

As though frozen in midair, Jacob stood with one foot ready to kick, his small fists doubled against John's chest while Robin's uncle held her arm by the wrist.

Robin jerked free from John's grasp. The last thing she needed was Miss Blair paying an early morning visit—in the barn—while she sat in a pile of straw. Wearing britches. She attempted to get her feet under her, but the slick soles of her new boots slid on the loosened muck.

"Miss Wenghold? Should I get help?" Anna gripped the fork with one hand, while she pinched her nose with the other.

Robin couldn't blame her. She shared the same sentiment—the aroma was less than that of roses.

Robin gulped and willed the lump in her throat to go down along with the pride she was forced to swallow. So much for praying. "No, Miss Blair. What you witnessed is not at all how it appears."

Robin's hair hung in her eyes, but to swipe it away would mean turning loose of the mess she clutched in her hand. She shrugged and wiped the remains on the leg of her men's britches.

Anna offered her white glove-encased hand then quickly withdrew it.

"Miss Blair, if you would like to go to the house, I will join you shortly. Perhaps we could have a cup of tea." Robin glared at her uncle. "Mr. Wenghold is relieving me from my present duties, you see."

Miss Blair seemed relieved for an excuse to exit.

"Well, now," John muttered when she was gone, "likely the whole town of Cedar Bluff is gonna hear about how John Wenghold's niece was found sittin' in a pile of muck, dressed like a man." He held out both arms for leverage and helped Robin to her feet.

"I imagine my being dressed as a man is the least of your problems, Uncle John. Now, if you don't mind keeping Jacob busy, I will attempt to entertain Anna Blair. Perhaps there will be a redeeming quality to this day yet."

"I don't want to stay here with him." Jacob pointed at Uncle John. "He's mean."

Robin sighed. She didn't have the time nor the energy to have this argument. "Jacob, Uncle John is not mean, and you will stay with him. Don't fuss with me."

Big tears swam in the boy's eyes. "But he was gonna hit you."

The older man knelt in front of Jacob. "Oh, son, I would never hit Robin. Never."

"But you said . . ."

"I know what I said, but it was an old man talkin' when he should've kept his mouth shut." He nodded at Robin. "You go on in and attend to Miss Blair. Me and Jacob will finish this man's work."

Robin squinted against bright sun when she stepped out of the barn. How had she managed to get herself into so much trouble in such a short amount of time? Her stomach growled in protest of the skipped breakfast.

Breakfast. Robin rubbed the back of her neck. To get even with Uncle John, she'd chosen to leave the kitchen in shambles—the kitchen Miss Blair was no doubt perusing at this very moment. Would she ever learn? How much more humiliation could she take?

She pried off her boots on the porch, stepped into the house, and answered her own question—*not a whole lot.*

Anna stood on a chair, a voiceless shriek emanating from her beautiful, contorted face. Beneath the table, feasting on bread crumbs, sat the fattest rodent Robin had ever laid eyes on. The critter seemed unperturbed by the commotion going on around it. She had complained to Uncle John that she'd seen signs of the pesky things. But he'd scowled. *"This ain't Chicago, missy. Them creatures come in and make themselves to home both spring and fall. I'll try to plug the holes they's coming in, if I don't forget."* It was rather obvious, at the moment, that he forgot.

"But they're dirty," she'd argued, "and if someone sees them in here they'll think I'm dirty, too."

John shook his head. "Every woman on this prairie has them things coming and going, and it don't have nothin' to do with dirty or not. They's field mice what wishes they were a house mouse."

Robin stomped her stockinged foot exasperated by the audacity of the creature, the silly behavior of Miss Blair, and her uncle's neglect. The thing skittered behind the cupboard.

"Was that . . . a rat?" Anna's gaze darted around the room.

"Miss Blair, I have no idea whether it's a fat mouse or a small rat. But no matter what it is, I'm so very sorry you had to encounter the intruder." Robin reached to help her guest from the chair.

Anna shrank from her grimy hands. "Oh, thank you, but I—I don't need help."

Robin stuck her hands in her pockets. With luck, the dirty crumb-eater would stay hidden.

"I can't imagine what you must think of us, Miss Blair. Let me assure, you, this is not a typical day. To explain would only confirm your worst imagination, so I won't even try. But do sit down—that is if you can find a spot that isn't occupied by debris of some sort." She pushed the remains of breakfast to one side of the table then went to wash her hands.

"Robin? You don't mind if I call you Robin, do you?" Anna brushed something off the chair before sitting. "I came this morning, wishing to become better acquainted. I . . . I very badly want to be your friend. And I need your help."

Robin dried her hands and set a plate of cookies and the teapot on the table. At least she had pretty teacups, thanks to Emma. "I don't mind at all. And I could use a friend, myself. But I can't imagine why you would need my help doing anything, Miss Blair."

Anna removed her gloves and ran a delicate finger around the rim of the teacup, a small frown resting between her eyebrows. "I do hope you won't think I'm being presumptuous, Robin. But Henrietta Harvey assured me you would be the best person to ask. I'm sure you're aware that Ty and I will be married at Christmas. Unless, of course, he insists he simply cannot wait that long." She smiled.

Robin shrugged so her shoulders wouldn't sink with her heart. No. She was not aware of that little piece of news but couldn't trust herself to utter a reply. A shrug would suffice.

"I'll be so busy planning and purchasing my trousseau, and seeing to ever so many small details. I fear I won't have the time nor the energy to sufficiently prepare the big house on Ty's ranch for my arrival. With no woman on the place since Grace Morgan's death, I'm certain it's in need of a thorough cleaning."

"And you're wanting my help with that?" Had the woman not taken a good look around her?

"I was hoping you would agree to do it—without my help."

Robin sank into the chair across from Anna. Her hands shook too much to do more than fold them in her lap. "I'm sorry, Anna. I wouldn't feel at all comfortable being in Mr. Morgan's home with no other woman present." It didn't help to look down—all she could see were men's britches.

Anna pushed her cup to one side, contents untouched. "I'm sure no one would think any less of you for helping a neighbor and a friend. Of course, you could take the boy with you, if that would make you more comfortable. As far as Ty is concerned, I doubt he would even notice you were there." She stood. "Mother agrees to pay you well for your labor."

Robin swallowed. "And when would you want this accomplished?"

"I've not yet told Ty, but he does so love surprises. Mother and I are planning a big Fourth of July picnic at the Hawk. We'll announce our engagement then, although it will hardly come as a surprise to anyone around Cedar Bluff. We've been promised since we were small children, you know." Anna turned the ring on her finger. "That would give you at least six weeks. Would that be sufficient? I know so little about such things. We've always had a housekeeper, you see."

"I don't think—"

Tears welled in Miss Blair's eyes. "Please don't refuse me, Robin. I have no other friends who would even listen to such a plea. It would mean so much to both of us." She kissed Robin's cheek. "Thank you."

Robin stared, unblinking. Her tongue stuck to the roof of her mouth and refused to let words pass. So the beautiful Anna Blair had no friends who would stoop to such a menial task? And Ty would hardly even know she was there?

Robin followed Anna onto the porch as the lovely, soon-to-be Mrs. Ty Morgan picked her way past one barn cat and three old hens that had somehow managed to escape their confines. She would need to remind Jacob again about latching doors behind him.

"Thank you, Robin. I'll tell Ty he can expect you," Anna called as she climbed into her buggy.

Robin covered her mouth with her hand as she observed a large chicken feather stuck to bottom of the pretty lady's dainty shoe.

Perhaps the day had been redeemed after all.

FOURTEEN

Ty removed his hat and wiped his forehead with his sleeve. The morning sun already burned through his shirt, but he wanted to check one more waterhole before heading back to the house. A swirl of dust advanced his direction, and he shaded his eyes to determine the origin. Who could be in such a hurry? Knowing a stranger lurked the hills made him wary. He gripped the reins with one hand and reached for his rifle. He relaxed when the dust settled enough for him to recognize his new cowhand.

"Hey, Boss."

"You're riding like something's on fire, Sam. You have trouble?"

Sam grinned. "No, but you might have. Was you expectin' company today, sir?"

"I don't ever expect company. You know something I don't?" Ty liked this cowpuncher. Hard worker. Looked you in the eye. If only he knew a little more about him, instead of having to wait and find out in bits and pieces. He smiled to himself when Sam leaned from the saddle to tell his big news—like he had a secret.

"Rusty had me choppin' burrs out in the horse pen, and I seen me this buggy a comin' down the lane. It drove straight up to the house, and a real fancy lookin' lady got out and went in like she owned the place. I thought you oughta know."

"A fancy lady? And how would you know, Sam? You've seen a lot of fancy women in your day, have you?"

He blushed. "No sir. Leastways not like this one."

"Did she have a boy with her?" Maybe Robin had forgiven him after all.

Sam shook his head. "No sir. She was all alone. But she didn't act like she was no stranger. Walked right in. Didn't knock—anyway, not that I could see."

Ty hung his lariat over the saddle horn. "Well, friend. I reckon we better go see who this fancy lady might be, and what she's doing in my house acting like she owns it and all." He grinned. "Thanks for the warning." He clicked his tongue, and Tag responded with his slow, easy walk.

Sam rode beside him. "Ain't ya even gonna hurry?"

Ty winked. "Nope. If she's as familiar with the place as you say, then she'll still be there. And if she's gone—well, I don't think there's a buggy Tag can't outrun." Maybe he should consider getting a dog. He didn't much like the idea of anyone coming onto the place and into his house uninvited.

When they reached the house Sam leaned toward Ty. "Don't you want me to go in with you, Mr. Morgan? Or maybe I should go 'round back in case she tries to escape."

Ty dismounted and handed Tag's reins to the other man. "I recognize the buggy, Sam, and I can pretty much guarantee I won't need any help." He grinned. "You mind watering this animal for me? Then you can go back to choppin' those burrs."

Sam's shoulders drooped. "I don't mind tellin' ya, it's a prickly job."

Ty brushed his britches with his hat. "Yeah. Well, I have me a feeling I'm about to step into a right thorny situation myself."

He opened the door, and Anna appeared to float down the open staircase, a vision of sunshine with her yellow dress billowing around her.

"Hello, Ty." She rose on tiptoe to kiss his cheek and wrapped her arms around his neck.

He stepped away from the embrace. "Anna, what are you doing here?"

"Is that any way to greet your future wife? The Ty I remember would sweep me up in his arms and twirl me around and around." She folded her hands at her waist. "Aren't you even a little happy to see me?"

He shook his head. "Did you honestly believe you could waltz back into my life, Anna? Surely you don't expect us to take up where we left off? If you'll remember, that little scene involved you walking away from me."

"I told you Sunday, I was wrong." She brushed at her cheek, but he saw no tears. "I still have your ring, Ty. And, if you recall, you told me that night you would always be here. I would know where to find you. You would never stop loving me." She crossed her arms and stepped forward. "Yes, I do expect us to resume our relationship."

Ty grasped the stair rail. "It's not that easy, Anna. A year is a long time. Things change."

Anna drew nearer. "And have things changed so much that you can honestly look me in the eye and tell me you no longer love me?" She laid her palms on his chest.

Ty's heart beat like a war drum at her touch. Could he tell himself he didn't love her? Had his pride been cut and peeled? After all, she left him behind to try to explain her sudden departure to everyone who thought they were a couple—and he couldn't. And he most certainly didn't know why she chose now to return. But the temptation to pull her to him flowed hot through his arms.

"May I assume your lack of words means you're thinking? Do you even see me, Ty?"

His gaze met hers and her beauty took his breath away. How often they'd stood in such an embrace—his arms encircling her tiny waist, his cheek resting on her head—while they talked of a life together. But now, when he looked at her, he questioned his heart. What was wrong with him? What did he want? One move her direction and he could claim his dream—a life with the one woman who'd occupied his mind for most of the past year. But things had changed.

"You have to give me time, Anna. It took me almost this entire year to come to grips with the fact that you chose to leave. I finally let you go. We have a lot of time to make up. There are so many questions I need answered. Don't push me."

Anna smoothed his hair away from his face and traced her finger down his cheek. "I'll give you time. I wanted to surprise you, but perhaps it's better that you know. Mother and I have planned a picnic for the Fourth of July, here at the Hawk. It would be the perfect time to announce our engagement."

Ty slammed his hand against the railing, and Anna flinched. "Did you not hear me tell you I need time? I'm not ready to promise there will *be* an engagement. Besides, there's been no woman in this house since my mother died. Take one good look around and you can see for yourself. I've barely been able to keep it presentable."

Anna's hands clenched at her side. "And I'm telling you, Ty Morgan. There *is* an engagement, and I have the ring to prove it. If you don't intend to honor that, then you will be the one to explain to our friends and neighbors. And don't forget the good people at church. You know this entire community expects us to wed, and they have since we were children."

"You didn't seem to see the need to explain your leaving."

"My leaving was no business of anyone around here. But my coming back is. I'm here, and I'm staying as your wife. Or you can have the distinct privilege of telling everyone why you refuse to honor our engagement."

"Anna—"

She raised her hand. "And you're quite correct in your assessment of the condition of this house. It does need a thorough going over, and I've arranged for Miss Wenghold to take care of it."

"You did what?" He closed his eyes. Surely she didn't ask Robin to clean his house. "Why, when you have a cleaning woman, would you ask her? How many people do you need to involve?"

Anna sat on the bottom step and motioned for him to join her.

"Why are you so angry? Is it because I didn't let you in on what I thought would be a wonderful surprise? Or is it because I asked Robin?"

"Both. And what made you think John Wenghold's niece would even consider such a task?" Why did she question his anger? What happened to the Anna who put other people first? What happened to the woman who cleaned this house when his mother became too ill to do it herself?

"Henrietta Harvey told Mother that John invited his niece to come to Kansas to help him. Something about it working both ways, since his brother left a lot of debt. I thought it would benefit her, and I didn't for one minute think it would upset you so."

"And how did Mrs. Harvey know this bit of news, Anna? I've never known John Wenghold to divulge anything vaguely familiar to family business, and I doubt his niece would tell her."

Anna shrugged. "I don't know. I'm only repeating what she said. But there's something you need to know that concerns Miss Wenghold."

Ty chewed on the side of his mouth. Had Anna been in the house long enough to find the picture Jacob drew for him? He did observe her coming down the stairs when he came in. With a sigh, he lowered himself to the step. "I'm listening."

Anna explained what she'd witnessed at John's place in the barn and in the house.

"You say the boy was screaming at John not to hit his mama?" Ty braced his elbow on his knee and rubbed his forehead.

"Yes. And Robin—" An odd look came to her eyes. "She was dressed like a man, Ty. I've never seen the like. I would have mistaken her for Mr. Wenghold had he not been in a tussle with the child. And I think maybe John had knocked her down because . . . Oh, Ty—the girl limped something awful."

He shook his head. "So naturally, you decided asking her to come here to clean would keep her safe? Is that what you're saying, Anna? And what did Miss Wenghold have to say about such a plan?" Plenty, he imagined.

"She tried to reason it wouldn't be proper for her to be at your home alone. But I assured her you wouldn't even notice her presence, and she could bring the little boy with her. I told her Mother would pay her well, unless you would rather take care of it." Anna smiled.

"And she agreed?" She may not speak to him, let alone take money from him.

Anna reached for his hand. "I didn't give her an opportunity to refuse. The poor girl needs to get away from that dreadful place." She ran her soft thumbs across his knuckles. "Maybe we could even work something out, after we're married, so she could continue to work for us. This is far too large a place for me to keep up by myself, especially with the entertaining we will be expected to do. And it would give her a steady income."

Ty stood. "You're forgetting, Anna. I'm agreeing to nothing. Have you already issued invitations for the picnic?" Did she honestly believe having Robin working for them would be an answer to any problem?

She nodded. "Protocol demands sufficient time to plan. Anything less than six weeks would be egregious."

Ty shook his head. "I do wish you would've talked with me about this first. I don't like it at all, and now you've managed to include the entire community."

Anna stood and squeezed his arm. "Ty Morgan—you know as well as I do that you have never been able to tell me no. Six weeks is a short time to get ready for such a gala event, but more than enough time for you to realize you still love me. Now, walk me to my buggy. Mother will be concerned I've not yet returned."

They reached the buggy, and she put her hands on either side of his face. "Look at me, Ty. Take a good long look so you don't forget. Then you go back into the house and think about all we've talked about." She kissed her fingertips then touched his lips. "That could be the real thing, you know. You only need to decide."

As she drove away, Ty pressed his fingers to his mouth. The real thing? How often, during the long nights this past year, he'd willed her to be in his arms with her lips on his. He could have taken her in his arms today. She let him know that with certainty. Why hadn't he?

He took the steps to his bedroom two at a time. He would change clothes, then hightail it over to John's. Would Robin speak to him? What had possessed her to dress like a man? And why had Jacob yelled at John not to hit his ma?

Ty grabbed a clean shirt from the wardrobe. As he turned away, he saw John's notice lying on the bed, and that revelation removed all doubt. Anna had seen it all. But did she want him to know? He sat by the window and leaned his head against the back of the chair.

Anna challenged him to remember her promise of kisses. But a small dimple, at the corner of a mouth he'd never tasted, niggled into his mind and squeezed into a corner of his heart.

Was it possible to love two women at the same time?

FIFTEEN

A shaft of noonday sun shone through the gap in the rafters of the barn, revealing the lingering dust in the air. John smiled down at the impish, dirt-covered face of the boy standing in front of him. "I tell you what, Jacob. I'd say you done a man's work this mornin'. Why don't you hustle on in the house and see what you can find to eat? How 'bout it?" He picked a piece of straw off the boy's shoulder and flicked it to the floor.

"What you gonna do? Aren't you hungry?" Jacob imitated John and wiped a finger under his nose then on the seat of his pants. "*Phew.* Robin missed all the mans' work, didn't she?" His forehead puckered. "Are you gonna yell at her again?"

John knelt in front of him. "I was wrong to get so all-fired foolish actin', Jacob. Sometimes even grown-up people like me have to say they's sorry. So, while you're a gettin' you something to chew on, I'm gonna go talk with Robin. I need to ask her to forgive me for them mean things I said."

"Where is she? Didn't she go with that lady to the house? She's real purty—that Anna lady—ain't she?"

John shrugged. "Guess you might say that. But if there's one thing a man has to learn, it's that sometimes purty ain't what's on the outside. You run on in now. Then stay put. You hear me? Don't go wanderin' off by yourself. Stay in the house 'til I get back." He gave him a swat on the behind and scooted him out the door.

"I will. Promise." Jacob scampered away.

John waited to make sure Jacob entered the house. He'd watched his niece limp her way to the creek after Miss Blair's buggy rolled from sight and determined then he would follow her as soon as he got the boy situated. He did need to apologize. That was plain as the nose on Albert Harvey's face. But somethin' a whole lot more important stirred around in his head. Why did the boy think he was gonna hit Robin? Was it because he'd come to think of her as a real ma? Or could it be some man hit that poor lady what laid out on that prairie?

From a distance he spied Robin with her back against a big cottonwood tree, hands in her lap. And she was still wearin' them men's clothes. Things must not have gone so well with Miss Blair. She gave him a sad smile when he reached her. His throat tightened with the knowledge he'd caused her pain. He lowered himself to the ground beside her. "Bad day get badder, did it?"

She nodded. "When I left the barn I thought the day couldn't get any worse. But it did."

Don't put it off, John. He took her hand. My goodness, did all ladies have such small hands? "Before we talk 'bout another thing, Robin, I need to say I'm sorry for shootin' off my big mouth like I did 'bout the way you was dressed and all. You caught me by surprise, and I guess I don't like surprises much."

She squeezed his hand. "I'm not without fault, Uncle John. I think I knew how you would feel. Emma warned me when I went to buy the clothes."

"That woman knows a lot about people's feelin's, don't she?"

"Did you hear Jacob refer to me as Mama?"

John scooted so he could see his niece's face as they talked. "I surely did, and that's another thing I want to talk to ya 'bout. But first off, I guess I gotta know if you forgive me or not. Sure hate to go to bed with anger in the house."

"Oh, dear man. You're forgiven. I'm not angry. I'm scared. I've been scared from the first day I got here. I didn't know what was ahead for me. I'm not sure I would have taken you up on your kind offer if I had."

"Would you rather be married to William Benson?"

"I don't know. No. I don't think so. When I think about it, things swirl around in my head. William doesn't know about Jacob. His offer may not stand if there is a child to consider. But as far as I'm concerned, that little boy and I come as a package."

"You mean, if he wants you *and* the boy, you might consider leaving?" He didn't much like the idea of that city fella takin' them away.

Robin smiled. "No. I'm just thinking aloud. Right now, my biggest fear is Jacob. Did his outburst mean he saw his mama being abused? I was so loved by my papa. Why would anyone put a child through such a thing? It was clear he wanted to protect me."

"And I didn't help none. Me and my thinkin' if I threatened to whup ya, it would change things. You gotta remember, I ain't used to havin' nobody but me to watch out for, and nobody else to boss around. Ain't no other woman ever lived in this house but my ma." He patted her hand. "I'm sure wishin' I could talk with Emma. See if she could shed some light on that whole thing with the boy."

"Are you going to town?" Robin picked at her fingernails.

"Nope. Too late in the day to start now. Ain't 'bout to leave you and the boy here all by your lonesome with someone nosin' around. See what tomorrow brings, I reckon."

"Where's Jacob? He won't wander off, will he?"

"Sent him to get somethin' in his belly. You hungry?"

"No, but I'll come in and help clean up the mess like I should've in the first place." She related the scene with Miss Blair, including the pesky rodent. "You were right about the pack rat. At least this creature was larger than any Chicago mouse I've ever seen."

"I'll plug them holes first thing. I never should've left the kitchen in such a fix. Reckon I was playin' the same game as you. Wanted to see how long it took before you hollered."

Robin laughed. "Then we've both learned a lesson, huh?"

"Yep. Did you find out what that Blair woman wanted so early in the morning?"

Robin nodded then wiped at tears spilling down her cheeks.

He studied the bark on the tree behind her. *What's a fella supposed to do? This havin' a woman around sure is different. One minute she's smilin' the next thing she's got water fillin' her eyes.*

"She and Ty are getting married. Anna and her Mother have a big party planned for the Fourth of July, and they will announce their engagement then. She asked me to ready the big house at the Hawk for the special event."

"She asked you to clean Ty's house? What right does she got to do that?" He slapped his knee. "Looks to me if Ty thought it needed cleanin' he'd ask you himself."

"Would he, Uncle John? Is that how Ty sees me, too? As a housemaid?" She palmed away her tears.

"Oh, girly. I didn't no more mean that than I meant I'd whup ya. Just an old man a talkin' again. You ain't nobody's housemaid. Especially Ty Morgan's. And for sure not someone Anna Blair can order around. Ya told her no' didn't ya?" He lifted himself from the ground and pulled Robin to her feet.

"I tried. Miss Blair is obviously not accustomed to having her requests denied." She dusted off the seat of her britches. "Let's go get that kitchen cleaned up."

He shook his head. "No. Me and Jacob made the mess, we'll clean it up. You take your time comin' in. Might be surprised what this old man can do."

"You know what I'd like to do? I'd like to try my hand at cleaning the barn. It would help work off my frustrations. But could you see that Jacob stays away? I need some time alone."

"Doggone it, girly. Didn't mean for this day to come a fallin' down on ya like this. I'll keep Jacob with me, you can bet on that. And I'll stay out of your way, too." He laid his arm across her shoulders. "I probably ain't supposed to be showin' you this, but if you was to go around to the other side of this tree you'd find what Ty calls his 'leanin' spot.' Might be good if you was to spend some time there a leanin' and thinkin'."

Robin peered at the tree. "Ty showed me the day we came fishing with Jacob, but I didn't recognize it. It's his place, Uncle John. I'm not sure, with all that has happened, that I should intrude on a private spot like that."

"Pshaw, girly. It ain't no more his private spot than it is mine. It's a hole in a tree. I don't see no reason you can't lean there if you was a wantin' to."

"That day we were here, Ty recounted some of the times he spent in that hideaway. Most of them were sad. I think he was even going to tell me about Anna Blair that day, but I interrupted him. In retrospect, I should have allowed him to talk."

"Well, you do what you've a mind to do. I'll keep Jacob away, and I don't think you'll have to worry none about Miss Blair finding ya. You know, my ma is the onliest woman I ever put my arms around, or my lips on, but sure if I don't feel like givin' you a hug right now." He pulled her to him and held her while she sobbed then dug in his pocket for his handkerchief and handed it to her. "I sure do hope you stick around, Robin. I imagine you're 'bout the best thing to happen to me for a long time. Your grandma Wenghold would be proud. Mighty proud."

John kicked a rock ahead of him and shuffled to the house. His ma would like this spunky daughter of Lionel's. It would break her heart to watch the little gal limp like she did, but it was strange how you forgot about it after you were around her a while. And the longer you were around her the prettier she got. Maybe because it wasn't only outside beauty. No, it went clear through. Like Emma.

He picked up the rock and chucked it at a fencepost. That Emma—she was some lady. He always wondered how George Ledbetter came to win her heart like he did. You'd never guess it. Why, the guy must have measured as much around his middle as he did from head to toe. But every inch of him was packed tight as could be with goodness. Did Emma miss that man as much as he did? Maybe he should ask her. But it was strange—when he was around that lovely lady he hardly even gave George a thought. Land's sake.

Maybe the best thing would be to take her to the hotel for a right nice steak supper. Now that would set tongues a waggin'. But it wouldn't bother him. Nope, wouldn't fret him at all.

Robin watched Uncle John trudge back to the house, and her heart swelled with the same kind of love she'd felt for her pa. Times like this she missed Pa so fierce it ached. But it had helped to have flesh-and-blood arms around her while she cried. Her uncle said he didn't want her to leave. And she didn't think it was just because he'd grown fond of Jacob either.

When Uncle John disappeared from sight, Robin slipped around the huge trunk of the tree and tucked herself into Ty's leanin' notch. Had he ever shown this special place to Anna?

Was it wrong to hope he hadn't?

Ty dismounted and wrapped Patch's reins around the hitching rail in front of John Wenghold's big stone house. The setting sun cast a golden hue to the surroundings. A magic time of day when everything seemed right and worries or problems disappeared in the beauty of it. But this evening he had too much on his mind.

Do I still love Anna? Could I be in love with Robin, too? Does Jacob have a pa? Does Robin know about John's quest to find her a husband? Does Anna? The questions assaulted him from every direction, like the hailstones the first night he'd met Robin. But that storm had ended. With no answers, tonight's questions continued to twist through his mind.

Ty knocked on the kitchen door. Ordinarily he'd walk right in, like he'd been doing since he'd begun his daily visits to the Feather. But he was hesitant to do that this evening. With all that had transpired in the last couple of days, he may no longer be welcome. Jacob answered, and when he saw it was him, the lad squealed and jumped up and down. "Ty, you're here! I been missing you. Did you come to read me a story?"

"Let him sit down before you try climbin' on his lap, boy." John pulled Jacob off Ty's leg. "Thought I told you to stay away." He grinned and motioned for Ty to sit. "Ya look plumb tuckered. Care for a glass of something cool? Me and the other man of the house was puttin' the last bite around supper."

The kitchen was nothing like Anna described. Floor clean. Stove clean. Nothing, except the dishes they used for their meal, seemed out of place. "Buttermilk sounds mighty good, John. It's been another hot one, hasn't it?"

He sat and took Jacob on his lap. "So, my little buddy, what have you been doing today?" He poked his fingers in the boy's ribs, and Jacob wriggled with laughter. "You smell like a horse barn."

"I know. Me and Uncle John worked like mans do. I pitched horse—"

"Jacob." John's voice was stern.

"I learned how to sling a pitchfork." The lad glanced up at John.

John winked at him. "He sure did. Was a big help, too." John set the drink on the table for Ty. "Got a few sweets left if you care to have one." He pushed a plate of cookies his direction.

"You make these, Jacob?"

"No. Robin made 'em. But she don't work in the kitchen no more. Uncle John hired her to muck out—"

"I did no such thing, Jacob." John scowled. "Ever have one of them there days, Ty, when ya should a stayed abed and waited for it to be over?"

"That's why I came, despite your telling me to stay away."

"Will you read to me, Ty?" Jacob jumped from his lap and grabbed onto his hand. "Come on."

"Jacob, leave him be. He ain't even swallered his drink." John pulled the boy onto his own lap.

Ty tickled Jacob's tummy. "It's too early, isn't it? I don't think Miss Robin would want you crawling into bed smelling like a horse.

"Robin isn't here. She won't know."

Ty didn't miss John's frown. "Not here? John, you didn't let her go off alone, did you?"

John shook his head. "I'm old, not stupid. She's on the place, just not in here."

Ty nodded. "Tell you what, Jacob, let's you and me go out to the pump, and I'll give you a cold water bath. How would that be?"

"But what if somebody sees me? I can't take a bath with my clothes on. Robin said."

"If Miss Robin scolds you, I'll tell her it was my idea." He stood and reached for the boy's hand.

Half an hour later, with a clean-smelling Jacob in tow, Ty bent to pull back the covers on the small bed. "I'm not sure why I'm nearly as wet as you were, my little friend. Here"—he patted the pillow—"lie down."

"Do I have to go to sleep? It's not even dark." Jacob pouted but wiggled onto the bed.

"It's plenty dark, fella. You promised you would settle down if I read to you. Now you've had your story. You don't have to sleep right yet, but you could lie here and think about what I read."

"Are there giants for real?"

"Goliath was real. But I'd rather have you think about the boy named David. He was brave, wasn't he?"

Jacob planted his feet flat on the bed and bounced his bottom. "I'm not brave. I get scared a lot."

He straightened the boy's legs and held them still. "Being afraid doesn't mean you aren't brave, Jacob. Brave is when you do the right thing, even though you are afraid."

"Oh." Jacob giggled as he fought to continue his bouncing.

"No more wiggling. You've worked hard today. Now you need to settle down and rest." Ty ruffled the boy's hair. "G'night."

"Wait. Aren't we going to pray?"

Ty sat on the edge of the bed. "Sure enough. Thank you for reminding me. How about you go first?"

Jacob scrunched his eyes and tucked his chin into folded hands. "Dear Jesus. Thank you for Robin and Uncle John and Ty and for cuz we don't have a giant living here anymore. And don't let Robin make Uncle John so mad any more, and let me be brave and let Ty teach me how to ride a horse, and don't let me be afraid of storms anymore. Amen. And, oh yeah, I almost forgot—let me have a new ma and pa and if you need ideas of who I want then I would say Robin and Ty, but Robin says I shouldn't try to get my own way when I talk to You. Amen again." Jacob squeezed Ty's hands. "It's your turn now."

Ty swallowed. "I think you said my prayer for me, Jacob. Thank you." He smiled. "Shut your eyes, and first thing you know it'll be morning."

"Will you still be here? I wish you could live at this ranch." Jacob turned on his side and tucked his hands under his cheek.

"I won't promise, Jacob. But I'll try to be back to read to you tomorrow night. How's that?"

Jacob yawned and nodded. "G'night, Ty."

Ty stood outside the closed door for several minutes. Why had the boy prayed about John being mad? Had he actually knocked Robin down as Anna suggested? That didn't sound like the John Wenghold he knew. And what would Robin think of the boy's prayer? He believed all things were possible with God. Why did this seem so impossible?"

John was in the kitchen when Ty came back downstairs but still no Robin.

"You get the boy down for the night, did you?"

Ty nodded. "Not asleep, but quiet for now. He grumbled about it not being dark, but it will be soon, and if he'll close his eyes it shouldn't take him long to drift off to sleep."

John pointed to the basket on the table. "Thought you might want this, Ty. As far as I can tell, Robin ain't et nothin' all day." He folded a towel and placed it on top.

"Where is she?" Ty peered under the towel and found a pot of coffee, two cups, and a plate of biscuits. "You think she's going to agree to a picnic?"

John shrugged. "Never hurts to try. You'll find her in the barn, I reckon. Oh, and Ty—don't let her come back in 'til the two of you talk." He wiped out the dishpan and hung the towel on the hook by the sink.

"About what?" Did John know Anna asked Robin to clean his house? Did he suspect Jacob drew his picture on the back of the crazy advertisement for a husband?

"A lot happened today. It started with me a fussin' at her like a silly old man and ended with Anna Blair paying a very untimely call—before noon."

"So you know about Miss Blair's request?"

"Did you put her up to it?" John stepped closer. "Cuz if ya did we'd better be havin' us a little talk."

"Anna paid me a most inopportune visit as well, John. And no, I did not know she was going to pull such a stunt. I'm sorry. I don't know what got into her. It's hard for me to believe she's being intentionally unkind, no matter how it seems."

"Did she tell you she walked in on a fight?" John sat down and dropped his hands between his knees. "I don't mind confessin' I'm plumb ashamed of myself."

Ty lifted the basket. "None of my business so long as no one got hurt."

John sighed. "More than one way to hurt a body. I reckon what comes out of a mouth can hurt as much as a punch in the gut. The pain of a punch goes away after a while. The sting of words can settle in like squatters and be just as hard to get moved out."

"Have you talked with her since Anna left?"

John nodded. "We done spoke our apologies."

"Then, if you don't mind, I'll go see what kind of fence mending I can do."

On the way to the barn Ty rehearsed his request for forgiveness.

How would he start this conversation—if she would even listen? John said words could hurt forever, but what about words never spoken? Anna intended to hold him to everything he'd ever proclaimed to her. This might be his last opportunity to voice his heart to Robin.

He stepped into the dusk darkened barn and lit a lantern. "Robin? Are you in here?" He found her asleep, propped in the corner of an empty stall. He shook his head. The girl indeed wore men's clothing, but only a fool would mistake her for a man. Her legs were stretched in front of her, crossed at the ankles. A dirty rag wound around both hands, which still held the handle of the pitchfork draped across her lap.

Ty set the basket on the dirt floor and knelt beside her. Pieces of straw adhered to her hair, which hung tangled across her shoulders. Long lashes curled against her cheek. A smudge of something graced her forehead. And she smelled like a barn. But this was the same woman who loved a little orphaned boy as if he were her own. The very same feisty lady who defied crusty old John Wenghold. The girl who made his heart skip when she smiled and caused him to wonder how it would be to come home every evening to someone like her.

He pulled a fragment of straw from her hair. Was this proper? To be here alone, wanting to wipe the smudge from her face and take the pitchfork from her rag-wrapped hands? What did John have in mind when he'd sent him out here like this—with orders not to come in until they talked? Shouldn't John himself have come with him and helped her into the house where they could talk with him as a witness? He was a preacher. Ty groaned. Yes, he was a preacher, but he was also a man.

"You're staring, Ty Morgan. I've told you before it makes me very uncomfortable when someone stares at me." Robin's eyes remained closed.

Ty jerked his hand from her hair. "How did you know it was me?"

She opened her eyes. "I smelled you." Her face remained expressionless.

"You smelled me?" Ty sat back on his heels and laughed. "Well, guess what—I can smell you, too."

Robin glared at him. "I'm so very sorry. Had you been invited perhaps I might be a bit more presentable, but I doubt I would've bothered." She tossed the pitchfork to one side. "Now, if you don't mind. I still have work to do."

"No, please, Robin. Let me explain." Ty grabbed her hands.

She attempted to pull them away then cried out in pain.

"Robin? Let me see your hands." Ty turned them palm up and his heart stuttered at the sight of the bloody rags. "Oh, dear lady. What have you done to yourself?" He tried to unwrap her hands, but the cloth was stuck.

"Don't. I can do it myself." She pulled at them.

Ty held fast. "Hold still or you'll make it worse." He fished the coffeepot out of the basket, relieved that it had cooled somewhat. "Here. This might be a little warm, but at least it will soak through enough to loosen this filthy rag. What were you thinking, Robin? Why didn't you stop? Don't you have any sense at all?"

She grimaced, and Ty bit his tongue. Why scold her? He was frightened, that's why. What if he hadn't come looking for her? What if John assumed she wanted to be left alone and went to bed? What if . . .

"Please, don't. That hurts." Robin struggled to free her hands. "Why are you so angry at me? No one asked you to come here, you know. I can take care of myself."

"Apparently not, Miss Wenghold. Do you have any idea what this kind of injury can do?" He continued to pour coffee onto her hands to release the crude bandage.

"It's just blisters. I'm not used to handling a pitchfork all day, that's all." She sniffed.

"You'll be lucky if you don't get an infection. And infection could lead to . . ." He didn't want to think about it. "We'll get some clean bandages on here, and in the morning I'm taking you to see Doc Mercer."

"That's silly. I won't go. And who do you think you are, giving me orders—threatening to take me to Doc Mercer? Go home. Don't you have some kind of animal or something that needs your doctoring skills there?"

Ty unwrapped the last length of cloth and took a closer look at her hands. He shuddered. Dirty, open blisters covered the palms of her hands. Loose skin curled at the edges and fluid seeped from the worst of them. She must be in terrible pain.

He raised his eyes and met her gaze. Tears puddled then ran down her cheeks. She sniffed them away. "Don't move your hands, Robin. Please." He lowered her hands to her lap, palms up, then wiped her face with his handkerchief. "Better?"

She shrugged.

"You want to know why I'm here?"

She nodded.

"I need your forgiveness. I wish, with all my heart, we could start over. I should have told you right away I was the preacher. If I could take Sunday back, I would. Robin, I never wanted to hurt you." He pulled a piece of straw from her hair and tucked the loose strand behind her ear. "Will you forgive me? Will you give me another chance?"

Robin's forehead wrinkled. "Anna came here today. I know about your upcoming marriage, and I congratulate you. She's very beautiful."

He couldn't argue with that statement. But did Miss Wenghold realize the effect she had on him? He longed to explain that marriage to Miss Blair may not be a sure thing. But a man didn't discuss such matters. Not between two women who, at this point, had him in such a muddle it was a wonder he could even remember his own name.

"Anna told me she asked you to . . . to—"

"Be your maid?" Robin interrupted. "Is that what you're trying to say?"

"I would never think of you in that manner." But what would Robin think if she knew Anna wanted to invite her to continue to work at the Hawk after their marriage? Robin was right. Being their maid was exactly what Anna inferred. "Besides, I won't allow it. Especially not with your hands like this."

Robin's eyes narrowed. "You won't allow it? Not with my hands like this? Well, guess what, Mr. Morgan? I heal quickly. In a day or two my hands will be good as new, and then I'll fulfill my obligation to see the grand house on your ranch is ready for the big day and the most important announcement." Fresh tears rolled down her face, and she raised her hands to wipe them away.

Ty grabbed her wrists and forced her hands back to her lap while he mopped his handkerchief across her face. "Look at me, Robin." He waited until she locked her gaze on his. He expected to see defiance. Anger. Condemnation. Instead, her dark eyes were wells of such sadness he could barely speak. What had he done to this girl? This . . . this woman?

"I wouldn't care if your hands healed right before my eyes, tonight, here in this dirty barn. You are not my maid, Robin Wenghold. Not mine. Not Anna Blair's. Not even your Uncle John's. You are a fine, wonderful, beautiful woman." He wiped her face again, but it seemed in vain as rivulets of tears continued to run down her cheeks. He ached to pull her to him, to tell her all that was in his heart. He wanted to hold her and feel her close but busied himself tearing the towel into strips and wrapping her hands. She winced with the movement but didn't make a sound. Ty appreciated her silence. He would have to look at her if she spoke—and if he did, he wouldn't be able to think. Why did this girl he'd known such a short time cause him to question his commitment to the woman he'd loved for most of his life?

He could have taken Anna in his arms this very day, in the home they were destined to share, and no one would have questioned their embrace. Anna had invited his arms and would have welcomed his lips. He was free to declare his love with all the words of endearment he could imagine. Anna was, after all, his betrothed. And she wore his ring to prove it. The same diamond and ruby circle of promise his mother wore from the day his pa asked her to marry him.

But what if Ma could know Robin? If she could help him choose, who would it be?

He finished tying the bandages then took her hands. "You haven't said you would forgive me."

Her gaze met his. "I forgive you."

Ty took a deep breath. "Robin . . . if we had more time—if things were different—would you give me another chance?"

Robin shook her head. "Time is not something either of us can promise. Any chance that might have been ours ended when Anna returned wearing your ring." Her smile belied the sadness in her eyes.

Ty touched the dimple at the corner of her mouth.

One small circle of gold and jewels and a promise that threatened to become a noose.

One small indentation at the corner of lips he had no right to claim, and a promise he was not free to make.

He groaned. *You are in so much trouble, Ty Morgan.*

SIXTEEN

"Why in granny's name didn't ya come get me?" John barked, while he unwound the strips of toweling from Robin's hands. *What was the guy thinkin' anyway?* He weren't thinkin' as far as he could tell.

Ty stuck his hands in his pockets. "You were the one who told me not to let her come in until we talked."

John discarded the last bandage and examined Robin's hands. "And I suppose you would've talked 'til the blood quit runnin' if you'd found her bleedin'. Go in the cupboard by the sink and bring me that squatty little green jar sittin' on the shelf."

"You have medicine?"

"Shore, I got medicine, but it ain't gonna do a lick of good sittin' on the shelf and you a standin' with your hands in your pockets. And bring me some fresh water when you come and another towel."

"I'm sorry, Uncle John. I don't want to be such a nuisance." Robin winced as he applied a wet cloth to her hands.

"Pshaw, child. Ain't nobody worth their salt what hasn't had blisters on their hands. I jist wish you'd a come in when they commenced hurtin'."

He blotted her hands dry and applied the salve from the jar. "Whooee, but this stuff does stink. Doc calls it goose grease. It's his own concoction. Supposed to be good for anythin' what ails a person." He laughed when Robin screwed up her face. "Told you it stank, didn't I?"

Ty's nose wrinkled, too. "How'd you come by this? I don't remember having anything like it at our house."

John wrapped clean bandages around his niece's hands. "Abe Mercer and me been friends since he come a ridin' into Cedar Bluff nigh on thirty years ago, lookin' for somewhere to hang his brand-new shingle. He's never been content to deliver babies and take out splinters. Nope. He sees himself as the one man what might someday be famous for findin' a cure for everything." He screwed the lid back on the jar. "This here stuff probably comes about as close as he'll ever get. Course, far as I know, me and Abe are the onliest ones to have any of it."

"You're sure it'll work? What if she gets infection?"

"Well, I used it on foot rot on my milk cow—and it got better. Even tried it on a bald spot and doggone if it didn't grow hair." He winked at Ty. "I'd say it'll take care of these blisters right fine."

Ty grinned. "I'm almost sorry I asked."

John shuffled to the cupboard and retrieved a bottle of brown liquid. "Here, Robin. You take a swig of this. It'll help take the sting right out of them hands. Help ya sleep, too."

"Is it liquor?" Robin frowned.

"Don't keep liquor around here. This here is laudanum. Good for pain."

"I'd like to clean up first, if you don't mind. I don't want to crawl into bed like this." Robin stood. "Being clean will help me sleep."

John slapped his forehead. "Jumpin' bullfrogs, girly. Never gave that a thought. You can't be gettin' them hands wet. How you gonna wash yourself? Why, I don't reckon you can even get out of them duds without help. And there ain't nobody in this house what can help ya, neither."

Robin slumped back into the chair. "I can't stay like this."

Ty stepped forward. "I could ride into Cedar Bluff and get Emma.

John shook his head. "Makes more sense to put Robin in the buggy and take her to town. Can't expect Emma to close the mercantile but reckon she'd have room for an extra body for a few days."

Robin fidgeted in her chair. "I can't leave Jacob."

"Never gave that a thought." John scratched his head. "Reckon Emma wouldn't mind if we was to take him along."

Ty sat across from Robin. "Don't wake him. I'll take Jacob to the Hawk with me until you're able to care for him. He prayed tonight I would teach him how to ride a horse." He grinned.

Robin's forehead wrinkled. "But would he be safe, Ty? I thought you had questions about Sam Mason."

Ty shrugged. "Sam won't hurt the boy. And if there is a connection then maybe it would be a good thing to find out what it is. We can't claim Jacob for a son until we know he doesn't belong to anyone else."

John cleared his throat. "Didn't know ya was plannin' on claimin' him for a son. Can't hardly be a son to the two of you if one of ya is plannin' to marry up with someone else, now can he?"

Ty's face flushed. "I spoke out of turn, John. I'm sorry." He stood. "I'll take good care of him, Robin."

"Does Jacob have clean clothes to take along?"

John puffed his chest. He was downright proud to tell this little lady he'd done everything he was supposed to do. And with luck, the boy wouldn't tell her about the white shirt that changed color when he washed it with the britches.

"Done took care of it, missy. Exceptin' for your . . ." He leaned toward her. "Well . . . some of your *personal* things. Didn't seem right to let the boy see me handlin' them so stuck 'em back to wait for you," he whispered.

"And you expect me to take dirty clothes to Emma's?" Robin's voice shook.

"Now, don't you go a tearin' up again. I'll tell Emma to give you anything you be needin' and I'll take care of it later. Don't ya fret no more about such things. Ty can figure out what the boy needs hisself."

"I'll hitch up the buggy for you, John. And, Robin, don't worry. I'll stay the night here, and we can go over to my place in the morning. You let those hands of yours heal."

John followed Ty onto the porch. "Did the two of ya ever talk, like I said?"

"We talked."

"And . . . ?"

"We talked, John. That's all I can say."

"*Humph.* Well, the way she was a lookin' at you, when you was a flappin' about claimin' Jacob for a son, there was a whole lot you didn't say."

John's words echoed through Ty's mind as he climbed the steps to check on Jacob. He and Robin never talked about making Jacob their son. What caused him to make that kind of statement? What must she think?

And what about Anna? Her response to Jacob didn't leave much hope she'd be open to the possibility of becoming a bride *and* a mother. But then, he could never take Jacob away from Robin anyway.

He peeked into the boy's room. Jacob lay on his tummy, with his rump in the air, sound asleep. Ty smiled. The boy resembled one of John's jumpin' bullfrogs in that position. Did the tyke ever wake up in the middle of the night? If he did, would he call for Robin? Maybe he should sleep close by.

The door to the room across from Jacob's stood open, he had only to take one step inside to know it was Robin's. He backed out. It just didn't seem right for him to be in there. There was a closed door at the end of the hallway. It would put him farther away from the boy, but he doubted he'd sleep anyway. He'd hear him if he called. He had to push against the door to get it open, and his heart sank. Enough moonlight shone through the bare windows for him to tell John used this room for storage. Though he could make out a bedframe, there was no way of knowing if it held a mattress. If so, it was piled high. There'd be no placed to stack the stuff if he did try to uncover it.

There wasn't even room on the floor to stretch out. He closed the door and leaned against the wall. Proper or not, what choice did he have? But it was only a bed. She wouldn't be in it—she wasn't even in the house or on the ranch. And Jacob would no doubt check there first if he needed someone. He took a deep breath then crossed the threshold into her room.

He lit the small lantern on the bedside table and sat down to pull off his boots. It had been a long day and it would feel good to stretch out. And he'd work hard to put out of his mind who might be lying beside him. The flame flickered as the breeze rustled through the open window and sent shadows dancing on the wall. A small rocker in the corner by the window held a blue and yellow quilt, and a picture on the table revealed images of three young girls—probably the Wenghold sisters. He reached for the picture. Could he recognize Robin? A gust of wind billowed the lace curtains when he lifted the framed photograph from the table and an envelope fluttered to the floor.

Ty studied the picture and smiled. Robin stood on the left, a rag doll draped over one arm and a large bow balanced on the top of her head. But the dimple at the corner of her mouth made positive identification easy. He leaned to replace the frame and retrieve the envelope.

Was it against the law to read the address? Or the return? If so, he was in big trouble. *Mr. William Arthur Benson, III.* His heart lurched. Robin had received mail from a man? The postmark read Chicago. An old beau? The *friend friend*? Perhaps the notice printed on the back of Jacob's picture was posted long before Robin ever set foot on the Feather. Was this William Benson someone who'd answered the ad? Someone interested in Robin as a wife? Why should this bother him so? He had a fiancée.

He paced the room, reading and rereading the return address. The guy must be mighty important to have his own printed stationery. His name was even printed larger and darker than the rest. He slapped the paper against his hand. Oh, but he wanted to see what this fella had on his mind.

He shoved the envelope back under the picture and blew out the lamp, then slipped across the hall to check on Jacob. He couldn't go back into Robin's room with that letter screaming to be opened. He had never been so tempted to deliberately go against his upbringing.

Jacob lay sprawled on his back, one arm slung across his face and one leg tangled in the sheet. What if this Benson guy took Robin and the boy back to Chicago? Could he let them go? Without a fight? He bent to straighten the covers, and the boy's face split into a grin.

"I fooled you, didn't I? Did you think I was sleepin'?" Jacob sat up and crossed his legs. "I play lots of tricks on Robin. Is she gonna tell me good night?"

"Yes, you did fool me, buddy. And no, Robin isn't coming up tonight. She hurt her hands cleaning the barn, and John took her in to Mrs. Ledbetter's. I'm going to stay here with you until morning then take you to my place tomorrow. Would you like that?"

Jacob's forehead puckered. "Is she gone forever, like my other mama?"

"No, no, little man. She'll be back when her hands are healed. Mrs. Ledbetter will take real good care of her." Ty smoothed the covers. "Now, you lie down here, and this time shut those eyes for real."

"My eyes aren't sleepy. Why do little kids have to go to bed before big peoples?"

A growl from beneath the open window sent a shudder down Ty's spine. In a flash, Jacob jumped from the bed and pulled back the curtains. "Tripper! Here, Tripper! I knew you'd find me." He ran from the room and Ty followed, taking the steps to the kitchen two-at-a-time.

"Jacob. Stop." He caught the boy as he reached the kitchen door. "Get back in here, son. You don't know who or what is out there."

"I know who it is. It's ole' Tripper." Jacob fought against Ty's arms. "Let me go."

"No, you're not going out there alone. Calm down and I'll go with you, but not without a lantern." The bark persisted until they stepped onto the porch. Ty held the light in front of him with one hand and grasped the boy's wrist in the other. The small flame revealed a medium-sized dog only a few feet from where they stood.

Boy and dog faced one another without a sound. Jacob trembled and Ty pulled the boy closer. Obviously there was something familiar, yet child and beast seemed hesitant to breach the distance that separated them.

A whistle from the shadows beyond the porch broke the eerie silence. The dog turned and trotted toward the sound, then gave one last look over its shoulder, whined, and disappeared into the night.

Ty peered into the darkness and tightened his hold on Jacob. Who was out there? He didn't dare leave the boy alone to investigate, nor could he take him on what might be a dangerous chase. How stupid. He hadn't even grabbed a gun before running onto the porch. So much for promising to take care of the little man.

Jacob wrenched away from Ty and shuffled back into the kitchen and up the stairs.

Ty followed and watched as the boy crawled into bed and turned his face to the wall. Ty sat on the edge of the bed. "Was that your dog, Jacob?"

He sniffed.

"Can you tell me who might have been out there with him?"

Jacob trembled and drew his knees to his chest, as though he wanted to make himself as small as possible.

Ty rubbed his eyes. Obviously the boy didn't want to talk about it. He lay down beside the child and put his arm around him.

Jacob turned and curled against his chest. "Don't leave me," the boy mumbled. He clutched Ty's shirt.

"I'm staying right here, buddy."

"Promise? Will you be here in the morning?"

"I'll be right here beside you, Jacob." He drew the boy closer. "You go to sleep."

He'd promised he would be there in the morning, but what about all the mornings to come? If he kept his promise to Anna, would it mean giving up this little guy cradled in his arms?

He held still and listened to the night sounds outside the window. Who'd been out there with the dog? Was it the boy's pa? Wouldn't a pa reveal himself? Jacob was only a little boy, yet he seemed to hide a man-sized secret. Was he in danger?

Once, during the long night, Jacob awakened and called out for Robin. Ty whispered, reminding him where Robin was, and Jacob snuggled closer—but not before proclaiming, "I want Robin."

Morning light filtered through the lace curtains, and Ty still lay awake. He'd fought a battle in his heart, and lost.

He wanted Robin, too.

SEVENTEEN

The pink rose-covered wallpaper in Emma's tiny spare room reminded Robin of their parlor in Chicago. She must remember to tell her sisters. Wouldn't Mama have been surprised to know the wall covering she'd so carefully chosen for their fancy city parlor, also graced the walls of Emma's simple Kansas bedroom.

"Robin? May I come in? I'd knock, but it's a little hard to do with only a curtain covering the doorway."

Robin pulled back the curtain and smiled at her friend. "Do come in, Emma. I was admiring your choice of wallpaper. Roses are my favorite flower. They were my papa's favorite, too."

"Then I made the right choice." Emma smiled and handed her a blue glass bottle. "Here, I want you to have this. With that Mr. Benson coming for a visit, I thought you might like something sweet to dab behind your ears. Besides, the Feather does have a way of sticking to a person."

Robin cradled the cobalt blue bottle in her hands. "Oh, Emma. How thoughtful." She removed the cork and sniffed the contents. "Ahh, rosewater. My mama always used rosewater. I don't suppose I'll ever forget how comforting that fragrance was to me. No matter if I laughed or cried—when Mama hugged me she smelled like roses, and it made me feel safe. Thank you, Emma."

"*Pshaw.* Go on with you, girl. Having you here these past days has been nothing but a pure pleasure. You're welcome anytime. You sure I can't come help you get ready for that Chicago fella?" She winked.

"I've been thinking about his visit. Guess there's no better time for William Benson the Third to see me like I am—the Feather and all. I only wish I knew how he will accept Jacob."

Emma's eyebrows arched. "He doesn't know?"

"Wren and Lark don't even know. I'm ashamed of myself for not corresponding with them sooner. But so much has happened I don't know where to begin."

Emma perched on Robin's bed. "You're not going to clean Ty's house, are you?"

Robin shrugged. "Ty said he wouldn't allow it, but I don't want to cause trouble with Anna Blair. I've given it a lot of thought. I don't think she meant to be unkind. She's used to having things her way. What would it hurt if I helped her? It would only be this one time. It's not like I would be a permanent fixture over there."

"Tell me this. Do you still have feelings for Ty Morgan? If you do, then you best stay as far away from there as you can. You go over and work in that house, and he comes in and the two of you talk there won't be anything but trouble and a whole lot of hurt. You mark my word."

The bell above the door jangled, and Emma stood with a groan. "Duty calls, I suppose." She kissed Robin's cheek. "You know, it's going to be mighty quiet around here without you.

Robin laughed. "I've been noisy?"

Emma smoothed her apron. "Not noisy, just present. Someone who would at least grunt when I was finished speaking my piece. George never talked much, but my goodness he was a dandy grunter."

"Robin? Emma?"

Emma smiled. "That would be your Uncle John."

"Ain't nobody in this here place what's waitin' for me?"

Robin put her arms around Emma. "Now, there's a grunter *and* a talker."

"And don't I know it." Emma wet her fingertips and smoothed her eyebrows.

"Wait." Robin dabbed a bit of rose water behind the woman's ears. "Cedar Bluff does have a way of sticking to a person." She giggled.

Emma blushed like a schoolgirl. "Now, don't you go getting ideas."

Ty lifted Jacob onto the saddle in front of him and clicked his tongue to let his horse know they were ready to move. Robin was home, and it was time to take Jacob back to the Feather. "Are Robin's hands still hurted? Do you think she'll remember me? Why do Tag's ears wiggle back and forth when I talk? I wish Tripper would come back. Do you think he got dead somewhere? I wish you would stay at our ranch all the time."

Ty sighed, grateful Jacob didn't seem to require answers to his questions. Right now he had too many of his own to try to keep straight. How he wished he could stretch the miles between the Hawk and the Feather to give him time to settle his heart. There was no question as to what to do about Anna. He'd made a promise, a vow. He would marry her. But oh, how he dreaded saying good-bye to what might have been.

"I see 'em! I see 'em!" Jacob shouted and waved his arms.

"I see them, too, little man." Ty nodded at John when they reached the house. "Evening, neighbor. You ready to have this little lightning bolt back in your house?" He handed Jacob down to John.

"Give you trouble, did he?" John ruffled the boy's hair. "Guess you can imagine how quiet it's been with him and Robin both gone. Plumb forgot what it was like before they came. Don't mind tellin' ya, I'll like it a whole lot better now that they're back."

"And I'll be the one checking to see why there's no noise coming from Jacob's room." Ty shook hands with John. "How is she?"

"Robin?" John raised one eyebrow.

Ty removed his hat. "You know good and well who I mean."

John shrugged. "Why you askin' me how she be? Her hands seem healed enough, if that's what you was a meanin' by 'how is she.' If you was a wonderin' anything else, I reckon you best be pointin' them questions at the lady yourself. It may be you need to finish up some talkin' you might've left undone when you was still in the barn."

"I've said all I'm free to say, John. I'll leave it at that."

"Yeah. Well, I'm only gonna say this one time so ya better be payin' some mind. Another week or so, and ya might be wishin' ya would've cut whatever ropes is a holdin' ya back. Never can tell who might beat ya to it."

Ty scratched his chin. Sometimes this old neighbor could be downright cantankerous. "Want to tell me exactly what it is you're trying to say?"

"Told ya I was only gonna say it one time, and I done did it." He turned his back on Ty. "Jacob, boy? Let's you and me go put this horse in the barn."

"Are we gonna put your horse in the barn, too, Ty?" Jacob took Tag's reins. "Can Ty stay here tonight? He'll get real lonesome at his house without me."

John shook his head. "Not tonight. Maybe if he gets lonesome enough he'll think about it."

Ty frowned. The sly old fox. He was up to something. What did he mean 'never can tell who might beat you to it'? Did he know about this Benson guy?

Robin stopped the sway of the swing with her good foot and clasped her hands in her lap. Why would Uncle John leave her alone with Ty? Didn't he know how awkward it would be?

Ty sat in the wicker chair facing her swing, his long legs stretched in front of him. "It's good to see you, Robin. I take it your hands have healed or Emma wouldn't have allowed you to come home."

"Doc Mercer's miracle cure did the trick." She wiped her sweaty palms on her skirt. "Did you and Jacob get along well?"

"Very well. Don't have to wonder what he's thinking, do you?"

"Did he ask you why the moon doesn't fall if stars fall? He asked me and I told him maybe you'd know." Banter about Jacob would keep things lighter.

Ty laughed. "That was thoughtful of you, Miss Wenghold."

Robin peered into the dusk. "Did Sam recognize him? Was there any trouble?"

"I didn't take any chances. Rusty knows I want to protect the boy and is aware of my suspicions that Sam might recognize him, so he sent Sam away for a few days."

She raised her eyebrows. "Away? Where? Could you trust him not to sneak back?"

"The Hawk's a big ranch, Robin. It wasn't hard to find a place to keep him busy. Rusty trusts him. Besides, if he's up to no good, we'll find it out sooner or later. Jacob was in no danger. I kept him with me all the time." He frowned. "Trust me. He was as safe at the Hawk as he's been over here."

"I wasn't implying he wasn't safe, Ty. I only voiced the same concerns I thought you had." Why was there a lump in her throat? She didn't want Ty to see her in tears, ever again.

Giggles and shouts announced Jacob's return. "Robin! I missed you." He hopped into the swing beside her and sent it swaying. "Ty has a swing, too. I liked it. But he don't cook good. Did you miss me?"

Robin pulled the boy onto her lap and wrapped both arms around him. "I missed you so much I won't ever let you go." She laughed while he struggled to get out of her grip. "Nope, little man. You have to stay here forever."

Jacob pried her hands away and scooted to the other end of the swing. "I couldn't get loose when Ty tickled me. He's bigger. And Ty teached me to ride a horse all by myself. Did you see me, Robin?" He straddled the arm of the swing and mimicked a riding motion.

Robin used her toe to stop the swing's movement. The rocking motion, and Ty's close proximity, did nothing for her swirling stomach. "Emma sent some cookies with us. Would you like a glass of milk and cookies before you go to bed?"

"Aww, do I have to go to bed?"

Ty chuckled. "Hey, buddy. You had to go to bed at my house, too, you know."

Jacob hopped from the swing and stood in front of Robin. "You should see my bed at Ty's house." He held his hand above his shoulder. "It's this bigger than me. Ty had to lift me in. You should stay all night there sometime, Robin. There's another room nobody sleeps in and it's real purty. It's yellow. I sawed it. And I bet Ty would help you get in bed if it's bigger than you. He's real nice."

John cleared his throat. "Ty, if you wouldn't mind fetchin' the milk from the well, I'll get some cups and the cookies. Jacob, boy, I'm thinkin' you probably ought to think about lettin' somebody else talk a while." He winked at Robin.

Both men left the porch with silly grins on their faces.

Jacob wrapped his hands around Robin's arm and laid his head on her shoulder. "I wish Ty lived here. Don't you?"

Robin couldn't answer. Why, oh why, hadn't she let Emma come?

EIGHTEEN

The unmistakable wail of a train whistle broke the stillness of the prairie, and Robin shifted on the hard wooden bench of John's wagon. If she didn't know better, she'd think he was being pokey on purpose. Though he'd never admit it, she believed her uncle to be as apprehensive about William Benson's arrival as she was. Now William would probably be waiting at the depot when they arrived. She'd so hoped she'd get there first and have time to . . . to what? The small train station in Cedar Bluff certainly didn't offer the amenity of a washroom so she could freshen up. Robin fingered the lace collar on the new blue dress Emma had tucked away in her valise as a surprise. How silly to be so nervous. She'd known William for as long as she could remember, but could she ever see him as more than a friend?

"I wish I could've stayed with Ty." Jacob huffed, crossed his arms, and stuck out his bottom lip.

Robin fought to keep her voice calm. "We've gone over and over this, Jacob." She had deliberately waited to tell the boy about William's visit until this morning. Perhaps that wasn't such a wise decision, but Jacob would surely announce it to Ty Morgan.

"Will he like me?" Jacob's eyes grew round. "Is he a nice man?"

Robin put her arm around the boy and pulled him close. "Do you think I would let him come for a visit, all the way from Chicago, if he were a bad man? Of course he's nice."

"But will he like me? Ty likes me. He told me when you was getting your hands all better."

"He told you? Did you ask him, Jacob? It's not polite to ask questions that might make people say things they don't want to say." She needed to avert his questions about William. She didn't know if William would like him. What if he didn't?

"Is that him a standin' there holdin' up the wall of the depot?" John flicked the reins across the horses' backs. "Hup there, you lazy animals. Doggone, the way you been lollygaggin' over every tuft of grass between here and the Feather, a body would think I never fed ya." He turned to Robin and winked. "That there fella don't look like no city slicker to me. Suppose your Mr. Benson got lost?"

Their wagon pulled along the station platform and Robin's breath caught. This man certainly didn't look like the William she remembered. Clad in dark gray britches and black boots—the white and gray striped shirt contrasting sharply with the tan of his face—this person didn't look like anyone she knew. But when he pushed away from the wall and stood, legs apart and hands behind his back, she recognized all too well his familiar stance.

Robin ducked her head. *Oh, dear little Wren, you did not exaggerate. He does look delicious.*

William Benson peered at the wagon approaching the station. The tilt of the woman's head left no doubt. He'd often teased Robin for her strange little habit of turning her head to one side when she studied something—or someone. *You even look like a robin, you know—cocking your head like that. That's what they do before they go after the worm.*

When the older man stepped from the wagon, William walked to the end of the platform and reached for his hand. "Will Benson, sir. I'm glad to meet you."

John laughed. "*Pshaw*. You ain't so glad to see me as you are that pretty little gal sittin' beside me. But to be mannerly, so I don't make her blush any more'n she already is, I'm glad to meet you, too."

William smoothed his mustache with his thumb and forefinger. "Hello Robin. You did get my letter, didn't you?"

"Course she got your letter," John grumbled. "You think we make a habit of meanderin' up to the train depot to pick up whatever warm body what might be tiltin' his shoulders against the wall?"

William nodded. "I guess that was a dumb question. Forgive me. It's just that you look a bit surprised."

"Well, she is surprised. And I'm downright befuddled. Ya certainly don't look like no city slicker to me." John walked all the way around him. "Nope, son. You ain't no city slicker."

"What's a city licker, Robin?" The little boy hadn't taken his eyes off him since they stopped the wagon. Wary? Frightened? Who was he? Why was he with Robin? He surely wasn't the older man's child.

William knelt on the platform. "A city slicker, young man, is what they call someone who doesn't know a thing about a ranch." He reached for the boy's hand. "My name is William, but you can call me Will. And you are . . . ?"

The boy didn't answer until Robin nodded. "Robin said I'm supposed to call you Mr. Benson. My name is Jacob. You can call me Jacob."

"Well, now, perhaps we can get Miss Robin to change her mind once we get better acquainted. Do you think that might be possible?" He winked at Robin, and nodded in response to her mouthed thank you.

John pointed to the leather valise. "This all you brung? Thought you was a stayin' a while."

"I thought I might purchase some items locally. Mr. Rempel mentioned Emma's Mercantile. Does she carry men's clothing?"

"She don't carry many fancy things. Got britches and shirts, I reckon." He grinned at Robin and her face turned red. Apparently, it was a private joke.

"Robin has some man clothes. You could borrow some from her." Jacob grinned. "She can't wear 'em no more cuz Uncle John gets—"

"That's enough, boy." John scowled.

The smile slid off Jacob's face, and he snuggled closer to Robin.

"If this is all you got, then we better get." John lifted the valise into the wagon.

"There is one more thing, but I'll fetch it, Mr. Wenghold." William pulled a large trunk forward. "I believe this belongs to you, Miss Robin." He bowed.

"My trunk! Oh, William, how did you know?"

"A little bird told me." He laughed. "As a matter of fact, two little birds made double sure I wouldn't forget it. Wren said you would be so happy to receive it, you might even give me a kiss." He leaned toward her.

"Stop it, William." She pushed him away.

"If I'd a knowed you was a gonna start courtin' before ya even got in the wagon, I'd a sent Robin in alone."

William settled the trunk into the back of the wagon and climbed in beside Robin. "Here, Jacob. Want to sit with me?" He placed the boy on his lap and wrapped his arms around his middle. "You know, Mr. Wenghold. I don't ever remember not knowing your niece. And would you believe, after all these years, I still haven't gotten a kiss from her?"

Jacob clasped his hands on top of William's. "Ty don't kiss her, neither. But I think he wants to."

"And who is Ty?" Surely Robin hadn't been here long enough to have a beau? Who would be available in Kansas? A cowboy? She deserved better than that.

"Ty likes me. He might be my pa someday. I been praying. Ty is big, like you Mr. Benson. And he's not a city licker, either."

NINETEEN

The first evening star was visible, though it was still quite light. Robin loved this time of evening, right before the last burst of sunset changed to the whisper-gray of night. Cicadas hummed their eerie undulating song and a mocking bird perched somewhere close by and whistled through its repertoire.

William came onto the porch and Robin took a deep breath. His apparent ease did nothing for her quaking nerves. If only she could have a few moments alone before the inevitable visit with him. *You two run along and enjoy the evening. Me and Jacob will tend to the cleanin' up in here.* Bless Uncle John. She'd take that up with him another time.

"Do you mind if I join you?" William pulled a wicker chair next to hers, then leaned back and crossed his long legs. "The meal was wonderful, Robin. But why do I get the feeling you stayed in the kitchen all afternoon on purpose? You've been avoiding me, you know."

She clasped her hands and willed them to stop shaking. "I haven't been avoiding you. I've been busy."

"You've been busy staying away from me, my sweet friend. This is William sitting here, not some stranger."

Wrong. He was a stranger. She expected the old William—the one who dressed in suits and stiff white shirts with black bow ties. The man she knew parted his hair in the middle and plastered it down with some kind of sweet-smelling oil. William Arthur Benson the Third—the banker's son from Chicago—was clean shaven, pale faced, and would never sit in the presence of a lady with his shirt collar open like that. She forced her gaze from his chest.

"I haven't seen you for nine months, William. In a way, you *are* a stranger. Why, after all this time, have you suddenly decided to come back into my life?"

"It isn't sudden, Robin. I asked you to marry me before your father died. You turned me down. I'm hoping you'll reconsider. You did read my letter, didn't you?"

Robin met his gaze. "Yes, I read your letter. But did you honestly think that by not contacting me in any way during that time, you would endear yourself to me? You're most confident that no other man in his right mind would consider courting a cripple, aren't you?" She'd just made trouble for herself. In the past William would not allow her to reference her limp, and from the expression on his face that hadn't changed.

William leaned forward and braced his forearms on his legs. "Stop it, Robin. I will not allow you to feel sorry for yourself. You know that."

"Nor will I tolerate your pity." She stood and crossed her arms. "I'll ask you again. Why are you here?" *Robin, why are you doing this?*

William stood and put his hands on her shoulders, forcing her back into her chair. "I'm here because I care for you, Robin."

What did she want him to say? That he loved her? She would argue that point, too. Why couldn't he be the old William? Not this . . . this handsome stranger who seemed as at home on the prairie as he did in Chicago.

"Look, Robin, can we start over again with this conversation? I didn't come to fight with you."

"Oh, that's right. You came to *care* for me."

William frowned. "And what is wrong with my caring for you?"

"Do you have any idea how many times I've heard Uncle John declare he'd best get out and care for them animals—they don't care for themselves, you know. You make it sound like caring is a chore to be accomplished." That was a childish outburst and she knew it. And the smirk on William's face indicated his knowledge as well.

"You're twisting my words. I didn't say I came to take care of you. I distinctly remember saying I came because I care *for* you—as in always have and always will. I don't see it as something I need to accomplish at all. Friends care, Robin."

"And that is how you see us? Friends?" She was talking herself into a corner. William wasn't afraid to meet her in the middle of the ring and punch back.

William shrugged. "I will always be your friend. Anything beyond that will be entirely up to you."

"So you want me to decide whether I want to remain only a friend, or return to Chicago as your wife. Are those my choices?"

William leaned back in his chair. "Husbands and wives have been known to be friends, Robin. Now you're making this sound like some kind of business transaction." He smoothed his mustache with his thumb and forefinger. "I think to be safe, we need to change the subject. Tell me about Jacob. Who is he, exactly? He's a handsome little tyke. I think he could charm the silver off a dollar."

Robin nodded, grateful for the change of focus. "He's a sweetheart, isn't he? Ty Morgan and I found him on the prairie."

"And who is this Ty? I never did get an answer, but he must be someone important to Jacob."

"I need to start at the beginning. Do you want to hear the whole long story?"

"How long? Will I need a cup of coffee and perhaps another piece of your apple pie?" He winked. "Like any man, I listen much better over a plate of sweets."

Robin smiled. He didn't look like her old friend, but he did sound like him. Her mama would say William Benson could smell pie baking before she assembled the ingredients. "This is the first apple pie I've baked since coming to Kansas. And, wouldn't you know—you just happen to show up in time to eat it."

William stood and pulled Robin to her feet. "And here I thought you baked it special for me. But, Robin, I didn't just happen to show up. I planned this trip well."

Robin poured William another cup of coffee while he smashed the remains of the pie onto his fork.

"You didn't like the pie?"

William shook his head. "Liked the pie, not the story."

"Because it doesn't have a happy ending?"

"It didn't have a happy beginning, Robin. And it still has no ending. I wish I could have protected you from the storm. And I wish Jacob . . . what will become of him?" William sipped his coffee. "Whew, that's hot. You must have refilled it when I wasn't looking."

"You seemed deep in thought. I'm sorry. I should have warned you. I don't know what will become of Jacob. I threatened to return to Chicago—once when I was very frustrated—but Uncle John said I couldn't take Jacob. And I can't leave him."

"Why didn't John want you to take the boy?"

Robin carried the dirty dishes to the cupboard then returned to sit across from him. "He thinks as long as there's a chance he has a pa, we need to wait."

William leaned back and crossed his arms. "I can understand his reasoning, Robin. Look, at the risk of another argument—and believe me, I don't want a fight—but let's say that at the end of this month you decide to return to Chicago with me. What *would* you do with Jacob?"

Robin frowned. "What do you mean? Are you saying you wouldn't want him with us? What would you want me to do with him?" She trembled. She didn't want another fight, but she'd fight with anyone in order to keep Jacob.

"I said I didn't want an argument. And I don't. I've been here less than a day. This little guy surprised me. I need answers to a lot of questions before I can make any statement you would probably want to hear."

"Like what? I've told you everything I know about him."

"How would Ty Morgan feel if you were to take the boy away? And what would happen if we did take him to Chicago and then a father came after him? Could you give him up? What would it do to you? Have you prayed about this? Maybe you should talk with your pastor. Perhaps he would be able to give you counsel."

Robin shook her head. "Our pastor would be no help. Believe me."

He raised one eyebrow. "It's not like you to speak unkindly about a man of the cloth."

She smiled and shrugged. "William, the preacher is Ty Morgan."

TWENTY

William's watch showed half-past midnight. The room was hot, no breeze came through the open windows, and scenes of the day's events insisted on being rehearsed. He slipped on his britches and padded barefoot down the steps and onto the porch.

"You couldn't sleep, either?"

William jumped at John's voice. "I hear you but can't see you."

"I'm tryin' to keep this wall from fallin' down. Keep your voice low, if you don't mind."

"Oh, I'm sorry. I don't wish to awaken anyone."

"Not worried about wakin' anybody. You got good eyes, son?"

William moved to John's side. "I don't wear spectacles, if that's any indication."

"I been a starin' at one spot so long I can't tell if they's somethin' a movin' out there or if I got myself spooked. Look yonder, toward the barn. There! Did you see somethin'?"

William peered into the darkness. He did see movement, but what would anyone be doing way out here at this time of night? "You have any idea who or what it might be?"

"They's been somebody snoopin' around. He's been seen here and over at Ty Morgan's, too. Usually on horseback, and never looks to be hidin'. Never gets close enough, or stays around long enough, for anybody to catch up with him."

"Want me to take a look? If it's the same person he wouldn't expect two men on your place, would he? Do you have a gun handy?"

"There's one a hangin' above the door in the kitchen. Can you manage handlin' a gun without shootin' somebody?"

William didn't answer but stepped inside and retrieved the gun. "Don't intend to shoot anyone, but if it's an animal, I might find the weapon useful, don't you think?"

"*Humph.* I knowed you weren't no city slicker the minute I eyeballed ya in town. Think you can stay out of sight 'til you get to the barn?"

"Trust me."

William slipped into the shadows, scolding himself as he crept toward the barn. Only a city slicker would go out at night without his boots. What was he thinking?

He stopped at the edge of the tree cover, his jaw stiff from clamping it shut so he didn't yelp as he encountered twigs and stickers along the way. He rubbed the bottom of each foot across his pant leg then leaned against the trunk of a tree to catch his breath. Did Robin know someone had been spying on them? What kind of danger was she in? Was Jacob in danger?

A twig snapped and a tingle ran the course of William's spine. Had he been stupid enough to let someone get behind him? Heavy breathing accompanied another crunch of undergrowth. William shouldered the gun and whirled to face his opponent.

"Don't ya dare pull that trigger. It's me."

William lowered the gun. "Well, you're lucky you didn't get shot, John Wenghold. I don't recall hearing you say you were going to follow me. If someone's still out there he's no doubt laughing his head off."

John stepped out of the shadows. "Keep the gun handy but come with me. I got me an idea." He walked a ways farther then stopped and cupped his hands to his mouth. "Hey you, whoever ya might be. We knows you're out there so ya might as well show yourself and tell us what ya got on your mind."

"That's a good way to get shot, you know." William stepped

between John and the barn.

"We don't aim you no harm," John shouted, "and I reckon if ya was intent on no good you would a done it long before now, so come on out."

They waited for a long minute before a silhouette of a man emerged through the open barn door and slid around the corner. William ran, but John moved in front of him, and he tripped.

Pounding hooves telegraphed a departing message then all was quiet.

William sat on the hard ground with his knees drawn up. "If you would have stayed on the porch this might not have ended in such a fiasco. Why'd you cut in front of me?"

"Well, if that wouldn't make granny's cat howl. I didn't do no cuttin' in front. You was so slow I done got ahead of ya."

"I couldn't go any faster. I'm barefoot."

"Barefoot?" John spit. "About the time I think ya might have a little bit of smarts, you go and pull some dumb trick. Don't ya know no better than to go barefoot out here? It's a wonder ya didn't step on somethin' sharp, or a snake, or somethin'."

"Did you think the guy was going to accept your invitation for a tea party? 'Come on out. We don't aim you no harm. Nice Mr. Bad Man.'" William mimicked John. "Why don't you leave him milk and cookies out behind the barn? After a while I bet you could get him to eat out of your hand."

John waved him off. "You can poke fun all ya want. But promise me you'll bust a gut to keep Robin and the boy in sight at all times. Never had me no trouble with anybody sneakin' around 'til they showed up. Me and Ty think it's the boy what brung it on, but we can't be sure."

William rose and dusted off the seat of his pants. "Does Robin know?"

"Yeah, she seen him one night."

"So, now what? You want me to stay up and watch?" William picked up the gun.

"Nope, no need. If the fella has half a brain he's done figgered out there's two of us. I doubt he'll be back tonight. I been thinkin' on havin' me a piece of that there apple pie, if you haven't already et it all. I was a wishin' we could maybe have us a talk without Robin or the boy listenin' in."

"Hate to tell you, I ate the last piece of pi—*Unh!*" William winced as he stepped on something sharp.

"Here. You wanna hold my hand so's you don't trip?" John slapped his knee. "I'm purty sure ya didn't eat the last piece of pie. I done figgered out where she puts the sweets when she don't want me or the boy to find 'em. B'sides that, a woman don't ever bake only one pie on Saturday when she knows there's company for Sunday." John wiped his hand across his face. "Ya know, it's a wonder that gun didn't go off when you went a slammin' into the ground. You did load it, didn't ya?"

William grabbed John's sleeve. "Are you telling me you keep an unloaded gun above your kitchen door? A lot of good that does. You think some intruder is going to politely wait for you to find your ammunition and load the crazy thing? John, you'll have to be more diligent if you're going to protect Robin and Jacob. You let me go out there with an empty gun, for crying out loud."

"Didn't let you do no such thing. I thought you'd have enough know-how to check. Always kept it loaded 'til the boy came. Don't take no fancy to him gettin' curious and tryin' to get it down."

"You got a point. You know, if that gun had been loaded chances are you would have gotten shot tonight, cutting in front of me like you did." William laughed. "If you don't mind, though, I'm gonna load this thing before I hang it over the door again. With us both keeping Jacob in sight it should be safe enough."

John shook his head. "Don't know much about kids, do ya? I didn't either before Jacob showed up. I'll tell you one thing I've learned—keepin' a boy like him in sight at all times is about like clutchin' a handful of water. What say I pound a couple nails up a bit higher? Maybe keep it out of his reach as best we can."

William hung the gun back over the door. "Probably should wait until morning to pound anything unless, of course, you don't mind Robin catching us cutting that other pie."

John motioned to the cupboard where the coffee cups were. "Since you're a gonna be around for a while, I reckon ya might as well make yourself at home. You can pour the coffee. I'll get what I can find tucked away."

William did as he was told, then grinned as John set a plate of cookies in front of him. "No pie? Thought you said she wouldn't have baked only one pie." He reached for a cookie. "Mmm . . . molasses. She remembered they're my favorite."

"Well, don't get so high on yourself, boy—they's my fav'rite, too." John put two cookies on the table by his cup. "As late as it is, I reckon I might as well come right out and speak my mind. What ya here for?"

William liked this man. "That seems to be the question of the night. Robin asked me the same thing earlier."

"So, what did ya tell her?"

"The same thing I'll tell you—I came because I care for her."

"Anybody send ya?" He reached for another cookie.

William took a sip of coffee. "Why would you ask a question like that?"

"Cuz Lionel Wenghold was my brother. He writ me a letter before he died—hadn't kept in touch like I should've—askin' me if I would think on making sure his daughters got took care of."

William pointed to the cookies in front of John. "So, who's taking care of whom?"

"Didn't know how to go about gettin' 'em out here, and I surely weren't gonna set up camp in Chicago. Didn't reckon on them comin' one at a time."

"Why did he ask you? I mean, if you didn't keep in contact, how did he know you would be the kind of person to honor his wishes?"

"Cuz we's Wengholds, that's how. Distance didn't erase our name or drain our blood. Did Lionel ask you to take care of Robin in particular?"

William nodded. "Robin and I grew up together, played together, went to school together. At some point, can't remember when, I appointed myself her knight in shining armor. Her limp made her a target for some awful mean pranks and a whole lot of ridicule. I tried to spare her as much as possible. Mr. Wenghold knew I wouldn't let anything bad happen to her as long as I could help it."

"You let her out of your sight long enough for her to make her way to Kansas. You don't think anything bad could happen to her out here? Jumpin' bullfrogs, man. Did you know she was caught in a twister the first day she arrived? If it hadn't been for Ty Morgan it's hard tellin' where she might've got blowed to."

"I've heard the story. This Ty must be quite the man—preacher, woman and child saver, successful rancher . . ."

John's eyes narrowed. "And a man what's so blamed honorable he's done got himself caught in a web that's more'n likely gonna strangle him."

"I didn't mean to disparage him, Mr. Wenghold."

"Ya sounded like a jealous schoolboy." John spooned sugar into his coffee. "If my brother asked ya to take care of Robin, why'd it take ya so long?"

"I asked Robin to marry me before your brother died. I thought it might bring him a small measure of comfort. She refused—quite adamantly, I might add. I'm sorry to admit my pride was wounded. I fooled myself into thinking that if I left her alone for a bit she would see she needed me and would reconsider the offer."

"The offer? Like ya was buyin' a piece of property? I don't know nothin' about a woman gettin' married, but I think I can pride myself on bein' a mite smarter than you."

"I didn't know she would leave Chicago. Actually, I was gone when Mr. Wenghold died. I returned as soon as possible when my father contacted me with the news that the Wenghold sisters were in financial straits. He'd also heard a rumor that Robin planned to go west to work on a ranch. I didn't get back in time to try to stop her."

"Where was ya? You rich kids travel to warm climates for the winter, do ya?"

William stood and took his cup to the sink. "I was on my Uncle Earl Benson's ranch in Wyoming Territory. I've spent my summers there since I was twelve years old. My father thought it would do me good to learn to work with something besides other people's money."

"You there all summer and winter?"

"No, no. I have an office at my father's bank. Your brother visited with me there in early September, shortly after his physician gave him the news he had only a few months to live. I proposed to Robin soon after. I reasoned it would give her papa comfort to know she would be provided for. When she refused, I sulked. A short time later we received word my uncle was injured, and it provided me an opportunity to leave Chicago."

"Did Robin know where you were? Does she know about this Uncle Earl?" John brushed cookie crumbs off the table.

"I guess I can't answer that. I'm not sure my whereabouts mattered to her. It wasn't unusual for me to be gone often during the summer. Our family owned a small private lake in Michigan. When I was younger, Mother and I would spend as much time as possible there, while my father stayed in the city. I don't recall ever talking to Robin about my Uncle Earl or my working on his ranch. And I certainly didn't know you existed until I returned and went to call on Robin."

"Do ya love the girl, Mr. Benson, or is it a sense of duty you got stuck in your feelin'? Robin ain't no dummy. She'll sniff you out like a dog huntin' a rabbit hole."

William shrugged. "I admire Robin. And I know I could learn to love her. Love, as I understand it, would only be a fickle emotion without friendship, admiration or respect, and the profound need to protect that which is loved. I'm hoping my time here will allow Robin and me to have a better understanding of where we are in this relationship. Or, perhaps, whether there even is a relationship."

John held his hand out to William. "I don't suppose you'd consider staying on here, should Robin decide to take you up on your so-called offer?"

William shook hands with the older man. "It would be tempting, but no. As much as I've learned to love this way of life while working for my uncle, in the end I don't want to set up camp on a ranch. I'll return to Chicago and my life as a banker—like my father and his father before him—with or without Robin."

"With or without the boy?"

William shook his head. "I don't know, sir. I don't know."

TWENTY-ONE

Robin tied the bow of her new straw bonnet under her chin. The trio of small burgundy roses along the brim complimented the lighter shade of pink of her dress. One last dab of rosewater on her wrists, one last pinch of her cheeks, and she was ready. Mama would no doubt have scolded her for being so vain. But Mama wasn't here. And was it so wrong to want to be pretty? To actually *feel* pretty?

Uncle John would no doubt wink, and Jacob was sure to blurt out something about her new dress. But she would *not* let anything spoil this day. How good it was to have her trunk again. And to make it even sweeter, her sisters had packed two new dresses. It must have cost them a fortune, but this morning it didn't matter. She would see they received payment later. For today, she planned to enjoy going to church with a new frock—and with William.

"Robin? You plannin' on havin' church in your room or you gonna hie yourself on down here so we can be a leavin'?"

"I'm right here, Uncle John. You needn't yell." Robin reached the bottom step and smiled at him.

"Well, if you don't look purty this mornin. Reminds me of them wild roses what grow along the creek." The older man stepped closer and sniffed. "And, by gum, you smell like 'em, too. Whooee, Cedar Bluff, Kansas. You best be lookin' out this mornin'."

"Uncle John, please don't say anything." She kissed his leathery face. "I'm sure Jacob will embarrass me enough. But I do so want to look nice."

John patted her cheek. "Oh, girly, I wish your Grandma Wenghold could see you. Ya remind me of her, you know?"

"I do? Thank you, Uncle John. I think that's the nicest thing you could say. I've never heard you talk of her without love in your voice. She must have been a very special lady."

"Special don't near say it all. But enough of that for now. Come along. Church won't wait for us, you know.

Robin stepped onto the porch and William's eyes widened. A slow smile spread across his face, and butterflies danced in her stomach while his gaze inched at a snail's pace from her bonnet to her feet, then back again. Her breath caught, and she bit her tongue to keep from gasping. William's dark suit accentuated his sapphire-blue eyes. His reddish brown hair swept away from his face and fell to the top of his crisp white shirt collar. Why had she never seen this side of him in Chicago? *He didn't look like this in Chicago. That's why.*

"You two gonna just stand there a gapin'. Ain't you never seed one another cleaned up before?

Jacob giggled and his shrill voice broke her reverie. "Look at me, Robin."

Goodness, but it was warm.

"Do you see me, Robin? Uncle John says I'm big enough to ride the horse Ty gave me all by myself."

Robin scowled at her uncle. "You aren't going to let him ride alone, are you?"

"He ain't gonna be by hisself. I'm lettin' you and William take the buggy, and me and the boy will ride horseback, and I got his horse tied to mine. No need to worry, though. By the time I was his age I was bouncin' on the top of a big ole' cow pony so broad my legs stuck out like oars on a boat."

"By yourself?"

"No. Your pa was with me. Hard to find a young'un on this prairie what don't learn to ride pert near as soon as he can sit by hisself. It's a necessity. I figger we're startin' two years too late with Jacob boy."

Robin shot a glance at William. Was he in on this?

He shrugged and winked.

She sighed. They outnumbered her.

"Your buggy awaits, my lady." William stepped to the porch and placed her hand in the crook of his elbow, then walked her to the buggy. He helped her in then climbed beside her and gave the reins a flip.

John rode alongside the buggy. "William, be sure and have Robin point out the wild rose bushes. Patch don't like to lollygag, so me and the boy will be pushin' on. We got plenty of time if you was wantin' to meander a bit." He tipped his hat. "See ya in church." He laughed as he rode away.

"You have rose bushes out here on the prairie?"

"We do, but that isn't Uncle John's reason for making the announcement." Heat bathed her face, and it was more than the morning sun.

William nudged her with his shoulder. "I didn't figure it was. And, by the way, you look beautiful this morning, Robin. Is the color of your dress the same as a wild rose?"

She giggled. "You catch on fast, Mr. Benson."

"Not fast enough, I'm afraid. But maybe my time here will make up for it. Now, is there anything I should know before we make our entrance into church this morning? Tell me about the good people of Cedar Bluff."

Glad for the change of subject, Robin did her best to introduce the people she knew through unbiased eyes. William could form his own opinion of the townsfolk when he met them.

A quiet churchyard greeted them, and it made her more than uneasy. Not only would they walk in late, but also the likelihood of finding a seat in the back was very slim.

William helped her out of the buggy, then placed her hand in the crook of his elbow "Are we late? I don't see John or Jacob."

Robin nodded toward the array of horses tied along the long rail.

"Their horses are here. I'm afraid we meandered a bit slower than we should have."

When they reached the door, William put his hands on her shoulders and forced her to face him. "The look on your face tells me more than anything you said all the way here. And I can feel you tremble. Is it my being here that has you so upset?"

She shrugged. "It's not you, William. You know how I hate limping in late to anything. Plus, I've only been here once before and that time I left before the service began. It's another long story I'm afraid."

"We'll walk slow. So what if we're late? You're a picture to behold, so why not give your friends and neighbors a chance to enjoy it?"

She lowered her eyes. "Don't tease me. Please."

William squeezed her hands. "I'm not teasing. I mean every word of it. I'm proud to walk in with you. And I don't think this is the kind of pride I need to confess as sin." He winked. "Come on, you can lean on me."

Robin swallowed. The last time she heard those words she'd been through a twister. Now her insides twisted. William's hand pressed warm on her back as they stepped inside the church.

"This is the day which the Lord has . . ."

Ty stopped, mid invocation, and in that moment of hesitation Jacob stepped into the aisle.

"Down here, Robin." His arms waved like signal flags. "We saved you a seat so Ty could see you in your purty new dress with Mr. Benson."

Heads snapped and smiles split faces as the congregation turned, en masse, to where the boy pointed.

"Keep walking. And smile," William whispered. He guided her forward, nodding in greeting to those along the aisle as they made their way to the front.

When they reached their pew Jacob slipped between them. "We're ready now, Ty."

A titter ran through the congregation as Ty cleared his throat and resumed the service.

"What took you so long?" Uncle John whispered out of the side of his mouth as people around them sat down once again. "I said meander, not stop for a picnic."

Robin shot Uncle John a glance she hoped would silence him for the rest of the service. He should know better than to tell the boy something he didn't want repeated. And to top it all off, Henrietta Harvey and Albert occupied the same pew.

"I think we should make young Jacob here our official greeter." Ty smiled at the boy snuggled between her and William. His smile stiffened when his gaze locked onto the man sitting beside her. "We do welcome you, sir. I'm sure you'll have time after church to mingle and be introduced. For now, would you all please turn in your Bibles to Leviticus chapter nineteen and verse thirty-four. 'But the stranger that dwelleth with you shall be unto you as one born among you, and thou shalt love him as thyself; for ye were strangers in the land of Egypt: I am the Lord your God'."

"Robin?" Jacob was on his knees on the pew, one hand cupped around her ear. If he said he needed to use the necessary she was going to make Uncle John take him out. She put her finger over the boy's lips so he wouldn't announce his plight to the entire gathering.

He took her face in both hands and forced her to look at him. "I just want to ask you something," he whispered. "Are strangers bad?"

Ty swallowed before he continued. He'd chosen today's text with Jacob in mind. Now there was another stranger in their midst, and Jacob's face beamed at him from his seat between this man and Robin. Mr. Benson, Jacob had called him. So this was the fancy-stationery man from Chicago? He'd expected a city slicker, not someone who appeared so comfortable in his surroundings. He'd need to work very hard to avoid looking at the front pew. And behind the Wengholds sat Anna Blair and her mother. Was there no mercy? "Could we all bow for a moment of silent prayer before I begin?" He took a deep breath to quiet his mind.

He longed to retreat to the small cloakroom. But John would sure enough follow him. *Lord, You're going to have to take over my words, my thoughts, and my actions. Right now, Father, I would give my ranch to know what it is You're teaching me, or what You want me to do. I'm engaged to Anna, but I can barely breathe with that other man next to Robin. The way he touched her, Lord . . . I know You have a purpose in all of this, but could You please let me know what it is?*

"Ahem."

Ty glanced up and John motioned for him to get on with it. He cleared his throat. "Amen. Now, once again we will turn our attention to the Word of God."

Somehow he managed to get through the service. He forced his gaze to stay behind the first two rows of worshipers. There was one more thing to attend to, and how he dreaded it. But even without looking, he could *feel* Anna's glare. He fought to keep his voice steady. "Before we close, I do have one more announcement." He stepped away from the pulpit. "I'm sure you're all aware we celebrate Independence Day this week. Anna and myself, along with Mrs. Blair, would like to invite you all to the Hawk for a picnic. I'll be pleased to provide the beef and drinks. And, ladies, this is a perfect opportunity for you to display your prize culinary efforts. We hope to see you all bright and early, and do plan to stay and enjoy the fireworks." Now, he needed only to get through the final hymn; then perhaps he could relax.

As soon as he pronounced the benediction Anna slipped her arm through his. "I thought sure you were going to forget our invitation. You stumbled around all morning, though I can't say I blame you the way that little boy seemed to want all the attention." She pulled a small piece of lint from the sleeve of his suit coat. "The least we can do is greet people as they leave. I'm sure they have more questions than your announcement made clear."

"Wait, Ty." Jacob's voice rang above the voices of the departing crowd. "Did you think Robin looked purty this morning? 'Scuse me. 'Scuse me, please." The boy tunneled through people around him, then tugged on Ty's hands. "Come tell—"

A dog barked and Jacob stopped and cocked his head. "Hear that, Ty? That's Tripper again." Before Ty could grab him, Jacob ran and shoved his way through the throng gathered at the back of the church.

"Jacob, wait! Don't go out there."

The boy dashed out the door.

"Wait here." Ty pulled away from Anna and shouldered his way through the remaining visitors.

"Sam! Rusty!" With luck, they would still be jawing with other ranch hands in the churchyard. "Get the boy!"

Jacob's little legs pumped down the street, and the dog ran and yelped in front of him as though it was a familiar game of catch-me-if-you-can.

Sam and Rusty mounted their horses and raced after the boy before Ty could get Tag untied from the hitching post. He turned to wait for John and met Robin's fear-etched face, her eyes wide.

"Who is it, Ty? Did you see anyone with the dog?"

"Can I help?" The Benson fella stepped forward. "I'm not sure if there's a connection with the dog, but someone came sneaking around John's barn last night. Tell me what to do."

"Take care of Robin for now, Mr. Benson. I'm going to try to get the boy and let my ranch hands search the area."

Take care of Robin. Had he actually told this stranger to do what he longed to do himself? Judging by the arm Benson had firmly around Robin's shoulders, it was obvious the man didn't need any coaching in that area.

By the time Ty rode to the end of the street, Sam and Rusty returned with the boy. A shudder coursed through him as he observed Jacob riding in the saddle in front of Sam. There was an uncanny likeness.

"You let me down. That was Tripper. Put me down!" Jacob kicked and screamed, but Sam rode up to Ty as though he didn't notice.

"We lost him, Mr. Morgan. We saw a man and then he was gone. He plumb disappeared into thin air and the dog with him."

Ty dragged the fighting boy onto his own horse. "Jacob, stop and listen to me right now." He put both arms around the boy to still him. "Do you know that man?"

Jacob struggled to be put down. "It was my dog. It was Tripper. And he was scared cuz everybody was chasing him." He sniffed. "Put me down. I want to find Tripper."

Ty wiped the boy's face with his handkerchief. "We'll find Tripper another time. But listen to me, buddy. Don't you ever go chasing after him again unless we're with you. Do you understand me?

"Why?" Jacob shook his head. "Tripper won't hurt nobody."

How could he explain to the boy that it wasn't the dog that concerned them? But if Jacob knew the man, he wasn't telling, and that put doubt in Ty's own mind. Why wouldn't the boy say? And if the man intended no harm, why didn't he reveal himself?

"Jacob, sometimes people ask you to do things for your own good. I'm telling you, for your own good, if you ever go running off like that again you're going to be in big trouble. Do you hear me?"

Jacob crossed his arms and stuck out his lower lip. "I hear, but I don't like it one bit. I'm telling Robin I'm mad with you."

Ty grinned and ruffled the boy's hair. "Well, you go right ahead and tattle, little man. You aren't the only one mad at me today."

He rode back to Robin and lifted Jacob into her arms. "He's okay."

"Was there someone with the dog, Ty?"

William took the boy from Robin. "We can discuss this later, Robin. I imagine this boy is hungry, and I know you packed a lunch, so what say we find us a place to eat. Would you care to join us Reverend Morgan? Perhaps you and Miss Blair know of a nice spot to picnic."

Though grateful for Mr. Benson's intervention, Ty didn't care to share a picnic lunch as a foursome. Neither did he desire to delve into the whole story with half of the church still waiting to see what caused all the commotion. With Benson's free arm around Robin's shoulders, and Anna's gaze shooting arrows his direction, the only thing that could make the day worse would be Henrietta Harvey inviting them all to her home.

"Oh, Reverend." Henrietta bustled toward them, arms flapping like wings, with Albert a few steps behind. "I told Albert, I said, 'Albert, I think it only right that we ask the newcomer to lunch.' Oh, I know it will be a houseful but my goodness, what's a little crowd. John, you're invited, and of course Anna and Florence."

"Why, how nice of you Mrs. . . . Mrs. Harvey is it?" William stood Jacob to his feet then took Henrietta's hand and brought it to his lips. "I'm sure another time we'd be more than tempted, but Miss Wenghold got up bright and early and packed a lunch for us to enjoy on the way home. I'm from Chicago, you see, so I'm most interested in observing all I can of your beautiful Kansas prairie in the short time I'll be here."

Henrietta pressed the hand William kissed to her cheek. "Albert, see there. Now you know how a gentleman should behave. Your dear Papa used to kiss my hand like that." She took a handkerchief from her sleeve and wiped her pudgy face. "Of course, Mr. Benson. I understand. Uh—did you say how long you plan to stay?"

Ty swallowed a chuckle as Henrietta's face turned as pink as Robin's dress.

"No, I don't believe that was stated. I will be here on an extended visit. How extended will depend on Robin." He smiled at the older woman. "I'm sure we'll see you at the celebration at Reverend Morgan's on Independence Day."

"Well, I would certainly hope so." Anna Blair greeted the small knot of people. "Robin, did you plan to keep this gorgeous specimen a surprise?"

Robin's brow furrowed as Anna extended her hand to William

The expression on Anna's face was new for Ty—like a cat that had cornered the fattest rat in the barn. Why? She could garner all the attention she needed by being Anna. Was it necessary to roll her eyes and lean a bit too close? Benson didn't seem overwhelmed by the recognition. Either he was accustomed to having women enthralled with him or Anna didn't make that much of an impression.

She turned to Robin. "Miss Wenghold, have you given further thought to my earlier request?"

Ty shook his head. "This is not the time to discuss it, Anna."

"But there's not much time, dear. And you know the house is nowhere near ready for guests."

Florence Blair stepped forward and nodded at Ty. "Anna, I've told you repeatedly that I would take care of this." She turned to Robin. "I appreciate your willingness to help, dear, but with your company, I wouldn't want to take you away. I've already arranged with our cleaning lady to take care of anything that needs to be done at Ty's." She smiled and squeezed Robin's hand then turned back to Anna. "Now, we are keeping these friends from their lunch and ours is waiting at home. May we expect you, Ty?"

"I think not today, Mrs. Blair. It's been a busy week, and I feel I need this Sabbath Day of rest.

"I don't know why you can't rest at our house." Anna pursed her lips in an exaggerated pout. "You know how I hate to be away from you."

"Let me walk you to your buggy, Anna." Ty took her arm and led her away. "I need to talk with my men to see if we can shed some light on what happened with Jacob. He may be in danger."

"Then let Miss Wenghold's uncle or her new man friend take care of it. Why do you find it your duty to care for the homeless child? If I didn't know better, I'd think you care more for that boy than you do for me."

Ty clenched his fists. Embarrassed and angered by her behavior, he tried to hurry her away. "I'm in no mood to argue. It's not a matter of how much I care for either of you. I'll see you in two days.

"I'm not waiting that long, Ty. I plan to be there tomorrow night if I can convince Mother. You will have accommodations for us, won't you? Perhaps your mother's large, cheery yellow room?"

Ty sighed. After she became bedridden, his mother had requested her bedroom painted a soft yellow to remind her of sunshine. And to him the room was nearly sacred. During the last year of her life she continued to conduct the daily business of the Hawk from her bed. Never complaining. Never failing to think of others first. She'd never known anything but love to emerge from that room. Beside that bed, in his mother's last hours, he'd made the promise to give her ring to Anna. That thought alone kept him from telling Anna there would be no marriage. If he'd learned one thing from both his parents, it was that you never went back on your word. Your word defined you.

He would keep his promise, but he would prepare a different room for Anna and Mrs. Blair.

TWENTY-TWO

Robin knelt by the open window and gazed into the first rays of morning as they unrolled themselves on the hilltops. She'd spent yesterday baking bread, molasses cookies, and three pies for today's Independence Day celebration. What would the day bring? How would they keep Jacob in sight with so many people present? William and Uncle John assured her they would help. And she knew Ty would see that Sam and Rusty remained on watch for any stranger who might mix with the crowd. Was she foolish to worry so?

She loved this time of morning, as she now loved this ranch. Could she return to Chicago after experiencing this prairie and the hills that cradled it? How she would miss the Feather and Uncle John. What would he do? Of course, there were still Wren and Lark. But the thought of her sisters being here without her caused a twinge of jealousy.

She stood and slipped her arms through the sleeves of her wrapper. She would check on Jacob, set out the fresh bread and extra cookies she'd made for a quick make-do breakfast, and then have time to get herself ready before their departure at nine o'clock.

One skinny leg hung over the edge of Jacob's bed, and his arms extended above his head. Even asleep, he looked ready to run. She planted a kiss on his forehead and turned to leave.

"I's foolin' you, Robin. My eyes have been awake for a long, long time. This is the day we go to Ty's, isn't it? Maybe me and you can sleep there all night cuz it's gonna be really, really late when we're done. And Ty wouldn't want us to travel in the dark, would he?"

Robin scooted his leg back onto the bed and sat beside the boy. "We won't stay all night. Remember, Mr. Benson is our guest and it wouldn't be polite for us to leave him here. Ty knows Uncle John and William will keep us safe. I don't want you even suggesting it. You hear?"

Jacob sat cross-legged in the bed. "Why don't you want to stay at Ty's house? He's real nice."

"Because we aren't married, Jacob."

"Oh." A small frown wrinkled across his forehead. "But sometimes Liam stayed all night with my—" He clapped his hands over his mouth and his eyes widened. "I gotta go use the necessary." He scooted off the bed and scampered down the stairs before his words registered with Robin.

Were those tears she'd seen in his eyes? Uncle John and Ty both needed to know what Jacob said. No. For now, she'd keep quiet.

She met Jacob as he came back into the kitchen. He wouldn't look her in the eye, and she determined to let the incident pass without questioning him. "Would you like a cookie and some milk or some bread and jam for breakfast?" She pulled out a chair.

"Can I have two cookies and bread and jam, too? I'm awful hungry." He tried to wink.

"Where did you learn to do that? Do you think that will make me let you have your way?" She grinned as she set the cookies in front of him and reached for the bread.

Jacob shrugged. "I seed Ty and Uncle John do it when you isn't lookin'." He stuffed half a cookie into his mouth.

So those two sneaks winked behind her back? That little bit of information she'd let pass, too. She finished putting the jam on Jacob's slice of bread and set it on the table. "You go gather the eggs when you're done eating, then wash your hands and come back upstairs. I'll lay your clothes out on the bed. Don't dawdle. We have a big day ahead of us."

"What's dawdle?" He wiped jam from his mouth with his fingers. "Does dawdle mean naughty?" He took a swig of milk.

"Dawdle is when you don't do your chores as quickly as possible. It means to move slow and not pay attention to what you're doing."

"What's pay attention?" He tried to wink again and used his other hand to make his eye stay shut.

She put her hands on her hips. "No more questions. Eat your breakfast, do your chores, then come back upstairs."

"Just one more question? *Pleeease?*" He stood beside the table a mustache of milk still covering his upper lip.

Robin wiped his face with the dish towel. "One more, but only one."

"If I don't do my chores fast, will Uncle John hit me?"

Robin sat and took the boy on her lap. She wrapped both arms around him and held him tight. "Jacob, your Uncle John would never hit you."

"He hit you." He turned and buried his head against her.

"No, he didn't, Jacob. He threatened to take me over his knee, but he never hit me. And he would never hit either of us."

"Would Ty or William hit me?" His voice muffled in the folds of her wrapper.

"Jacob, now *I* have a question." She held him away from her and forced him to look into her face. "Did your pa hit you? Did anyone hit you? Ever?"

Tears puddled in the boy's eyes, and he wiped at them with a vengeance. His mouth opened, as though he was going to say something, then he shook his head and scooted out of her embrace. With one hand he pulled his eye down into a wink, then scooted away from her. "I won't dawdle. Promise."

"Oh, sweet boy. I would . . ."

The door slammed behind Jacob as he raced outside.

". . . Give my life for you." She leaned her head on the hard back of the chair. Perhaps that's what his mama had done. Ty and Uncle John needed to know. Remaining quiet could do more harm than good.

She was halfway up the stairs when the door opened again. "Jacob, is that you so soon?"

"No, it's me." Uncle John stood at the bottom of the stairs. "Jacob done passed me like a little windstorm. Is they problems?"

She went down to join her uncle. "We'll have to talk fast."

"Well, don't reckon you're waitin' on me. Talk."

Robin set more cookies and bread on the table and told him what she'd learned. "You want coffee this morning, or a glass of milk?"

"Coffee. So, are you a thinkin' this fella what the men saw yesterday might be somebody what hit the boy? Who do ya reckon this Liam might be?"

"I don't know." She poured his coffee then sat down across from him. "But I think we'd better keep a close eye on the little man today. I'd insist we stay home, but that would disappoint him so much. By the way—did you know you and Ty taught him to wink by your shenanigans behind my back? Now he thinks if he winks it'll make everything okay." She laughed. "I promised his mama we'd take good care of him and see to it that he grew into a man she would be proud of. I don't know what I'd do if something were to happen to him."

John reached across the table and patted her hands. "First place, ain't nothin' gonna happen to the boy without a fight from me and Ty and his men. And me and your Chicago friend done got it planned how we're not gonna let him out of our sight today."

"Do you think William likes him?"

John shook his head. "I can't never figger out why it is you young'uns always ask me the questions you oughta be a askin' each other. If you's wantin' to know how William feels about the lad, then you're a gonna have to ask him yourself. I ain't talkin for nobody 'cept me."

"Have you seen William this morning? I know he's been getting up early to ride out into the hills every morning."

"He was out helpin' me but then stopped to go along with Jacob. They'll be in shortly, I reckon.

"Then I'm going to go get ready. You can put the dishes in the sink. It won't hurt to leave them this morning." She kissed John on the cheek. "I'm not sure why I cry so easily. I don't suppose my grandmother Wenghold shed many tears, did she?"

"Not a Wenghold borned what was ever ashamed of tears. She told us boys—me and your papa—it would be a sad day if we was ever to marry a dry-eyed woman. A little salt water runnin' down your cheeks don't mean you're weak. Nope, the way I understand it, the Lord even bottles up them tears they's so precious to Him. You run on now and get yourself all purtied up."

By the time they arrived, the Hawk was bustling with buggies, wagons, and men and children on horseback. Sam and Rusty seemed in their element as they directed the varying conveyances to positions out of the way of the activity. Long tables stood under the shade of the trees, already laden with food as women proudly unpacked their baskets and unwrapped their prized offerings.

"Look, Jacob. You won't have any trouble finding someone to play with." She slipped her arm around his shoulders. "But you must let us know where you are if you leave this front yard."

Jacob leaned his head against her arm. "Do I have to play with them?"

"Don't you want to meet some new friends? You'd have fun."

"Can I stay with Ty or Uncle John?"

William tousled the boy's hair. "Hey, fella. Mr. Morgan is going to be pretty busy with all the guests here today. I don't know very many people here either, so what you say you and me stick together?"

Jacob's brow furrowed. "Are you scared cuz nobody knows you?"

"Not scared. But I would feel better if I knew you'd be my friend today."

Jacob shrugged then smiled. "I'd rather be with Ty, but I reckon you'll do." He turned to Robin. "Who's gonna be your friend? Will you be sad all alone?"

"I won't be alone. I see Dolly over there under the trees, so Emma is here. And you and Uncle John and William are here. Maybe I'll decide to stick with you, too."

"Aww, mens don't need no ladies followin' 'em around, do we, Mr. Benson?"

William laughed. "Hey, speak for yourself. We men think it quite nice if a pretty woman like Robin wants to stick around with us. What say we let her?" He winked at the boy.

"Well, while you two decide if I can be your friend, I'll put my food on the table and find Emma. We'll meet back here at the wagon when they're ready to eat. Will that give you enough time to be alone with your friend, Mr. Jacob?" Robin reached for the basket of food.

Jacob made circles in the dirt with the toe of his boot. "Can we eat with Ty?"

William shook his head at Robin before she could answer. "Guess what? I just happen to have a ball in the wagon. Would you like to play catch? You think you can throw it to me hard enough?"

Jacob's eyes lit up. "I can throw it harder than anybody."

"Well, that settles it. We'll be over there in the grassy area by the wagons if you want us Robin."

She raised her eyebrows. "Where in the world did you find a ball? You surely didn't bring it with you, did you?"

"Shh." He leaned to her ear. "I have a secret supplier. I can't tell."

John harrumphed. "They's gonna be callin' for dinner before the likes of you decide what to do. Don't know why that's such a big decision."

Robin giggled. "I'm going to set my food on the table, then find Emma. Want to come along?"

"Now what makes you think I'm gonna spend my day sittin' with you petticoats? I'll find Emma by myself when I'm good and ready." He raised one eyebrow. "Or Emma will find me if she's a lookin'."

Laughing, Robin crossed the lawn to join the other ladies. She recognized a few of them from church, but it helped to know Emma would be by her side. She tried to concentrate on the new dress her sisters had included in her trunk—white lawn fabric, with clusters of red roses embroidered on the skirt. A white dress out here on the dusty prairie wasn't practical, but she'd worn it anyway. And William's reaction when she'd come down the stairs this morning made it all worthwhile. His eyes had widened as he gazed from her shoulders to the hem and then into her eyes. Not knowing what else to do, she'd turned away.

"You're beautiful," he'd whispered. "Why has it taken me so long, Robin?"

She fiddled with her hands. You didn't tell a man he was beautiful, but she did find him quite handsome. Still amazed that he appeared so much at home here on the Feather, she admired his blue-striped shirt, open at the neck and sleeves rolled to reveal tanned, muscular arms. Today he wore dungarees, like most of the men, and his black boots were polished to a satiny finish. No one would guess he was a Chicago banker.

Emma smiled as Robin approached. "You look like one of them white prairie flowers, Robin. I declare. Is this a new dress?" She helped Robin unload her basket.

"Shh. I don't want the other women to think I'm trying to show off. My sisters packed it in my trunk as a surprise. Isn't it perfect for Independence Day?" She made a small curtsey and hoped no one besides Emma observed.

"Are you ready for the day?"

Robin nodded and forced a smile. "Ready or not, it isn't going to change anything, is it? I'm glad William is here. You haven't met him yet, have you? You missed a lot of excitement in church Sunday."

"Didn't miss a thing. Leastways didn't miss the telling of it. Henrietta Harvey was waiting for me to unlock the door first thing Monday morning so she could fill me in on every little detail." She wrinkled her nose in imitation of Henrietta. "I says to Albert, I said, 'I must let Emma know the news. Why, to think! A right-good-looking young man all the way from Chicago sitting there beside John Wenghold's niece, just like he belonged here.'"

"You knew he was coming, Emma. I'm anxious for you to meet him."

"I didn't finish my story. Henrietta barely got the words out of her mouth when who should walk in the door but the right-good-looking young man himself."

Robin frowned. "William was in the Mercantile? Monday?"

"Sure thing. Do you think he brought those blue britches from Chicago? He came walking in as if he did that every Monday morning of his life. First he bowed to Henrietta, kissed her hand, winked at me, and announced he was looking for the nicest throwing ball I might have for a very special little boy. I thought Henrietta would swoon plumb off her feet." Emma laughed.

"Well, that explains his secret supplier. I didn't know he left the ranch. I was so busy getting ready for today I all but ordered the men to stay out of the house. Did he say anything?"

"Well, of course he said something." Emma laughed. "You think we just stood and stared at one another?"

"You know what I mean, Emma. You're as bad as Uncle John. I suppose you'll tell me that if I want to know anything I'll have to ask him."

Emma nodded. "I'm not saying we're in cahoots, but your Uncle John's a wise man."

"Oh, Emma. I know William came to find out if we could have any kind of relationship that might end in marriage. He told me that much in his letter. I feel like one of those mannequins you have in your window. William and I have always been good friends, but this is very awkward. And he's different out here."

"Different?" Emma frowned. "Different in what way? He's still a man, isn't he? Still your friend, isn't he?"

"It's because he is a man. I've never seen him so . . . so manly. And when he looks at me, it's not at all the way he used to look at me when we were just friends."

Emma patted her hands. "I doubt either of you expected the other one to be different. People have a way of remembering the what-was's without giving any room for the what-is's. Give it time, Robin. He's only been here a short, short while." She hooked her arm into Robin's. "Now, let's meander a bit and enjoy this wonderful Hawk ranch. Back behind the house is perhaps one of the most beautiful views of this prairie you'll find anywhere. It's remarkable to think Ty's grandparents got a wagon over these hills all those years ago. And they traveled alone, so the story goes."

The panorama was everything Emma promised. A small bench beckoned Robin, and she sat with her back against the rough bark of a large cottonwood tree. Its heart-shaped leaves danced above her as a breeze tiptoed through on its way to the hills. "Oh, Emma, this is beautiful. I could stay here all day."

"Well, you sit, girl. I want to see if Florence Blair needs help. I doubt she can depend on Anna. I'll meet you at John's wagon come lunchtime."

Robin drank in the view and the stillness. It was hard to believe a place of such solitude existed with all the activity and noise surrounding her. A few large, flat rocks lay here and there, as though they may have been stepping-stones, or perhaps marked boundaries of some kind. How she wished she could share this with her sisters. What fun they would have conjuring up make-believe stories of days gone by. Ty never talked about his parents, but what gracious people they must have been. The large rambling house indicated they'd planned on it housing many people at any given time. And the wraparound porch held an assortment of small tables and chairs, along with two large swings.

"It's quite impressive isn't it, Miss Wenghold."

Anna's appearance startled her, and she cringed at the thought of needing to make conversation. "It is at that, Miss Blair. And so very welcoming."

"Yes, well, the Morgans were known for their hospitality, though their choice of guests was often questionable. I don't suppose Ty's mother ever turned away a soul."

"She must have been a wonderful lady. It would be no small job to keep a place like this running efficiently."

"I can assure you the new Mrs. Morgan does not intend to follow in her footsteps. In fact, I commented to Ty that perhaps after we wed you might consider working for us on a regular basis. You know, cleaning house, preparing the evening meal, laundry, and such. I will certainly need help. As mistress of this lovely place, I will be expected to entertain often, and I certainly don't want to become a charwoman in the process."

"And Mr. Morgan agreed to this arrangement, did he?" Robin fought to keep her voice steady.

Anna's eyes narrowed. "No, as a matter of fact. He seemed to think you would consider yourself our maid, though I assured him you we would treat you as one of the family. That is, of course, if you'll still be here. Tell me about that handsome man beside you in church on Sunday." She leaned closer. "Is he by any chance one of those who answered your uncle's advertisement for a husband? Quite exciting, I must say—not to know who might be showing up next."

Robin stood. Oh, if only she could run. "My uncle's advertisement, Miss Blair? And how, may I ask, could you have seen it?"

"Oh, well, you see after I left your house that day, I came here to visit Ty and he—"

"Ty's aware of this, too?" Her heart thumped and heat rushed to her face. Would he think she'd agreed to such a scheme? What must he think of her?

"I don't know how he could not be aware. The advertisement lay on his bedside table, in plain sight. But honestly, Miss Wenghold, there's no reason for you to be so upset. Your guest is quite handsome, and I'm sure you must know that as well. And I believe Henrietta Harvey understood he was from Chicago. One would never know it by looking, would one?"

"Miss Blair. How many people here today know about my uncle's ridiculous scheme?"

Anna arched her eyebrows. "Ridiculous? I think he must be thinking only of your own welfare. How else would you find someone willing to take on a . . . a fatherless child and, oh, I know this is going to sound especially cruel, but we're all aware of your infirmity. You have such a burden to bear. It would be wonderful if you were to find a husband by any means."

"Oh, there you are, dear." Florence Blair bustled around the corner of the porch. She smiled at Robin and slipped her arm around Anna's waist. "You have five minutes to freshen up before we start the activities."

Anna nodded at Robin. "It's been so nice visiting with you, Miss Wenghold. I do hope you'll consider what we've discussed." She turned. "I'm coming, Mother, but don't start until Ty and I join you, please."

At her daughter's departure, Mrs. Blair stepped closer to Robin. "I'm glad you and Anna can be friends. She hasn't many, you know. I'm quite guilty of being far too lenient with her. I suppose I made the same mistake as many mothers—attempting to be a friend rather than the parent. You see, her dear papa died when she was yet much too young to remember him. I'm sure you understand, practically being a mother to that small child, and with no man to help." She smiled and laid her hand on Robin's arm. "But I see your situation may soon change. I do hope you will decide to stay in our fair community. There are not many young married couples in the area. How lovely if Ty and Anna were to have friends close by."

"And why wouldn't I stay, Mrs. Blair?" Robin regretted her sharp words, but she had to know if this woman also thought William had answered the advertisement.

A small frown flitted across Mrs. Blair's brow. "I . . . I suppose I assumed the nice young gentleman . . . well, Chicago is such a lovely place, and I couldn't blame a young woman for preferring the city over our humble, rough prairie."

Robin clenched her fists. Why hadn't she followed her instincts and stayed home? It wouldn't have changed anything, except she wouldn't have known what people were thinking. She extended her hand to Mrs. Blair. In spite of this conversation, she liked the woman.

She didn't for a minute believe she intended to be cruel. Her daughter, on the other hand . . .

"If you'll excuse me, Mrs. Blair. I believe I shall find Mr. Benson and Jacob. I do thank you for the obvious effort you've put into making this day special for . . . for everyone."

TWENTY-THREE

Ty folded his arms along the top rail of the fence and peered at the hills beyond. If only he could talk with Pa again. A heaviness squeezed his chest and he took a deep breath to rid it. This should be a happy day. A day to remember forever. Engaged to a beautiful woman, owner of the biggest ranch in the area, and by the number of people around the grounds, he was blessed with friends and neighbors. Why, then, did he feel as though he were suffocating?

"Thought I might find you out here." John Wenghold propped his foot on the bottom rail. "Ya reminded me so much of your pa a standin' here it gave me a start."

Ty nodded. "I could always count on him being here every evening before bedtime. I'd sidle up to him and do my best to hike my foot up on that bottom rail like you did just now. 'What'cha doing Papa?' I'd ask him the same question every time, but he never scolded me. His answer never varied in all those years. 'Lifting my eyes unto the hills from whence cometh my help.' I miss him. Wish I could ask him one more time."

John clapped him on the shoulder. "Never enough one-more-times. A body keeps a wantin' more. As old as I am, I still miss my pa." He crossed his arms on the rail and glanced sideways at Ty. "Ya don't have peace about what's happenin' today, do ya?"

Ty turned and braced one shoulder on the fence. "None at all. But it's my own fault, I suppose."

"Why'd you let things go this far? Ya had a choice, didn't ya?"

He smiled at his neighbor. "Pa taught me a lesson concerning choices once."

"I'm listenin'."

"He caught me with a cookie in one hand and the other hand in the cookie jar. 'You have permission for that, son?' he said." Ty laughed. "I can still see the furrow in his brow. I told him I did. Papa cocked his head and one eyebrow raised to his hairline and asked if I had permission for two cookies. I knew better than to lie, so I swallowed and said, 'No, sir, but I can't decide which one I want.' Then Pa asked me what difference it made. I should've known there was a lesson in it."

John chuckled. "And the lesson?"

"Mama made molasses cookies that day and decorated some of them with sugar. I argued the one with sugar would be the best because it was the prettiest, and with the sprinkles it had to be the sweetest."

John cocked one eyebrow. "Reasonable thinkin'. Though sure is funny how things come back to haunt ya, isn't it?"

"Those are the words Pa used. He knelt down in front of me and looked me square in the eyes. 'Son,' he said. 'All your life you're going to have to make choices. I think you know the difference between good and bad, so I don't expect that to be so hard. But it's deciding between good and good that'll give you trouble.'"

"Bet you never expected them two good things to be women-folk, did ya?"

"Never. Pa told me it was the inside of a cookie that made the difference. The sugar made it look pretty, but what was inside was what really mattered. 'Choose wisely, son,' he said, 'because a man is defined by the choices he makes and the words he speaks. You don't go back on either. A good choice will bless you, while a bad choice can haunt you forever.'"

John scratched his head. "You think askin' Anna to marry ya was a bad choice?"

Ty turned and peered across the prairie again. "Asking her to marry me wasn't a bad choice. It's the promise to always be here if and when she ever decided to return that haunts me. I gave my word, John."

"Guess you never figgered on a little bird flyin' in, did ya?"

He laid his forehead on his crossed arms. "Didn't expect that little bird to limp into the middle of my heart. And"—he met John's eyes—"Anna has changed."

John turned and braced his back on the fence. "And supposin' Anna would've showed up without Robin bein' here? Is those changes so big you can't abide by your word?"

Ty shrugged. "I don't know how to answer that. Maybe if I had more time."

"I ain't never had no young'uns askin' my advice. And it don't look like you got more time. But I reckon when your days on this ole' earth are done, they ain't gonna carve into no headstone how many cows ya grazed, or how big your house was, or how much money ya had in the bank. The Bible says it's better to choose a good name than all them other things people call riches. And a man's word *is* his name. It takes a big man to do what's right even when his heart is a thumpin' the other way."

"What will become of Robin and Jacob?"

"Ya think the Lord don't know where they's at? Don't tell me ya think you're the onliest one who can take care of 'em. I think you're still wantin' both cookies, Ty. It don't work that way. Next time you'll know better than to fill your mouth with words so quick. Tell me this, which one of them sweets did ya choose way back then?"

Ty groaned and put his face on his arms again. "The one with the sugar sprinkled on top."

John pushed away from the fence. "Habits are formed early, ain't they? You can't be lifting your eyes unto them hills as long as you got your face buried like that. I'm gonna go back and find Robin. And whatever decidin' you gotta do better be done in a hurry, cuz I think that's Florence Blair standin' by the bell, and I reckon she's lookin' for you."

Robin turned from Mrs. Blair and limped around the side of the house as fast as her bad leg allowed. Her insides trembled so she imagined it showed, even at a distance. How dare Anna Blair suggest she might consider being their housekeeper. The raw nerve of her to indicate that the only way she would ever find a husband was to advertise for one. How could William's gaze make her feel so beautiful this morning, and Anna's smile make her feel so ugly a few short hours later?

On the front lawn, William and Jacob were still playing catch, and as soon as she drew near enough to be heard, she yelled for them. *Please, Lord, this would be a very good time for You to start answering my prayers. Let Jacob cooperate and William not ask questions. I need to get out of here. I can't face one more minute of humiliation.*

"Jacob, go get in the wagon." She struggled, unsuccessfully, to keep her voice steady. "Now."

William put his arm around her waist, brow wrinkled. "Robin, what is it? Can you tell me?"

She shook her head. Hadn't she prayed he wouldn't ask questions? "Please, don't ask. Not yet. I need to get away from here. Jacob, you're coming with us."

"But I don't want to leave. Me and Mr. Benson is having fun."

William pointed to the wagon. "We're leaving, Jacob, and it will do you no good to argue."

Jacob crossed his arms and shook his head.

Robin grabbed the boy's shoulders and turned him to the wagon. "I need you to cooperate. Get in. Now." She couldn't stop the tears.

"Are you sick, girly? You done look like you been kicked." A wrinkle settled between John's eyebrows. "What's happened, William?"

William shrugged. "I don't know, sir. But this isn't the time to pry. It's obvious she's quite upset and wants to go home. Perhaps I'll know more later."

Robin shook her head. They were all discussing her as if she were a child—as if she wasn't even there.

William cupped his hand to yell at Emma, who was rushing from the house toward them. “I’ll explain later. Would you mind bringing John home?”

Emma waved him on. “Was already figuring on it.”

“Pack rats got the paper, Uncle John?” Robin glared at him. “How could you?”

TWENTY-FOUR

A bell clanged across the grounds of the Morgan ranch to signify the start of the day's events. From his perch on the wagon seat, William guided the horses through the swarm of people scrambling toward the big house.

"Can't you make them go faster?" Robin leaned forward on the seat beside him. "I want away from here."

His mind whirled. What had upset this girl so? "I don't want to draw attention to our leaving. As soon as we're over the hill and out of sight I'll get you home as fast as I can."

As they neared the top, a lone man on horseback slipped over the crest and a dog ran in front of the rider, yelping.

From the seat between William and Robin, Jacob cocked his head. "Tripper! It's Tripper." The boy scrambled over Robin and hung one leg off the side of the wagon. "This time I'm gonna catch him."

William lunged for him, but missed. The boy jumped from the wagon and rolled as he hit the ground. Robin screamed and William jerked the reins. But Jacob leapt to his feet and raced after the dog.

"Jacob, get back here." Robin gasped and yanked on William's shirtsleeve as the tall grasses and rolling terrain swallowed the boy.

"William, do something! That man is just sitting there. What if he's after Jacob?" She stood at the same time William snapped the reins. The sudden lurch sent her backward over the side of the wagon.

He clutched for her, but came up empty.

Robin hit the ground and lay motionless, and his heart plunged. He vaulted from the wagon before it quit rolling and bolted to where Robin lay. He flinched at the sight of blood pooling beneath her head. He couldn't leave her, but could he dare trust this stranger with Jacob? It seemed his only choice.

Robin moaned, and he stood and cupped his hands around his mouth. "She needs help, Mister! Please."

As though he'd only been waiting for permission, the man spurred his horse and galloped past them toward the throng of neighbors.

Ty tugged the bell's rope once more, and his heart wrenched at the same time. One year ago, amidst the pain of Anna leaving, he'd made her a promise. Today, amidst the confusion of her return, he would honor that vow.

"You seem deep in thought." Anna slipped her arms around his neck and kissed him on the cheek. "I hope it concerns me." A small crease flitted across her brow. "Why do I get the feeling you would rather be anywhere but here today? Are you having second thoughts?"

He folded her hands in his and gazed into her eyes. If he looked deep enough, maybe he would catch a glimpse of the Anna he thought he knew so well. "Are *you*? Are you sure this is what you want, Anna? No running away this time."

She met his gaze. "You do love me, don't you? The proposal, the ring, the promise—I didn't imagine all that, did I?"

He sighed. "I love the Anna I knew all my life. The little girl who cried when she found a broken robin's egg on the ground. The young lady who insisted we couldn't have a party without inviting everyone we knew because she didn't want to hurt anyone's feelings. The woman who stood beside my mother's bed, bathing her face with a cool cloth and singing hymns. That's the Anna I love. I don't know the Anna I'm looking at now."

"Help! Anyone!"

Ty turned on his heel to see a lone rider pummeling through the crowd.

"There's been an accident," the stranger yelled.

Ty turned and rushed to meet him. The man reined to a halt and leaned from his saddle. "Mr. Morgan, you best get a doctor. A young woman is hurt badly. You've no time to waste." With that, the stranger turned his horse, and the crowd parted like the Red Sea as he galloped away.

Ty scanned the area and shouted for his hands. "Sam. Rusty." Where were they? He'd told them to watch for any stranger that might make an appearance. Who was this man, and how did the man know him by name? He sprinted to the barn for his horse.

John raced toward him, his face ashen. "I think it might be Robin. She and William left with Jacob a few minutes ago. I can't see well enough from here, but I'm thinkin' it's my wagon sittin' out there."

"Robin left? Why?" Ty mounted Tag. "Find Doc Mercer. I know he's here somewhere."

When Ty got closer, he recognized John's wagon, and made out the form of a man kneeling a short distance from it. His heart constricted. William Benson, stripped to the waist, cradled Robin in his arms. Blood soaked the shirt wrapped around her head.

He spurred Tag harder.

Benson's stricken face met him as he dismounted. "She's hurt bad, Morgan. Real bad."

Ty swallowed past a dry throat. Dark circles under Robin's eyes gave color to her otherwise lifeless face. He dismounted and knelt beside William. "We've got to get her back to the house. But the wagon's too rough. Can you lift her up to me on my horse?"

William shook his head. "I'll carry her."

"It's a long ways, man. It would take too long."

"She can't be jostled. She's bleeding something awful. Can't you see?" William wiped his eyes with the back of his wrist.

See? Or course he could see. Ty stood and jammed his hands

into his pockets to keep from pushing Benson aside and pulling the stricken Robin to himself. He rubbed the back of his neck. What was he thinking? What kind of man was he? A few short minutes ago he was standing beside Anna, waiting for their engagement to be announced. Now his empty arms ached to hold another woman, and he was willing to fight for the chance. Only the arrival of Emma with Doc and John crammed into her buggy kept him from making a fool of himself.

John's feet hit the ground before the buggy stopped, and he was at Robin's side in three long strides. He cupped his hand around Ty's shoulder. "Is she still with us?"

"Barely, I think." He turned to Abe Mercer. "Can't you do something to make her stop bleeding? I can't bear to think of her dying here on this dirty piece of ground."

Doc nodded. "Give me time, son—I'm doing what I can." He cradled Robin's head in his hands while Emma unwound Benson's makeshift bandage. "It's not unusual for a head wound to bleed like this. What concerns me most is what might be happening on the inside, where we can't see."

He inspected the wound, then stood and wiped his hands on his handkerchief. "One of you young fellas needs to hold her so we can keep her head from bumping around while we get her back to the house. John, you're gonna have to hoof it back on your own, if you don't mind. Emma you best ride along with us. I'll be needin' your help to get her settled."

"I'll hold her." Ty stepped toward the buggy. "But you'll have to lift her up to me, Benson."

William shook his head. "No, Morgan. She's with me." He rose with Robin in his arms.

John turned on the two men with a vengeance. "Look, you fellas better be prayin' you get another chance to argue over which one of ya gets to do what with this little lady. But now ain't that time."

"I'll ride ahead then, and have a room ready by the time you get there." Ty reached to touch Robin's face then quickly drew back.

The sight of her lying against Benson's bare chest sickened him. "You'll need a shirt. I'll see what I can do."

TWENTY-FIVE

"You have guests, Morgan. I'll let you know if anything changes with Robin." William finished tucking the shirt Ty had loaned him into his britches and brushed past him.

"The guests can wait. Robin is more important at this point." Ty stopped outside Robin's door and braced his shoulder on the wall to face Benson.

The last time he'd stood outside the closed door to this room, his pa had lain in the big mahogany bed. It was the only time he could remember being denied access to his parents' room, and the first time he experienced how deep the pain of love could be.

"Where were you taking her in such a hurry?"

The muscle in Benson's jaw tightened. "She asked to be taken home."

"Did she say why? Was she ill?"

William shrugged. "I've told you what I know. I saw her and Emma stroll to the back of the house. She returned a short time later, quite upset, and demanded I take her home."

Ty arched one eyebrow. "Demanded, Benson? I've never known Robin Wenghold to demand anything."

William gave a wry smile. "And you've not known Robin as long as I have."

The familiar scent of lilacs announced Anna's presence, and Ty moved from the wall.

"Well, you boys look like you're going to race to see which one can get through the door first when it opens." Anna placed her hand on Ty's arm. "Do you suppose you could tear yourself away long enough for Mother to finish the announcement this little accident interrupted?" She smiled at William. "I do believe Mr. Morgan will take nearly any opportunity to stall our engagement, Mr. Benson. Do you suppose you'll have such groom-to-be jitters?"

The muscle in William's jaw twitched. "I would hardly call it a little accident, Miss Blair."

She turned her gaze to Ty. "How serious are her injuries? I'm not as uncaring as you seem to think. I was only suggesting that while people are still gathered we might at least make our announcement. You aren't helping anyone by standing here in the hallway."

Ty closed his eyes. "Not now, Anna. There will be no announcement tonight. Your mother and I already discussed it."

Anna slammed her hands on her hips "You went to Mother instead of consulting me? Why, might I ask?"

Ty took Anna's arm and gave her no choice but to follow him back to the stairway. "Robin Wenghold is lying in that room near death. Your mother understands the gravity of her injury and knows how very rude it would appear for us to continue the celebration as though nothing happened. Anna, please. Think of her."

"I'm thinking of *us,* Ty Morgan. And I'm frightened. You have no intention of going through with this marriage, do you?" Her voice shook, but her eyes remained dry.

He ran a hand through his hair. "This has nothing to do with my commitment to you, nor is it the time to discuss it. A guest at my ranch was injured. That's my concern."

Anna brushed her fingertips down the side of his face. "I think your concern runs much deeper than you care to admit. We'll discuss it later. For now, what can I do to help?"

Before her gaze hardened, Ty caught a glimpse of the Anna he once knew. "Perhaps you can help your mother dismiss these people with as much grace as possible."

"Boss?" Rusty called from the bottom of the steps. "Sorry to interrupt, but I think maybe you and that Mr. Benson might want to hear what I've got to say. We were able to catch up with young Jacob. He's down in your study—him and that dog." He shrugged. "I couldn't convince him to come without the hound. But he thinks he's in trouble. I ain't told him nothin' about Miss Robin. Figgered that was your job."

Ty gripped the stair rail. Jacob. Why hadn't he noticed Jacob wasn't with Robin or William? How distraught Robin would be if something happened to the tyke. He moved Anna to one side and peered down the hallway. "Benson? I think you need to come with me."

William paused at Robin's door then joined Ty as they descended the stairs. "Did something happen?"

"I'm not sure. Rusty seemed to think we needed some privacy." They reached the bottom and Ty motioned for them to follow him. "We can talk in my office. Rusty, did you say anything to John?"

"Yeah. He's gonna check with Mrs. Ledbetter first to see if there's anything she needs before he comes."

"Good. Emma will know what's needed."

Ty stepped into his study and found Jacob crouched by the wall, clinging to the dog. The boy's eyes were wide, and with one hand he twisted the hair on the dog's neck around his fingers.

Ty knelt beside Jacob. "So, this is Tripper? You finally caught him, didn't you?"

Jacob sniffed. "Is you mad with me?"

Ty patted Jacob's head. "No, little man. I'm not mad at you. Tripper looks like a mighty fine dog."

Jacob nodded. "I told you he wouldn't never hurt me. Where's Robin? I want Robin to see Tripper."

Images of Jacob's dead mother and the small storm-tossed child of a few short weeks ago swirled through Ty's mind. How could he tell this child that the woman he'd so quickly claimed at his new mama was injured? Would it bring bad memories? Would he equate being injured with never coming back? And what if Robin died? With no evidence that Jacob had a pa, and nothing legal to bind him to anyone else, what would happen to this little man?

William sat on the floor and folded his legs to make a place for the boy, then picked him up and settled him on his lap. "Jacob, I think we should keep Tripper as a surprise for Robin when she wakes up."

Jacob squirmed to look up at Benson. "Why's she sleeping in the daytime? She don't never sleep if it's daytime."

William took a deep breath. "Do you remember a little while ago when we were going back to the Feather, and you saw your dog?"

Jacob nodded.

"You were pretty excited, weren't you?"

"Yeah, I wanted to catch him, and I did." He rubbed his face in the dog's hairy neck. "See, he likes me."

"He sure does. And you know what? Robin likes you, too. She was so excited you might catch your friend here that she stood up to watch you. But then she fell out of the wagon and bumped her head. It made her real sleepy, so for a while we need to be very quiet and let her sleep."

"All night? Then she won't get to see Tripper 'til morning. That's a long time. Will she get waked up in the morning?"

William lifted his eyes to Ty.

Ty swallowed, but words wouldn't come.

William sighed then ruffled the boy's hair. "Well, it might even be longer than all night, Jacob. Sometimes when a person gets a bad bump on the head it makes them sleep for a long time. So we'll have to see. Do you think you can remember to be real quiet when you're in the house?"

"What if she don't wake up? My mama went to sleep after the big storm, and she didn't ever wake up. I hollered and hollered at her, but she kept on sleeping and sleeping. Will Ty have to dig a hole for Robin like he did for Ma?"

He scrambled from William's lap and threw himself at Ty's leg. "I don't want you to dig a hole, Ty. Cuz then I'll have to say good-bye to Robin, too. Please don't dig a hole." Sobs shook his small body. "Promise ya won't dig a hole."

Ty's chest tightened until he could hardly breathe. He gathered Jacob in his arms and rocked him. How he longed to say what the boy wanted to hear. But words were cheap—the price of a promise too high.

The door opened and John entered the room, his gaze resting on each of them. Deep furrows lined his brow above sorrow-filled eyes. He ran his tongue over his lips. "Men, I think we best be talkin' to somebody what knows a whole lot more than we do right now."

He bowed his head, and the rest of them followed suit. "Father in heaven . . ." John's voice trembled. "I don't reckon You can hardly miss a whole roomful of bawlin' men like we are. But sure as the sun rises ever' mornin', we need Your help right now. There's a little gal soft and sweet as her name a layin' real hurt upstairs. I don't know about the rest of these cowboys, but I can tell Ya for sure I love her more'n I ever thought I could love somebody other than my own ma. You knowed what You was doin' for sure when You packed all that feistiness into such a small package. You done could see ahead how much she was a gonna need it as she went through life. Well, now, we're a beggin' You to put all that fight into one big punch and bring her through this bump on the head just like she was before it happened. We'll surely be beholdin' to Ya for hearin' our puny prayers. And we be askin' Ya this in the name of Your Son, Jesus. Amen."

Amens echoed through the room.

John blew his nose then stuffed his handkerchief into his pocket. "Okay, Rusty—you wanna tell us why you called this meetin'? I'd surely like to know how it is that stranger got so close to the house without bein' seen." He leaned on Ty's desk.

Rusty widened his stance and squared his shoulders.

Ty held his breath. His foreman was a gentle giant, but he didn't cotton to anyone insinuating he wasn't doing his job. John may have met his match.

"We saw him—me and Sam. We watched him for a long time, but

he wasn't doin' nothin' but sittin' there lookin'. We figured as long as he didn't make a move to come closer, we wouldn't bother him none."

"Well, he sure 'nuff got close without any interference."

"And it was a good thing he did." Ty interrupted. "His quick action got help to Robin sooner than either Sam or Rusty could have."

"That's right, Mr. Morgan." Rusty relaxed his stance. "We saw the boy run for the dog, but then everything happened so fast. We was still tryin' to keep track of Jacob; then Benson was on the ground, and the next thing we knew the stranger came thunderin' in."

"Good thing he didn't have a gun."

"Let him finish, John." Ty nodded. "Go on Rusty."

Rusty shoved his hands in his pockets. "Well, sir, after we caught up with the boy and his dog, Sam took off after the stranger. I waited to see if he'd come back, but he's been gone a long time. I'm wonderin' if I should try to find him, but I didn't know what to do with Jacob."

"You think Sam might be in trouble? Or is there more?"

"I've known Sam Mason since we was pups, and I never knowed him to be so upset as when we caught up with the boy and this here dog. His face turned white, and he looked me in the eyes—you know how he does—and he said, 'Rusty, you take the boy and the dog back. I've got me some man-fetchin' to do.' Then he spurred his horse without nary a glance back. He can take care of himself, that's for sure. I'd just feel better if I could go lookin' for him."

Ty's chest constricted. What if Sam caught up with the man and did something foolish? They might never find out who he was or what he was doing hanging around their ranches. "You want me to send one of the other men with you?"

"No sir. I don't think that'll be necessary unless you don't hear from us for a couple of days. Hard tellin' how far he might have to chase him. But if I know Sam, he won't quit as long as he can keep him in sight." Rusty patted Jacob on the head. "Take care of that pooch, boy."

The minute Rusty left the room, John slammed his hand against the closed door. "I don't like it, Ty. Not one bit. Sam knows somethin' he ain't been lettin' us in on. No sir, I think he's up to no good."

Ty shook his head. "I don't like it either, but I don't think Sam would do anything to cause harm. My bet is he caught the guy and is trying to decide what to do with him."

"Don't know that it's up to him to figger out. Bring him back here. If he's the boy's pa, then we'll decide what to do with him." John walked to the window and pulled the curtain aside.

"Tripper's ears get all pointy when you talk loud." Jacob pulled the dog closer to his side. "Look, Mr. Benson. Are my ears all pointy?"

William laughed. "No, Jacob. Your ears are fine."

Ty shot a withering glance at John. "Your ears are fine, but Mr. Wenghold has a big mouth."

Jacob traced his own mouth with his fingers. "Will my mouth get big when I get old and talk loud?"

"Oh, for . . ." John's face matched the red bandana he swiped across his mouth.

Ty met William's gaze and they exchanged smiles.

TWENTY-SIX

Somewhere in the timber beyond the house an owl hooted its mournful call as Ty stepped onto the porch and lowered himself to the swing. A lamp burned on the small table by the open window and revealed Anna's mother as she sat in his mother's favorite chair. Florence Blair had been an incredible help, and he didn't have the heart to ask her and Anna to leave, especially to journey home in the dark. So far he'd managed to avoid any further confrontation with his so-called fiancée. But the staccato of approaching footsteps signaled that was about to end.

"May I join you?" Anna stood in front of him, arms folded.

He scooted to one side, and she slid beside him and slipped her hand into his. "How is Miss Wenghold?"

His shoulders tensed. Perhaps if he could see Anna's face he could discern whether there was real concern there or merely polite curiosity. "Doc says the next hours, or maybe even days, are critical."

"Do you plan for her to stay here until she's fully recovered?"

He nodded. "She'll be here until Doc Mercer tells me she's well enough to be moved. Then it will be her decision."

"But wouldn't she be more comfortable in her own bed at her uncle's ranch?"

Ty laid his head against the back of the swing. Why did she choose now to challenge him? "She's too critical to move. Doc won't let anyone in to see her. Not even her uncle."

"I don't want her in our bed, Ty. Couldn't she at least be moved to another room?"

"It's not *our* bed, Anna. It was my folks' bed, in my folks' room, and she stays where she is."

She placed her hand on his chin and turned his head to face her. "What if her head injury leaves her . . . well, even more crippled than she is already? What would become of the little boy? Her uncle couldn't care for him, and I doubt her mail-order beau would—"

Ty jumped from the swing with such force that it hit the side of the house. "What do you mean, her mail-order beau? Why would you make a statement like that? Did Robin tell you that?"

Anna put her hand to her throat. "No. I assumed—"

"You assumed what?"

"I saw something that indicated she might—"

"You saw *something*? What did you see, Anna? And where did you see it?" Ty balled his hands into fists and paced. "Tell me. What exactly did you see?"

"I saw an advertisement."

"And where exactly did you see this? Was it posted publicly? Was it in a newspaper? Tell me. I want to hear it from you."

Anna jumped to her feet, hands clenched at her side. "Fine! If you must know, I saw it on the table by your bed—the day I came to tell you that Mother and I were planning this picnic to announce our engagement." Anger laced her words.

"And did you happen to see the picture Jacob drew for me on the back of the advertisement?"

Anna shook her head "No, I . . . I didn't see a picture. Only the advertisement. I thought . . . I thought maybe you'd answered it." She toyed with her ring.

Ty's pulse pounded in his ears. Could it be *Anna* was responsible for Robin's hurried departure and thus her accident? "And because your love for me is so strong, and you trust me implicitly, you were suspicious instead of discussing it with me. Am I correct? Did you tell anyone else what you observed in the privacy of *my* bedroom?"

"Anna Kathryn." Florence Blair stepped from the shadows. "I would be interested in knowing that myself. Ty, please accept my apologies for intruding. I never planned to eavesdrop. However, I couldn't help but overhear. I was right inside." She motioned toward the open window.

Anna flipped her wrist in dismissal. "Mother, this doesn't concern you. This is between me and Ty."

With chin raised, Mrs. Blair turned to face Anna. "Oh, but it does concern me, daughter. I heard you tell Ty we planned this big celebration. You told *me* this was Ty's idea—that he could hardly wait to make the announcement, that in fact he was so anxious to be married he was pressuring you to move the wedding date to early autumn." Her voice broke. "You lied to me, Anna. I want to know how many other lives you've affected with this charade."

Anna sank back into the swing. "What makes you think I told anyone, Mother? Why are you so quick to accuse me of bearing tales?"

Florence clutched Ty's arm. Her chin quivered and eyes clouded, but she spoke with authority. "Perhaps I question you, my dear, because Henrietta Harvey asked me Sunday morning if the young man who accompanied Robin Wenghold was, by chance, one of her mail-order beaus."

Ty groaned. "Anna, surely you must realize that by telling Henrietta you might as well announce it from the rooftops of Cedar Bluff. Why her, of all people?"

Anna glared at him. "I thought she would be able to tell me if Robin had received letters from men, and if any of them were from you. But I honestly thought she would be sworn to secrecy since Albert is the postmaster."

"Secrecy to whom?" Ty shook his head. "Did you think she would tell you and no one else? Are you truly that privileged?" He leaned toward her. "Did you ever tell Robin you saw the advertisement?"

Anna crossed her arms, her mouth tight.

Ty lifted her chin. "Look at me, Anna, and for once tell the truth."

Her gaze locked on his, dark and defiant. "I only asked if Mr. Benson answered the advertisement."

"And when did this conversation take place? Today?" Ty ran his hand through his hair. "Is that why she left in such a hurry? Because you chose today, when practically the entire community was present, to humiliate her regarding something over which she had no control?"

"How do you know she had no control?" Anna stood, her voice shrill. "I saw the look on your face when they walked into church. You were as surprised as anyone to see your Miss Wenghold on the arm of that man. Who is he, Ty? Do you know him? How do you know he isn't mail order? Henrietta said Robin got a letter from some man from Chicago. Doesn't it seem a bit strange that she would be getting correspondence from someone that far away? He could very well be some poor city-slicker looking for an unclaimed treasure who just might be in line to inherit a large Kansas ranch."

"I'm wondering"—William Benson strode from the shadows of the wraparound porch— "why my relationship with Robin, or my reason for being here, should concern either one of you?"

Ty pinched the bridge of his nose. "I didn't realize you were still up." The last thing he wanted was another person in on this conversation.

"Yes, that's obvious." William nodded his direction, his eyes narrow and dark. "I owe no one this explanation, but for Robin's sake I will say this one time, and then consider the topic closed to further discussion." The muscle in his jaw tightened, and his hands clenched at his sides.

"I'm here at my own insistence, Miss Blair. Robin and I grew up together. In Chicago, to be exact. We are lifelong friends. I proposed to that sweet girl once before she left. She turned me down. So I invited myself to Kansas to see if I might convince her she made the wrong decision. I can assure you, I answered no advertisement. I came with the intention of staying one month. I will now stay until such time Robin tells me to leave—if God answers my prayer that she survive."

He turned on his heel, then hesitated and turned back. "By the way,

Morgan, is there somewhere in town where I might send a telegram? I believe Robin's sisters need to come at once."

"Mr. Rempel at the train depot could take care of it for you. Uh . . . could I perhaps help in the purchase of tickets for their travel?"

William shook his head. "That won't be necessary. I'll contact my father at the bank and he will see to the arrangements from that end. I'll go to town first thing in the morning. I pray Robin is still with us then."

He turned to Anna. "Where I come from, a gentleman would never divulge his financial situation to a lady. But since you question my integrity I will apprise you of the fact that I could, and would, buy the Feather *and* the Hawk should their owners ever decide to sell."

Ty gazed into the stricken face of Florence Blair. She touched his arm and her hands trembled. "I'm so very sorry, Ty. I so hoped we might be of help to you, and instead this only adds another dimension of pain for us all. I know this is a lot to ask or expect, but do you think it possible someone could hitch up our buggy so we might return to Cedar Bluff?"

He squeezed her hand. "I don't want to let you drive across the prairie this time of night. You needn't leave, Mrs. Blair. Your help has been invaluable, and I'm sure Emma would agree."

Anna's mother shook her head. "Oh dear boy, you remind me so very much of your mother. Never would she admit to any kind of inconvenience or insult placed on her by others. None of us know what this night will bring for sweet Miss Wenghold. I do hate to take you away, but allow this old lady to leave with some bit of dignity, though she must skip out in the dark to retain it." Her chin quivered, but her lips curved in a faint smile.

He put his arm around her shoulders and walked her to the door. "And I must insist on accompanying you. I'll have Rusty hitch your buggy and saddle my horse. We can leave when you are ready."

"It shan't take long. Come, Anna. I need your help, and I will brook no further displays of your bad manners."

TWENTY-SEVEN

Ty looped Tag's reins over the hitching post in front of the church. The painfully silent ride alongside the Blair buggy into Cedar Bluff only added to the anger, sorrow, and regret that burned in his gut. A huge question still hung above today. Memories haunted him and the future troubled him. What future? And with whom? Anna? How could they build a marriage upon a foundation of deceit?

He didn't bother to light a lamp, but made his way down the aisle and slid into the front bench. A sliver of moonlight beamed onto the small, square table altar and illuminated the open Bible and the gold cross set behind it. Other times he would picture this as God's finger, showing him the way. Tonight it mocked him. *Where's your faith, preacher boy? Don't you tell others His Word has all the answers? Don't you remind them to go to the Cross? Are you saying it works for others, but not for you? Are your problems too big—your God too small?*

He knelt and buried his face in his hands. Not since the night Anna walked away from him had he experienced such anguish—such hopelessness. That night he would have given anything for Anna to come back to him. That night there was not another woman or a small boy to consider. A year ago he promised he'd never let himself love again. A year ago there was not Robin or Jacob. That night he promised he'd never forsake his first love—he would always be there. Tonight, he regretted the promise.

A draft whispered through the room, and the scent of lilacs announced a visitor. He rose and faced the woman destined to become his wife. "What are you doing here, Anna?"

She approached his bench. "I needed time alone, away from Mother. I didn't know you were here until I saw Tag tied outside."

"Your mother needs you, Anna. She appeared exhausted. Surely you observed that."

She sat on the front bench and turned to face him. "We've been home for two hours. I made peace with Mother. Now I've come to seek forgiveness from the Lord . . . and from you."

Two hours? Had he been on his knees for two hours with no answers? He stood and paced. "I've replayed the night you walked away from me over and over trying to find an answer. What did I do? Why did you stop loving me? When did you stop loving me? The same questions day after day, night after night."

"Ty, please let me—"

He raised his hand. "I'm not finished. When no answers came, I begged God to help me get past the questions and learn to live without you. I thought He heard my plea. At last I could go to bed at night and not dream of you. I could wake up in the morning and walk and breathe without every step and every breath packed with memories of you."

The moonlight streaming through the windows glistened off the tears on her cheeks, but her tears failed to move him. "Then you came back. Why? I'm finding it more difficult each day to believe it has anything to do with your love for me."

Anna gazed into the night. "I left because I was frightened. So deep-down afraid that the only thing I thought I could do was run and hope it would go away."

He sat beside her. "Frightened of what? Me?"

She shook her head. "The love you had for this land, for your ranch, scared me to death. I saw you so weary after a day in the hills that you hardly had energy to climb off your horse. I watched men like your father and John Wenghold grow old and tired ahead of their years. I witnessed your own mother's red, blistered hands in the winter and sunburned face in the summer, working alongside your papa. I didn't want to compete with wind and grasshoppers and the terrible storms that rage on this prairie. The Hawk is a demanding mistress. She would always come first—and I've never been second in anything." She lowered her gaze.

"So what changed your mind? The Hawk is still here. My love for this land hasn't changed. Yet you've insisted on our marriage since the day you returned."

Anna twisted the ring on her finger. "Nothing I have to say will endear me to you."

He gritted his teeth. "Nothing you've done since returning has endeared yourself. But try me. I deserve to know."

She took the ring from her finger and clutched it in her hand. "While gone this past year, I met a man. He declared his love for me early in our courtship then hesitated to make any further commitment. Returning to Kansas was my way of forcing him to realize he couldn't live without me."

"Then I'm right in assuming this whole thing was nothing more than a charade? And I was a decoy? At what point did you intend to admit what you were doing? At the altar?"

"I never planned to deceive you. At least not initially. But then I walked into church that Sunday morning, expecting to see your face light up at my presence, and instead I saw your eyes seek those of a stranger sitting with Henrietta Harvey and holding a little boy on her lap."

"And the old habit of always winning grew too strong, right? Is being first so important that you would deliberately set out to cause pain and ridicule to another person? And not only to Robin but also to me? You would marry me so you could declare yourself a winner in a contest not even declared? Why?"

She shrugged. "I told you, I've never been second in anything. It frightens me to be anything else."

"And you see Robin as competition?"

Her gaze met his and she gave a faint smile. "No longer competition, Ty. She's the winner. And I don't concede often."

He slammed his hand on the bench and Anna flinched. "And what has she won, Anna? Humiliation? Embarrassment? An injury so severe she may not survive?"

Anna handed him the ring and closed his hand around it. "No, Ty. She's won your heart. I've watched you—oh, how I've watched you. Did you know your eyes even change color when she enters a room? And tonight, on the porch—you grieved for her. I'm not sure I ever witnessed your heart so openly as I did when you came back to the house after her accident. Not even the night I broke our engagement. Now, I'm breaking it again." She loosed her clasp on his hand. "You're free to declare your love for her. You do love her, you know. And I believe she loves you, too. Only she's too naive to know it. It will be up to you to tell her."

Ty studied the ring in his hand then sought her eyes. "I would have married you. You do know that, don't you?"

She laid her hand on his arm. "And how foolish and miserable we both would have been. One too selfish and one too honorable to admit they were wrong. I ask your forgiveness, Ty. I'm sorry I've caused so much pain . . . to so many people."

He lifted her chin. "You have my forgiveness. Now you must forgive yourself."

TWENTY-EIGHT

The clank of the stove lid roused Ty from fitful slumber. He braced his elbows on the table and wiped both hands across his face, then rubbed the back of his neck. "You rattled that thing on purpose, didn't you?" He squinted through tired eyes at Doc Mercer who stood with coffeepot in hand. "Is . . . is Robin still . . . ?"

Doc frowned and waved the coffeepot in the air. "You think I'd be down here having coffee if she was worse . . . or gone? There hasn't been much change, but she's still with us."

Ty breathed a deep sigh of relief. "Then would you mind pouring me a cup of that coffee?"

"Would if I could. You didn't do a very good job of tending to the fire, and there's nothing but grounds in this pot. Must have boiled dry. What are you doing down here anyway? By your appearance you haven't changed clothes since yesterday."

Ty stirred the coals, threw on a couple of sticks of kindling, then waited for them to blaze. "I took Florence and Anna Blair back to town last night and didn't get home until late. Planned to drink one last cup of coffee and rest for a minute, but I must have fallen asleep." He added more wood and dropped the lid back on the stove. "Shouldn't take too long before we'll have fresh brew."

"You need a wife. Hear tell Mrs. Blair was about to announce your engagement when all the fracas started. You and Anna have been engaged for a while, haven't you? Reckon that's one fire you didn't let go out, huh?" Doc laughed at his own joke.

"It's a long story and not one I care to repeat." Ty patted his shirt pocket. "Nothing left but what's in here." He pulled out the ring. "This, a cold stove, and nothing but dregs in the bottom of the pot pretty well sums it up."

"That little gal upstairs have something to do with it?"

Ty shrugged. "It's not her doing, if that's what you mean."

"Well, none of my business. To tell the truth, I'm kind of glad to catch you here alone. Something's been weighing on my mind all night." Doc made circles on the table with his empty cup.

"Serious? Does it concern Robin?"

"Tell me, what do you know about that little fella you call Jacob? He doesn't belong to Robin, does he?"

"No. We found him on the prairie the day after the twister." Ty continued the story, surprised Doc hadn't already heard it from John. The doctor sat quiet for a long time after Ty finished.

"I didn't answer your question, did I?"

Doc shook his head. "There's still time. I'm not through yet. How attached to the boy is Robin?"

"Very attached. If his pa were to show up and want to take him, I'm not sure she would let him go without a fight. At the least, it would break her heart."

"And this Benson fella? Does he have any connection to the youngster?"

Ty shook his head. "No, he's an old friend from Chicago."

"You ever see that dog the boy has with him before yesterday?" Doc retrieved the coffeepot from the stove and filled their cups.

"You know something, don't you?" Ty handed Doc the spoon holder and pushed the sugar bowl toward him. "You could use a little sweetening." He grinned.

Doc spooned two heaping spoons of sugar into his coffee then methodically stirred, tapped the spoon on the side of his cup, licked it, and put it on the table. "If you had a wife, she'd see to it there was at least a saucer to put my spoon on, and maybe a cookie or two."

Ty crossed his arms and leaned back in his chair. "Look, Doc, yesterday was a terrible day. I've had a long night, and today isn't starting out too well, either. Say your piece so I can get on with what has to be done around here."

Doc frowned and peeped over the top of his glasses. "Son, I took an oath, way back when, that I would do everything in my power to protect the privacy of my patients, as well as use all knowledge I had to diagnose and treat the ailments of any and all who came my way. Right now I'm weighing that pretty blamed serious, because to protect one, I very well could be doing harm to the other. Can you understand my dilemma?"

"I'm trying. Go on."

Doc stirred another spoon of sugar into his coffee. "Three or four days after the twister a man came knocking on my door late one night. A man close to my age, clean, well spoken, but plumb tuckered. First thing I noticed was his eyes. You can tell a lot by a man's eyes, you know. His were the saddest eyes I ever did see, but they never wavered. No matter what questions I shot him. I trusted him right off."

"Why did he come to you? Was he sick?" Talking about the man's eyes brought back Ty's first meeting with Sam. He'd had the same thought. Not that Sam's eyes were sad, but that he had a habit of looking at you straight on like he had nothing to hide.

"He said he had a heart condition. But the longer we talked, and after I examined him, the more I began to think maybe his heart wasn't sick, but he was heartsick. Does that make sense?"

Ty frowned. "Maybe the reason for the sad eyes? What did you do for him?"

"Mostly I listened and tried to answer his questions. If I'd known then what I know now I could've helped him a whole lot more." He leaned toward Ty. "He asked whether I had maybe treated a young woman for injuries after the storm. Had I seen any signs of a young boy. You starting to see a puzzle come together here?"

Ty stood, arms crossed. “Did you ever see him again?”

Doc nodded. “Comes around a couple of times a week. We talk, play a game of dominoes now and then, usually share a cup of coffee, then he leaves. But here’s the clincher—that dog your young Jacob claims is Tripper—it’s been at my table more than you have.”

Ty pinched the bridge of his nose. Then there was a connection between the stranger and Jacob. But why, if he didn’t intend harm, wouldn’t the man come to the ranch and identify himself? And why was he so willing to help yesterday then take off like he did? If only he’d had this information before Rusty left. “Do you know where he goes? Where he might be now? Two of my good men are out looking for him, and it’d be a mighty big help if I could ride after them and tell them where to look.”

Doc cleaned his glasses on the front of his shirt. “I know, but like I said—what goes on between me and my patients is private. Not likely they’ll find him until he’s ready to be found. But there’s more.”

“Doc?” William Benson entered the kitchen. “Sorry, don’t mean to interrupt, but Emma wants you upstairs right away. Robin opened her eyes then closed them again. But she’s very restless.”

“We’ll have to finish this later, Ty.” Doc scooted his chair from the table. “You get any sleep, Benson?”

“Enough for now.” William turned to Ty. “If you don’t need me here, I’m going to ride into town and send that telegram.”

Ty sighed. Had William been with Robin all night? Shouldn’t he be the one with her? After all, this was his home. Instead, he was downstairs sleeping with his head on the table. “Do what you have to do. I’m sure we can handle things around here.”

“Oh, I wasn’t concerned about you handling things. But Robin calms when I hold her hand.” He turned without giving Ty a chance to reply.

TWENTY-NINE

William stepped from the depot, pleased that Mr. Rempel had readily complied with his wish to send the telegram. If everything went according to his calculations, Robin's sisters should arrive on Sunday. *Oh, Lord, please get them here in time.* He hadn't been in Kansas a week, but it seemed a lifetime. The next three days would be an eternity.

He spurred John's horse, and the gelding settled into a smooth lope. Anxiety to return to Robin pushed him. The need to sort through his thoughts restrained him. The anguish on John Wenghold's face since Robin's accident confirmed the man's love for his niece. A fact William hadn't taken into consideration when he began his quest. Nor had his plans included a small, impish boy.

To do anything other than follow in his father's footsteps, and his grandfather's before him, had never been a question nor an option. Though he enjoyed summers on his uncle's ranch, he was always anxious to return home. He liked living in the city and the amenities it afforded. Besides, it was family tradition.

But the Feather was Wenghold family tradition. Robin's father had intimated as much when they'd visited before his death. He lamented the fact that neither brother took the time to stay close. What right did William have to ask Robin to leave now? And how would he explain to his father should he decide to stay?

William reined the horse to a walk. Clouds obscured the mid-morning sun, and the breeze, though quite warm, brought the refreshing scent of rain. Maybe if he got caught in a downpour it would wash the cobwebs from his mind. Though he prided himself on his ability to keep long columns of numbers and facts with precision and accuracy, the tangle of emotional events thus far encountered left him weary and unable to decipher.

William stopped the horse at the crest of a hill and crossed his hands over the saddle horn. A shaft of rain darkened the horizon across the distant hills and swept the prairie as it advanced toward him. He gulped deep drafts of air and welcomed the sting of expanded lungs. Since Robin's accident his breaths occurred in shallow gasps of fear as he attempted to fit together the prior chain of events.

He rotated his shoulders, but the questions refused to slide off. Who was the stranger, and what role did he play in Jacob's life? How would that change Robin's decisions? William's spine tingled as the one piece of the puzzle he very much wanted to ignore, niggled its way onto the table of his mind—

Exactly where did Ty Morgan fit?

A gust of wind blew warm rain through the open window beside Robin's bed, and she jerked when a drop landed on her cheek.

Ty smiled. "Was that cold?" He wiped the droplet away. "Maybe I should close the window."

It seemed foolish to talk to her when she didn't seem to be aware that anyone was in the room. But he'd follow Doc's orders. He glanced at the small bed they'd set up for Emma. Doc had finally convinced her to rest in another room while someone stayed with Robin. He envied Emma. His body longed for the stretch-out sleep he'd missed since Robin's injury. Though grateful Benson had not yet returned to challenge his position at her bedside, the lengthening shadows in the room confirmed that another long day had failed to produce any change in her condition.

Robin moaned and turned her head to one side.

Ty brushed his hand across her forehead and smoothed away a strand of hair. "Are you in pain? Of course you are. I wish you could tell us where it hurts. Would a cool cloth feel good?" A small frown crinkled between her eyebrows then vanished. "I'll take that as a no."

Robin moaned again, and Ty clasped her hands in his and knelt by her bed. There was a time, not so many days ago, when his heart ached to pursue his feelings for this girl. But Anna and the promises he'd made stood in the way. Now Anna had released him from those promises, but Robin couldn't hear what he wanted to say.

What *did* he feel for her? It was no longer pity. He reserved that emotion for Anna now. It was as though he had watched a long-ago-dream come true then disintegrate before his very eyes. But did he love Robin? Anna seemed to think he did. He'd never doubted his love for Anna before she left for Pennsylvania. Had he not loved her? Had it only been a physical attraction?

He could at least console himself with the fact that what feelings he had for Robin were never based on physical appearance. She was lovely, but it was more than that. She was feisty, opinionated, determined, and stubborn to be sure. She was also strong, caring, loving, and brave. But then, the same things could be said for John Wenghold.

Ty laid his head on the bed beside Robin's hand and welcomed the veil that slowly dulled his eyes.

The sun punched an occasional hole through the gauze-like curtain of clouds scudding low across the hills as William approached Morgan's ranch the next morning. The rain had prompted him to stop at the Feather for the night, but now he regretted that decision. A hush pervaded the surroundings. Though men and horses moved around the yard, it lacked the usual bantering that accompanied the morning's push of activity. He entered the kitchen, and a knot settled in his gut, and then grew larger when he observed Doc slumped over the table.

William laid a hand on his shoulder.

Doc jerked.

"Sorry. Didn't mean to startle you, Doc. Didn't you go to bed last night? Is she still with us?"

Doc rubbed his eyes with his palms. "As far as I know, she is. I sent Emma to another room to rest, but Ty's with her. I gave him orders to come get me if there was any change."

"Morgan's with her?" William smoothed his mustache. "Is that a good idea?"

"Why wouldn't it be? Left you with her, didn't I?"

"Yes. But Robin knows me."

Doc hooked his thumbs in his suspenders and leaned back in the chair. "She knows Ty Morgan, too. I reckon she's seen more of him than she has of you lately. Ty won't do anything to upset her. He's a preacher, don't forget."

William stopped at the stairs. "Yeah, but he's also a man. Doesn't seem right he's there all alone. At least Emma was in the room when I stayed with her."

"Look, son, this isn't Chicago. I don't carry a nurse around with me to mollycoddle all the gossipers. Sure as I had a woman traveling along they'd have something to say about that, too. That little gal is hurt bad. Somebody needs to be with her, and blamed if I'm gonna start splitting hairs over who she knows best and which one of you should or shouldn't be left alone with her." He stood and peered into his cup. "One thing's for sure—if Ty don't get him a wife one of these days I aim to quit coming out here. Haven't had a decent cup of coffee since Florence Blair left."

William took the steps two at a time. Regardless of Doc's tirade, he didn't like the idea of the preacher, or rancher, or whatever he might call himself today being alone with Robin. He liked it even less when he opened the door and found Morgan on his knees, his head on the bed beside her, and her small hand encased in both of his resting against his cheek

He crossed the room in one stride, and tapped Ty's shoulder, motioning for him to get to his feet.

Ty stood, and Robin's hand dropped lifelessly to the mattress.

William leaned to whisper. "I'm back. You may leave now." He motioned to the door.

A frown furrowed Ty's forehead. "Did Doc give orders for me to leave, or is this your idea?"

William moved between Ty and the bed. "What difference does it make whose idea it is?"

"Do you mind telling me what your problem is?" He nodded toward Robin. "This is no place to discuss whatever burr you have under your saddle. The least we can do is step out into the hallway." The floor creaked as Ty moved for the door.

William followed and shut the door behind him then turned to face the preacher. "I'll only say it one time, Morgan. Did you—?"

Ty scowled. "Believe it or not the last thing I remember is praying. I must've fallen asleep."

William scoffed. "Prayer is always a good excuse, isn't it?"

Ty shrugged. "Look, Benson—I talked to her, like Doc told me to do."

"And what did you talk about? Did you tell her you loved her? And did you expect her to believe you if you did? Do you love her, Morgan? Yesterday you were all set to marry Miss Blair. What happened? Is it your nature to divert your love every time the Kansas wind changes direction? If you can change your heart so quickly, how do I know you aren't just wanting Robin so you can keep the boy?"

Ty shook his hand in William's face. "Whatever has happened between me and Miss Blair is strictly our business, Benson, and I don't intend to discuss it with anyone. Why're you here?"

"I'm here to take Robin back to Chicago." He pushed Ty's hand away.

Ty gave a shove and William's head hit the wall. "Because you love her, Benson? Or because you feel sorry for her? What if she doesn't want to go?" Ty moved to the door of Robin's room.

William pushed away from the wall and stepped in front of him. No way was he going to let Ty Morgan back in that room with her. "I promised Robin's pa I'd take care of her. The best way I know to do that is to marry her. I respect her, I admire her . . ." *And I'll learn to love her.* But he didn't dare voice that to Ty Morgan. He straightened and jutted his chin. "She'll go with me. What's to keep her here? You?"

"She deserves better than that, Mr. Big City Man." Ty poked William's chest with each word. "You think she won't know the difference between me loving her because of who she is, or you marrying her because you promised her pa? I'll keep her here or bust your face trying."

William grabbed Ty's hand. "You have a woman, Morgan. What difference does it make to you why I ask Robin to marry me? I don't think you're man enough to bust my face."

Ty pulled his hand out of William's grip and gave him a shove.

William's shoulders hit the wall. So he wanted a fight? Good! He'd give him one. He'd fought more than one fella in order to protect Robin.

Their boots hit the floor like hammers, and their elbows knocked against the wall while they pushed and shoved at one another.

"Stop it." John Wenghold stood at the top of the stairs, eyes blazing. "You two itchin' for somethin' to do, are ya? Well, I'll tell you one thing, you done come lookin' in the wrong place. Both of you get your sorry behinds down them stairs and out of this house."

Ty pointed at Benson. "He accused me of—"

"I don't care a feather in granny's gray bonnet who said what or why. You two hotheads act worser than a couple of bull calves out rompin' on them hills, buttin' heads and bawlin' like you was important."

"John, I never—"

"I told ya I don't wanna hear it, Ty Morgan. I oughta take a horsewhip to your backsides."

"We're not children, Mr. Wenghold." William wiped a hand through his hair.

"Oh? Well, you sure nuff coulda fooled me. Now git!" He followed them down the stairs. "Good thing Doc isn't in here or he'd skin you both."

"I talked to him a while ago," William said. "I told him no good could come of leaving Morgan alone with her."

"Hush your yammerin'." John shoved William ahead of him when they reached the barn.

William squinted to adjust to the dark interior, and his nostrils quivered. Was it the barn, or this whole situation that smelled so bad?

John leaned against the nearest stall and crossed his legs at the ankles. "Look, you two. Ever' day that little gal don't wake up is gonna heft another load of worry on all our shoulders. Robin can't help what's happenin' to her right now. She hurt her head. But we gotta keep ours with some sense in 'em. You buttin' them hard knots on top of your shoulders ever time you see one another don't do nothin' to help her get well."

William took a deep breath, and wished he could breathe fresh air. He'd not apologize for defending Robin, but his behavior had been less than that of a gentleman. He smoothed his mustache then reached for Ty's hand. "I'm sorry. I allowed my concern for Robin to outweigh good manners."

Ty shook his hand. "Apology accepted. And I'm sorry I gave you concern."

John nodded. "Well, now you done shook like gentlemen, suppose you find a wall to lean on and cool off for a bit, or balance yourselves on one of them milk stools hangin' on the wall."

"You figure to keep us out here all day?" Ty stuck his hands in his pockets.

"What I figger is, Doc will let us know when and if we can see the little gal."

"You aim to keep me out of my own home?"

"If that's what it takes to keep you from causin' commotion. That's my niece in there. I ain't proud that I never knowed her 'til a few weeks ago, but I don't aim to let you two hotheads do nothin' that will make it worse for her. Now tell me, Benson—did ya get the telegram off to her sisters?"

William pulled two stools from their nails on the wall and handed one to Ty.

"I did. They should be here by Sunday."

THIRTY

Robin fought to surface from the deep pit that threatened to suck her into its depths. Noises from somewhere vibrated through her body, and her head throbbed. Angry voices sounded familiar. She tried to open her eyes and strained to climb through the fog that clouded her vision.

Where was she? If she yelled, would anyone hear her? She tried to call out, but her head hurt with the effort. She pulled her arms from whatever encased them and her hand struck something hard and cold, then the crash of splintering glass broke the silence. The door opened, and she made out the unmistakable form of Emma Ledbetter.

"Goodness, child. What a way to wake up. You needn't have thrown the lamp you know." Emma stooped and kissed her forehead. "But it's worth anything you broke to see your pretty eyes open."

Robin reached for her head, but Emma caught her hands.

"Don't take the bandage away, Robin. You fell from John's wagon. Do you remember?"

Robin closed her eyes. "Emma? Where am I? Why are you here? I heard angry voices. It sounded like Uncle John. And . . ." She wanted to rub her head to take away the pain but Emma gripped her hands.

"Yes, John was one of them. But don't fret, sweet girl. Everything is all right. You keep resting. I'll be right here. Doc had Ty move a bed into the room so I can be close."

She turned her head and tried to make the room come into focus. "I'm at Ty's?" A flash of memory came and her pulse raced. "Where's Jacob?"

"He's with the hands at the bunkhouse. He's fine. All the men will look out for him."

"Emma, was there a man trying to get Jacob?" A tear slid down her face and trickled into her ear. If only she could make her brain put all the pieces together.

"There was a stranger, but we don't think he meant any harm to Jacob. It was a good thing he was there, too. William sent him back here for help after you fell."

William. His was one of the voices she heard—William and Ty and Uncle John. "Is William still here? And where's Uncle John?"

Emma smiled and wiped Robin's face with a damp cloth. "The last time I saw him he was scolding Ty and William all the way down the stairs."

"Why?" Robin pushed the covers away. "Where's Jacob?"

Emma cradled Robin's head. "I told you, sweetheart. Jacob's with some of Ty's men. They're taking good care of him." She lowered Robin's head to the pillow. "Now, promise me you'll stay quiet while I go fetch Doc. He'll want to see you now that you're awake. Promise?"

"Oh, Emma. I don't have the strength to do anything but shut my eyes. But I want to see Jacob."

"Don't know as Doc will let anybody that rambunctious up here yet, but I'll put in a word for the boy."

The door clicked behind Emma, and Robin squinted through bleary eyes. The room had yellow walls—like sunshine. Her room at home had yellow walls, too.

She clutched at the covers as she felt herself slip into the pit again. *I don't want to fall. It's so far down and so hard to get back to the top. I want to go home.* As she spiraled, her own voice taunted. *Home? Where's home?*

John moved from the wall when Emma came into the barn hightailin' toward him. Tears rolling down her face could mean only one thing—something happened to Robin. With two steps he met her and gathered her to him with one arm while she sobbed.

Ty and William jumped to their feet, their faces white.

"Oh, John," Emma's voice cracked.

John put his other arm around her. One hand patted her back. "Emma girl. Is Robin . . . ?"

She nodded and dust flew as both younger men bolted for the door. John wanted to join them, to get to his niece as quickly as possible, but he still held Emma in his arms.

"When?" He croaked out the words.

"Shortly after you came out here with Ty and William." She stepped away from him and pulled a handkerchief from her sleeve. "Robin wants to see Jacob."

John held the woman at arm's length. What did she just say? "She wants to see Jacob? Then she isn't . . . she didn't . . . ?" He pulled her to him once again, sagging with relief.

A long minute later, Emma was still clutched to his chest. He could get used to his arms being full of this woman real fast. "I thought you was a tellin' me that she done—that she was gone for good."

Emma leaned away to look at him. "Oh, heavens, no, John!"

"Land's sake, Emma girl. I thought my heart was gonna stop right there."

She wiped her eyes on the front of his shirt. "You love that little girl, don't you, John Wenghold?"

He kept one arm around her while he fished in his pocket for his bandana. Sure would be nice if he didn't make such a snort when he blew his nose, but likely she'd understand. "I surely do. Funny how she sorta hobbled her way in, you know? But I'm thinkin' we better put them boys' hearts to rest. The way they lit out of here, I reckon they's thinkin' she's dead, too."

Emma slipped her arm around his waist as they walked to the house. "Doc was going into the house when I came to get you. I reckon he'll put a stop to any of their foolishness. It wouldn't surprise me if she's asleep again. She's very weak."

"Wait a minute, Emma girl." John slipped his hand into hers and pulled her to a stop. "I . . . well, I reckon I been alone so long I'm plumb addlebrained when it comes to sayin' anything to a woman. But I sure do 'preciate all you've done for us since that little bird showed up out here in this wild country." He wanted to say more, but Emma got all teary-eyed again. What did a young man say to a lass to make her all buggy-eyed and giggly? If things kept going smooth for a couple days he'd see if William would give him some hints. He'd ask Ty, but the last look he saw on Anna Blair's face wasn't anything he ever wanted to witness on Emma's.

Ty and William hovered outside Robin's door, anguish filling their faces.

John shook his head. He should've hollered at 'em right away. "I'm sorry. The two of ya ran before Emma could finish tellin' us what she came to tell us in the first place. Emma weren't cryin' cuz Robin is dead. Them were glad tears. Robin woke up."

Ty thrust his hands in his pockets. "Then why won't Doc let us in? He said one of us should bring Jacob in first."

"Cuz it ain't you Robin was wantin'. She woke up askin' to see the one man in her life she probably loves the most. And it weren't none of us a standin' here wastin' time when we could be fetchin' the boy."

Ty's face crumpled as he reached for Emma. "Is it true? She's alive?" Tears streamed down his face. "Thank You, Lord Jesus. Thank You for keeping her. Thank You for giving me one more chance to tell her all I've wanted to say for so long." He bolted down the steps in two leaps, calling for Jacob before he hit the yard.

William wiped his face. "I suppose you think that display proves who truly loves Robin?"

"Does it?" John shrugged. "I'm not the one to say, you know."

William sighed. "I told you before. I came to keep a promise to Robin's pa. I'll do anything to make sure she's safe and financially secure. She knows I care for her. I've never declared any more than that."

John glared at him. "Are you sayin' you don't love her?"

William lifted one shoulder. "I suppose I do love her, but perhaps not in the way she deserves. It would be unfair, at this point, to insist she make a choice. From all indications, Ty Morgan has more than just a desire to see her cared for. I think he truly loves her and the boy."

Emma laid a hand on William's shoulder. "There's been question in your mind about the boy returning to Chicago, hasn't there?" Emma's lip twitched.

John pulled her closer. This time he'd be ready if she needed an arm around her.

William nodded. "Jacob is well entrenched here. He has so many people unwilling to part with him. I thought it would help Robin be able to leave him, and give us a chance to build our marriage before having children of our own."

"She won't leave him, William," Emma said. "Women's hearts are different, I suppose. But she'll give you up before she'll turn loose of the boy."

He nodded again. "I can see that now. But tell me this—will she give Ty Morgan up to keep the boy?"

John shook his head. "She won't ever have to decide between the two, William. Ty couldn't leave the boy any more than Robin could."

"But you're leaving out the fact that there's still a stranger lurking. What if he shows himself and lays claim to Jacob? What then?"

"You got me in a corner, son. I don't have any idea what would happen, other than I could pretty well guarantee there'd be one whale of a fight. What I think I'm hearin' is you don't relish none of that."

William shrugged. "I'm saying if the stranger is Jacob's pa, then he'd have first rights to the boy. I think there are courts that would agree."

"Maybe in Chicago there are courts like that." John swiped his hand through his hair. "Out here we'd ask the man what took him so blamed long to come after him. Why sneak around? You love someone, you go after 'em. It don't take no fancy court to decide somethin' like that."

William smiled. "You're trying to tell me something, John. Spit it out."

John nodded. "I knowed you weren't no city slicker. What I'm a sayin', and you listen up. You knowed Robin all your life. You watched out for her and all, but you never could up and say you loved her. Now, you flip that gold piece over and you got a man what only has knowed her for a couple of months, and he can't wait to tell her them words."

"You know for a fact Morgan's engagement to Anna Blair is off?"

"Doc told me Ty showed him the ring hisself. I ain't heard it from Ty."

William's gaze darkened. "It seems a bit unfair for us to stand outside Robin's room and try to make a choice for her. I won't make a scene, but neither will I sit back and presume we know what's in her heart. So what if Ty's engagement is off. If he can change his mind with every twist of the Kansas wind, then Robin will only become another victim of Morgan's storm, won't she? How do you know he won't marry her just to keep the boy? Is that any better than my reasons for being here?"

John wiped his hand across his mouth. Doggone if William didn't have a point. "What you're sayin' is you aim to fight for Robin's hand? You maybe done chawed off a hunk of life what might end up tastin' bitter before you get it swallered."

William rubbed the back of his neck. "I'll take my chances. I invited myself here, but I won't leave unless, or until, Robin tells me to go."

"I reckon that's fair enough. But ya know you and Ty will most likely be buttin' heads again, don't ya?"

William shook his head. "You needn't worry, John. We'll behave like gentlemen."

"Humph. Ain't nothin' gentle about neither one of ya. Guess we'll have to see if lovin' the little lady what's layin' in that bed yonder can make men out of ya."

John winked at Emma. Yep. A good woman could sure make you

feel like a man. His heart nearly thumped out of his chest. *Jumpin' bullfrogs. Am I in love? Now wouldn't that buy granny a new hat—and a pink feather to put in it?*

THIRTY-ONE

"Did Robin wake up? Can I bring Tripper for her to see?" Jacob jabbered and jumped in Ty's arms all the way to the house. "She'll like my dog, won't she? Why you carryin' me? I'm big now."

"I know you're big, but I can still walk faster than you can. And to answer your first question, yes, Robin woke up, and she wants to see you. But you can't take Tripper in the house."

"But she wants to see him, I know she does. Can I, please?"

Ty stood Jacob on his feet when they reached the porch. "She'll see him when she's feeling better." He knelt in front of the boy. "Now, listen to me. Robin is awake, but she's still very hurt, so you have to promise you won't talk loud or jump on the bed. You do what Doc Mercer says. No arguing."

"Can she talk to me?" He opened the kitchen door. "Can I tell her I gots Tripper?"

"You can tell her, but keep your voice soft."

Doc Mercer met them at door. "You take him on up to Emma, Ty, then join me and John down here, if you don't mind."

"I can't see her?" Ty wanted to argue, but he wouldn't—not in front of Jacob.

"Not yet. Just do as I say and you can maybe look in on her later. Depends on what Emma says."

Jacob was halfway up the steps when Ty caught up with him. "You mind Emma, now. You hear?"

Jacob reached for his hand when they got to the top. "Are you mad with Doc Mercer?"

"Disappointed, Jacob. I wanted to see her, too."

"I'll tell her, okay?"

Ty smiled at the boy. "Yeah, you do that. I'll see you after bit." He trudged down the stairs to join the other men already seated in the kitchen.

John shoved three pieces of pie around the table as though he were shuffling cards. Ty gritted his teeth. His mother would be ashamed for company to see the chips in her white ironstone plates, even if it were only men.

"Where did this come from?" Ty sighed and stuffed a bite into his mouth. He couldn't remember when he'd last had food. "Mm-mm, apple. And the tip is the best bite, you know."

"Robin brought the pie along for the celebration. It'll go to waste if we don't eat it." John cut his triangle into two pieces. "Now, if you had any smarts you'd be a followin' what I did and you'd have yourself two of them tippy mouthfuls." He grinned and waved a forkful under Ty's nose.

"You don't have more pie, John, just more pieces." Ty nodded toward Doc. "You have something on your mind?

"Humph, he ain't had nothin' on his mind for as long as I ever knowed him." John smashed his fork on the crumbs of crust on his plate.

Doc reared back in his chair. "Well, at least I *got* a mind which is more than I can say for some other old codger sitting at this table."

Ty took a deep breath. "Stop it."

The two older men jerked at his outburst.

He knew he was being short with them, but he was losing his patience. "I got more worthwhile things to do than listen to the two of you harp at each other. If you have something important to say, Doc, then spit it out. Otherwise, I'm out of here and you can find me upstairs with Robin."

"I got plenty to say, young man." Doc peered at him over the rim of his glasses. "That man, the one you call the stranger—"

Voices and the telltale thump of boots clipping across the porch stopped their conversation. In chorus they turned toward the door.

Rusty held the door open while Sam and another man came inside. Ty recognized the stranger as the one who'd alerted him of Robin's accident—the same one Doc mentioned. Could this be the man who'd watched them from a distance? He appeared harmless enough. Ty nodded to Rusty and Sam. "Good job, men. Thanks."

"Mr. Morgan? Uh . . ." Sam stepped closer to the man. "We didn't 'xactly catch him, sir. He was a sittin' waitin' on us. Just took us a spell to find him. I don't reckon you'll understand this, but . . ." He removed his hat and twisted it in his hands.

Ty's spine tingled. He had a hunch whatever Sam was going to say was nothing he wanted to hear.

Something poked into Robin's ear, and she flinched to move it away.

"Can you hear when you're sleepin?"

Jacob! She struggled to open her eyes, and a giggle rewarded her efforts. "Did you stick your finger in my ear?" She smiled at the impish face before her. "It tickled, you know."

"Could you hear me? I said 'Robin, Robin,' but you didn't open your eyes."

"I'm so sleepy it's hard to wake up fast."

He poked his elbows onto the bed and leaned closer. "I'm sorry you got hurted. Ty told me I can't jump on your bed, but I didn't even want to. He's dis'pointed cuz he wanted to come see you, but Doc said I could go first. Ty's mouth did this." Jacob used his fingers to pull his mouth down at the corners. "Then I told him I'd tell you he was dis'pointed and he did this." He pushed his lips into a grin. "Can we go home when you get all waked up?"

Robin shook her head, and waves of pain threatened to throw her into the pit once more. She grabbed for Jacob's hands to keep from plunging into the void.

"Um . . . That kinda pinches when you hold so tight." Jacob's breath brushed Robin's cheek.

"I need to hang onto you, little man, so you won't run away from me again." The throb in her head couldn't compare to the pain she would incur if anything ever happened to this little boy.

"Did you think I was running away? Would it make you sad?"

Robin squeezed his small hands. "Very, very sad."

"I tried to catch up with Tripper and my . . ." He pulled on his hands, but she held tight.

"Jacob, who was the man with the dog? With Tripper? You know him, don't you?" Could Emma hear this conversation? Should she call for Uncle John?

The boy's face crumpled. "If I tell, will I be in trouble? Mama said he'd find us, but I couldn't tell." He sniffed. "I can't wipe my nose when you hold my hands so tight."

"If I let go, will you tell me who the man is? You won't be in trouble. I promise.

Jacob sniffed again. "I guess you'll have to hang on to 'em, cuz I promised Mama, and it would make her sad if I told. I'll wipe my drips like this." He wiggled his face on his sleeve.

Robin attempted to focus on the boy's face, but the room spun, taking Jacob's image with it. "Jacob, is the man your pa?" Was that her voice? It seemed so far away. She slipped off the edge of the precipice into the deep again, and a small voice ricocheted off the walls as she tumbled.

"I don't have a pa . . . pa . . . pa . . ."

Ty's heart constricted as his gaze darted between Sam and the older man. His idea of who or what the stranger might be never wore a face so etched in care or eyes so full of sadness. The man stood straight and tall beside Sam. Older, by far, yet his broad shoulders and large hands suggested strength. Only when Doc Mercer shook his hand did the man's eyes waver.

"Obed, my friend. Won't you have a seat?"

The man gave a wan smile. "I believe Sam needs to be heard, then I'll let Mister Morgan decide if I'm still welcome at his table."

"Sam?" Ty nodded.

Sam's shoulders straightened. "Sir, this here is Obed Mason."

Ty gasped. "Mason?" Fear and dread wrenched his heart, and his pulse hammered in his ears.

"Yes, sir. This here is my pa."

"Your pa?" Ty's mind reeled. What about the dog? How did Jacob fit with both of these men. Jacob with his big blue eyes? Surely this Obed person wasn't the boy's pa, too?

John slammed his hand on the table and coffee sloshed from the cups. "Move your mouth enough to ask the man why he was sneakin' around, Ty. I told you from the get-go the kid knew somethin'."

Obed squared his shoulders. "Believe me, Mr. Wenghold. If I'd been sneaking, you would never have seen me."

"You knew we were on to you?" Ty motioned for them to sit. "So why didn't you come on in instead of just watching? Sam? Did you know it was your pa all along? Because if you did, young man, I've lost my trust in Rusty's word."

"You can leave my son of out it," Obed said. "He hasn't laid eyes on me for over ten years. Men change in that time and so do boys." He put his hand on Sam's shoulder. "He wasn't keeping anything from anyone. I imagine the last person he expected to see out on this prairie was this old hill-man from Missouri."

Rusty fingered the crease in his hat. "Boss, I done heard this story so if you don't mind I'll be checkin' on things outside."

"One question before you go, Rusty." Ty pointed to Obed Mason. "Is this the same fella who rode in the night of the storm?"

Rusty shook his head. "No sir. Not the same man." He put his arm around Sam's shoulders. "Glad to be your friend, Sam Mason."

He nodded at Obed. "You, too sir. Just wish it would've had a better endin' for ya."

John leaned toward Obed. "What does he mean, better endin'? You got your son, didn't ya? Or was you wantin' somethin' else?"

Obed folded his big hands on the table. "Finding Sam, here, was an act of grace on God's part, Mr. Wenghold. I came looking for my girl, Sam's twin sister."

Ty frowned. "Twin? You told me your sister was younger, Sam."

"She was, by five minutes." He grinned.

John scowled. "I reckon you knowed by now there ain't been but one woman around here all the whilst you been spyin' around. What made ya think you'd be findin' your little gal in these hills, anyway?"

Doc punched John in the shoulder. "You old piece of crow bait, let the man talk. I've already told you I know him so why are you acting like he's an enemy?" He scooted his chair from the table and motioned for John to follow. "You cut us all another piece of Robin's pie and I'll pour the coffee."

John shook his head. "I don't aim to miss nothin' this fella has to say. You wanna stuff your mouth to keep from yammerin', then you go right ahead."

Ty placed his hand on John's arm. He loved this crusty old neighbor of his, but there were times he wanted to stuff a rag in his mouth. "I apologize for the interruptions, Mr. Mason. Please continue."

Obed turned to John. "I knew where my girl was headed, Mr. Wenghold. She left a note in my barn telling me she was leaving Missouri. Said her man planned to start his own ranch in Kansas, and she was sorry for taking the wagon and horses. I left as soon as I could pack a little grub and a bedroll. I figured she had a good day's travel ahead of me."

"Ya up and lose her, did ya?" John crossed his arms. "One man a travelin' on horseback shoulda been able to catch up with a team and heavy wagon if ya pushed."

Ty shook his head. "John, please."

"Oh, I pushed, Mr. Wenghold. But I didn't want the lowdown

weasel she was with to know I was following them." Obed seemed to wrestle for control. His eyes dulled but never wavered as his gaze met Ty's. "That's my girl's grave out on the prairie not so far from here. Sam's sister."

Sam bowed his head briefly.

Obed leveled his gaze at Ty. "Was it you who found her?"

Ty nodded. "The day after a twister went through these parts. We found her and Jacob. Still don't know how he managed to escape. But how did you know it was your daughter? Jacob either couldn't, or wouldn't, give us a name to put on the marker."

"I came across my team of horses dragging their harness close to fifteen miles east, near a town called Elmira."

"Nobody with the team, I take it?"

"No one. The horses let me approach them. Called them by name, Pete and Charley, and they came right to me. Other than a couple of cuts they were in good enough shape. I led them on into Elmira and was able to sell one of them and the old horse I was riding to a farmer. I needed the money and a new mount. I threw my saddle on Charley and continued my search. Not the smoothest ride, but that horse could plod for days on end. I didn't know how far I'd need to go, or how long it would take me. But I wasn't going to quit until I found my girl."

Ty nodded at John. "That answers why the horse he rode didn't look like a cow pony."

Obed shook his head. "Not many cow ponies in my part of Missouri. The horse I rode until then was the same one I rode to visit from church to church back in the hills. Didn't need to be sleek or fast, just sure-footed.

"Go on, Mr. Mason." Ty urged. "I'm sorry we keep interrupting. We had a lot of questions, and you're answering them."

"When I found the wagon all busted, and no horses, I knew I'd found my girl. I didn't even need to read the name on the marker."

Ty's spine tingled. "This man she was with—was he Jacob's pa? He told us repeatedly that he didn't have a pa."

"I don't suppose anyone could answer that question. After my wife died and Samuel took off, my girl turned real wild. I doubt she could've named which one of the untamed hill-bucks she kept company with fathered the boy."

Ty studied his hands. What a difficult question for a father to have to answer. No wonder his eyes held such sadness. But what if the lowdown weasel he described returned and tried to claim Jacob. "Is there any chance this fella will show up and lay claim to the boy?"

Obed's eyes brightened. "No chance at all. I found him before I found my girl. I don't know if he got caught in the twister, or if his horse threw him. Maybe both. I found him at the bottom of a small ravine—dead. And, God help me, I left him for the animals. He'll never be able to hurt my girl, or her little boy, again."

"Ty, come quick. Robin waked up again and she—" Jacob leapt from the bottom step into the room. "Papaw?"

Ty's heart constricted as the boy rushed into the older man's embrace and flung his skinny little arms around his neck. Tears wet Obed's face.

"I knew you'd find me. Mama said you would, but I wasn't ever, ever supposed to tell. I didn't tell. Never. Mama will be happy with me not telling, won't she?"

Obed swiped at his cheeks. "Very happy with you, Jacob."

"Mama went to sleep when it stormed." He rubbed his eyes. "I couldn't wake her up so Ty put her in a big hole." He laid his head on Obed's chest and scrunched his eyes.

Obed rubbed Jacob's back.

"But then Robin and Ty found me. That makes us happy, doesn't it?"

"Yes, it does, son."

Jacob raised his head and clapped his hands. "Oh, yeah, I almost forgot. Ty's supposed to go talk to Robin. Emma said." He pulled Obed's nose. "Rosy, Posy got your nosey." He crammed his hand in his pocket and squirmed until his back rested on the older man's chest, clasping the man's big hands in front of him. "I didn't jump on the bed, Ty."

"Good boy, Jacob." Ty stood and ruffled the boy's hair. "I guess we'll have to finish this conversation later, Mr. Mason, but I do have one more question."

"I would imagine you have many questions, Mr. Morgan. And I can't blame you. What bothers you the most?"

Ty forced his eyes away from Jacob. "Do you plan to . . . head back to Missouri?" He trusted Mason understood the question.

"Ty Morgan?" Emma called from the top of the stairs. "You best get up here, and bring Doc with you."

Ty took the steps two at a time. Mason's answer would have to wait.

John eyed the family threesome still around the table. Doggone, if he didn't feel as welcome as a pebble in a shoe just sitting there. The others chattered like he wasn't even in the room. "I reckon you'd like a place to bed down for the night?" He shot the question at no one in particular.

Obed's steady gaze met his. "That would be more than I could expect, Mr. Wenghold. I've been housed quite sufficiently in a place not so far from here." He smiled down at Jacob on his lap. "I no longer need to ride into the shadows, you know. That is, if you don't mind my hanging around in the daylight."

"You'd leave the boy here, I reckon?"

Jacob's eyes widened. "I want Papaw to sleep with me and Tripper. He misses Tripper."

Sam stood and laid his arm across his pa's shoulders. "We can put him up in the bunkhouse, Mr. Wenghold. It'd be more comfortable than the cave he's been sleeping in. Plus, me and my pa, we got a whole lot of catchin' up to do. If you're worried about us leavin', we ain't gonna."

"Seems to me catchin' up is what your pa done did."

Obed shifted Jacob to one arm and stood, his large hand wrapped around the boy's legs. "I don't know if you can understand this, but the only catching up a man can do is with words. A man ought to live in such a way there'd only be tomorrow to look at, with no regrets. Redeem the time, John Wenghold. Redeem the time."

John slumped back into his chair. Jacob's giggles floated through the open door and twisted around his heart. He'd been getting along real good all by himself for many a year. But suddenly he'd never felt so alone.

William stepped into the shadows as Sam, Jacob, and the stranger strode past him. He hadn't intended to eavesdrop. It took restraint to keep from following Ty Morgan to where Robin lay. Had she called for him, or was it only Emma? And why did they need Doc in such a hurry?

Dusk threw its first blanket of darkness across the hills. Everything surrounding him spoke of peace, yet a sense of impending doom settled across his shoulders. If the two older Masons should decide to go back to Missouri, they surely would take Jacob with them. Wouldn't they? And without Jacob, Robin might be more willing to return to Chicago. The boy was the one obvious bond between her and Ty Morgan.

Who was he kidding? Jacob indeed played an important part in the strange chain of events that had led to this moment, but the boy wasn't the only link between Robin and Ty.

John stepped from the house into the shaft of light brightening the porch. "Thought I heered somebody out here." He scratched his shoulder on the porch pillar across from William. "You got big ears, do ya?"

"Never found a good time to interrupt the conversation."

"T'weren't none. Leastways not 'til Emma hollered for Ty."

"Is Robin worse?"

"Well, I reckon you done heered the same thing I did. Nobody come back down the steps a tellin' me nothin' so I can't rightly answer that question." John grunted as he lowered himself to the porch. "Did you get a gander of that man we've been callin' the stranger?"

"Not a good look. Saw he was big, not much else."

"Ain't nothin' like I thought. Fact is, I kinda like the fella. But I'll tell you one thing for downright certain. Like him or not, if he tries to take Jacob off this prairie before Robin is well enough to deal with him herself, he's done chose a battle he ain't gonna win."

"Whose battle will it be, John? Robin's? Or could it be you aren't willing for either Robin or Jacob to leave this prairie. The boy's grandfather has every right to take him back to wherever it is he calls home. And I have my doubts Robin will want to stay only to become your housekeeper or Ty Morgan's second choice." If only his confidence matched his words. By the looks of things, she wasn't Ty's second choice, but she didn't know that yet. Would it make a difference if she did? "Now, if you don't mind"—he gave a nod in John's direction—"I think I'll see if Doc will let me sit with her for a spell."

John stood and placed one arm across the doorway. "You might as well plunk your behind right down on them steps cuz Ty's up there with her now."

William pulled John's arm from the doorway and sidled through. "Then I'll plunk my behind, as you suggested, on the floor outside her room. The man has to sleep sometime. Good night, John."

THIRTY-TWO

Robin attempted to focus on the faces of Emma and Doc Mercer as they bent over her bed. "Please let me try to sit, Doc. I fall into a hole when I'm lying down, and I need to talk to Ty."

Doc shook his head. "It's against my better judgment, Robin. But if there's no fresh bleeding, maybe it won't hurt for a bit." He turned to Emma. "Suppose you could help me sit her up so I can examine those bandages? I'll hold her head if you can lift her shoulders."

Emma leaned and put her arms around Robin's shoulders. "I tell you girl, you do beat all. Ty could wait, you know. He isn't going anywhere. You can talk to him tomorrow, or the next day if need be. Girl, you've got a bump on your head big enough to swing a rope around."

"Please don't scold me. You have no idea how good it feels to sit up." Robin clutched at the covers hoping the room would stop spinning. "You did tell Ty I wanted to talk to him, didn't you?"

"I'm here."

She jumped at the sound of Ty's voice behind her.

"But Doc said I had to keep my mouth shut until he knew why Emma hollered for us."

"I didn't hear you come in." How long had he been standing there? Had he seen how helpless she was? "Can you come around where I can see you?"

Ty rounded the bed to kneel in front of her, and his face blurred as she squinted to focus. She giggled. "I'm sorry, but my eyes are doing funny things. Did you know you have only one eye, but two noses?" He also had a chin covered in at least a day's worth of whiskers and a smile that took her breath away.

One set of lips under the two noses ventured closer. "And you have purple eyes. A couple of nice shiners." He touched her cheek. "But I'm glad those eyes are open."

Doc probed Robin's bandages. "Doesn't look like you did any damage by sitting up, but I'd rather you lie back down again."

Robin shook her head. Goodness, it hurt. "Not until I talk with Ty."

"This a private talk?" Doc twirled his glasses in his hand.

"If you stop twirling those glasses you can stay." Robin closed her eyes against a wave of dizziness. "I think Jacob knows the man who owns the dog, Ty. But he won't tell me."

Ty pried her fingers loose from the bed and wrapped them in his. "Sam and Rusty found the man, Robin. I've been talking to him. Turns out he's Jacob's grandfather, and he's also Sam's pa."

Her stomach clenched and she gripped Ty's hands. "Are they going to take Jacob away from me?" Her head throbbed. "Don't let them take him. Please."

"Robin, they're his kin. I don't know that we can keep them from claiming what is rightfully theirs."

"He's not property. He's a little boy. He's happy here." How could she ever go on if she lost Jacob? Surely Ty wouldn't let them take him. Ty loved him, too. Didn't he?

"And that little boy didn't hesitate a minute to throw his arms around his grandpa's neck. It's obvious he loves the man, Robin. And is loved in return. He'd be happy with his grandpa, too. But they aren't going anywhere soon. Sam promised me they wouldn't leave. For now, you rest, so your head will heal."

"*Humph.*" Doc bumped Ty out of the way and put his arm around her shoulders. "If you were wanting her to rest and heal you should have kept your mouth shut. Now, let's get you back in that bed, little lady."

"Please, can't I sit for a bit? You said there wasn't any fresh bleeding."

Doc shook his head. "It's nighttime. You need to sleep."

"No, please. Everything spins, and it gets so dark when I close my eyes. It's like something pulls me down, down, down." She shuddered. "It's so deep and frightening. So full of shadows, and I don't know who's behind them."

"Could we sit her up in the chair so she doesn't have to try to hold herself up, Doc? I can lift her into it." Ty winked at her, then helped her put her arms around his neck and pressed her head to his shoulder before Doc could object. "Lean on me. I won't drop you."

Her head swirled as he lifted her and carried her to a chair by the window. She might be safely seated, but no matter what Ty said, she'd been dropped. He would marry Anna Blair, and Jacob would be taken away. She didn't have the strength to fight, but she still had one choice. "Could I ask one more favor?" She pulled her hands from Ty's grip.

Ty studied his empty hands before turning his gaze to hers. "I'll do anything you ask."

"Would you tell William I wish to talk to him, if it's not too late?"

A muscle in Ty's jaw twitched as he stood and crossed his arms. His eyes darkened, but didn't leave hers. "The night's still fairly young. I doubt he's sleeping."

She willed her voice to remain steady, though her throat tightened with unshed tears. "That's not what I meant, Ty. If he'll come, could we please be left alone?"

Ty reached for her hand. "Not until I talk with you first." He'd come close to losing her, and he wasn't going to let it happen again.

"You can't be alone with either one of the hotheads, Robin. And that's final." Doc shook his finger at her. "It's enough that this fella picked you up and moved you like I wasn't even here."

"Then the two of you will just have to stay and listen to what I have to say." He certainly didn't relish having an audience, but if that was the only way he could declare his love for her before she talked to William, then so be it. Ty dropped to one knee and gripped Robin's hands. "I won't have William talking you into going back to Chicago with him. Don't leave."

Robin frowned. "If I lose Jacob, I'll have no reason to stay. William would provide a home for me, and my sisters would be secure. Uncle John could continue to live as he has for the past who knows how many years. It would solve a lot of problems."

"But you do have a reason to stay, Robin. Stay for me. Give me a chance. Give *us* a chance. Please."

"We discussed this once before, Ty. You gave up your chances with me, or anyone else, when you gave that ring to Anna Blair." She pulled at her hands. "Let me go. And please accept my apology for interrupting your engagement party."

"I'll turn loose of your hands. But I'll not let you go." He stood and wiped a hand across his brow. "Look." He pulled the ring from his pocket and held it in the air. "You, too, Emma and Doc. Anna no longer has my ring. She gave it back the night you were injured, Robin."

Robin lowered her gaze. "I'm sorry, Ty. I had no way of knowing. Is it . . . my fault?"

Ty bent again and cupped Robin's chin in his hand. "Look at me. Yes, it's your fault, but it's nothing you did. You didn't know my feelings because I never told you. I couldn't. I was obligated to keep my word to Anna. But she released me from that promise, and we parted as friends."

"And now, suddenly, you have feelings for me?"

"It isn't sudden at all. I had feelings for you from the minute I first laid eyes on the dimple at the corner of your mouth." A tiny hint of the dimple appeared, and he caressed it with the tip of his forefinger. "Those feelings only grew stronger when you sent me out to care for my friends after the twister, instead of staying with you. I've watched you with Jacob and with your Uncle John. Then those stupid blisters on your hands because you were too stubborn to quit."

Ty kissed her hands, desperate to convince her. He didn't know how to make himself any clearer. "Robin, please . . ."

"You'd better leave, Ty. She's plumb worn out." Doc motioned to the door. "It's late and tomorrow's another day."

Ty shut the door behind him, and nearly stumbled over William sitting on his haunches outside Robin's room. "Don't even think about going in there, Benson. Doc told me tomorrow's another day. That goes for you, too."

Robin ran her hands along the arms of the chair. "Let me sit here for a bit, Emma. The breeze feels good coming in the window."

Emma adjusted the blanket over Robin's knees. "Oh, sweet girl. Did you listen to Ty at all? He was trying to tell you what you've wanted to hear all this time. And you sent him away."

Robin swiped at her tears. "Three words, Emma. Why is it so hard for a man to say the three words that would make all the difference?"

Emma wiped Robin's tears. "If you weren't hurt so bad, sweet girl, I do believe I'd shake some sense into you right now. Those words are hard for a man, sometimes. You must learn to listen to what he's saying to you without him ever opening his mouth."

"Didn't George ever say he loved you?"

Emma's eyes clouded. "In a thousand different ways, and very few of them needed words."

"But didn't you want to hear him declare it?"

Emma blushed. "The first time I ever heard those words come out of George Ledbetter's mouth was the night I became his wife. Believe me, Robin. They were worth waiting for. I don't know, to this day, that I'd have believed him so much if he would've said them any sooner."

"You mean you married him without him ever telling you?"

"I knew down deep in my soul that he loved me and that one day all those words would come a bubbling to the top. Ty's a deep-hearted man. He has words he's longing to say when there isn't anyone to listen but you and him."

Robin whispered, "Is Doc Mercer still here?"

Emma shook her head. "No, sweet girl. He followed Ty out. But he'll be back. I doubt he'll let you sit for long."

No sooner had Emma uttered the words, than Doc entered the room and shuffled to her chair. "I think you've had enough excitement for one night. Let's get you laid down again, and I'll be finding me a place to stretch out for the night."

Robin laid a hand on Doc's arm. "I'm so sorry you've been away from your office for so long."

Doc winked at her. "*Pshaw*. I've only been here a couple of days. People know where to find me. Albert said he would post a note on my door, and I'm sure Henrietta will keep her eyes peeled for anyone who even comes close to the office. And you know, I spent more time than this a couple of years ago, waiting for a Henry babe to decide he'd make his appearance." He turned to Emma. "I could use your help getting this little gal back to bed."

Robin shook her head and tried to ignore the pain. "Please, let me stay here. Couldn't I sleep here in the chair?"

Doc shook his head. "We can't take a chance of you falling. Even the slightest bump could start that bleeding again. I want you back in bed, but I won't make you take the laudanum right away." He helped Emma get her settled then pushed his glasses up on his nose. "I'll check on you in a couple of hours. If you're still awake then I'll listen to no more argument. Agreed?"

Emma huffed. "You go on to sleep, old man. I'm right here and will check on her myself."

"Won't argue with you. Wake me up if she needs anything."

"I will if it's something I can't take care of myself. Now, good night." She shooed him away with a flick of the wrist.

Doc shuffled from the room, and Emma straightened the light blanket covering Robin.

Robin clutched at the older woman's hand. "I know Doc wants me to sleep, but can we talk for a while?"

"Why, sure we can, child. Let me pull up a chair so I don't get a crooked back from bending over, then you talk away. Mighty good to have you back with us again. Now, what's troubling you?"

"I'm so afraid."

"Of what, dear girl?"

"I don't even know if I can put a name to it. When I close my eyes, I'm afraid of falling so deep into a pit I can't get out, and no one will know where I am. But then I'm afraid to open my eyes. Afraid this bedroom will be my home forever. Afraid I'll not be strong enough to care for Jacob, and afraid his grandfather will take him away. Afraid William will go back to Chicago without me, and afraid to hope that Ty wants me to stay."

Emma slipped her other hand around Robin's and a determined look lit her eyes. "I'm not the one you need to talk to."

"I know, but *Ty's* the preacher. I can't talk to him, Emma."

The smile lines deepened around Emma's mouth. "Well, I think we could even bypass the good preacher and go right to the One who's in charge in the first place." She groaned as she knelt by Robin's bed. "You may have to holler at Doc to get me up again."

"I've prayed, but God either doesn't hear or doesn't care to answer my prayers."

"Oh, sweet girl. The Lord hears every prayer, even those not spoken. As for caring—why else would He let his only Son die for you? He cares all right. But I don't mind doing the talking while you listen."

Only the ticking of a clock and Emma's rhythmic breathing broke through the silence that pervaded the room. *Is she praying? How am I supposed to listen when she's not saying anything? Should I worry about her? She did groan when she knelt.*

As though she could read her thoughts, Emma patted her hands. "Father God, meet us here in this silence because You tell us to be silent and know that You are God."

Robin counted the ticks; then she counted her own breaths. *This is talking to the One who's in charge?*

Emma went on. "You tell us that if we wait on You, our strength will be renewed and we will rise up with wings like eagles. So we're waiting, Lord."

Another long moment passed and Robin wanted to scream. *Why isn't she praying? Why does she insist on reminding God of what He already said? Why isn't she telling Him to make me unafraid? Why isn't she asking Him to take away the dark pit, and to let Jacob stay, and to show me which man I should choose?*

"You tell us to trust in You with all our hearts and not to lean on our own understanding. We're trusting, Lord."

No, Emma. We aren't trusting. We aren't waiting. We aren't praying. She tried to pull her hands away, but Emma squeezed harder.

"We welcome You to this bedside because You tell us where two or three are gathered together, You will be there also."

Is that true? Is God really here? A shiver ran across her shoulders. *If so, where is He? Why don't I feel Him?*

"We acknowledge Your presence in our lives even before we were formed in our mothers' wombs."

But if God knew me then, like Emma says, couldn't He have made me with two good legs?

"We know You don't make mistakes, Father."

No mistakes? What about my leg? And why would He let a little boy lose his mama, or a grown lady fall from a wagon and get hurt her head so badly she's forced to stay in a bed, helpless as a baby?

"And because You are God, You know our thoughts even before we think them."

Another shiver escaped and trickled down her spine. *He knows my thoughts? All the times I've kept quiet but words warred in my mind? The accusations, the doubts, the fears? Even now? This very minute?*

"And we ask You to forgive us for all that which we fooled ourselves into thinking we could hide."

Oh, Emma. How could you know?

"We confess our unbelief and doubts that You answer, when You tell us to call on You and You will show us great and mighty things that can't even understand. We confess fear, even after You tell us to 'fear not' because You are with us. We confess reluctance to ask for direction, when You have promised You will guide us."

How does she know what He said? Can she hear God speak? Why can't I hear Him?

"Now, Father, I claim the rest for Robin that You promised for all those with heavy burdens who would come to You. I claim the forgiveness You promised to give if we would confess our sins. I ask that You show Robin that You are able to do exceeding abundantly above all that she could ever ask or think. And I give You alone the praise for hearing and answering this prayer. In the name of Your Son, Jesus Christ. Amen."

Emma groaned again as she got to her feet, then bent and kissed her on the cheek. "There, now. That wasn't so hard, was it?"

"But . . . but Emma, you never even mentioned Jacob or Ty or William."

"Didn't need to. He knows all about them. He knows your thoughts, and He has His own thoughts for you—thoughts of peace and not of evil, to give you an expected end."

Now Emma was just frustrating her. "What end? What does that even mean? How do you know this, Emma?"

"He wrote me a letter, Robin. And He wrote it to you, too. It's all there in the Bible for you to read over and over again."

"Can . . . can you show me?"

"I'll write down all the places we talked about tonight. You can read it for yourself. But for now, you just close those pretty eyes and rest. I'll be right here beside you. And so will He."

The clock chimed twelve and Robin still lay awake. At some point Emma blew out the lamp, but enough light filtered through the open window to make out the older woman sitting beside her. "Emma? Why aren't you in bed?"

"Oh, I just had a few things to discuss with Jesus."

"I thought you already prayed." She attempted to shift positions but her shoulders wouldn't move.

Emma bent closer. "Do you hurt? I can give you laudanum to help you sleep?"

"I'm tired of lying in one position, but I can't get myself moved. Would you mind helping me? My hips and shoulders burn."

Emma rolled her gently to her side then propped a pillow behind her back. "Is that better?"

Robin tucked one hand under her cheek and reached for Emma with the other. "Thank you. You've done so much for me. I wish you would rest."

Emma's smile radiated in the moonlight. "Real rest comes as much from the condition of the heart as the position of the body, dear girl. Don't you worry about me. But the next time that clock dings I want your eyes to be closed."

Robin giggled. "And if my eyes are closed you'll think I'm asleep? What happened to the condition and position theory?"

Emma shook her finger. "You're getting your sass back. That's a good sign. I can rest sitting up, but you can't sleep with your eyes open. Argument closed."

"Emma?"

"Go to sleep, girl."

"One more question. Then I'll sleep. Promise."

"You're worse than Jacob. Okay. Ask away."

"Who's running the mercantile? I hate that you've had to close down to be here with me."

"Don't you fret your pretty little head. Henrietta Harvey has the key and everyone in town knows where to go if they need anything. There, now. Shut those eyes."

Robin brought the wrinkled hand to her lips. "I love you, Emma Ledbetter."

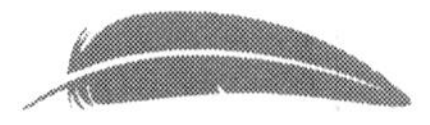

THIRTY-THREE

"Kind of early in the mornin' to be so long-faced, ain't it?" John stroked his horse's velvet nose. "Reckon I know how ya feel, Patch, ole' friend. Most likely a good run would do us both good."

With one foot in the stirrup he hefted himself into the saddle and made his way out of the barn and across the yard. He nodded to one of Ty's ranch hands. Did the kid have any idea how lucky he was having his day all ordered out ahead of him? Sure beat thunder out of feeling like a yo-yo toy, never knowing if you were going to be yanked to the top or left spinning down at the bottom. Only thing a body could hope for these days was for the string to get shorter so you bounced to the top sooner.

Once away from the house, John nudged Patch with a spur and headed him for the Feather. Tomorrow the sisters should arrive—*Lord, have mercy*—and he wanted to tidy up the place a bit for Robin's sake. It helped that William could describe them, but he didn't look forward to having more females around.

John relaxed his grip on the reins and settled into the saddle. The big gelding rode as smooth as a rockin' chair on a lazy Sunday afternoon and would take him home without further prompting. With a good horse under him, the sun warm on his back, and the wind cool on his face, there wasn't much more a man could ask for—unless it would be a fine God-fearing, pie-baking woman waiting for him when he got home. And if she smelled like wild roses, that would be nice, too. The thought left his fingers tingling and his face burning like he was standing over a branding fire. *Now why would I be havin' them kind of ideas goin' through my skull when that sweet little niece is a layin' at Ty's house and the Obed fella might be gonna take Jacob away?*

They topped the hill overlooking the Feather, and John reined his horse to a stop. He never would've imagined thoughts of a woman would fill his mind so. It was his brother's fault, that's for sure, up and dying and making him promise to take care of his nieces. He snorted. It wasn't Emma's fault Lionel died. Maybe he should blame George for leaving Emma alone like he did.

A rabbit darted through the grass and Patch gave a leap. John grabbed the saddle horn, and the horse lowered his head and humped his back. One more stiff-legged hop and John's grip loosened. His teeth clamped onto his tongue as the ground rose to thump his nose. Blood mingled with the dirt under his face. He rolled to his side, squinted through one eye, reached for his handkerchief and groaned as he focused on the hem of a ladies skirt. Well, hadn't he just been thinking how nice it would be to have a lady waiting? *Maybe I've done died and went to heaven.*

"Oh my, my, my. John Wenghold. No wonder you didn't answer your door. I was just a telling Albert, I says to him. 'Albert, you just scurry on over to—'"

"Henrietta Harvey . . ." John rolled back to his stomach and rested his forehead on his folded arms. *Either I'm not dead or I'm not in heaven.* "What are you a doin' way out here this time of day? Never mind, I'm sure you're gonna tell me." He sat up and pinched the bridge of his nose.

"No, no, no. Don't lean forward. Here . . ."

A female voice he didn't recognize clanged from one ear to the other like the clapper on a bell. Then someone grabbed a hank of hair, pulled his head backward, and shoved something sweet smelling up his nostril. John opened one eye. It just wasn't right to have some stranger digging in his nose like that.

"There. You may have to breathe through your mouth, but that will stop the bleeding."

John dropped his head.

"No, keep it back. I know what I'm doing. Oswald is forever coming home after a fight with his face all scuffed. I keep a box of rags right by the kitchen door ready to jam up his nose."

"Well, jumpin' bullfrogs, missy." John opened both eyes. "Who are you and who is Oswald?" Two orbs, black as coffee, sitting on each side of a freckle-sprinkled snip of a nose stared back at him. He sucked a mouthful of air. "How long you gonna make me sit like this? I can't hardly breathe, you know"

"Oh, you'll breathe. It just makes it hard to talk because I'm holding your head so far back. Mrs. Harvey, you count to one-hundred, very slowly, then we'll check to see if the bleeding has stopped." Her black eyes twinkled as she leaned closer. "I'm Wren. You know—Wren Wenghold, your niece—one of Lionel's girls that you never took the time to meet. Oswald is one of the children I care for. I work as a nanny for the Wesley family in Chicago."

"Wren?" He tried to raise his head but was promptly yanked back again. "You weren't supposed to get here until tomorrow."

"Well, it's like I was telling Albert, I says to him—"

"Don't talk, Mrs. Harvey—count. How far are you?" Wren hid a grin with her fingers.

"Thirty-four . . . thirty-five—"

"Mr. Benson knows all the right people, I suppose. We had a private car on the train just for me and Lark. He's very rich, you understand."

Henrietta gasped. "Oh my, then I do hope Albert will—"

"Mrs. Harvey. Please."

"Thirty four . . . thirty five—"

John put his hand around Wren's wrist. Goodness, she was small as a bird. "If you don't let me put my head up we'll be a sittin' here all day," he whispered. "I'm not sure the woman will get them numbers said all the way past thirty-five."

Wren turned loose of his hair and he patted her hand.

"Where's Albert? Don't tell me Henrietta done drove you behind that sorry horse of theirs all the way out here alone?"

Wren straightened.

Land's sake. Even all up and down she's no taller than a fence post. Sitting on the ground he hardly had to raise his eyes to see the all of her.

Wren smiled. "When you came flying off your horse our direction, Albert flew the other way on his. Mrs. Harvey sent him to find a Mr. Ty somebody."

"That would be Ty Morgan. But I don't know how Albert would have gotten past me without me layin' eyes on him."

"Well, your head was in the dirt, Uncle John. Now, where's my sister? I thought she would be here to meet us." Wren brushed at her skirts. "And William? I have a special message for William from his father."

John frowned. "Didn't Mr. Benson tell you why we sent for ya?"

"Only that Robin was anxious to see us and William wanted to surprise her. She will be surprised, won't she?"

John reached for her hand. "Here, see if you can pull hard enough to help me up." She had a surprisingly strong grip. Once on his feet, he brushed his pants off and widened his stance to steady himself. "Now, there ain't gonna be no easy way to say this, so I'll just tell you right off—Robin was hurt bad in a fall from a wagon, and we thought it best if you sisters was here. Doc Mercer thinks she'll get better—in time. But for now she can't be moved."

Wren's forehead ruffled. "So she doesn't know we're here? She must've been hurt very bad for William to send for us. But you haven't answered my question. Where is she?"

John put his arm around her. This little bird was dry-eyed and calm. Only her pale face and wide, dark eyes gave evidence she understood. "She's at Ty Morgan's ranch. We was all there for a celebration when she was hurt."

Henrietta's counting threatened to drown out their conversation, but at least the woman was past forty now.

"I see," Wren said. "And I imagine Albert will give the news that we've arrived? I must tell Lark. She'll be wondering what's keeping us." Her chin quivered. "I do so want to bury my face and cry, but I've been reading about Kansas ever since I knew we would be coming here one day, and I've learned that women must be strong to live on this prairie."

"Cryin' don't mean you're weak, Wren."

"Are you sure?" She sniffed.

"Dead certain."

"Well, then . . ." Tears dripped from her eyes, but didn't get to her chin before she wiped her face with his sleeve and gave him a smile. "There now, enough of that. I believe you need to meet Lark, Uncle John, then perhaps you can instruct us how to get to this Mr. Ty's ranch." She gathered her skirts in both hands. "You can stop counting now, Mrs. Harvey," she called over her shoulder as she marched past.

John shook his head. He didn't know how she did it, but Henrietta Harvey seemed almost speechless in her presence. *Wait 'til Emma meets this one.* He stomped both feet to make sure they were on the ground. The last time Emma came to mind he ended up eating dirt.

The girl sitting ramrod straight in the wagon looked nothing like the other sisters. Her red hair was pulled so tight away from her face it made her look all squinty-eyed, and her mouth puckered like she'd just taken a bite of green persimmon.

John nodded when Wren introduced them. "Lark. Glad to meet ya at last." He extended his hand.

She clutched her own hands away from him so tight her knuckles were white.

"Yes." Her head bobbed stiffly in his direction. "We could have become acquainted much sooner had you accepted Papa's numerous invitations to visit Chicago."

John pulled his hand back. It seemed foolish to dangle it out there like a worm on the end of a fishing line when it was plain as day she wasn't going to take the bait. William was right—this one would be hard to describe. Though Emma would likely win her over in short time. While Lark's lips remained pursed in disapproval, the way she glanced from side to side told him she was more fearful than haughty.

"Did ya have a good trip?" The furrow in the middle of her forehead should've answered his question.

"Mr. Wenghold"—she rearranged her lips enough to spit out the words—"our trip was an unnecessary expenditure. I have neither the time, nor the means to repay Mr. Benson for such an extravagant excursion to a part of the county I have no desire to see, nor plan to ever make my home." She shuddered as she glanced behind her.

Wren frowned. "Lark, that was unkind. Mr. Benson failed to tell us Robin has been badly injured in a fall. William sent for us, not for our pleasure, but for Sister's sake."

Lark's shoulders drooped and her face softened. "Please accept my apologies, Uncle John. Had I known the genuine reason for our hurried trip, I would have attempted to be more . . . more . . . Oh, Robin would be so ashamed. It's this . . . this sea of grass with nowhere to go should we need refuge. And the hot wind. I've never been away from Chicago. I had no idea such wildness could be found."

John reached to pat her hand, pleased she didn't pull it away. "I felt the same first time I laid these country eyes on Chicago. Never could figure out how a body learned to find their way home when all them buildings looked alike. But don't you fret none. Ain't nobody here gonna bother ya, and before long you won't feel so lost. Now, what say we get you girls to the Hawk so you can see that sister?" He gave her fingers a squeeze.

"I would like that, but shouldn't we wait for Mr. Harvey to return? You don't suppose he ran into Indians, or his horse threw him, do you? He's been gone such a long time."

"Oh my, my. How sweet, Miss Lark." Henrietta nudged John away from the wagon. "You know, I said to Albert soon as I laid eyes on you, 'Albert', I says, 'Albert, now there's a young lady with good sense.' I could tell, you know. Mothers know those kind of things. No fancy hairdo and your brown dress and all. Brown just happens to be Albert's favorite color. Has a brown neck dressing that's been his favorite since his papa passed."

Well, jumpin bullfrogs. That little gal is blushin' so you can't hardly tell where her face leaves off and her hair starts up.

Henrietta tipped on her toes and reached for Lark's hand. "Oh, I just knew it. Look at those long slender fingers. You do play the piano, don't you? Oh, you must play for us while you're here. Do you by any chance sing, also?"

"You have pianos out here?" Lark's face lit with excitement. "I didn't suppose I'd see a piano until I returned to Chicago."

John squeezed Lark's fingers. "They's a pianer sittin' in the parlor at Ty's ranch. His mama could make real purty music with it. Once Robin wakes up, I'll be obliged to sit and listen to you tickle them keys all day if you got a notion to do so."

She returned the squeeze. "Thank you."

He nodded.

"Uncle John?" Her eyes twinkled when she smiled.

"Yeah? Can I do somethin' for ya?"

"Do you have any idea how utterly absurd you look with Wren's lace-edged handkerchief dangling from one of your nostrils?"

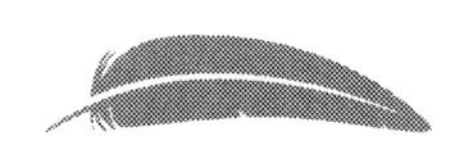

THIRTY-FOUR

"There, now, Ty Morgan, don't you worry about John. I counted all the way to ninety-nine before we got here so the bleeding should have stopped."

Ty reached for Henrietta's pudgy hand.

"Oh, and I have a little surprise for you," she said. "Right here in my reticule, if you would be so kind as to help me out of this wagon."

Listening to this woman babble was one thing, but it was the twinkle of victory in William's eyes as he'd escorted the sisters to see Robin that irked him. And Doc was no help—telling Benson to take all the time they needed because it would do Robin more good than any medicine.

Henrietta straightened her skirts. "Hand me my parasol. It's right there behind the basket of food Florence Blair sent along. She's such a dear, and Anna, too. They're leaving, you know? Oh, of course. If anyone would know it would most certainly be you. Oh, those dear girls from Chicago. I was just telling Albert, I says to him, 'Albert, even though these young ladies have come to see their sister, I doubt they will want to start cooking right away,' so it was indeed a blessing that my dear friend thought of sending—"

"Yes, it was very thoughtful, Henrietta. I will send her a note of appreciation along with you when you return to Cedar Bluff, if you don't mind. I'm sure you're anxious to get back to town, what with the post office and all."

Henrietta patted his hand. "Never you mind the post office. I just put a note on the door saying we went on an errand of mercy to deliver food and cheer to Ty Morgan. Now, if you would be so kind as to offer me a cup of cool water, I must get out of this sun. With skin as lovely as mine I mustn't expose it to the harsh elements."

Ty ducked as she flipped open her parasol. "Would you please hold this for me, Ty? I mustn't forget your surprise." She handed him her parasol while she dug in her reticule, then fanned herself with the envelope she brought forth. "Florence Blair asked that I deliver this. Of course, I was only too willing—knowing you must be most anxious to hear her news." She sniffed the envelope. "Oh my, Florence has such lovely things. Even her stationery is scented."

Ty took the letter. "Let's get you out of this sun, Henrietta." He took her by the arm, picked up the basket of food, and urged her toward the house. Mrs. Blair had not penned the missive he held in his hand. He recognized both the handwriting and the scent of lilacs. *Anna.*

Ty opened the kitchen door to find Emma facing John, one hand on the old man's shoulder. He set the basket of food on the table. "Get too crowded up there?"

Blushing, Emma took a step back. "That, and this crazy old man needed more attention than Robin." She handed John the wet cloth she held in her hand. "Here, put this on the back of your neck."

She motioned for Henrietta to sit. "How nice of you to bring food. Heaven knows no one has taken the time to do much cooking since Robin's accident. Could I get you a cup of cool water?"

"I'd like buttermilk, please, Emma." Henrietta fanned herself with her hands. "Florence Blair sent the food. She's leaving town, you know. I'm sworn to secrecy—though everyone knows I would never divulge a confidence—but John, I don't suppose you could ever guess whom she will visit?"

John snorted. "If you're sworn to secrecy I ain't supposed to be guessin', am I?"

"Oh, you funny man." Henrietta covered her mouth with three fingers and batted her eyelashes. "Do the initials E. P. remind of you anything? I did offer to find an address, you know."

Emma sloshed the glass of buttermilk into John's lap, and Ty squelched a laugh.

"Oh, how clumsy of me. I'll get you another one, Henrietta."

"You mind gettin' me somethin' to sop this stuff off my lap?"

"Use the cloth from the back of your neck." Emma was back in a minute and set a fresh glass of refreshment on the table for Henrietta.

"This rag is wet." John's scowl deepened. He mouthed to Ty, *What'd I do?*

Emma sat beside Henrietta and folded her hands on the table. "How thoughtful of Florence to take time from her busy schedule to think of us."

"If you'll excuse me, ladies—and gentleman—I have some business to attend to." Ty nodded to each. He winked at John. "Looks like you're in good hands.

Henrietta would no doubt keep them occupied long enough for him to read Anna's letter. He climbed the stairs then paused outside Robin's door. Should he knock, and let Doc know where he was? That was unnecessary. Doc knew he was across the hall.

He moved a soiled shirt from the rocking chair by his window and stretched his legs in front of him as he slid one finger under the rose-shaped seal. He unfolded the paper and Anna's familiar fragrance wafted through the room.

My Dearest Ty: It's only fair that you hear what I have to say from me, before dear Henrietta tells you. By the time you read this, Mother and I will be on our way to Pennsylvania. I intend to finish my schooling, and Mother will visit an old friend, Eunice Parker, for a few weeks. I want to thank you, once again, for your forgiveness. When I think of how badly I hurt so many people it breaks my heart. I thank you, too, for praying that night in the church for peace that would pass all understanding. You shall always be my first love, Tyler Morgan, and a piece of my heart will remain in these hills forever. But my fervent prayer is for Robin to recover and take her rightful place as the mistress of the Hawk. Your mother would have loved her. Farewell, my dear friend. I seal this letter with all the love of our youth and one last kiss. I wish you only joy and happiness.

Anna Kathryn Blair

Emma and John were still in the kitchen when Ty emerged from reading Anna's letter.

"Bad news, Ty?"

He shook his head at Emma's raised eyebrows. "Later, Emma."

Laying a hand on John's shoulder he motioned for him to follow and headed for the bunkhouse. "Have you seen Sam or his pa this morning? I need to talk to him and would like for you to be in on the conversation."

"He weren't around when I rode out. Ain't seen nobody since then 'cept a whole bunch of womenfolk a squawkin' around like hens what just saw a fox."

"It was quiet when I brought Henrietta to the house. That hand on your shoulder wasn't making a sound." Ty grinned.

"Don't get no ideas. Henrietta and her talk of E.P. done took care of any notions you might think on. And I stink like sour milk."

Ty glanced at John. He'd sure like to ask him about *E.P.*, but he'd save it for another time. "Where is Henrietta? You didn't let her go to town alone, did you?"

"Didn't let her, but reckon I didn't stop her neither. Albert will find her if she has trouble on the way home. Surprised you didn't hear her leave. That woman can out-puff Kansas wind." He grabbed Ty's arm. "Jumpin' bullfrogs, you're gonna walk me to my death if you don't slow down a mite. Remember I done lost a whole lot of blood. What's your big hurry? Sam said they weren't goin' nowhere."

They reached the bunkhouse, and Ty fished the letter from his pocket. "Here. Read this."

John hitched one foot up on the small bench on the porch of the bunkhouse and mouthed each word as he read. He refolded the letter and handed it back.

"Well?" Ty peered into the older man's face.

"Well, what?" John wiped his forehead with his bandana. "If you is a askin' me what to do next, don't."

"Could you talk with Obed and find out what he plans to do with Jacob? Robin deserves to know."

"And I'll ask you again—what's your hurry? Doc ain't sayin' when or if she'll be able to even go back to the Feather, let alone tryin' to keep up with the little tornado."

"What if she wouldn't have to go back to the Feather?"

"You aim on keepin' her here, are ya?"

"It's on my mind, yes."

"And that Benson fella has it on his mind to take her back to Chicago. You're both a forgettin' Robin's got a mind of her own. Seems to me she's the one what needs to be answerin' your questions instead of me."

"I can offer her more, John. And if we can keep Jacob—"

"You offerin' her a ten-room house to clean and a boy to raise is more? A bunkhouse full of men to cook for is more? More than what, Ty? Ya got a ranch to run and a church full of people what think they own ya, and you owe them."

Ty clenched his fists. "My ma did it. And so did yours."

"Neither my pa or yours could offer anything else. It was all they knew, this land and cattle and all that goes with it. But William can give Robin a choice. Ya need to let her be the one what decides."

"What choice? Stuffy old ladies playing cards all day and planning dinner parties where everyone dresses like monkeys and smiles when they don't feel like it? Are you telling me William Arthur Benson the Third doesn't have a ten-room house, and that he won't one day want to fill it with his offspring?"

"I'm tellin' ya that somebody else would be cleanin' them rooms. Robin wouldn't need to tote water from the well or tramp outdoors when she was wantin' to use the necessary. And they could probably convince one of her sisters to be their nanny." John shook his head. "Don't forget my brother left three of them little birds in the nest. Robin ain't gonna want to fly away and leave the other two clingin' to a branch what's just a flappin' in the wind."

"I thought your offer of a home included the sisters. I can't lose her, John. I want to talk with Sam and his pa. I'm as fond of the boy as Robin, and I intend to do everything I can to convince them to stay on here."

"What you gonna do with another old man? Ain't I enough bother?"

Ty shrugged. "Maybe Emma could put him to work in her mercantile."

John knocked on the bunkhouse door. "I'll listen to you, Ty. But don't you go puttin' ideas in Emma's head."

"Why not give Emma a choice? Let her make up her own mind, John? Could it be the Eunice Parker mentioned in Anna's letter might be the initials E.P. that Henrietta mentioned? She's from here originally, isn't she? You ever heard of her?"

John's mouth hung open, his hand in the air.

At that moment, Obed opened the door with his finger over his lips. "The boy's still sound asleep. Would you mind if we stayed on the porch?"

"Is Sam still asleep?" Ty grinned as John ducked his head. "Mr. Wenghold, here, is real good at giving advice, but doesn't much like to listen to it, even if it's his own."

Obed chuckled. "Haven't you ever heard it's more blessed to give than to receive? I'm sorry, but I was a preacher too long to let that opportunity pass. Sam rode out earlier with a young man by the name of Albert. I think they were going to try to get your horse, Mr. Wenghold."

"I reckon my horse would've found his way back without their help, but I'm obliged." John moved to a chair on the porch. "I got throwed this mornin' by that crazy animal, and I'm not too proud to tell ya these old bones hit the ground mighty hard. Think I'll sit a spell."

"Did you sleep at all, Mr. Morgan?" Obed lowered himself to the porch with a groan. "Me and Sam sat up till daybreak. Guess we both got some stuff off our chests, and tucked away a whole lot more in our hearts."

Ty took advantage of the opening. "I know it's soon to be asking, but have you given any thought to what you will do with Jacob?"

"Oh, I've been giving that question thought since the day I left Missouri looking for my girl. But I never expected to find Sam, too. That puts a different curve to the road I planned to take."

Ty's pulse quickened. Maybe he could help straighten that curve a bit. "You mentioned being a preacher. Do you have a church waiting for you in Missouri?"

"Son, I don't have anything or anyone waiting for me anywhere. The powers that be sent a young man from the city to fill the pulpit full-time before I left, and it made leaving a whole lot easier. The neighbor's put his plow in what little ground I have, and he's welcome to my cabin. I figured I would catch up with my girl, then go wherever she headed."

"Then you won't be taking Sam back to your farm?"

"I don't think I could get Sam to leave here. You've been downright good to him. If you hadn't given him a job, we'd never have met up again. I'm grateful."

Ty paced the length of the porch. "Mr. Mason? Would you still preach if you were to find a church?"

Obed's eyes misted. "You going to build me a church, young man? And what would I do with Jacob? Being a preacher involves being away from home so much. Sam would be the first to tell you I wasn't there when he needed me the most. Finding Jacob gives me a second chance."

"Would you be open to listening to a plan that might help us all?"

Obed nodded. "Talk away. All I have right now is time."

THIRTY-FIVE

William lit the lamp on the bedside table in the bunkhouse. Alone at last, he could read the message his father sent with Wren. Doc had given strict orders no one was to see Robin again until after noon the next day. The only consolation being Ty couldn't see her, either. He slipped off his boots and propped his feet on the bed while he read.

Dear Son: I trust the Wenghold girls arrived safely and in time to see their sister. I thought it best not to apprise them of her condition since they were traveling alone. I hope that didn't cause undue anxiety when they arrived.

It is difficult for me to write this letter. Lionel Wenghold was one of my dearest friends, and I would never want to be accused of dishonoring him in any way. However, your mother and I are very concerned over your seemingly over-exaggerated need to marry Robin to insure her future well-being. She is a fine girl, but you must consider your future as well. With her known infirmity and the unknown complications that might arise from this injury, you would, we fear, be taking on not a helpmeet, but rather an unnecessary burden. Lionel's wish was only to see that his girls were provided for, and I'm prepared to purchase their home at above-market price. By investing the money, and their being able to live so unpretentiously out on the prairie with their uncle, they would be assured of a rather substantial monthly income.

This matter concerns us so greatly that we're asking you to return to Chicago as soon as you can make arrangements. In time, I believe you will see the wisdom behind this appeal. Your mother's cousin sent word her daughter, Lucille, will travel to Chicago for the summer and wishes to stay with us. She will need an escort to the various functions she will attend while here. This would be a very advantageous arrangement, William, and there is no room for further discussion.

William Arthur Benson, II

William wadded the letter and threw it at the wall. This was absurd. He was a grown man, not some irresponsible boy. His father knew why he'd made the trip to Kansas. He also had to be aware of how much he desired to carry on the family tradition of banking.

He slammed the door behind him then stomped to the house. With any luck at all, he would find John alone and—

"You better think twice before you go marchin' into the house like what you is doin' now."

William stopped short. The light from inside spilled onto the porch, revealing John and Emma in the swing.

John eyed him. "You come lopin' up here like you got a race to win."

"I guess you might say I do. I hoped you could maybe help me." He propped one foot on the porch. "But I don't want to interrupt anything."

Emma smiled. "You're not interrupting a thing, William. I need to check on Robin, anyway, if John will just stop this swing so I can get up."

"Well, I say he done come between me and a nice breeze what was a blowin' in my face, but I reckon I can stop it long enough for you to get to your feet." John helped Emma stand. "Now, you get some rest, you hear?"

Emma patted William's shoulder as she passed him. "Watch him, William—he's bossy tonight."

John waited for Emma to enter the house then moved to a chair on the porch "Now, what's got you in such a lather?"

William handed him the letter from his father and waited while John positioned himself to see it from the light which filtered from inside—then waited for what seemed a lifetime while John mouthed each word. Finally, he methodically folded the paper and handed it back.

"You ain't thinkin' I'm gonna tell you what to do, are ya?" John drummed his fingers on the arm of the chair.

"I hoped you would, but I knew you wouldn't."

"Seems to me we done had this conversation before, but I'll ask ya again—why did you come here in the first place?"

William shrugged. Why did he come? Guilt? Duty? Maybe his parents were right in calling his motives overly exaggerated. "I promised her pa I would look out for her. I thought by making her my wife I would be doing that."

"Do you love her?" John leaned toward him. "Can you look her in the eyes, like I'm a lookin' into yours, and tell her you love her?"

"I'm willing to marry her."

John leaned back, his arms across his chest. "That's the wrong answer, son. Let me ask you this—are you just as willing to give up a position in your papa's bank?"

"I don't know anything else. It's what I've been trained to do since I was old enough to tell a dime from a nickel." He wiped his forehead with the flat of his hand. "It's the only way I know to provide for Robin."

"You worked on your uncle's ranch, didn't you? That ain't providin'? Tell that to Ty if you got the nerve."

"Ty's working his own ranch, sir, not his uncle's. There's a difference."

John leaned forward and rested his forearms on his knees. "And they's a difference between money and providin'. See, you can trot on down to your fancy bank ever' day and count money and loan money and lose money and bring home money, and still not be providin' for your family. If you don't love her, you can't tote home enough dimes and nickels to call it providin'." He leaned back in his chair and crossed his arms again. "Now, you be thinkin' on that before you go tryin' to convince Robin, or yourself, that marryin' up with you is what's best for her."

"This probably isn't a fair question, but I'm going to ask it anyway. You want her to marry Ty, don't you?"

John's big hand clamped his shoulder. "Don't matter what I want. You two is so bent on decidin' who gets to hitch up with that little gal you haven't had sense enough to ask her who she wants. Now don't ask me no more foolish questions. I'm tired and so are you. Ain't nobody gonna bother that girl 'til Doc says they can, so ya might as well get some sleep."

William sat on the porch long after John went in. Lightning flashed behind a towering thunderhead, accompanied by a long roll of thunder. There was a storm brewing out on the prairie, but it couldn't be any worse than the one churning in his gut.

THIRTY-SIX

"Where are my sisters, Emma? Why haven't they been in today?" Robin pulled her gown closer. If only she could get dressed again. She didn't like sitting around in nightclothes.

Emma finished tucking the blanket around her legs. "Wren insisted on being taken to the Feather. She wanted to inspect it to make sure she had everything she needed before they brought you home."

"Did Uncle John take them?"

Emma smiled. "Your Uncle John is sly as a fox. No—he made sure he was too busy, and gave Sam Mason that little work detail."

"Oh dear. Now what's he up to, do you suppose?"

"Think, Robin—only try your best to think like John Wenghold. What was the first thing he wanted to do when you arrived?"

"Find me a husband?"

Emma nodded.

"But he wrote that silly notice. He was going to get one through advertising."

"Only because there was no one here for him to manipulate, other than Ty. And he did try that route, you know. Just didn't give the man time enough to make up his own mind."

"Oh, poor Sam." Robin laughed. Mercy, but it did feel good to laugh without her head pounding. "Did Lark go along? Her presence alone will probably stifle any notion of romance if Sam is so inclined. She's hardly stepped foot outside this house, according to little sister."

"Lark is frightened, Robin."

"Of this prairie? These hills?"

"No, I would expect that's the least of her concerns. I think she's afraid because she doesn't know what will happen next. Where you will be. Where that will leave them. Where that will leave her. I think life in general scares her."

"But she knows the plan is for her to come here, too."

"Was she that much different in Chicago, Robin? Did she have friends there? Did she ever go out on her own?"

Robin shook her head. "I'd have to answer 'no' to all those questions. We were all excited when she accepted the position at the music school. It seems the one place she feels confident."

"And if and when she comes out here, she'll leave that one place. She's secure with her music. She knows what to expect of her students, and she knows that what she's able to give them is what they need."

Emma opened the window by Robin's chair. "I'll make more of an effort to visit with her. Maybe ask her to help more. My mama used to make me dry the dishes, even after my Pa died and there was only the two of us. I could never understand it. The woman could bake bread, plant taters, and sew a dress all in the same afternoon. But she needed help with the dishes?"

"I'd imagine she was tired by then."

"Nope. It wasn't her being tired at all. She was wise. It took me lots of years to come to the full knowledge of that dish-drying time. See—that's when we talked. I'd prattle away about everything and nothing, and she'd listen and smile and ever so often ask me a question to keep me going. I got so used to telling her all my little-girl troubles that by the time I was old enough to have real problems it wasn't hard at all to keep right on talking."

"Papa was like that at our house," Robin said, touched at the memory. "We sisters tried hard to never upset Mama. But Papa would sit all night with a forkful of potatoes midair and regale us with tall tales or listen to us chatter. Then Mama would scold, 'Lionel, either eat those potatoes or lay your fork on your plate. How will our daughters ever learn manners with you waving food like a flag.'"

Emma laughed. "My George would have been like your papa, had God blessed us with children." She wiped her eyes. "But you know, I just had a thought. There's a piano sitting down in Ty's parlor. Probably hasn't had a note of music come out of it since Grace Morgan died. Maybe—"

"Oh, that's a wonderful idea. And did you know Albert Harvey also has an interest in music? Do you suppose—?"

"You leave it to me." Emma patted Robin's hands. "We'll have a musicale to celebrate when you get well enough to come down the stairs. See—now it's up to you." She straightened the pillow on the bed. "But for now, Robin, we've kept poor William waiting long enough. He's been propping up the wall in the hallway since Doc said he could see you. I think we best let the poor man in."

"Wait." Robin reached for the older woman's hand. "I'm scared, too."

Emma sat on the side of the bed and took both of Robin's hands in hers. "And what frightens you most?"

She shrugged. "Perhaps the same things that weigh on Lark's mind. What happens if I don't get well? What will become of Jacob, of Wren and Lark? Uncle John can't be expected to care for all of us if we aren't able to contribute to the work."

"And . . . ?"

"And will Ty or William either one want me if I become an invalid? William has a bank to run, and a wife would be expected to entertain, be active in the social community, volunteer for various causes. And Ty has this ranch and all that comes with it. I don't think I even begin to realize what all that would include."

Emma leaned to embrace her. "Such big worries for such a little lady, Robin. But you're trying to borrow what isn't for loan—strength for tomorrow—before you've used up this day's supply. And you know what? I have a feeling by the end of the day a whole lot of questions will be answered for you." She gave her shoulders a squeeze. "Now, may I let William in?"

Robin nodded. "Will you stay?"

"No, sweetheart. There isn't a man alive who wants an old widow lady hanging around while he's trying to declare what's on his mind. But I'll be close by if you need me." She winked and held the door for William.

Robin's lips quivered as she attempted to smile at her caller. Why was he dressed as a banker today? It made her uncomfortable, though this was the William she'd known in Chicago.

He reached for her hands. "I never wanted my coming to be so awkward for you, Robin. But I think you know why I'm here."

She nodded. "I know what you stated in your letter, but I'm not sure that's why you're sitting here now."

"I need an answer, Robin. Your sister brought word from my father, requesting that I return home as soon as possible. I can't . . ."

"But I thought you were staying for a month. Is something wrong? Your mother's not . . ."

"No, everything is fine at home. It's complicated. But I can't leave without knowing if we are to have a future together."

"But I . . . we don't know what will become of Jacob yet. I'm not well enough to travel. There's so much we don't know. How can I make a decision so soon?" If Emma thought William's visit would answer questions, she was wrong. He'd only raised more.

A frown settled between his eyes. "It's not so soon, Robin. We've known one another since we were children. And you know my intentions. Surely you've had time to consider my offer."

"Is that what this is, William? An offer? A business proposition? Is that why you're dressed in your suit?"

He released her hands and stood. "My suit and all it represents is who I am, Robin, what I can give you. It's assurance that you and your sisters will be cared for."

"And what will become of Jacob?"

William turned to the window. "He has a grandfather and an uncle who will look after him."

"But he needs a mother and father." Her heart thumped. How could she make him understand? She couldn't leave Jacob. She couldn't.

"And will he have that if you stay?"

She shrugged. "I . . . I can't answer that. I would hope—"

"You hope . . ." William dropped to his knees beside her. "And does that hope include Ty Morgan?" He cupped her chin in his hands. "Look at me. Do you love him?"

She could hardly breathe. It was one thing to think about it. It was quite another to be forced to voice it.

William kissed her hands. "Your silence screams at me. I think I knew before I asked. I just wasn't sure *you* did."

"Are you angry with me?"

"No, my dear friend, but only if you'll promise to be happy. Morgan doesn't deserve you. But then, neither do I."

"What if he doesn't love me in return?" She hadn't meant to voice the question aloud, but there it was.

"Oh, sweet Robin. I knew the first time I saw him look at you that he loved you. I just didn't know how he was going to manage loving you with Miss Anna Blair in his life, too.

She studied her hands folded in her lap. "If Anna were still in the picture, would that change your proposal to me? Do you truly love me, William, or did you make a promise to Papa to look after me?"

He squeezed her hands. "What makes you think your papa asked me to look after you?"

She laughed, recognizing his hedging for what it was. "Because I know my papa. I also knew when you proposed to me before Papa died that it was to bring comfort to him, not happiness to you. I love you for it, William. And I know marriage must be built on friendship, too. But I don't want to be a project. No girl wants to settle for that when her life's dream is to be loved for who she is alone."

He touched her face. "You need to know that I reached a turning point in my life while here. But believe me, you were never a project. Had you told me you loved me I would have found a way to make it work."

"That sounds so arduous—*to make it work.*"

"Banking is my life. Believe it or not, I love the smell of Chicago as much as you've grown to love the scent of rain on this prairie. I look forward to putting on my crisp white shirts and stodgy ties, and walking, cane in hand, the few blocks to my office. And I would love walking home each evening knowing you were waiting for me."

"And I would hate it, and you would grow to resent a marriage based on a promise you made to a dying man. In retrospect, I think Papa would hate it, too. You know, you aren't the only one he asked to look out for me. Perhaps he wanted me to have a choice. He often lamented I had so few opportunities. One day, according to him, the world will change and people who are different in the eyes of some, will be accepted in the eyes of many."

"You seem much more at peace with accepting yourself. No more kicking against the pricks so to speak."

"I blamed God for so long. I was angry and resentful because He didn't answer my prayers the way I wanted. I decided if I didn't get my way, then He wasn't listening. Emma set me straight on that one. I've a ways to go, but I now realize He's my friend and desires only my best. And His best and my idea of best might be worlds apart."

"Worlds apart like Chicago and Kansas?" He smiled at her.

"Maybe." She searched his face, no longer caring there were no signs of love written there. "Promise me we can still remain friends, William."

"Only if you promise to invite me to the wedding." He kissed her on the nose. "Now my sweet, sweet little bird, I shall return to Chicago. But remember, I'm only a telegraph message away."

"You will always be much closer than that. There's a special place in my heart with your name on it." Her fingers tightened around his. It was scary to let go.

The light coming through the crocheted curtains in Robin's room cast lacy shadows dancing across the pale yellow walls. A slight breeze billowed them, like a hoop under a lady's skirt. Robin folded her hands on her lap. It seemed such a long time ago that she'd worn a dress of any kind. Doc said another week before she could attempt walking alone, but only in the bedroom with Emma present. She hated that William's last memory of her would, no doubt, be a contrast of his business suit and her cotton wrapper.

The chatter of voices downstairs signaled her sisters' return from the Feather, and she welcomed the *thump, thump, thump* of footsteps on the stairs. At last—someone to talk to. She closed her eyes and played the game which had become the one entertainment she was allowed—guess who's coming? She'd wait until they entered to open her eyes and confirm her prediction. But this time she needn't play. Even with all the stomping, Wren's steps were as telling as her giggle.

"Robin? Robin, are you awake?" Wren bustled through the open door and perched herself on the edge of the bed, arms folded across her chest. "That Sam Mason makes me so mad. Do you know what he did? I told him I was going to come right back here and tell you, but he said you weren't his boss. Can you believe the nerve? Of course you're his boss, and I told him just wait and see. And he just laughed. Do you know what he did?"

Robin took a deep breath and willed Wren to take one, too. "No, I don't know what he did, but I'm sure you would like to tell me. But, Wren, he's right. I'm *not* his boss. He answers to Ty Morgan or Rusty or Uncle John."

"All men, and what do they know about cleaning a house?"

"You expected him to clean house at the Feather? It shouldn't have taken much work, Wren. Except for a few dishes in the sink the day we came for the celebration, I left it clean and tidy. There hasn't been anyone there except, perhaps, Uncle John."

"*Humph*. You think Uncle John picks up after himself? There were dirty socks by his chair in the living room. Dirty socks in his bedroom and two pair under the kitchen table."

Robin giggled. "That's all? Dirty socks? So what did you do, or say, to Sam Mason to get you in such a dither?"

"I'm not in a dither. Mr. Mason is the one who got all steamed up, then he laughed at me when I"—she leaned to whisper—"fell on my bottom."

Robin put her hand to her mouth. This was not a good time to be amused, at least for Wren to see. "You fell? How? Did he trip you? Why are you so upset with Sam?"

"He let go of the sock."

Robin chewed on her lower lip—hard. She might not be able to squelch this giggle. "And were you *in* this sock? I'm afraid you've lost me."

Wren stood, hands on hips. "Lark went upstairs to check the bedrooms for clean bedding, and Sam just stood there doing nothing, and I asked him why couldn't he help instead of gawking, and he said he wasn't gawking, but he didn't know what to do, and I told him to look around, there was surely something he could find that needed picked up or put away." She huffed before taking a deep breath.

Robin held up a hand. "Slow down. Speak one sentence at a time, Wren. I'm listening, and I'm a captive audience. So you asked him to look for something to do? Did he?"

"He was disgusting. He picked up one of Uncle John's dirty socks and held it away from him as far as his arm would reach with one hand, and pinched his nose shut with the other, and he was smiling. I could see him smile. 'Here,' he said, 'is this what you wanted me to do?'"

"And?" There must be more to this story.

"And I told him he needn't be so smarty, and I grabbed to take the sock from him, only he wouldn't let go, so I pulled harder, and he gave a yank, then let go and I . . . I fell on my bottom. And he laughed. He makes me so mad." Wren fell to her knees, laid her head in Robin's lap, and sobbed.

Robin stroked her sister's hair. "I think you're more embarrassed than angry, Wren. And no doubt you've held in a whole lot of tears since your arrival. You go ahead and cry. I'll ask Emma about the socks. I'm wondering if Uncle John's changed clothes at all."

Emma stepped into the room with an armload of folded laundry. "Well . . . Oh, I'm sorry to intrude. Is this a private conversation?"

"No, Wren and Sam just had a little tussle. But Wren said John has dirty socks strung throughout his house. Do you think he's even changed clothes since I was hurt?"

Emma placed the stack of laundry on the bed. "I'll put this away later." She sat on the edge of the bed. "John has changed his clothes. I've made sure of that. I've done laundry here, and Sam Mason has helped, if you can believe that—"

"I can't believe it." Wren's muffled voice interrupted.

"Wren, let her finish."

"I was going to say that John has gone home on occasion when you were still not with us."

Robin giggled. "So you think he just went home to change socks?"

Emma shook her head. "No, no. That dear man has been nearly out of his mind with worry for you, Robin. You have to remember he's been alone for a long time. I don't think he ever thought he'd love you like he does. I suspect each pile of socks represents a place he sat and prayed. Don't ask me why I think he took his socks off to do it." She grinned. "Now, tell me about this tussle between Sam and Wren."

Robin relayed the story, grateful Wren couldn't observe Emma's face. "I think it might be a good idea for Wren to help you with dishes tonight. Perhaps she could dry them for you."

Emma nodded in understanding. "I would like that very much." She stood and patted Wren's back. "In fact, dearie, if you think you've had your cry, I could use your help right now."

Wren stood and wiped her eyes with the hem of her skirt. "Mama would fuss at me for doing this, wouldn't she?"

"Not for crying, Wren, but she *would* admonish you to use your handkerchief, and she would insist you carry a lace-edged one."

Wren giggled. "I stuffed that one up Uncle John's nose the first day we came. I don't know what became of it, but I don't think I want it back. I do have another one." She reached into her pocket and retrieved her handkerchief and an envelope. "Oh, Robin. I forgot to give you this." She handed her a letter. "I hope you're not mad at me. Henrietta Harvey gave it to me before she left that day she brought us here. She said I should keep it until you were well enough to read it. You are well enough, aren't you?"

"I suppose that depends . . . Who's it from?" Robin sniffed the envelope. Lilacs. Why would Anna Blair be sending her a letter?

"Wren, why don't you and me go down and see if we can get something rounded up for supper. That will give Robin a little privacy to read her letter. You can come back up for a while this evening."

Robin turned in her chair to take advantage of more light from the window. Her heart tripped. Ty said she'd broken their engagement. What possible reason would she have to write to her—and have it hand-delivered? She slipped her finger under the wax seal.

Dear Robin: I simply do not have the words to sufficiently express my deepest regret for the way I treated you these past weeks. I have no right to expect it, but from the bottom of my heart I ask your forgiveness.

At a time when you needed a friend, I behaved as though you were my enemy. You were not, Robin. I am my own worst foe. I was jealous and deceitful. And I knew from the first encounter that you would one day emerge the victor in a battle you never chose and a war you didn't know had been declared.

I don't know what will become of you and William, but you need to know that Ty Morgan loves you. I've never been more sure of anything in my life. I've watched him since that first Sunday in church. And the day you were injured, I knew without a doubt that his heart belonged wholly and completely to you. And I believe you love him, too, dear girl.

I have visited with Ty, and he has graciously forgiven me for the charade and torment I put him through. He is an honorable man. He deserves someone like you, and I pray you will give him an opportunity to prove his love for you.

This is not the way I would have chosen to speak these words.

However, Doc Mercer would not give me permission to visit with you, and by the time you are well enough to read this on your own, Mother and I will be on our way to Pennsylvania. I've asked your sister Wren to determine the best time to give you this letter.

Get well, dear Robin. Ty and that little boy need you. My prayer is that you will become the mistress of the Hawk. Ty's mother would have loved you. I hope we might one day become friends.

Sincerely, Anna Kathryn Blair

THIRTY-SEVEN

Robin stood in the middle of the bedroom at Ty Morgan's ranch. As eager as she was to return to the Feather, how she would miss these cheery sunshine yellow walls where she'd been nestled since her injury three weeks ago. Time played tricks with her, but within these walls she'd experienced such comfort and healing—and a newfound relationship with the Lord. And did she dare hope—the love of Ty Morgan himself?

"Robin?" Lark's face revealed frustration. "I . . . could you help me fasten this string of pearls? I don't even know how."

Robin stepped behind her sister to close the clasp on the string of pearls Emma had insisted on loaning her. She caught her sister's gaze in the mirror. "You look lovely. I'm glad you consented to Emma's offer of a new dress. The soft green looks beautiful with your red hair." She leaned and kissed the top of Lark's head.

Lark smoothed the hair away from her temples. "I don't know, Robin. My hair feels as though it will fall in my face, and I've never worn jewelry, you know."

"I do know, and that's why I'm insisting you wear it tonight. And your hair is very attractive. Wren did a fine job of arranging it. It just feels loose because you're so used to pulling it back so tight. I don't think I've ever seen you look this happy. Could Albert Harvey have an influence?"

Lark turned and grasped Robin's hands. "Albert told me my voice was as beautiful as my face. Can you believe that? Robin, no one—other than Professor Lucas—has *ever* called me beautiful. Not even Papa.

"Professor Lucas called you beautiful?" Robin frowned. This was not the time to voice her concerns in regard to that little bit of news. She was up and around, feeling like her old self again. Lark and Albert were giving a musicale, and Ty had invited the neighbors far and wide to celebrate.

"Professor Lucas says nice things to all his students, Robin. I only mentioned it because sometimes I pretend he meant it special for me." She blushed. "Silly of me, isn't it?"

"If Albert told you something so sweet, then believe him. Albert is not a man of words he doesn't mean."

Lark laced her fingers together. "It was sweet of him, but I shan't make more of it than it can ever be."

Robin bent to check her own hair in the mirror. "Why can't it be more, Lark? Don't you like him even a little bit?"

Lark stood. "Here, sister"—she patted the back of the small chair in front of the dressing table—"you need to sit a spell before descending the steps."

Robin seated herself. "Nonsense. I've been up and down these steps countless number of times this past week. But I'll sit to please you. Now, sister, you are ignoring my question."

"I do like him, Robin. He is every inch a gentleman. But please try to understand what I'm going to tell you. This isn't the best time, but I'm not sure there would be a good time."

Robin pivoted in the chair. "That sounds so gloomy, Lark."

"It isn't so bad. I just don't want you, or Albert—and especially not Mrs. Harvey—to get false hope of my returning to Kansas anytime soon. I . . . I don't want to leave Chicago."

"Lark? Of course you're coming to Kansas. We made a promise to Uncle John. Papa would be ashamed if we were to ever break our word. And . . . and what else would you do?"

Lark pulled at the lace on her cuffs. "I can stay in Chicago and teach."

"You can teach out here, Lark. I'm sure you would find families who would love for their young daughters to have an opportunity to have music lessons."

"How many families do you know? Two? Five? That would not earn my living and you know it."

Robin stood and put her arms around Lark. "Perhaps making your own living won't be a concern. Albert seems interested."

Lark wiggled loose from her embrace. "Don't tease, Robin. It's not like you to poke fun."

"I am not teasing, nor poking fun. But you must promise you will give this more thought. We can't decide tonight."

"I know. I didn't intend to even broach the subject until closer to my leaving. I *will* give it more thought. But please don't pressure me, nor say anything more about Albert."

Hearing voices downstairs, Robin linked her arm in Lark's. "No pressure. Now, I think we have guests to greet." She stopped her sister before they reached the bottom step. "I want you to know how very proud I am of you, Lark. I never had a formal 'coming-out' party, you know. Mama wouldn't allow it since I wouldn't be able to dance. Thank you for making my 'coming-down' party so very special."

Ty slipped his arm around Robin's waist as they walked into the night. "I have permission from both Doc Mercer and Emma—you may accompany me on a stroll, my lady."

"Ah, but you've not asked *my* permission." Robin smiled up at him.

"You're right, I haven't." He turned to her with mock gravity. "Miss Wenghold, might I have the distinct pleasure of accompanying you on a stroll around my barnyard?" The dimple perched on the corner of her mouth gave him confidence to continue. "We shall observe, by the light of the moon, the cow, the horse, and the . . . and you, of course." He dared to smooth the tiny wrinkle that settled on her forehead then let his finger brush the corner of her mouth. "Do you know that from that very first night I saw you, that little dimple has haunted me? I've wished I could somehow put it in my pocket for safekeeping."

Robin lowered her eyes. "And what would you have done with it then, Mr. Morgan?"

He gazed into her eyes. "All those days, when we didn't know if you would make it through this injury, I would have done this . . ." He cupped her face in his hands and traced the corner of her mouth with his thumb. "I'd have put it back on, and then"—he brushed his lips across the dimple—"I would have sealed it to stay forever, just like that." What was he thinking? She'd done nothing to invite such behavior, and he'd just taken advantage of her need to stay close to him so she wouldn't fall. Yet, she'd not pushed him away. And even now, she stepped closer and laid her head against his chest.

"I've asked Doc Mercer if I might go back to the Feather, and he's given his permission. Wren wants to go over again tomorrow and make sure things are still in order, then Uncle John will take me home the next day. Jacob will accompany us."

"But . . ."

She lifted her head and put her fingers across his lips. "Shh. Please don't say anything more, Ty. Tonight has been more than I ever dreamed. My sisters are here. Lark was brave enough to sing. So many people I didn't know telling me they've prayed I'd recover. And now . . . this moonlight stroll. Don't spoil it with words you might come to regret later. Remember?"

"Robin . . . please."

"I'm quite tired. I think I best start back. I'm surprised Doc hasn't come looking for us."

He put his arm around her waist as they followed the path back to the house. He'd told Doc to leave them alone. He'd told Emma, too, and persuaded Sam to take Jacob to the bunkhouse for the night. This wasn't the way the evening was supposed to end.

Robin undressed and climbed into bed with only the light of the moon streaming through her window. The house had been eerily quiet when she and Ty returned, and he waited at the bottom of the stairs for her to say she'd reached the top safely before saying good night. She had stood in the dark hallway, and it seemed forever before the soft click of the door told her he had gone.

She turned onto her back and put her hands behind her head. Should she have stopped Ty from speaking? He had declared his love—at least that's what Emma called it—but that seemed ever so long ago. What if he was going to say he spoke too soon, or that he'd only offered marriage to keep William at bay, but now he could see it would never work?

Something pinged against her window—or had she imagined that, too? Her pulse raced. Another ping, this time unmistakable. She slipped out of bed, opened the window, and knelt in front of it. Ty stood, bathed in moonlight, under the tree that provided shade for her room during the heat of day. "What are you doing? Is something wrong with Jacob?" If she didn't keep her voice down, everyone in the house would be awake.

"You didn't answer me." He moved away from the tree and widened his stance.

"I didn't answer you? What was the question?" She'd stick her head out a bit more, but she hadn't bothered to grab her wrapper.

"No question. I said good night, and you didn't answer."

"This is crazy, Ty. Good night."

"No wait. I . . . I'm not done."

"Ty, please . . ."

"Don't leave, Robin. Promise you won't leave until we can talk again. But I have to go to town tomorrow. I need you to promise you'll be here when I return. Please."

"I told you. Uncle John will take me the day after tomorrow. Now, may I go to bed?" Would he detect the smile in her voice?

"Robin? Wait."

Okay, let see how serious you are, Mr. Morgan. "Ty, unless you sing to me, I'm going to bed and that's where you need to head yourself."

"You think I can't, Miss Wenghold?"

In the moonlight his teeth shone even and white. *Why am I noticing his teeth? Robin, have you lost all decorum? You're in your nightclothes, hollering down at a man, chancing the entire household hearing, and you notice his teeth?*

"I don't doubt your ability, Mr. Morgan, only your nerve to do such a thing."

Ty clasped his hands to his chest and stepped forward. "'Believe me, if all those endearing young charms, which I gaze on so fondly today . . .'"

Robin grabbed the curtain and wrapped herself as best she could. The room was dark. Could he really *gaze fondly*?

"'. . . Were to change by tomorrow and fleet in my arms like fairy wings fading away. Thou would still be adored . . .'" He opened his arms and raised his hands toward her. "'. . . As this moment thou art . . .'"

She couldn't let him continue. The richness of his voice tingled down her back, seeped through her body, and tied a knot in her stomach. She wrapped the curtain tighter. Surely he must be able to tell even from down there that her face was burning.

"All right," she said, trying to keep her voice low. "Good night."

"I'll go only if you promise to meet me tomorrow under the big cottonwood tree in the back. There's a bench for you. Wait for me. Please."

Robin reached above her head and pulled the window shut. Why did he have to ruin it? She'd been sitting on that bench when Anna Blair confronted her. So much had happened since then. But couldn't he have picked a different place? She'd not promised. Dare she peek to see if he were still there?

She peeked. He was still there, his long frame propped against the trunk of the tree. He wiggled his fingers at her, and she ducked below the sill.

Uncle John's jumpin' bullfrogs, I've been caught.

"Lark?" Robin approached the big cottonwood tree. "I wondered where you were. You didn't answer when I called." She lowered herself to the bench beside her sister.

Lark shrugged. "I thought if I came out here for a while I might be able to see what it is that endears this Kansas prairie to you so."

"I've asked myself that a good number of times. I'm not sure I can give you an answer. Not one you would understand, anyway."

"Does it ever just . . . stop? Look. As far as you can see it moves, in ripples, in waves. It never quits. The heat. The dirt swirls down the lane twisting and turning, you don't know which way to move to escape its wrath. And that buzzing noise undulates in my ears day and night to where I can't tell if it's my pulse pounding or those ugly green insects. Even at night the noises don't stop, and the heat doesn't relent." She covered her face with her hands.

Robin slipped her arm around her sister's shoulder. "Lark? Remember when Mama and Papa took us to Lake Michigan?"

Lark sniffed. "I suppose you are going to tell me your prairie is like that lake."

"It is, in a way. We couldn't see the other shore, but we knew it was there somewhere, and in between there was another whole world. This prairie ebbs and flows just like that water, sister. Some mornings the grasses barely ripple, other times they toss and roll like waves. Remember the roar the waves made as they were driven by an unseen force upon the shore? There are days when the house at the Feather shudders just like that when the wind rushes across the grass."

"You've learned to love it, haven't you?"

"Ty says you learn to love it or you leave. I didn't believe it at the time. All I could see is exactly what you see. But then I became her friend and found just how beautiful she was."

"She? Kansas has a gender?"

Robin laughed. "Oh, sister, I asked the very same thing. Then Ty explained how much this Kansas-land is like a woman—gentle enough to cradle the creatures nestled in its bosom—wild enough, unpredictable enough to be exhilarating, thrilling, even dangerous."

Lark's face turned pink. "Robin Wenghold, Mama would take to her bed with that description. What do you know about a woman being . . . being wild or thrilling?"

"I don't. I only want you to see this country like I see her. You were afraid of the vastness of the lake, too. Remember? Then Papa picked you up and walked into the water with you. He waded in a long distance before it got deep enough to get your toes wet, then you cried when he made you get out. That's how I feel. I got my toes wet on the back of Ty's wagon, jumped into the deep when we found Jacob, and now I can't bear the thought of leaving. I don't want to get out, Lark."

"Albert says I haven't given it a chance. Maybe he's right."

"You need to give Albert a chance, too. Please consider it. At least say you'll come for an extended visit before you decide. Plan for next summer."

Lark stood and smoothed her skirt. "We have one more week here, Robin. I'm not ready to promise for next summer." She kissed Robin's cheek. "Ty will come looking for you here when he gets back from town, and I don't think he would be pleased to find me with you."

"You heard?" Robin laughed.

"If he'd been in Chicago the neighbors would have summoned the constable. Maybe the prairie has more advantages than meets the eye—or the ear." She turned and called back over her shoulder on her way to the house. "Ask him if he knows 'Aura Lea.'"

Robin lowered herself to the bench under the tree. She'd expect that retort from Wren. But Lark? And she was even smiling.

THIRTY-EIGHT

Robin leaned her head against the rough bark of the tree. Sunshine peeking through the branches above dappled the ground with shadows. In the distance a meadowlark warbled and she laughed aloud. Lark would not appreciate knowing she was perhaps named after such a raucous bird. She closed her eyes and let the music of the wind in the grasses fill her heart. If only Lark could come to know this land's melody, its rhythm.

"Wake up, Robin. We have somethin' 'portant to show you."

Robin woke with a start. She'd only meant to close her eyes for a short time. Now Ty stood before her, holding Jacob by the waist while the boy rubbed his nose on hers and waved a piece of yellow paper in front of her eyes.

"Why do your eyes look all funny? It looks like those round things are gonna roll on top of your nose." He giggled. "Me and Ty have been talkin' like mens. You wanna talk? First you gotta read this."

"My eyes are funny because you're so close I have to look cross-eyed." She moved his head away. "That's better. Now maybe the two of you should sit down."

Ty settled on the ground in front of her, pulling his long legs up and resting his arms across them. Jacob leaned his bony elbows on her knees.

"Well, which one of you is going to tell me what's so important you interrupted a perfectly good nap?" She took the envelope from Jacob.

"No. Let me. Let me. Then you can read it." Jacob's mouth twisted as he worked to open it. With his chest puffed with pride he handed her the folded note.

"Purchase of home complete. Sisters may stay as long as necessary. Say yes to the next question the boy shoots your way. That's an order. Always your friend. William.

She looked at Ty. "Do you know what this says?"

His eyes twinkled as he pulled a matching envelope from his pocket. "Uh-huh. Got one, too. Mine came with instructions. Did yours?"

She nodded.

He winked at the boy. "Jacob, I believe it's your turn. Do you remember what we practiced?"

Jacob hopped on one foot and giggled. "I 'member real good." He stood straight and tall, hands to his side. "*Ahhemm.*" He pulled one eye shut with his fingers. "Me and Ty was wonderin'—would you be my mama?"

"Wha—?"

Jacob clapped his hands. "Please, please say yes cuz if you be my mama, then Ty says he will be my pa, and I been prayin', and Papaw says it's okay with him and Uncle Sam—that's what I call him now 'stead of just Sam—says it would be fine and dandy, and—"

Robin cocked her head and smiled. "You're making a child do your bidding?"

His gaze didn't waver.

Her throat tightened as he leaned toward her and brushed his hand along her cheek.

"I know how hard it is for you to tell him no."

"Jacob, can you give me one good reason why I should say yes?" She couldn't look away.

Ty shook his head. "No, Jacob. It's my turn now." He held the telegram before her again. "Because this says you must follow instructions."

"That's it? Because a man in Chicago said I should?"

Ty rose to his knees, his eyes still locked onto hers. "No. Because this man in Kansas wants you to. Say yes, Robin, because we love you."

"*We* love you? I thought you wanted to answer for yourself. It was your turn, remember?" She held her breath as he brushed his hand across her lips.

"Say yes, Robin, because *I* love you."

"You love me?"

Ty pulled her to her feet and slipped both arms around her waist, drawing her close. He smiled. "I. Love. You."

"But what if—"

He shook his head. "No buts, Robin, and we'll face the what-ifs together."

"And Jacob? Can we keep Jacob?"

His chuckle rumbled along her cheek. "Obed Mason has agreed to become the new preacher, so he'll be staying. But he wants Jacob to have the advantage of both mama and papa. I told him I'd be his papa, but I'd need to shop around for a good woman to play the other part."

She leaned away from him. "That's not funny, you know."

He cupped her face in his hands. "Then say yes."

Robin closed her eyes and her head nodded against his.

How could she answer when his lips covered hers?

EPILOGUE

"If we ain't a sorry mess." John eyed the knot of people sniffling and wiping their cheeks. "Ain't this supposed to be one of them happy-from-now-on times?"

A driving rain forced the onlookers to stay indoors while Robin and Ty hurried to their buggy. Jacob's hand-scrawled *Just Married* sign hung limp, but matched the wet faces of friends gathered at the back of the church.

"Kinda fittin' isn't it? She flew in on a storm, Ty hitched up with her in one. Guess this is one Robin what won't be leaving come winter. What you think about that, Emma girl?"

"No amount of thinking could have prepared me for what God provided so exceeding abundant. Jacob's got his ma and pa, plus a grandpa and uncle. The church has a new preacher, and before winter a little Wren will make her nest at the Feather."

Lark averted her eyes when John drew her to him. "And I'll look forward to your arrival next spring."

She shrugged and pulled away. "Spring is a long way off, Uncle."

"Are you and Emma gonna get married, Uncle John?" Jacob skipped circles around him. "Cuz you're standin' awful close. Ty and Robin liked to stand close, too. That's why they got married."

"Oh, Brother Mason." Henrietta's lace jabot fluttered as she pushed and singsonged her way through the throng.

"Oh, brother, is right," John muttered. Emma's elbow dug into his ribs.

Henrietta puffed to a stop in front of Obed. "I just says to Albert, I says, 'You know, son, we must ask the new preacher for Sunday dinner.' My, what a fine strong voice you have. Why, I just loved the way you pronounced them husband and wife. It was so . . . so manly sounding." She fluttered her eyelashes and fanned herself with her gloves.

Obed bowed. "I do thank you, Mrs. Harvey. I'd be most happy to accept your invitation." He grinned at John. "Mr. Wenghold has told me all about your delicious ham and sweet potatoes and what a fine hostess you are."

John squirmed. *Jumpin' bullfrogs.* Emma's elbow nearly sliced clear through him. What he told the man was to be careful because Henrietta's hams were dry as dirt in the middle of a Kansas summer.

"He did?" She swished her gloves at John. "Why, John." Her cheeks glowed pink.

Emma stepped on his toe. "Yes, John, aren't you just a talker?"

Henrietta bustled a bit closer, and John's eyes watered from the heady scent of cloves.

"Why don't you plan to come, too, John? I've plenty of room at my table for two men. And guess who will be there? E.P. Does that give you a hint?"

Emma slipped her hand into John's and bent his little finger back. Doggone. If that Harvey woman said one more word he would be sore for days. "I'm sorry, Henrietta. I done got other plans, but I reckon the good Reverend here would enjoy a sittin' and eatin' ham with ya."

Her face drooped. "Well, I suppose if you have other plans—"

"Oh, he has plans all right, Henrietta." Emma pinched his elbow as she turned and stalked to the front of the church.

Now wouldn't that make granny's cat howl. "Emma, wait." He followed her, clamped his elbows tight to his sides, made sure his feet were out of the way, and plunged his hands into his pockets before starting a conversation. He peeked around the brim of Emma's bonnet. "Now, you wanna tell me why you is so het up?"

She crossed her arms over her bosom. "And what makes you think I'm *het up* as you say?"

"Mostly cuz you done smashed my toe, pert near cracked a rib, and bent my little finger like a twig. Is that a new bonnet?" *A smart man would've mentioned the new bonnet first thing, John Wenghold.*

Emma turned and fluffed the large bow under her chin. "You noticed?"

The twinkle in the woman's eyes made his mouth go dry. "Course I noticed—first thing." He ran his tongue over the roof of his mouth. No blisters so far, but they'd sure be coming if he couldn't change the subject.

"But you didn't say a thing." She lowered her eyes.

"Well, now, I was a-waitin'."

"Waitin' for what? The rain to stop? Henrietta Harvey to invite you for lunch?"

She was gettin' all het up again. Best way to stop a stampede was to get in front of the lead animal and pray they'd turn. A fella only had one chance before he got trampled. He reached for her hand and took a deep breath. "I was a waitin' 'til we could be alone, Emma girl. Thought I'd buy you that steak dinner I owe you—unless you want to bargain for the whole critter."

Emma smiled and hooked her arm in his. "John Wenghold—did your mama ever tell you you'd get blisters on your tongue if you told a lie?" She squeezed his arm. "But I'll take that steak dinner. And I'll expect the first waltz at the Christmas dance, too."

Christmas? John dared to put his arm around Emma's waist. Would he ever learn the ways of this woman?

Lark pressed her forehead against the window as the train carrying her and Wren back to Chicago prepared to chug away from the Cedar Bluff depot. She would miss her sister, but how good it would be to see her music students again. They depended on her. She'd not had anyone depend on her before she began teaching. Robin was the oldest, and by virtue of birth was the leader. Lark cast a sideways glance at her little sister preening herself in the window's reflection next to her. Wren was the cute one—the saucy, flighty, fun one—who assumed everyone must love her. A lot like Robin's prairie, she surmised—unpredictable, ever changing, and you learned to love her or leave her alone. Lark smiled at the comparison. She'd need to remember to tell Robin.

She'd also need to think of a way to make her sister understand she had no intention of returning to Kansas. At least not for an entire summer and certainly not to make it her home. Professor Lucas intimated that perhaps she might be interested in a year-around position at the school. She'd wait to apprise Robin of that bit of information, however. Robin's scowl whenever his name was mentioned signaled a concern she didn't care to pursue.

"Wren? Goodness, girl. Will you get away from that window? You're using it as a mirror but the people on the platform must think you're making faces at them."

"Maybe you should be the one looking out the window, Lark." Wren winked.

"Who taught you to wink, Wren Elizabeth? That's vulgar."

"Jacob taught me, believe it or not." Wren shrugged. "I'm going to miss him something awful. Robin's so lucky. A new husband and a child without ever having to . . ."

"That's quite enough, Wren. You needn't spell it out nor announce it to the people across the aisle."

"Well, are you going to look or not? You're so busy scolding me that you'll miss it. The train is already moving."

"Oh, what could be so important that you risk creating a scene to make sure I see it?" To stop Wren's insistence she turned to comply. The faces were beginning to blur as the train picked up speed—but not enough to distort that of Albert Harvey. Why was he there? She had explained there could be nothing more than an interest of music between them and asked him not to come to see her off. But there he stood, one hand in the air in a farewell gesture that now included all those with windows facing the depot.

"Did you see him, Lark? I think he was looking for you. Poor man's arm is probably sore from holding it in the air for so long. Did you . . . did he declare his intentions?"

Lark rolled her eyes. Even the woman across the aisle seemed poised for her answer. "Would you please keep your voice down? *If* Albert had any intentions and had thus declared them to me, do you think I would make a public announcement?"

"You needn't be so prickly, Lark. I only asked because . . ." She leaned closer. "Did you know Uncle John was going to advertise for a husband for Robin? What if he decides to do that for us? Wouldn't you like to come back to Kansas with intentions, even if it's Albert Harvey?"

"Robin wouldn't allow Uncle John to mail order a husband for her, and I doubt she'd allow him to do anything of the kind for us. Now, you might as well relax. We've a long ride ahead of us." She leaned her head against the seat and closed her eyes. Albert was a nice man, but Professor Lucas's offer was much more palatable than a lifetime in the company of Henrietta Harvey.

"Please don't go to sleep, Lark. I'm not through talking. I'm not taking any chances. I'm going to do my own advertising."

Lark bolted upright. "You're what? That's utter nonsense. You'll do no such thing. For shame. How can you even entertain such an idea?"

"Oh, gracious. You'd think I was going to rob a bank. I don't intend to sit back and let Uncle John order me a husband. I've already thought of a discreet notice I can post in only the finest newspapers."

"There is nothing discreet about advertising for a husband, Wren." She cast a furtive glance around her. How many travelers had heard this declaration?

"You go ahead and scold and scoff all you want. I'm a grown woman and I can make up my own mind. I will return to Kansas predisposed."

"Predisposed? Wha . . . ?"

Wren giggled. "It means prepared. I found it when I was searching for words to put in my advertisement. I'm going to be prepared, sister. Just you wait and see."

♥

ACKNOWLEDGEMENTS

To our sons and their wives: *Kip and Becky, Rob and Tami,* who have encouraged me this entire journey. I love you all so very much, and value your prayers and encouragement. They think I am going to get rich . . . and they will inherit it. Won't they be surprised!

To my critique partners, past and present: *Sara, Cherie, Susie, Jennie,* and *Peg,* who have had the courage to read my work, chew it up, spit it back at me, and rejoiced when I've finally gotten it right.

To my writing group: *Christian Writers Fellowship,* in Girard, Kansas, who have listened, critiqued, encouraged, and taught me so much.

To the "cabin" critters: *Debi V., Deb R., Sara, Susie, Susan, Laura,* and *Christy,* whose brains storm better than Kansas. And they bring chocolate.

To *Deb R.,* for the edit and encouragement.

To my beta reader: *Jeanie,* who has endured the many, many changes that occur during the birth of a book. And who is a constant encourager, and prayer warrior.

And my beta "listener," hostess with the mostest, and sweet cousin *Kathy* who has the patience to listen to me read my story to her, stops me when she doesn't understand what in the world I was trying to say, and tries very hard not to go to sleep while I'm reading.

To the Hinkle family: *Sam, Karen, Mason* and *Kensi,* who live on the Rocking SK Ranch, which in my story is the Feather. I've combined the father and son's names to give to one of the characters in this story. Karen is also the photographer for my author's picture. Sam and Karen have supplied me with old pictures of the ranch home (built around the time of the Civil War) and have given me an open invitation to tramp around their ranch any time.

To our grandchildren: *Rachel, Leah, Kirsten, Seth, Amy,* and *Drew,* who are a constant joy and encouragement . . . and who keep me on my knees in prayer. I've begged for pink kneepads for years—so far, they've not paid heed.

I'm so very thankful for the part each of you have played in bringing this, my debut book, to fruition. You believed in me. What a precious gift. I love you all.

UPCOMING TITLES

in the Brides of a Feather trilogy by Julane Hiebert

Wren

COMING IN MARCH 2016

Lark

COMING IN JULY 2016

Visit Julane's website: julanehiebert.blogspot.com

Wings of Hope Publishing is committed to providing quality Christian reading material in both the fiction and non-fiction markets.

Made in the USA
Lexington, KY
09 July 2016